The Great Mirror of Male Love

IHARA
SAIKAKU

The Great Mirror
of Male Love

Translated, with an Introduction, by

PAUL GORDON SCHALOW

Stanford University Press
Stanford, California

Stanford University Press
Stanford, California
© 1990 by the Board of Trustees of the
Leland Stanford Junior University
Printed in the United States of America
Original Printing 1990
Last figure below indicates year of this printing:
02 01 00 99 98 97 96

CIP data appear at the end of the book

Stanford University Press publications are
distributed exclusively by Stanford
University Press within the United States,
Canada, Mexico, and Central America;
they are distributed exclusively by Cambridge
University Press throughout the rest of the world.

FRONTISPIECE: Acknowledgment is made to the Boston Museum of Fine Arts for permission to use the print "Wakashu with Samisen," attributed to Hishikawa Moronobu, dated about 1685. James Michener says of the print, "This rare print has for years been known as the portrait of a yūjo (courtesan) but is actually the portrait of a wakashu (effeminate young man) as can be seen from the sword and the small shaved portion of the head. This wakashu plays as his dainty friends dance on the stage" (Michener, *The Floating World of the Japanese Print*, p. 26).

COVER ILLUSTRATION: Acknowledgment is made to the Tokyo National Museum for permission to use the six-fold screen "View of the Nakamura Theater in Edo," attributed to Hishikawa Moronobu and dated about 1688. The theater's crest originally bore the stylized figure of a crane, but in 1688 it was changed to the ginkgo leaf—seen on the banner over the theater entrance—because of a government edict forbidding use of the crane image. The same edict required Saikaku to stop using the crane character in his pen name, which literally means "west crane." The folding screen depicts a line of kabuki wakashu dancing across the stage while theatergoers, including samurai disguised under sedge hats, take their seats for the day's theatrical events.

For my father
Frederick Martin Schalow
(April 30, 1921–March 15, 1977)

Contents

Introduction

The Great Mirror of Male Love is a complete translation of *Nanshoku ōkagami* (1687), a collection of 40 short stories by Ihara Saikaku (1642–93) depicting homosexual love relations between adult men and adolescent boys in seventeenth-century Japan. A feature of premodern Japanese culture was that male homosexual relations were required to be between a man and a boy, called a *wakashu*.[1] When a wakashu reached the age of nineteen, he underwent a coming-of-age ceremony that conferred on him the status of an adult male, after which he took the adult role in relations with boys.[2] The first twenty stories in *Nanshoku ōkagami* highlight wakashu from the samurai (warrior) class whose lives exemplified the ideals of boy love; the second group of twenty stories shifts its focus to kabuki actors, who exemplified boy love in their own way, serving as boy prostitutes in the theater districts of Japan's three major cities, Kyoto, Osaka, and Edo (now Tokyo). Books on sexual love, such as *Nanshoku ōkagami*, flourished in the seventeenth century in response to a demand from Japan's emergent urban class of merchants and artisans, called *chōnin* (townsmen). These books reflected the cultural assumption that romantic love was to be found not in the institution of marriage, but in the realm of prostitution. Recreational sex with both female and young male prostitutes was a townsman's prerogative if he could afford their fees, and he chose between them without stigma. A cult of sexual connoisseurship grew up around each: *nyodō*, "the way of loving women"; and *wakashudō* (abbreviated to *shudō* or *jakudō*), "the way of loving boys." Both "ways" harked back to nonprostitutional classical archetypes. In the case of nyodō, this was the courtier's love of women (*joshoku*, female love) codified in such literary classics of the Heian Period (794–1185) as *Ise monogatari* (mid-tenth century; McCullough, tr., *Tales of Ise*) and *Genji monogatari* (early-eleventh century; Seidensticker, tr., *The Tale of Genji*), whereas the prototype for shudō was found in literary depictions of male love (nanshoku) among samurai and the Buddhist clergy.³ Saikaku structured his depiction of male love in Nanshoku ōkagami around the samurai tradition, juxtaposing it with kabuki boy prostitution so that samurai glory might be reflected on the townsman's version of shudō. This desire for reflected legitimacy derived from the fact that, by the mid-seventeenth century, townsmen had acquired wealth but still lacked social status, being ranked below farmers in the neo-Confucian social order that predominated during the Edo Period (1600–1868).⁴ One critic accounts for Saikaku's idealization of samurai in the first half of Nanshoku ōkagami as "an attempt to ingratiate himself with the government,"⁵ which was of course run by upper-echelon samurai. But Saikaku's flattering portrayal should be understood as an artistic device, not as a sign of genuine deference to his social superiors. Regarding Buke giri monogatari (1688; Callahan, tr., Tales of samurai honor), published the year after Nanshoku ōkagami, another critic points out that, "Far from adopting a pious approach, Saikaku gave full rein to his keen insight into the contradictions of the age and piled irony upon irony in his depiction of the samurai characters who people his tales."⁶ The attitude Saikaku showed toward samurai in Nanshoku ōkagami was dictated by his desire to create an idealized vision of male love. Once his artistic needs were met, Saikaku was perfectly capable of making samurai look foolish, which he did with great skill in the present translation in 7:4, "Bamboo Clappers Strike the Hateful Number." The technique of juxtaposing samurai and townsmen—to elevate the lower-ranking townsmen—that Saikaku employed in the structure of Nanshoku ōkagami was developed further a decade or two later in Edo-style kabuki, where popular stage heroes such as Sukeroku assumed a dramatic double identity that allowed them to embody the ideals of their townsman audience while holding the status and lofty values of the samurai class.⁷

The subtitle of Nanshoku ōkagami is Honchō waka fūzoku, "The Custom of Boy Love in Our Land," and the book bears the date Jōkyō 4 (1687) and two of Saikaku's signature seals, Kakuei and Shōju, following the preface.⁸ The collection is divided into eight sections (*kan*), each containing five chapters or stories. This format was typical of Saikaku's short-story collections, but *Nanshoku ōkagami* is about twice the length of his other books. Since the depiction of male love is evenly divided between samurai wakashu and kabuki wakashu, each half could almost stand on its own as an independent work. Aside from simple juxtaposition, Saikaku seems to have made little effort to integrate the two halves. In the introductory chapter, "Love: The Contest Between Two Forces," he establishes a fictional locus for the book's composition in a remote corner of Edo. (The illustration acompanying the text depicts a room where lectures on boy love are being given. Samurai boys are studying a book that may well be *The Record of the Origins of Boy Love* mentioned in the text.) This locus in Edo is consistent with the first four sections about boy love in samurai circles, but it contradicts the central position of the Kyoto-Osaka theater districts in sections five through eight, which deal with kabuki actors. To that extent, the introduction serves the first half of the work better than it does the second half. On the other hand, when the introductory essay turns to discussing the differences between male and female love, the imagery and examples in the chapter are taken almost entirely from townsman life in the Osaka area. At the end of the essay, when the authorial voice mentions gathering material for the collection like seaweed in Osaka Bay, the focus is clearly on the latter four sections. The discrepancy between the fictional Edo location and later Osaka imagery suggests that the two halves required very different introductions and that Saikaku was only partially successful in joining the two into a coherent conceptual framework.

"Great Mirror" in the title is borrowed from the twelfth-century *Ōkagami*, a historical romance detailing the illustrious political career of Fujiwara Michinaga (966–1027) with idealized biographies of the men who surrounded him at the Heian court.[9] Saikaku imitated the biographical format of *Ōkagami* in dividing *Nanshoku ōkagami* into 40 chapters, each a biography of an ideal samurai or kabuki wakashu. Saikaku had used "Great Mirror" in a title two years before in *Shoen ōkagami* (1685; *The great mirror of loves*), where he first followed the 40-chapter format to present the biographies of female prostitutes in the pleasure quarters. Saikaku took his cue for incorporating "Great Mirror" into the titles of these collections from his contemporary, Fujimoto Kizan (1626–1704), who a few years earlier had published *Shikidō ōkagami* (1678; *The great mirror of the way of love*) and first gave "Great Mirror" the slightly erotic connotation that Saikaku exploited. In the opening chapter of *Nanshoku ōkagami*, Saikaku employed the title in its literal sense when he stated, "I have attempted to reflect in this great mirror all of the varied manifestations of male love." Elsewhere in the text he used the word *kagami*, "mirror," in its colloquial sense to describe certain youths as "paragons" or "models" of male love to be emulated by all boys.

Saikaku depicts two types of men in the pages of *Nanshoku ōkagami*: connoisseurs of boys (*shōjin-zuki*) and woman-haters (*onnagirai*). Shōjin-zuki had a nonexclusive interest in boys, which means that they generally were married, maintained households, and continued to have sexual relations with women. Onna-girai, on the other hand, did not marry, and they completely rejected women as sexual partners. The former group had what we would call in modern parlance a "bisexual" identity, whereas the identity of the latter group is close to our modern conception of "homosexual." Since both groups could engage in man-boy sexual relations without stigma, their appreciation for boys did not serve as a distinguishing feature. As a result, sexual identity for men with an exclusive preference for boys was constructed from their sexual antipathy to women, and they thus got the name "woman-haters." Interestingly, Saikaku structured *Nanshoku ōkagami* not around the "bisexual" ethos of the shōjin-zuki, but around the exclusively "homosexual" ethos of the onna-girai. This separated his depiction of male love from any that had come before.[10] In a cultural idiom of connoisseurship, the onna-girai symbolized the single-minded devotion demanded by the way of boy love and was thus the logical figure around which Saikaku would build his literary paean to male love. Because he adopted the onna-girai's extreme stance toward female love rather than the shōjin-zuki's inclusive position, Saikaku was obliged to write disparagingly of women in the pages of *Nanshoku ōkagami*. But Saikaku's misogynous tone, which many readers of this translation will find offensive, is directed not so much at women as at the men who loved them. By denigrating the love of women, Saikaku sought to belittle the connoisseur of female love and thereby entertain a male audience that got reading pleasure from seeing boy love elevated.

Tradition and Innovation

Mishima Yukio once boasted that his novel *Kamen no kokuhaku* (1949; Weatherby, tr., *Confessions of a Mask*) was the first important work to deal with the topic of homosexuality in Japan since Ihara Saikaku's *Nanshoku ōkagami*.[11] A comparison of the two books is instructive about the very different literary traditions in which the two writers worked. Mishima wrote *Kamen no kokuhaku* in a Western literary idiom characterized by a dual strategy of masking (hiding the fact of homosexual love) and signaling (revealing it).[12] This literary strategy developed because writers did not feel free to write openly about homoerotic feelings or homosexual relations.[13] The strategy is employed in works as varied as Shakespeare's sonnets, which obscure the gender of the addressee but give clues to their homoerotic reading; Proust's *A la recherche du temps perdu*, in which the gender of certain characters is switched to avoid stigma while revealing the psychological reality of homoerotic relationships;[14] and Mann's *Der Tod in Venedig*, in which homoerotic feelings appear to serve as a metaphor for aestheticism, physical and spiritual decadence, and death. In each case the need to mask was the result of stigma, but the need to signal came from the writer's desire to let his true feelings be known. Mishima's literary treatment of homosexuality in *Kamen no kokuhaku* owes much to this Western tradition of masking and signaling, but it stands apart in one important respect: by acknowledging the mask, the novel becomes all signal, a "confession." In Mishima's words, "only a mask which has eaten into the flesh, a mask which has put on flesh, can make a confession."[15] By presenting itself as a frank confession and revealing the masked aspect of the literary strategy employed in writing about homosexuality, *Kamen no kokuhaku* changes the nature of the sign so that it no longer indicates the writer's desire to be known, but to hide. This is what Mishima meant when he stated in the introductory note to the novel: "Many writers, each in his own way, have set down their 'portrait of the artist as a young man.' It was precisely the opposite wish that led me to write this novel. In this novel I, in my capacity as 'the person who writes,' have been completely abstracted. *The author does not appear in the work.*"[16]

Ihara Saikaku wrote about male homosexual love in an entirely different idiom, yet he shared with Mishima a talent for innovation. Popular literature in premodern Japan did not depict male love as abnormal or perverse, but integrated it into the larger sphere of sexual love as a literary theme. Such a tradition had no need for strategies of masking and signaling. Sexual and romantic relations between men and boys, like relations between men and women, were discussed in terms of connoisseurship. Sexuality was simply another aspect of social life that provided a forum for proving one's sophistication and culture. Treatises on female love such as Fujimoto Kizan's *Shikidō ōkagami* and the ubiquitous critiques of courtesans in the pleasure quarter (*yūjo hyōbanki*) were products of the townsman's pursuit of sexual sophistication via female love. Similarly, philosophizing treatises on boy love such as *Shin'yūki* (1643; *Record of heartfelt friends*) and kabuki actor-evaluation books (*yakusha hyōbanki*) aided samurai and townsmen in their quest for sophistication through boy love.[17] In a context of connoisseurship, books about sexual love in Japan developed not masking and hiding strategies, but an ornate and complex iconography of symbols.

The iconography of female love included the legendary lovers of the past, beginning with the quintessential Arihara no Narihira (825–880) of *Ise monogatari* fame; his foil, the bungled lover Taira no Sadabumi (d. 923) in *Heichū monogatari* (late-tenth century; *Tale of Heichū*); Prince Genji in *Genji monogatari*; and assorted others from *Heike monogatari* (thirteenth century; McCullough, tr., *The Tale of the Heike*) and later works. Ninth- and tenth-century "passionate poetesses" such as Ono no Komachi and Izumi Shikibu were also part of that iconography. Chinese archetypes likewise loomed large among the icons of female love and included the beautiful but ill-fortuned Yang Kuei Fei; the tragic Chao Chun, sent by her emperor to the Huns as a token of friendship; and the

Hsiang Fei "fragrant concubines" who followed their emperor in death rather than live without him. The iconography of male love centered on the elite circles of samurai and Buddhist clergy. The characteristics of the samurai tradition were its emphasis on loyalty between lover and beloved and the mutual aid each, as a samurai, could provide the other. *Shin'yūki*, for example, built its rationalization of the connoisseurship of boy love around compassion (*jihi*) and empathetic love (*nasake*). The book urges samurai wakashu to respond to the sexual overtures of adult men and thereby fulfill their destiny as handsome youths. Although couched in Buddhist religious terminology, the lesson is essentially secular. *Dembu monogatari* (c. 1624–43; *Tale of a country bumpkin*) was the first book to argue in debate format the relative merits of boys versus women as sexual partners. The existence of such debates, called *danjo yūretsu ron*, suggests that though male love was not stigmatized, it was practiced by only a minority of men and thus required defense vis-à-vis female love. Since these debates were motivated by a desire to justify boy love, those who preferred boys are described, in the vocabulary of connoisseurship, as cultured and having discernment (*tsū*), and those preferring women as uncultured and undiscerning (*yabo*).

The Buddhist priestly tradition of homosexual love emphasized the power of love between priests and their acolytes to produce spiritual enlightenment.[18] One of the primary icons in this tradition was Kūkai (Kōbō Daishi, 774–835), founder of Shingon (True Word) Buddhism in Japan, who was attributed with the introduction of male homosexuality from China early in the ninth century. Numerous sources repeat this legend, and by the seventeenth century Kūkai was firmly established in the literary iconography as a virtual patron saint of male love; in certain literary contexts the mention of his name or the name Mt. Kōya, where Kūkai founded the great temple complex of Shingon Buddhism, immediately signaled homosexuality. This legend served as a legitimizing sign in an increasingly secular society, where religious symbols were given new content.[19] Japanese court poetry (*waka*) composed by priests to celebrate homoerotic feelings was another important aspect of the Buddhist tradition of boy love. This aspect of the tradition was given coherence in a waka collection called *Iwatsutsuji* (1667; *Rock azaleas*) attributed to Kitamura Kigin (1624–1705).[20] The collection gets its title from an anonymous love poem in *Kokinshū* (905; McCullough, tr., *Kokin Wakashū*) which is attributed in *Iwatsutsuji* to a disciple of Kūkai, Shinga Sōzu (801–879). The poem itself became another important symbol in the iconography of boy love and appears in "The ABCs of Boy Love," the second story in this collection. "Memories of love revive, like rock azaleas bursting into bloom on Mount Tokiwa; my stony silence only shows how desperately I want you!"[21] The poem's emphasis on unspoken love results not from stigma but from the poet's position as a priest who had ostensibly renounced the world of physical passion and should no longer be susceptible to a boy's (or woman's) attractions. It is a Buddhist poem, expressing the yearning of an enlightened mind to break the lingering power of sexual and emotional bonds.

In *Nanshoku ōkagami*, Saikaku makes full use of these and other features of the standard iconography of Japanese male love, but he is not content to end there. He deliberately distorts the iconography of female love and invents a new set of icons for male love as an alternative framework for discussing sexual love.[22] In both the preface and introductory chapter, he shows just how inventive he can be in creating an aesthetic basis for the choice of boys over women as sexual partners. For example, *Nihongi* (720; Aston, tr., *Nihongi: Chronicles of Japan*) had been used by proponents of nyodō to argue for female love's superior sophistication on the basis that it was established by the gods as a "natural order." Kitamura Kigin says as much in his introduction to *Iwatsutsuji*: "To take pleasure in a beautiful woman has been in the nature of men's hearts *since the age of male and female gods.*"[23] In the preface to *Nanshoku ōkagami*, Saikaku cleverly places the "historical origins" of boy love in the period of the age of gods (*kamiyo*) prior to the appearance of male and female gods in the fourth generation, thereby asserting boy love's chronological precedence over female love. By focusing in jest on the three all-male generations of the kamiyo, he is able to beat Kigin at his own argument.

Saikaku employs a different strategy in the introductory chapter to bolster the pedigree of boy love. This time he uses outright misrepresentation of the *Nihongi* creation myth in order to put proponents of female love on the defensive, depicting the love of women as a late-coming sexual pleasure of dubious legitimacy that has somehow distracted men from the archetypal love of boys. There is a story in *Nihongi* in which a wagtail bird educates the god and goddess Izanagi and Izanami about sexual intercourse by shaking its tail at them, since they seem to have been confused about how to go about the required act of procreation.[24] In Saikaku's humorous version, the wagtail inspires Kuni-toko-tachi to attempt anal intercourse with the boy Hi-no-chimaru, "boy of a thousand suns." The name is Saikaku's invention and has obvious links to the sun goddess Amaterasu, who played a crucial role in the creation myth. Saikaku locates the lesson in anal intercourse on the dry riverbed under the mythical floating bridge that linked heaven and earth in the age of gods, a place certainly recognized by Saikaku's readers as a reference to the dry riverbed of the Kamo River in Kyoto at Shijō, one of the centers of boy prostitution in the kabuki theater during Saikaku's day.

Saikaku then invents an etymology for an ancient name of Japan, *seirei koku*, "Land of Dragonflies," which he claims derived from the fact that dragonflies were observed to copulate by mounting from behind in what Saikaku calls "the position of boy love." This allows Saikaku another chance to facetiously assert the ancient pedigree and "natural" legitimacy of male love over female love in Japan. (The actual origin of the name was a word play: the Japanese word for dragonfly, *akitsu*, echoes the two middle syllables of the mythological second island, Toyo-aki-tsu-shima, "island of bountiful harvest," produced by Izanagi and Izanami in the creation of the Japanese archipelago.)[25] Finally, Saikaku invents a variation of the story of Susa-no-wo's marriage to Kushi-nada (Inada)[26] with misogynous motives, first to say that Susa-no-wo's interest in women developed only after he was no longer able to attract boys, and next to link the socioeconomic burden of marriage and childrearing with man's inability to resist the inferior love of women.

The introductory chapter of *Nanshoku ōkagami* also cites Chinese historical precedent to legitimize male love, showing that it was not peculiar to Japan. Three legendary cases are mentioned, each of which were synonymous with male love in Chinese literary discourse on the topic: Wei Ling-kung's relationship with Mi Tzu-hsia in the fifth century B.C.; the first Han emperor Kao Tsu's love for his minister Chi Ju; and the sixth Han emperor's relationship with Li Yen-nien, brother of his favorite concubine Li Fu-jen. Sai-kaku returns to the universal nature of male love in the closing lines of *Nanshoku ōkagami* when he mentions its existence in India, China, and Japan and states that, "This way of love is not exclusive to us; it is practiced throughout the known world." References to the practice of male love outside Japan lent an air of continental sophistication and, by extension, legitimacy to the discussion.

Saikaku freely borrows and fabricates literary legends to sub-stantiate the importance of male love, at the same time mocking the legitimizing use of those very icons by the absurdity of his claims. The first literary figure whose reputation he exploits in this manner is that of Arihara no Narihira. Narihira's romantic prow-ess earned him the appellation of "the god of *yin* and *yang*" (the god of love between men and women). Saikaku invents a sexual relationship lasting five years between Narihira and "Ise's younger brother, Daimon no Chūjō." If this person had any historical ref-erent in Saikaku's mind, it may have been Prince Koretaka (844–97), whose sister is identified as the Ise shrine virgin of story 69 in *Ise monogatari*. Narihira is known to have served Koretaka in an official capacity, and several of his poems addressed to Koretaka imply a strong emotional, but almost certainly not sexual, bond between them. Saikaku then states of Narihira that, "After coming of age, he abandoned his would-be lover and set off for the Nara capital. The purple cap that he wore surely makes him the father of all kabuki actors." In mentioning a "would-be lover," Saikaku was probably referring to the legend that attributed the anonymous *Kokinshū* love poem about rock azaleas to Shinga Sōzu, its com-position inspired by a secret love for Narihira. The purple cap Sai-kaku claims Narihira wore is a transformation of the purple robe in the first poem of *Ise monogatari*[27] and helps link Narihira to a contemporary custom among kabuki boy actors of covering their heads with purple kerchiefs. Saikaku's linking of the actor's purple

kerchiefs with the purple robe in Narihira's poem creates a clever
but farfetched bit of humor that would have appealed to a readership that knew the kabuki theater well. Saikaku then asks wryly
of Narihira, in reference to his supposed authorship of *Ise monogatari*, "How is it that he later turned his back on male love to
write a tale about the love of women?" Saikaku concludes the section by stating, "As an adult, Narihira still preferred the company
of boys to that of women. The fact that he is remembered as the
god of *yin* and *yang* must cause him no end of vexation in the
grave." Saikaku feels justified in reinventing the "Narihira" icon
to fit his discourse on boy love, and his readership no doubt enjoyed
the clever literary antics.

Saikaku does not stop with Narihira but also manipulates the
literary reputation of the courtier-monk Yoshida Kenkō (1283–
1352) to invent a new icon for male love. Kenkō was author of
Tsurezuregusa (mid-fourteenth century; Keene, tr., *Essays in Idleness*), a work still regarded as among the most beautiful statements
of Japanese aesthetics in the language. Saikaku was no doubt aware
of the homoerotic quality of parts of Kenkō's essays and may have
taken them as his cue for claiming that Kenkō had "sent thousands of love letters to a nephew of Sei Shōnagon named Kiyo-
wakamaru." This is an absurd claim not only because there is no
evidence that such letters existed, but because more than three centuries separate Kenkō from Sei Shōnagon (tenth century). The absurdity conceals a serious desire to base concepts of legitimacy not
on the strength of legend or precedent, but on personal aesthetic
considerations.

In the opening chapter of *Nanshoku ōkagami*, Saikaku develops
the aesthetic basis for choosing boy love by listing 23 pairs of characteristics comparing women and boys as sexual partners. In each
case, the boy is meant to seem more aesthetically appealing than
the woman, and Saikaku clearly intends the contrast to put the boy
to good advantage. The first three examples illustrate Saikaku's
approach.

Which is to be preferred: A girl of eleven or twelve scrutinizing herself
in a mirror, or a boy of the same age cleaning his teeth?

Lying rejected next to a courtesan, or conversing intimately with a
kabuki boy who is suffering from hemorrhoids?
   Caring for a wife with tuberculosis, or keeping a youth who constantly
demands spending money?

In the first case, Saikaku is describing the age when boys and girls
first become aware of themselves sexually. The girl fusses over her
outward appearance in a mirror, whereas the boy is concerned
about the less noticeable but in some ways more important clean-
liness of his teeth. The preference implicit here is for the boy's more
innocent and perhaps less calculating concern with hygiene than
with superficial appearances. In the second case, neither situation
with courtesan or actor allows sexual intercourse for the paying
patron, but the "intimate conversation" possible with the kabuki
boy provides a recompense of sorts, suggesting a nonsexual satisfaction found in having an affair with an actor that is lacking with
a courtesan. The third example juxtaposes two financially draining
situations, supporting a sick wife versus supporting a spendthrift
boy. Again the implication is that the sick wife represents a hope-
less situation, whereas the boy, in spite of his spending habits, offers
some pleasurable compensations. The misogyny implicit in the 23
pairs of comparisons listed by Saikaku is made explicit at the end
of the list. "In each case above, even if the woman were a beauty
of gentle disposition and the youth a repulsive pug-nosed fellow, it
is sacrilege to speak of female love in the same breath with boy
love. A woman's heart can be likened to the wisteria vine: though
bearing lovely blossoms, it is twisted and bent. A youth may have
a thorn or two, but he is like the first plum blossom of the new
year exuding an indescribable fragrance. The only sensible choice
is to dispense with women and turn instead to men."
   One critic has asked with regard to the misogynous tone of *Nanshoku ōkagami*, "Was Saikaku, who had written so differently of
women in his earlier works, now revealing his true preferences?"[28]
Saikaku exalted male love and denigrated female love in *Nanshoku
ōkagami* not as an attempt to signal masked homoerotic feelings,
but to entertain his readership. He showed great creativity in the
way he manipulated legends and icons of male love for the pleasure
of his readers, but he was bound by the overall constraints of the

literary tradition in which he worked. Masking and signaling of "true preferences" was foreign to that tradition. Not until Mishima, almost three centuries later, would another Japanese writer make similar innovations, but then in a literary tradition in which masking and signaling were real issues.

Saikaku's Oeuvre

Economic and social conditions in the seventeenth century led to the emergence of a flourishing publishing industry centered in Kyoto. For the first time in Japan's history it became possible for writers to live exclusively on their earnings, and Ihara Saikaku was the first to actually do so. As a popular writer, Saikaku's primary purpose was to entertain his readership, something he accomplished by drawing on an extraordinarily vast store of literary knowledge, life experience, and his own creative genius. His earliest venture into prose in 1682 was a great commercial success, and Saikaku quickly developed a sense of himself as a popular fiction writer. With that new-found identity came ambitions to reach beyond his native Osaka. When he undertook the writing of *Nanshoku ōkagami* in 1687, it was with the express purpose of extending his readership and satisfying his ambition to be published in the three major cities of his day, Osaka, Kyoto, and Edo. He chose the topic of male homosexual love because it had the broadest appeal to both the samurai men of Edo and the townsmen of Kyoto and Osaka, his regular audience.

Ihara Saikaku was known for most of his life primarily as a poet of comic linked verse (*haikai no renga*) in the Danrin school of Nishiyama Sōin (1605–82) and became the de facto head of that school after his mentor Sōin's death. Haikai was called comic not for its humor but because it allowed a broader range of poetic diction and linking techniques than did standard linked versification of earlier centuries. Saikaku's idiosyncratic poetic instincts demanded a freedom of expression that made him chafe at even the relatively limited restrictions of Danrin haikai, causing his critics to categorize his verses as belonging to the *Oranda-ryū* or "Dutch" school of haikai composition, named after the foreign residents of Nagasaki who represented in their speech and dress everything

that was outlandish to the Japanese. Saikaku turned to writing
short stories only in the last decade of his life, but that decision
changed popular prose fiction in Japan forever and assured Saikaku of a place in the pantheon of Japan's and the world's literary
giants.

Thematically, Saikaku's books formed the centerpiece of a new
genre of popular literature called *ukiyo-zōshi*, books of the floating
world, which depicted the pleasure quarters, theater districts, and
daily life of townsmen.[29] Ukiyo originally referred to the floating/
fleeting world of Buddhist impermanence, but by Saikaku's day
"floating" meant having fun, or the ups and downs of everyday
business. He began as a regional writer whose books appealed to
the townsmen of Kyoto and his native Osaka. In particular, Saikaku's ukiyo-zōshi were instrumental in establishing Osaka as a
publishing center able to rival Kyoto, though it would never equal
Kyoto's great publishing houses in size or scope.[30] In the course of
Saikaku's decade-long writing career, he explored various aspects
of the floating world in books generally divided into three main
categories: those about romantic love (*kōshoku-bon*); those about
samurai (*buke-bon*); and those about the economic life of townsmen
(*chōnin-bon*). There are titles that do not fit into any of these the-
matic groupings; for convenience's sake, such titles can be put into
a fourth miscellaneous category.

Nanshoku ōkagami is significant in Saikaku's oeuvre as a bridging work between kōshoku-bon and buke-bon, since it includes
aspects of both. One critic suggests that, "To write comprehensively
about homosexuality, Saikaku was obliged to include samurai, and
this seems to have sparked his interest in the general subject of
warrior life."[31] For that reason, *Nanshoku ōkagami* is sometimes
called the first of Saikaku's buke-bon.[32] This categorization is plausible, since Saikaku wrote three books about samurai immediately
after *Nanshoku ōkagami*, beginning with a collection of vendetta
stories, *Budō denrai ki* (1687; *Record of the transmission of the martial
arts*), followed by *Buke giri monogatari* and *Shin kashō ki* (1688; *The
new kashō-ki*). In each, some aspect of samurai existence provided
a loose organizing theme for a collection of stories. Another critic
has placed *Nanshoku ōkagami* in a group of works "concerned with

the various bonds between men,"[33] but this categorization obscures the basically sexual nature of the book's theme. Saikaku surely saw male love as an integral part of sexual love and thus compatible with the theme of his books on love. In the opening lines of his first work of prose fiction, *Kōshoku ichidai otoko* (1682; Hamada, tr., *The Life of an Amorous Man*), Saikaku specifically states that the way of love consists of two paths (*shikidō futatsu*), joshoku (female love) and nanshoku (male love).[34] To separate *Nanshoku ōkagami* from the category of kōshoku-bon is to reveal a reluctance to think of male love as a legitimate form of sexual love, a reluctance Saikaku would not have shared. In the final analysis, *Nanshoku ōkagami* belongs squarely in the category of kōshoku-bon. Saikaku conceived of and executed *Nanshoku ōkagami* as a kōshoku-bon, and it is only in retrospect that it can be appreciated as a bridging work to buke-bon.

There is a logic in *Nanshoku ōkagami*'s appearing when it did, for Saikaku had been covering various aspects of sexual love in his kōshoku-bon in a way that, in retrospect, appears surprisingly systematic. What motivated this systematic coverage was an ever expanding readership interested in books about sexual connoisseurship as it was being practiced in the pleasure quarters and theater districts of the day. Prostitution was ubiquitous throughout Japan, particularly in villages along Japan's major routes of transportation, both roadways and waterways. But it was elevated to a cult of connoisseurship primarily in the pleasure quarters and theater districts of Kyoto, Osaka, and Edo. The major courtesan's licensed quarters were Shimabara in Kyoto, Shinmachi in Osaka, and Yoshiwara in Edo. The theater districts for boy prostitution that figure most prominently in the second half of *Nanshoku ōkagami* were Shijō-gawara in Kyoto, often called "the dry riverbed" (*kawara*); Dōtombori in Osaka, called "the moat" (*hori*); and Sakai-chō, Fukiya-chō, and Kobiki-chō in Edo.

Saikaku's first work, *Ichidai otoko*, depicted the love life of its protagonist, Yonosuke (literally, "a man of the world"), from his precocious sexual awakening at the age of six to his final departure by boat for the imaginary Isle of Women (*nyogogashima*) at the age of 60 after having exhausted all the sexual pleasures Japan had to offer. The opening chapter states that during his lifetime his lovers numbered 3,742 women and 725 boys, not to mention the male lovers he enjoyed while still a handsome wakashu. The topic of boy love appears in only a few narratives and often for humorous effect, as at age ten when Yonosuke seduces a surprised samurai and causes him to abandon his wakashu lover.[35] The book parodies *Genji monogatari* in the 54-chapter format shared by the two books and in the theme of obsessive love. Yonosuke is of course a purely plebeian hero, lacking both the pedigree and courtly sensibility of Genji, but his insatiable lust more than makes up for those minor deficiencies. In effect, Saikaku had translated the sexual connoisseurship of the earlier Heian court into an idiom accessible to contemporary townsman readers. Attesting to the book's popularity, a pirated edition appeared shortly afterwards in Edo with illustrations by the great seventeenth-century woodblock artist, Hishikawa Moronobu.

Ichidai otoko represented the full range of possibilities in shikidō, the way of love, and the general trend from then on in his kōshoku-bon was for Saikaku to develop specific aspects of shikidō including female love, male love, and female viewpoints of love. The popular and commercial success of *Ichidai otoko* inspired Saikaku to produce a sequel, *Shoen ōkagami* (subtitled *Kōshoku nidai otoko*, "Another amorous man"), in 1684. In the sequel, Yonosuke's illegitimate son appears on the scene to pick up where his father left off, but he does not share his father's bisexuality and the focus is narrowed to nyodō, the love of women in the pleasure quarters. Prior to Saikaku, actors and courtesans had not been deemed worthy of literary treatment except in hyōbanki that concentrated on physical description. *Shoen ōkagami* was the culmination of a trend making courtesan-evaluation books more literary in quality.[36] Similarly, the second half of *Nanshoku ōkagami* represents a parallel development in critiques of kabuki actors. Saikaku wrote an actor-evaluation book called *Naniwa no kao wa Ise no oshiroi* (1683?; *Ise makeup on Osaka faces*), of which only sections two and three survive.[37] Though "it is considered the first hyōbanki to attain the level of creative literature,"[38] it should be considered an evolutionary step towards the literary depiction of actors that Saikaku fully achieved in the second half of *Nanshoku ōkagami*.

There is strong internal evidence that Saikaku conceived of *Shoen ōkagami* and *Nanshoku ōkagami* as a pair. They share the "great mirror" in their titles and identical formats of eight five-chapter sections. One is a collection of biographies of exemplary courtesans, the other of exemplary wakashu. Both contain parallel phrases in their opening chapters.[39] *Shoen ōkagami* asks, "Why in the world did [Yonosuke] make the dangerous ocean crossing to get to the Isle of Women, when right in front of him he had the female love of beautiful courtesans in Yoshiwara, Shimabara, and Shinmachi?"[40] Similarly, *Nanshoku ōkagami* asks, "Why in the world did 'the man who loved love' [Yonosuke] waste such vast quantities of gold and silver on his myriad women, when the only pleasure and excitement to be found is in male love?"[41] In addition, both contain similar scenes near the end where the narrator describes how he will do penance for the suffering he caused to female or young male prostitutes who gave themselves to him unwillingly—out of economic necessity, for example—during his life of love.[42] In the framework of Saikaku's kōshoku-bon, *Nanshoku ōkagami* stands overall as a humorous refutation of the ethos of female love in *Shoen ōkagami*.

It has been observed that the concern with sexual love in seventeenth-century Japanese popular literature represented a shift of focus in Tokugawa aesthetics from a negative and pessimistic Buddhist view of humanity to a pragmatic, hedonistic view emerging from the positivism of neo-Confucianism.[43] For the townsman, sex and romance represented a forum for the assertion of personal, private experience in a highly regimented world where chances for individual expression were deliberately minimized by the Tokugawa bakufu as potentially threatening to government control.[44] Bold expressions of romantic love frequently got people in trouble with the authorities by forcing them to violate the social constraints that confined them. This was the theme of Saikaku's next collection, *Kōshoku gonin onna* (1686; de Bary, tr., *Five Women Who Loved Love*). Five women who let passion get the better of them are spotlighted in five separate chapters, and all but the last are executed for their transgression, whether it be murder, adultery, or arson. The final heroine is rewarded with a happy ending, perhaps because the man she nabbed was a confirmed woman-hater whose

heart she worked hard to win. Here, as in *Ichidai otoko*, Saikaku
seems to have used male love primarily for humorous effect in a
larger context of heterosexual love, this time from the female
perspective.

Saikaku further explored the female viewpoint in love with *Kōshoku ichidai onna* (1686; Morris, tr., *The Life of an Amorous
Woman*), essentially a female version of Yonosuke's story, except
that whereas Yonosuke experienced ever richer pleasures during
his "rake's progress," the female heroine's only progress in *Ichidai
onna* was downhill. She begins at the pinnacle of the world of pleasure as a beautiful, high-class courtesan and in the course of the
book slides to the level of a common street-walker, now hideously
ugly, obliged to beg for customers. *Ichidai onna* is an obvious
parody of the confessional literature of the thirteenth and fourteenth centuries, in which monks and nuns recounted the course
of their lives leading them to enlightenment. She, too, achieves a
dubious enlightenment in the end, but only after an apocalyptic
vision (which smacks of sacrilege) at a temple where she has re-
treated to worship and do penance.[45] Her first-person account includes the description of a sexual encounter with the mistress of a
house where she was hired to serve as a maid. It is one of the few
depictions of female homosexuality in Japanese literature.

> "You are to sleep in the same bed as your mistress," I was told.
> Since this was a command, I could not gainsay it. Having joined my
> mistress in bed, then, I expected that she would ask me to scratch her hip,
> or something of the sort. But once more I was to be surprised: for now I
> was bidden to take the woman's part, while my mistress assumed that of
> a man and thus disported herself with me during the entire night. I had
> indeed been reduced to a sorry pass! The Floating World is wide and I
> had worked in many different places; but never before had I been used
> like this.
> "When I am reborn in the next world, I will be a man. Then I shall
> be free to do what really gives me pleasure!" Thus did my new mistress
> voice her fondest wish.[46]

The intent here is humorous, much like the humorous use of male
love in *Ichidai otoko* and *Gonin onna*. Presumably, if there had been
an audience for it, Saikaku could have written as sympathetically
about female homosexuality as he did for male homosexuality in

Nanshoku ōkagami. This oversight is the only asymmetry in Saikaku's coverage of the realm of sexual behavior in his kōshoku-bon. One reference work discusses the relationship of *Nanshoku ōkagami* to *Ichidai onna* and *Gonin onna* in jaundiced terms that distort the essentially complementary nature of Saikaku's kōshoku-bon: "The stories about women deal with the same human passion but remind us of the truer human experience that pleasures are fleeting, that enjoyments are small, and that both have their price, in experience as well as coin. The later stories catch fire as they deal with lovers in the toils that ruin them, or as the exigencies of age make sexual satisfaction more arduous. After these stories of women, the stories of male homosexuality in *Nanshoku ōkagami* have a routine character like the catalogue of Don Giovanni's amours sung by Leporello, without the grace of such music."[47] If Saikaku structured *Nanshoku ōkagami* around the theme of exclusive male love so it would appeal to a readership predisposed to the topic, just as he structured his other kōshoku-bon around the theme of female love for those inclined to its pleasures, then the stories in *Nanshoku ōkagami* would not have seemed "routine" to his intended audience. The music was there for those who had ears to hear it.

Immediately after completing *Ichidai onna*, which appeared in the third month of 1686, Saikaku turned to writing *Nanshoku ōkagami*. It would be the longest work he ever wrote, almost twice the length of this other kōshoku-bon. He probably submitted the completed manuscript to his Osaka publisher late in the summer of 1686. The process of publication took a full three or four months, due to the unusual length of the manuscript. Japanese publishers did not normally use movable type (though it was known from sixteenth-century Jesuit and Korean presses and sometimes used), probably because they felt that movable type was incompatible with flowing Japanese script and did not produce an aesthetically pleasing product. The process of publication was thus quite labor intensive and involved having a professional calligrapher hand copy the manuscript onto sheets of paper just as it would appear when printed. The paper sheets were then pasted onto blocks of cherry wood, preferred for its characteristic close grain that allowed a smooth printing surface. Then, the white parts of the page were carved away by a skilled carver, preserving the handwritten quality of the script. The wooden blocks were washed to remove any remaining paper or paste in preparation for the actual printing, which was done woodblock style. Each block was re-inked and rubbed to produce two printed pages of text per sheet. Illustrations, included here in the translation, depict highlights of each of the stories. They were also produced in woodblock and had to be printed at appropriate points in the text. Saikaku himself did the illustrations for his first book, *Ichidai otoko*, for *Shoen ōkagami*, and for *Saikaku shokoku banashi* (1685; *Saikaku's tales of the provinces*), but for subsequent works he used the services of professional illustrators. The illustrations for *Nanshoku ōkagami* are done in the style of a Kyoto artist named Yoshida Hambei (fl. 1660–1700). Nothing is known about the process of choosing which scenes to illustrate. It does not seem likely that Yoshida Hambei read through the text and picked the scenes he liked best. Saikaku probably specified the scenes he wanted illustrated, and may even have given sketches or guidelines on the manner of illustration he envisioned, given his talent in that area.[48] In the kabuki section of *Nanshoku ōkagami*, some critics speculate that the monk who appears in several of the illustrations is the narrator, whom they equate with Saikaku.[49] Two years after his wife's death in 1675, Saikaku is known to have shaved his head in the manner of a monk and retired from business activities to devote himself to his poetry, but we have no way of confirming if the man in those illustrations is in any way meant as a true depiction of Saikaku himself, though the suggestion is intriguing.

Nanshoku ōkagami was released on New Year's Day, the day publishers marketed their most promising books in order to have the greatest possible impact on the public. It was customary in townsman society for people to pay bills and collect debts twice a year, once at mid-year and once at the end of the year. New Year's Eve was particularly important as the time when all remaining debts for the year were expected to be settled. Publishers released interesting books during this season to exploit the fact that merchants had ready cash with which to buy them. The publishing houses that cooperated in printing and distributing *Nanshoku ōka-*

gami were Osaka Fukaeya, operated by Yasui Kahei; Kyoto Ya-
mazakiya, operated by Yamaoka Ichibei; and Edo Yorozuya, operated by Yorozuya Seibei. *Nanshoku ōkagami* was bound in several
formats, which varied according to the edition and distributor. The
first edition, distributed from Osaka and Kyoto, seems to have been
bound in a ten-volume format in which sections two and seven
were each divided into two volumes. For the second edition, which
the Edo publisher joined in printing and distributing, an eight-
volume format was used with each section representing a single
volume. A seven-volume format also survives in which sections
seven and eight are joined in a single volume.[50]

Because *Nanshoku ōkagami* was Saikaku's first major book to
bear the imprint of an Edo publisher, it is thought that Saikaku's
Osaka publisher had established links with Edo specifically for that
book's regional distribution.[51] The creation of the network may
have been motivated in part by an awareness that Edo publishers
had been making money from pirated editions of *Ichidai otoko*
since 1684.[52] By chance, that network was first made use of to dis-
tribute another book of Saikaku's, *Honchō nijū fukō* (1686; *Twenty
cases of filial impiety in our land*). Saikaku wrote the slender volume
shortly after he finished the manuscript of *Nanshoku ōkagami* in
the summer of 1686, apparently at the insistence of his publisher.
It was immediately rushed into production to capitalize on the
popularity of a book on the theme of filial piety from a rival publisher in Kyoto. Saikaku responded not with a straight imitation
but with a parody, choosing to write on unfilial behavior instead.
Its subject matter was inappropriate for a New Year's release (too
inauspicious), so it was marketed in the eleventh month of 1686,
just prior to *Nanshoku ōkagami*. Strictly speaking, then, *Nijū fukō*
became the book that marked Saikaku's debut as a nationally recognized writer (*santoban sakka*) published in the three great cities
of Osaka, Kyoto, and Edo, but only because a network had been
established for the publication of *Nanshoku ōkagami*. In terms of its
structure, content, and appeal, it was *Nanshoku ōkagami*, not *Nijū
fukō*, that reflected Saikaku's efforts to achieve national recognition
and signaled a new stage in his identity as a writer of popular
fiction.

Saikaku's Style

The stylistic debt Saikaku's prose owed to his training in haikai can hardly be exaggerated.[53] Of particular importance in shaping Saikaku into the short-story writer he became were his early solo compositions called *dokugin* and, later, 24-hour *yakazu* or "arrow counting" haikai competitions in which he engaged. (Yakazu haikai were imitations in linked verse of the archery endurance contests popular among samurai at the time.) The first of the solo sequences was *Osaka dokugin shū*, composed in 1673, followed in 1675 (shortly after his wife's death) by *Dokugin ichinichi senku*, 1,000 verses composed in a single day in her memory. The first of the 24-hour yakazu haikai competitions took place in 1677 with a sequence of 1,600 verses. When another poet beat that number, Saikaku countered with a 4,000-verse sequence in 1680, known as "Saikaku's Great Arrow Counting" (*Saikaku ōyakazu*), followed by his final effort in 1684 of 23,500 verses. All were recorded and published but for the last sequence, which was so fast and unrelenting in its pace that the officials overseeing the competition were able only to tally the verses, not record them. Due to their length and speed, Saikaku's yakazu sessions virtually eliminated the distinction between poetic and prose composition, being similar to stream-of-consciousness recitation. Given his success in such exercises, his subsequent entry into writing prose seems almost inevitable.

Nanshoku ōkagami represents some of the best writing that Saikaku ever did. As one critic notes, "*The Great Mirror of Manly Love* has often been praised for its style.... The simpler manner Saikaku had adopted in *Twenty Cases* [*Nijū fukō*] and other miscellaneous works, no doubt in order to please readers unable to follow the intricacies of his haikai prose, would predominate in most of his subsequent writings, but here he returns to the more complex and beautiful style of his kōshoku stories."[54] Saikaku apparently geared the difficulty of his prose, its complexities and embellishments, to what he thought his audience could handle. In certain works, particularly the later chōnin-bon, his style was less allusive, even spare, with fewer rhetorical complexities and haikaiesque embellishments. This increased their appeal to the average townsman reader for whom the books about economic life were designed. But *Nanshoku ōkagami* was meant for a sophisticated audience, on par with the audience for *Ichidai otoko* and the other kōshoku-bon, who brought with their appreciation of sexual connoisseurship a grasp of the complexities of haikai composition and the literary language of the classics.

The major element of haikai poetics in Saikaku's prose is the continuous and discontinuous linking of images. Saikaku's narratives are as concerned with the relationships of images as in actions in the way they tell their tales. In general, the movement of events in Saikaku's haikai short stories, what is called the story line, is propelled more by imagery than by action. Frequently, the more imagistic the story and typical of Saikaku's style, the less it has been appreciated by critics. In the case of *Nanshoku ōkagami*, the bias toward action-oriented plots shared by many critics has meant that the literary quality of the samurai half of the book has been overrated, and that of the kabuki half of the book underrated.[55] The degree to which narrative movement based on human activity is subsumed by imagery in developing a particular story is frequently determined by Saikaku's method of composition. When he worked from written sources, his rendition of events took on a more conventionally prosaic quality, whereas when he composed spontaneously from his own experience and imagination there were fewer impediments to the linking of images, allowing a purer yakazu haikai mode of composition that bordered on stream-of-consciousness writing. To look at a page of *Nanshoku ōkagami* in the original is to realize the stream-like nature of the prose. There are no breaks for paragraphs and no punctuation marks to end sentences or to distinguish quotes, only small circles after phrases. The meaning of these circles is the subject of debate, but they may represent a vestige of haikai phrasing that Saikaku was unable to abandon when he turned to prose.[56]

"The ABCs of Boy Love" (1:2) is an outstanding example of Saikaku's more spontaneous and unfettered short stories. One commentator criticizes its lack of plot and logical consistency, calling it a failed piece of writing.[57] Such criticism ignores the powerful uni-

fying images that successfully counteract and indeed derive power
from the erratic movement from scene to scene. The strongest of
these elements is geographic. All of the place names mentioned in
the story are located in the northeastern environs of Kyoto. In particular, the Kamo River unifies the story from beginning to end as
it "flows" in and out of the narrative, from the opening scene
where its waters give a mountain hermit pause for reflection, to
the closing lines when it is offered to quench the thirst of a dying
wakashu. Logical transitions may seem abrupt or disjointed, but
the overall effect is of a coherent whole because of the almost me-
lodic repetition of certain local motifs. Locus, and changes in locus,
sustain motion in the story more than human action does, giving
the tale lyrical consistency. The early descriptive passages of life in
isolation in the mountains are among the most evocative in the
work. Saikaku was able to write so beautifully because the story
dealt with invented material of a nature personally familiar to him.
Nothing intervened in the haikai mode. Scenes flowed from his
writing brush as spontaneously as spoken verses in a yakazu competition. For Saikaku and his readership, the method of telling was
the primary pleasure of the tale.

When writing about the samurai and their world in *Nanshoku
ōkagami*, Saikaku frequently relied on written sources for his material. Townsmen's access to information about the samurai way of
life was limited, and although Saikaku may have had more opportunities for direct contact as a teacher of comic linked-verse composition because he dealt with lower-echelon samurai as students,
he nevertheless could not be as intimately familiar with events in
the heart of castle towns, especially of a historical nature, as he was
with events in the kabuki theater. Though it is true that Saikaku's
"long association with the *haikai* world had afforded him innumerable opportunities for contact with samurai,"[58] the degree of
first-hand knowledge of samurai life is incomparably less than his
knowledge of his own class, and this fact affected his narratives in
various ways. Certain of the samurai stories, for example, are closer
to the standard style of seventeenth-century narrative in which they
were originally recorded, and they reflect Saikaku's unique haikai
mode of imagistic composition only slightly.

One such story is 3:4, "The Sickbed No Medicine Could Cure."
It recounts an actual incident that took place in Edo in 1640 involving the murder of a rival suitor for the affections of a samurai
youth, and the subsequent seppuku (ritual suicide by disembowelment; "harakiri") by the youth and his male lover. The same incident had been treated earlier in *Fūryū saga kōyō* (1683; *Beautiful
autumn leaves in the hills of Saga*) and would later appear in *Nanshoku
giri monogatari* (1699; *Tales of male love and honor*), indicating the
durable appeal of the story for Edo Period readers. An early account
of the incident, *Mokuzu monogatari* (ca. 1640; *Tale of seaweed*), was
written soon after the actual events and remained forgotten at Keiyō-
ji, the Buddhist temple in Edo where the double seppuku took place,
until the late-Edo novelist Takizawa Bakin (1767–1848) made a copy
of it in 1809 and suggested the connection with Saikaku's story in
Nanshoku ōkagami. On that basis, it was assumed for many years that
Saikaku worked from a copy of *Mokuzu monogatari* when he wrote
his version of the story for inclusion in *Nanshoku ōkagami*, but recent
scholarship has proved that the resemblance of Saikaku's version to
Mokuzu monogatari is only superficial and that the language of
Saikaku's narrative is strikingly similar to another early account of
the events, *Amayo monogatari* (ca. 1640; *Tale for a rainy night*).[59] It
should be remembered that in Saikaku's day writers borrowed freely
from earlier materials to an extent unimaginable under modern
plagiarism laws and unthinkable nowadays to any self-respecting
creative writer. The point for Saikaku was in the telling, or in this
case the retelling, but this particular retelling provides little enjoyment of Saikaku's haikai style.

Saikaku accomplished a more interesting retelling in 1:4, "Love
Letter Sent in a Sea Bass," where he seems to have digested and
reworked the prototype more completely. The story was inspired
by historical events that occurred in 1667 involving a young samurai named Mashida Toyonoshin (Jinnosuke in Saikaku's version)
from Bizen Province. Saikaku's major change was to transpose the
events from Bizen to Izumo Province on the basis of a powerful
literary association that the sea bass (*suzuki*) had with the town of
Matsue in Izumo. The association stems from the fact that there

are a province and a lake of the same name (Sungkiang in Chinese) that are connected with the sea bass in ancient Chinese poetic references. The shift of province motivated by literary factors extraneous to the factual aspects of the account immediately reveals Saikaku's focus on poetic association and image in the way he retells the narrative. Certain similarities in vocabulary and story line can be observed between Saikaku's version of the tale and the two surviving historical accounts (*jitsuroku*) of the same incident, but "Love Letter Sent in a Sea Bass" is so thoroughly injected with Saikaku's haikai sensibility that it stands independently as a distinct literary product.[60]

In general, when Saikaku's source for a story is a written one, it leaves its mark to varying degrees on his retelling. Saikaku comes closest to his own unique haikai style when he is free of outside influences and constraints on his diction, sentence structure, and overall narrative technique. This freedom is most evident in the second half of *Nanshoku ōkagami*, dealing with boys in the kabuki theater. Saikaku knew many of the actors personally that he wrote about, and thorough familiarity with them and their way of life freed Saikaku to produce some of his most inspired narratives. The last two stories in the book—"The Koyama Barrier Keeper" and "Who Wears the Incense Graph Dyed in Her Heart?"—are as rambling and loosely structured as any in Saikaku's oeuvre. Whether or not they succeed as literature, in translation or in the original, must be left to the individual reader, but they would seem to represent the narratives that best reflect the special prose style that Saikaku evolved from his yakazu haikai compositions.

Saikaku is thought to have abhorred revising anything he had written. This was not laziness, but an integral component of his concept of the writer's art. One critic has noted that "In the afterword to the text of his second [yakazu] performance, published one year before his first novel, Saikaku hailed the value of impromptu, colloquial literature. There was no need, he said, for the poet to spend months polishing a sequence of verse. Wit and speed were the ideals, replacing the pedantic wordplay and labored allusions to classical literature that had previously characterized haikai. Gone was the expectation that the work would necessarily endure.

It was a playful composition, intended to give delight beyond literary circles, a popular entertainment for the moment."[61] This philosophy can be extended to Saikaku's prose. It was intended as a moment's effort, presented for a moment's pleasure. He would undoubtedly look with bemusement at a translation made three centuries later, such as this one, of material he had composed in such a spirit. In assessing his style, it is important to remember the qualities he valued and judge the success or failure of his prose accordingly, not on qualities foreign to his aesthetic.

Cultural Setting: Samurai

Since male love was a normal component of male sexuality, it was governed by ethical constraints very much like those governing sexual relations between men and women, particularly in the samurai class. According to Saikaku's depiction in *Nanshoku ōkagami*, the beginning of a relationship between a wakashu and an adult samurai was normally accompanied by a formal exchange of written and spoken vows, giving the relationship a marriage-like status. The verbal exchange of vows was formulaic and involved a promise to love in this life and the next (one step beyond our "till death do us part"). The wakashu Sannojō's vow with Kan'emon recorded in 2:3, "His Head Shaved on the Path of Dreams," is fairly typical:

"Promise me your love will never change," Sannojō said.
"It will never change."
"Promise never to forget me."
"I will never forget you."

Occasionally, as in the case of Daiemon and Tannosuke in 1:5, "Implicated by His Diamond Crest," we are told that no formal vows were exchanged, but this did not seem to affect the quality of their commitment, since they ended up dying for each other.

As in marriage, sex was only one element of the man-boy relationship. The adult male lover (called a *nenja*) was supposed to provide social backing, emotional support, and a model of manliness for the boy. In exchange, the boy was expected to be worthy of his lover by being a good student of samurai manhood. Together they vowed to uphold the manly virtues of the samurai class: to be loyal, steadfast, and honorable in their actions. Not infrequently, the sincerity of the vow was proved by self-mutilation such as cutting the flesh on the arms or legs or severing parts of fingers. One example of self-mutilation in *Nanshoku ōkagami* appears in 2:5, "Nightingale in the Snow," when a samurai named Shimamura Tōnai pledges himself to two youths. Vowing to be faithful in his love, he bites off the last joint of each of his little fingers and gives one to each of the boys as proof of his sincerity. Kabuki actors and female courtesans sometimes imitated such acts of devotion, called *shinjū*, by mutilating themselves for a favorite patron to prove the sincerity of their love, but their actions were more easily interpreted as self-serving, done in the hope of being ransomed from contracts in theaters or houses of prostitution. A samurai wakashu's ultimate proof of love for his nenja was seppuku, but for a kabuki actor the ultimate sacrifice was to abandon the stage and enter Buddhist orders. The pages of *Nanshoku ōkagami* are filled with samurai or kabuki wakashu driven by emotions or circumstances to make their ultimate sacrifice.

Besides nanshoku and shudō, the term *kyōdai keiyaku* (brotherly troth) is used in Saikaku's narratives to denote male homosexual relations. It appears in only two stories, 4:2, "The Boy Who Sacrificed His Life in the Robes of His Lover," and 4:3, "They Waited Three Years to Die," and seems to designate a form of male love unknown in townsman society in which an adult male samurai and his wakashu lover were separated in age by only a few years. The term suggests the fictive kinship roles played by each in the relationship, one taking the role of elder brother (*ani-bun*) and the other taking the role of younger brother (*otōto-bun*). This hierarchy was central to all forms of Japanese male love and presumed a male/superior, female/inferior hierarchy of sexual activity in which the female or boy (inferior) is penetrated by the adult male (superior).

A wakashu was identified essentially on the basis of his long-sleeved robe and his hairstyle. In reading *Nanshoku ōkagami*, close attention must be paid to the way hairstyles and robes are described, for they are often the only clues to a boy's age and availability. At the age of eleven or twelve the crown of a male child's head was shaved, symbolizing the first of three steps towards adulthood. The shaved crown drew attention to the forelocks (*maegami*), the boy's distinguishing feature. At the age of fourteen or fifteen the boy's natural hairline was reshaped by shaving the temples into right angles, but the forelocks remained as *sumi-maegami* (cornered forelocks). This process, called "putting in corners" (*kado o ireru*), was the second step towards adulthood. From being a maegami (boy with forelocks), the wakashu had now graduated to being a sumi-maegami (boy with cornered forelocks). The final step, completed at age eighteen or nineteen, involved cutting off the forelocks completely; the pate of his head was shaved smooth, leaving only the sidelocks (*bin*). Once he changed to a robe with rounded sleeves, the boy was recognized as an adult man (*yarō*). He was no longer available as a wakashu for sexual relations with adult men like himself but was now qualified to establish a relationship with a wakashu.

A careful reading of *Nanshoku ōkagami* makes clear that the constraint requiring that male homosexual relations be between an adult male and a wakashu was sometimes observed only in the form of fictive role-playing. This meant that relations between pairs of man-boy lovers were accepted as legitimate whether or not a real man and real boy were involved, so long as one partner took the role of "man" and the other the role of "boy" in the relationship. Saikaku seems to underscore the importance of sexual roles as fictive role-playing rather than a reflection of reality by making it a central issue in the first narrative of *Nanshoku ōkagami* immediately following the introductory chapter. In "The ABCs of Boy Love," Saikaku introduces two nine-year-old boys (eight years old by Western count), Daikichi and Shinnosuke, whose relationship embodies the ideals of male love. They are mere children, too young even to be called wakashu, but they are old enough to have learned to play their future sexual roles, not unlike the way young children in most societies play "house" in imitation of their parents to prepare for their future roles as mothers and fathers. But Saikaku's purpose was not to instruct his readers on the nature of fictive role-playing, but to entertain them. After the grandiose

pedigree for male love Saikaku concocted in the introductory chapter, this depiction of two children as male lovers served as an amusing contrast.

In the final story of section four, the last in the samurai section,
Saikaku depicts a case in which a wakashu plays the fictive adult
male role in a relationship with another wakashu. The story is
about Geki, a wakashu who has "put in corners." The narrative
states that, though still a sumi-maegami, Geki had been involved
since the age of sixteen in a relationship with another boy in which
he played the role of adult male. This seems to have caused no
particular problem and was accepted by the people around him,
since the adult male/wakashu paradigm was fictively preserved.
The reverse situation, in which an adult male plays the role of
wakashu, appears in the story immediately before Geki's, "Two
Old Cherry Trees Still in Bloom." Saikaku praises the two lovers,
now aged 63 and 66, for their years of devotion. "Having lived
together all these years, they truly deserved to be emulated as models of the way of love for all who love boys." Yet their depiction
seems intended for humorous effect. In fact, the man playing the
wakashu role is labeled an eccentric in a headnote to the story,
reflecting that society was probably less comfortable with an adult
man retaining the boy's role than with a boy playing the adult role.
This is perhaps not surprising, since the latter involves the antici-
pation of a mature future role, but the former means retaining an
immature role and abandonment of adult male prerogatives.

The coming-of-age ceremony, which involved shaving off the
forelocks and adopting male dress, is taken very seriously in the
pages of *Nanshoku ōkagami* as a dividing line beyond which a boy
was off-limits to adult men. In one narrative, a boy undergoes the
ceremony deliberately to avoid a man's advances, and in another a
wakashu is punished for infidelity to his daimyo lord by being
ordered to come of age, thus becoming inaccessible to the other
man. The idea of a ceremony having the power to change one's
sexual status is a familiar one in Japanese literature, where taking
Buddhist vows is frequently depicted as capable of removing a person from the world of sexuality. In *Genji monogatari*, for example,
several court women separated themselves from Genji's sexual ad-

vances by taking the tonsure, turning a fundamentally religious act into an act of escape or even retaliation.

As previously stated, the ultimate sacrifice for male lovers was to die for the sake of their love. This was expected of both nenja and wakashu alike and occurs repeatedly in the first half of *Nanshoku ōkagami*, usually in response to an interloper trying to inject himself into the relationship. Responses to the interloper vary, depending on the circumstances in each narrative. In some cases, such as 1:4, "Love Letter Sent in a Sea Bass," the lovers duel with the interloper and kill him. In other cases, when the interloper makes advances to a boy already in a relationship, the boy attempts to protect the life of his male lover by dueling with the interloper alone. Or, if the interloper demands that a man relinquish his claims to a boy, the man refuses and fights the interloper. Common to each case is the underlying principle of samurai honor (*giri*) that requires a man to fulfill his commitments and, in this context, prove himself worthy of male love.

One aspect of samurai honor was the vendetta, a formally sanctioned procedure that allowed a samurai to avenge the unjust death of a superior, usually his daimyo lord or a family member, to whom he was under some sort of obligation. Unless a samurai undertook to clear the reputation of the one who died unjustly, it remained a blot of shame on both of them. A samurai who took private revenge could be punished with death, but successful completion of an officially sanctioned vendetta was rewarded and deemed a mark of great honor. The vendetta involved several prescribed stages: locating the man responsible for the unjust death of the person being avenged; announcing the name of the avenger and the act to be avenged; a duel to the death; and, if successful, presentation of the man's head to the official who authorized the vendetta.[62] In 2:1, "A Sword His Only Memento," the wakashu Katsuya follows the prescribed ritual meticulously and, with the help of his lover, completes a successful vendetta against his father's murderer.

Another aspect of samurai honor was seppuku. In the process of maintaining one's honor, it sometimes became necessary for a samurai to break his lord's laws. If the authorities understood the mitigating circumstances, he might be cleared of blame. More likely, he would be allowed to clear his reputation as a lawbreaker by committing seppuku. If conducted without approval of the authorities, seppuku was nothing more than a dramatic gesture that might rehabilitate a man's honor in the minds of some people but lacked official meaning. When officially sanctioned, however, it allowed a man to die honorably. Seppuku involved disembowelment with a short sword, followed (in the seventeenth century, at least) by decapitation by one's second (*kaishaku-nin*). It took place in front of official observers who certified that the seppuku was properly conducted. When a samurai was denied the honor of committing seppuku, he was executed like a common criminal by beheading or crucifixion, methods that stripped him of his honor forever (unless, of course, his ignoble death was later successfully rehabilitated by a vendetta).

In the first half of *Nanshoku ōkagami*, samurai honor is the principal source of drama. At the end of 4:3, "They Waited Three Years to Die," Saikaku concludes one tragic tale of death and suicide for the sake of male love with a fairly typical refrain: "Thus do those born in the lineage of the bow and horse die valorous deaths, their honor to be sung by future generations." But he follows it with an unusual caveat that must be understood as an aside to his townsman readers, for whom the samurai way of life (and death) must have seemed unnecessarily severe: "The details of this case were written down so that the example of these men would be more widely known, but their great love and strict adherence to honor have overwhelmed my heart with sadness. I shall put down my writing brush and leave the story, imperfect though it be, to pine for their memory."

A samurai's greatest treasure was his sword. An especially prized sword was given a name, or referred to by the name of the swordsmith who made it. Before a fight, the sword got careful attention, which included a final sharpening. For a samurai to lose his sword was the worst shame imaginable, and to lend it to another man was a sign of the greatest trust. Swords were divided into two categories, long and short. In general, only samurai were allowed to wear both long and short swords. A long sword (*katana*) had a blade over two *shaku* in length (about two feet), whereas the blade of a short sword (*wakizashi*) was one *shaku* eight *sun* in length (about one foot, ten inches) or smaller. The long sword was used in fighting duels, the short sword for hand-to-hand combat and committing seppuku. The category of short swords was further divided based on length: there were large short swords (*ōwakizashi*) up to two *shaku* in length, and small short swords (*kowakizashi*) under one *shaku* two *sun* in length (about one foot, two and a half inches).

A samurai's existence revolved around his service to his daimyo lord. Masterless samurai, men who lost their positions and had no lord to serve, figure prominently in many of Saikaku's narratives in the first half of *Nanshoku ōkagami*, as do wakashu in the personal service of a daimyo lord. It was not unusual for a daimyo lord to have a group of several boys attending to his needs. He might have sexual relations with one or more of them if he so desired. Such wakashu attendants, called *koshō* (bodyguards) or *daimyō gomotsu* (lordly possessions), were kept under strict surveillance and their activities severely limited by the laws of the daimyo household in which they served, due to the risk inherent in their direct, personal access to the lord. In many of the stories, the wakashu's decision whether to obey those laws or violate them is the pivotal dramatic moment of the narrative. The wakashu Katsuya in 2:1, "A Sword His Only Memento," reminisces with an old compatriot he encounters by chance on the way to perform a vendetta against his father's killer. "Remember when we were both in service at Edo? You sent me many letters expressing your love for me. I was very grateful for them. Unfortunately, I was sharing the lord's bed at the time. Though I wanted to respond, I was unable to. Those days are gone now. I can only rejoice that we have met again. At last we can spend the night together, conversing to our hearts' content."

Katsuya's faithful adherence to the daimyo's laws are in stark contrast to their bold violation by Korin in the next story, "Though Bearing an Umbrella, He Was Rained Upon." Korin took a secret lover and paid for it with his life in one of the most brutal scenes in the book. The daimyo lord cuts off Korin's arms one by one and then beheads him, as much for his personal betrayal and deceit as for his crime. In other stories, wakashu attendants fare better at the hands of their daimyo lords even after worse betrayals, but they all risk their lives when they take outside lovers. This is one of the contradictions of samurai life that seems to intrigue Saikaku: men and boys violate the bond of trust with their lords in order to establish an emotional and sexual bond with each other. This contradiction creates a dilemma for the partners that often ends in death.

On occasion, the lovers are fortunate enough to receive a pardon such as occurs in 3:5, "He Fell in Love When the Mountain Rose Was in Bloom." The wakashu Shume clearly deserves the pardon because he acted manfully in dealing with the revelation of the masterless samurai Gizaemon's confession of love. Gizaemon gave up his position and became a masterless samurai because of his obsession with Shume. The narrative comments disapprovingly, "He was in love, to be sure, but no samurai should so disgrace himself in society's eyes. That he should have fallen so low could only be attributed to a remarkable karmic bond." A Buddhist excuse for Confucian failings is common in Saikaku's tales; Buddhist belief in karma allows characters to transcend the rigid and narrow requirements of honor and gives a human face to events that often seem inhuman. Chikamatsu Monzaemon (1653–1724) worked similar resolutions in his puppet (jōruri) and kabuki plays when he had ill-fated lovers die for the sake of a Confucian duty while looking forward to sharing rebirth in a Buddhist paradise. The Confucian dilemma and Buddhist solution was a dramatic formula that worked equally well for both Chikamatsu and Saikaku.

Cultural Setting: Kabuki

The first few chapters in the second half of Nanshoku ōkagami incorporate what amounts to a brief history by Saikaku of the kabuki theater.[63] Entertaining skits and dances that came to be known as kabuki were first performed on the dry riverbed of the Kamo River in Kyoto in the early years of the seventeenth century. The legendary founder was Okuni, a shrine dancing girl from Izumo whose dramatic routines created a sensation in the capital. Kabuki developed from this simple prototype into more complex performances by men, women, and boys that served as thinly disguised vehicles for showing off their physical attractions. Men played men's roles, women and girls played female roles, and boys played boys' roles on the early kabuki stage. Unfortunately for ka-buki as a dramatic form, the erotic appeal of female and young male prostitution tended to overwhelm whatever artistic merit it may have had. The dry riverbed in Kyoto was a playground for the recreation of townsmen and townswomen, but it was consid-ered off-limits to the samurai and courtly elite. Nevertheless, its pleasures exerted a certain pull on the upper classes, as is apparent from contemporary folding screens depicting kabuki theaters in which samurai, faces hidden under sedge hats, mingle with towns-men in the audience. By 1629, the Tokugawa authorities found it prudent to ban women from the kabuki stage because of the un-wholesome mingling of classes and social disruption caused by ri-valries for the affection of kabuki actresses, particularly between samurai. Once banned, this early kabuki came to be called *onna kabuki* (women's kabuki) to distinguish it from the *wakashu kabuki* (boys' kabuki) that followed, in which some boys took over wom-en's roles while others continued to act boys' roles on stage. Those who specialized in women's roles were called *onnagata*; in girls' roles, *waka-onnagata*. Actors of boys' roles were *wakashugata*; lead-ing men were *tachiyaku*; and later, the role of antagonist branched off and was called *katakiyaku*. In addition, dramatic stage displays by jesters (*dōkekata*) continued to be popular in the kabuki theater.

Much to the chagrin of the authorities, kabuki next became a vehicle for displaying the physical charms of beautiful boys, whether as wakashugata or as onnagata. During the reign of the third Tokugawa shogun, Iemitsu, the social problems produced by this situation were not addressed, possibly because he was known as something of a connoisseur of boys himself.[64] Within a year after his death in 1651, boys were finally banned from the stage, first in Edo and then in Osaka and Kyoto. Theater proprieters negotiated with the authorities and were eventually allowed to reopen the theaters under certain stipulations: the name kabuki was forbid-den, and the name "Mime Theatrical Show" (*monomane kyōgen zukushi*) replaced it; actors were told to reduce eroticism and in-crease the realism and dramatic quality of their roles; and, perhaps most important, boy actors were required to shave off their forelocks in the manner of adult men (*yarō*). In samurai society this would have disqualified them from boy prostitution, but townsmen were imaginative when it came to subverting the intent of bakufu laws, especially when they could make money by doing so. As Saikaku says with obvious delight in 5:5, "Votive Picture of Kichiya Riding a Horse": "It used to be that no matter how splendid the boy, it was impossible for him to keep his forelocks and take on patrons beyond the age of twenty. Now, since everyone wore the hairstyle of adult men, it was still possible at age 34 or 35 for youthful looking actors to get under a man's robe. How strange are the ways of love!" The new creation came to be called *yarō kabuki* (men's kabuki) since adult men—or at least men and boys with the hairstyle of adult men—played men's, women's, and boys' roles.[65]

The kabuki actors Saikaku highlights in his narratives are almost all historical people whose existence and characteristics can be verified from independent sources, such as contemporary theater records, actor-evaluation books, and woodblock prints of actors. There was a close link between haikai composition and kabuki, revealed in the fact that it was the norm in Saikaku's day for actors to have a separate haikai name (*haimyō*) that they used when writing comic linked verse. Saikaku had personal contact with many actors through haikai composition. Some were students of his whose verses he included in his collections of comic linked verse, such as *Dōtombori hanamichi* (1679; *Dōtombori grand finale*). Others he knew from parties he must have attended in the theater districts of Dōtombori in Osaka and Shijō-gawara in Kyoto. He would have been invited to such parties, at which boy actors provided the entertainment, as a sophisticated observer and participant, someone whose status as a connoisseur of the "floating world" would have been unassailable and whose presence made the parties special. In his literary depictions, Saikaku shows himself to be a sympathetic guest. He freely points out exploitation, emotional pain, and socially or personally destructive acts by both patrons and actors in the pages of *Nanshoku ōkagami*. As one scholar has noted, "Saikaku saw the tawdry aspect of the entertainer's life for what it was. With the greasepaint and the fame came a salary that could never cover an actor's expenses and the resultant need to find a pederast for a

patron."⁶⁶ Nevertheless, Saikaku's sympathy stops short of unam-
biguously condemning these problems as evil. The reason for his
ambivalence is the importance he places on first-hand experience.
To be truly human, he seems to say, means to feel pleasure, to feel
pain, and to at least attempt to satisfy one's desires and even ob-
sessions. He ultimately cannot side with those advocating sacrifice
and control, but argues for the value of expression and experience,
the same stance he took in his career as a haikai poet. Some boy
actors were undoubtedly exploited by their proprietors and patrons
(who in the Japanese context ought not to be labeled "pederasts"),
but Saikaku makes it clear that many of the boys fit perfectly into
the role of theatrical idol and enjoyed the stardom it allowed them.
The personal rewards could be substantial, and they often balanced
the physical and emotional toll. Saikaku's depictions were always
meant to show both the good and bad as integral to the human
drama.

The townsmen Saikaku depicts in the narratives were probably
very much like his real-life cohorts in pleasure. The theater districts and pleasure quarters were a world set apart from everyday
concerns. When men entered it, they used code names to symbolize
their entry into a separate world of connoisseurship. In 7:4, "Bamboo Clappers Strike the Hateful Number," for example, the name
Shiroku (six + four), which when added equals ten, is the code for
a name containing the character ten (*jū*) such as Jūbei or Jūrō. The
theater district was a place men went for pleasure-seeking, sometimes spontaneous and sometimes carefully planned, and Saikaku
expends considerable artistic effort in his narratives to recreate for
his readers that comforting world of pleasure and illusion, the
"floating world" from which his ukiyo-zōshi took their name. But
Saikaku never lets visitors to the floating world escape entirely in
his narratives. Reality constantly impinges on the mood of fun,
both in the stories' content and in the way they are structured. This
confrontation with reality gives the stories a dimension lacking in
purely escapist literature, such as that produced by writers of *ge-
saku* ("playful compositions") later in the Edo Period.

Reality intrudes into the fragile mood of pleasure in Saikaku's
stories through the haikaiesque technique of *kyōzame*, "waking

from the spirit of fun." This word occurs several times in *Nanshoku ōkagami*, and the technique can be observed in several places where the word itself does not appear. In 7:1, "Fireflies Also Work Their Asses at Night," the actor Fujimura Handayū is entertaining at a party when he complains about the difficulty of his double life as stage actor and boy prostitute. In response, we are told that "the roomful of patrons was somewhat taken aback and laughed awkwardly." The narrative had been building an illusion of carefree fun that Saikaku then deliberately destroyed to reveal its illusory nature. This act of sabotage owes much to the haikai technique of juxtaposing irreconcilable or contrastive images. Predictably, its effect is to heighten the reader's awareness of the spirit of pleasure.

Patrons are not the only ones Saikaku makes squirm. Actors are confronted with uncomfortable reality in "Bamboo Clappers Strike the Hateful Number" when they are asked to reveal their ages. The truth would be a great embarrassment, since none of them is a true wakashu, and we are told that, "They were beginning to lose their party mood." In 8:3, "Loved by a Man in a Box," a party participant who some commentators equate with Saikaku himself makes some clever comments about how great the affection of kabuki actors must be that they are capable of giving themselves physically to patrons at their very first meeting. This comment naturally has a dampening effect on the men's enjoyment, since they would like to flatter themselves that the boys truly are in love with them, but the story tells us that "these were smart actors doing the entertaining tonight and they did not let the spirit of the party falter for a minute." Later in the narrative, the same group of men have a strange encounter with a doll capable of speech that has an unfortunate effect on them: "Their feelings of amusement disappeared and all the evening's pleasures went to naught, instantly forgotten." Examples of the technique of kyōzame abound in the kabuki narratives. This sort of interruption of the mood of fun occurs because Saikaku relentlessly probes the fragility of the illusion of pleasure created in the dynamic between boy actors and paying patrons. Saikaku was not satisfied to depict pleasure-seekers without also pointing out the ironies in their pleasure. It is in this sense that he can be called a realist.[67]

Besides the obvious rivalry between connoisseurs of boy love and connoisseurs of female love, several other rivalries are developed in the kabuki half of *Nanshoku ōkagami*. One of these is between the Osaka man and his Kyoto rivals. Since Kyoto was the overwhelming center of townsman culture in Saikaku's day, the Osaka native was at great pains to prove himself their equal in sophistication. Saikaku repeatedly reminds his readers of the rivalry, whether by boasting of what Osaka has to offer, as implied in the title of 6:5, "A Terrible Shame He Never Performed in the Capital"; or by revealing a certain envy for what Kyoto offers, as in 8:1, "A Verse Sung by a Goblin with a Beautiful Voice," in the following passage: "So, this was the capital. People in Kyoto had eyes and noses like everyone else it seemed, and even though this group hailed from Osaka their arms and legs were attached in much the same way."

Saikaku also exploited the sense of rivalry between the city dweller and provincial types, as might be predicted in a literature of connoisseurship in which sophistication was often contrasted with its lack. In 2:4, "Aloeswood Boy of the East," the narrative contains the snide comment, "For someone from the country, he had quite sophisticated tastes." In 5:5, "Votive Picture of Kichiya Riding a Horse," the actor Tamamura Kichiya has a strange encounter: "As he crossed the crumbling bridge at Shijō, he was spotted by a most unusual-looking man who could not have been more unmistakably from the north country if he had worn a sign around his neck announcing the fact." These remarks in Saikaku's stories served to flatter his urban(e) readers who thought themselves sophisticated in their tastes. But provincial types are not the only people Saikaku takes aim at in *Nanshoku ōkagami*. He manages to criticize just about every stratum of society, from townsmen and actors to the shogun himself, in the course of telling his tales. He makes fun of merchants for their stinginess when he writes, regarding the buying of an actor, "No matter how much they loved him, it must have taken tremendous resolve to pay the fee. But then, no one knows better than a merchant that you get what you pay for." He depicts the greed of drum-holders (entertainers at parties), who come across as shameless sycophants. Saikaku repeatedly pokes fun at the hypocrisy of Buddhist priests, who have forsworn physical pleasures but, in many cases, continue to practice them. He teases strict Confucianists for their stern faces and inability to have fun. He deflates samurai self-importance in the whisker-shaving scene in 7:4, "Bamboo Clappers Strike the Hateful Number." He even makes a veiled criticism of the fifth Tokugawa shogun Tsunayoshi in 5:2, "He Pleaded for His Life at Mitsudera Hachiman": "There is in present-day society a glut of both wild puppy dogs and ready cash, a state that results in widespread ostentation and wasteful spending." Tsunayoshi had promulgated laws of compassion toward animals (*shōrui awaremi no rei*), particularly dogs, beginning in 1685. The laws became extremely unpopular due to the severity of punishment for their violation.[68] Saikaku took risks when he made such criticisms, but he seems to have escaped censorship. The result was that his readers enjoyed a running commentary injected into Saikaku's narratives, sometimes between the lines, that criticized contemporary society from every imaginable angle.

Just as the life of samurai revolved around service to their daimyo lord, the life of kabuki actors revolved around the kabuki theater. The names of most of the major theaters of Saikaku's day appear in *Nanshoku ōkagami* or are represented by actors in their troupes. The theater year began in the eleventh month when new actors debuted in the *kaomise* (face-showing) season. When actors switched theaters, which was not at all uncommon, they did so at this time. A successful actor with considerable box office draw might stay with a single theater his entire career, whereas lesser actors were let go or moved in search of better opportunities. A boy actor could join a theater troupe as early as age eleven or twelve. If his career followed the normal progression, he would begin as an actor of girls' or boys' roles and graduate later into women's and men's roles. The promotion to adult roles was customarily followed by a name change. Name changes also occurred in conjunction with a new theater affiliation, particularly if the actor was identified as the protégé of someone in the theater.

It is often difficult to trace the career of a kabuki actor from beginning to end because, except for the very famous ones, no clear records remain to tell us when name changes were made. Evalua-

tion books concentrate on actors popular during a particular theater season and tell very little about an actor's history, so the only
way to follow developments in an actor's career is to compare several hyōbanki over a period of time and see how he is described or
which names appear and disappear from year to year. The major
actor-evaluation books that have been utilized for biographical information about the actors Saikaku introduces in the pages of *Nanshoku ōkagami* are, in chronological order of publication: *Yarō mushi* (1660; *Actor bugs*); *Mukitokoro* (1662); *Yarō daibutsushi* (1668;
The actor's great buddha); *Yakusha hyōban gejigeji* (1674; *Actor's furry
caterpillar critique*); *Shin yarō hanagaki* (1674; *New flower fence of
actors*); *Kokon yakusha monogatari* (1678; *Tales of ancient and modern actors*); *Yakusha hakkei* (1680; *Eight views of actors*); *Omowaku
uta-awase* (1681; *Match poems as you please*); *Naniwa no kao wa Ise
no oshiroi* (1683?; *Ise makeup on Osaka faces*); *Naniwa tachigiki mukashi banashi* (1686; *Stories of long ago heard on the run in Osaka*);
Yarō tachiyaku butai ōkagami (1687; *The great mirror of leading male
actors onstage*); *Yarō yakusha fūryū kagami* (1688; *Mirror of modern-
day male actors*); *Yakusha ōkagami* (1692; *The great mirror of actors*);
Yakusha ōkagami gassai (1692; *The great mirror of actors in living
color*); *Yarō sekizumō* (1693; *Actor sumo wrestlers*); *Kokon shibai
hyakunin isshu* (1693; *One hundred actors from ancient and modern
stages*); *Yakusha gozen kabuki* (1703; *Actors' kabuki performed in the
lord's presence*); and *Yakusha rongo* (1776; Dunn and Torigoe, tr.,
The Actor's Analects).

The last one, *Yakusha rongo*, is the only one of these actor-
evaluation books available in English translation.[69] Originally published in 1776 by the Hachimonjiya publishing house, it is a collection of writings, some of them by contemporaries of Saikaku, about
the practice and aesthetics of kabuki acting in the late seventeenth
and early eighteenth centuries in Kyoto and Osaka. The section
called *Mirror for Actors* (*Yakusha kagami*) by Tominaga Heibei
(mentioned in Saikaku's narrative "A Verse Sung by a Goblin with
a Beautiful Voice"; see 8:1 note 12) is of particular interest to
readers of this translation of *Nanshoku ōkagami* because it gives an
insider's view of kabuki that lends support and credence to Saikaku's account. One chapter of *Mirror for Actors* begins, "In plays in

former times the theme of male love very often occurred. Principal
actors playing young men often received larger salaries than those
playing women. At that time homosexual love was the rage in all
the quarters of the town."[70] It then proceeds to record the plot of
a play, "Visiting the Family Shrine," having a shudō theme. In it,
a daimyo lord pays a visit to his family shrine to worship; he and
his retainers enter the shrine while the lower attendants (yakko) in
his retinue wait outside:

Some yakko gaze at the view, and discuss the beauty of the young men.
"Yasanojō is best." "No, I've fallen for Tomoya." Thus they were gossip-
ping when a warrior emerges: "What are you chattering about? Just one
more word from you about my lord's beloved..."; thus does he upbraid
them. They cry out in alarm and flee with not one glance behind them.[71]

The play then goes on to enact the jealousy between the lord's
former "beloved," Yasanojō, and Tomoya, who now enjoys his
lord's affection. The scene culminates in humiliation for the daimyo lord, a not uncommon conclusion to comic plays. Tominaga
Heibei ends the chapter with the comment, "Thinking of it now,
it seems stupid that such a piece was a great success, but the audience at the time thought that such plays were amusing, and the
actors took a great deal of trouble over learning and playing
them."[72] Saikaku depicts that audience in the pages of Nanshoku
ōkagami and makes the theater come alive in a way that allows us
to reconstruct the mood of early Genroku kabuki. The shudō
pieces are largely lost and have passed from the modern repertoire,
but the aesthetic of boy love that inspired them is preserved in
Saikaku's prose.

The Translation

    The present translation is based on the printed text of the origi-
nal 1687 edition of Nanshoku ōkagami in Nihon koten bungaku
zenshū, volume 39 (Shogakkan, 1973), as annotated by Teruoka
Yasutaka. Several other annotated versions were also regularly con-
sulted: Teihon Saikaku zenshū, volume 4 (Chuo Koronsha, 1964);
Taiyaku Saikaku zenshū, volume 6 (Meiji Shoin, 1979); Saikaku
rinkō, volume 5 (Seiabo, 1962); and Gendaigoyaku Saikaku zenshū,

volume 3 (Shogakkan, 1976). A photo-facsimile of the Akagi Bunko copy of a second edition of *Nanshoku ōkagami* is available in *Kinsei bungaku shiryō ruijū, Ihara Saikaku hen*, number 7 (Benseisha, 1975), from which the illustrations for this volume were taken. Throughout the introduction and notes to the translation, I refer to the author of *Nanshoku ōkagami* as Ihara Saikaku, or just Saikaku as he is most commonly called in Japan. His real name is thought to have been Hirayama Tōgo, and in the course of his haikai and literary career he used a variety of pen names. He first used the name Saikaku ("west crane") in 1680, but his books continued to appear with the signature seal Kakuei ("crane everlasting"), an earlier pen name. From 1688, the year after *Nanshoku ōkagami* was published, Saikaku was obliged to sign his books Saihō ("west phoenix"), due to a government edict forbidding the use of the character for "crane" in names, since the name Tsuruhime ("crane princess") was being used by the newborn daughter of the shogun Tsunayoshi.

Various English translations of the title *Nanshoku ōkagami* have been used over the years by scholars discussing the book: *Conspectus of Sodomites*; *Mirror of Sodomy*; *Great Mirror of Pederasty*; and recently, the accepted translation, *The Great Mirror of Manly Love*. No one changes a generally accepted title lightly, but it seemed sufficiently important to me to preserve the formal symmetry of nanshoku (male love) and joshoku (female love) that I was willing to dispense with *Manly Love* and translate the title as *The Great Miror of Male Love*. Throughout the translation I have followed the policy of treating Japanese words that have entered the English vocabulary, such as shogun, daimyo, and seppuku, as if they were English. I dispensed with macrons over long vowels in such words and in commonly known place names: Kyoto rather than Kyōto, and Osaka rather than Ōsaka.

I have generally tried to discuss Japanese sexuality using native terms and concepts: nanshoku (male love); joshoku (female love); shōjin-zuki (connoisseurs of boys); onna-girai (woman-haters); nyodō (the way of loving women); shudō (the way of loving boys). I have sometimes used the word homosexual as an adjective meaning "same sex," as in "homosexual relations" or "homosexual love."

I have entirely avoided using culturally loaded vocabulary such as gay, straight, sodomy, sodomite, pederast, catamite, and heterosexual or homosexual (as states of being). These are all perfectly good words, but they do not seem appropriate in a cross-cultural, historical context because they can be misleading, describing Japanese reality in terms that distort it. I have tried hard to be conscious of cultural biases and avoid them so that what I have written about Japanese male love will be as useful a basis as possible for future researchers to build—and improve—upon.

The translation began as part of a doctoral dissertation in Japanese literature at Harvard University under the guidance of Professors Donald H. Shively and Howard S. Hibbett. It was Professor Shively who initially inspired my interest in *Nanshoku ōkagami* and the theme of male love in Japanese literature, and Professor Hibbett who gave me the encouragement and support that made completion of this project possible. I acquired the necessary skills for reading and interpretting Saikaku from my study with Professor Maeda Kingorō of Senshū University, first in 1980–81 in a seminar on Saikaku that he conducted as a Visiting Scholar at Harvard's Yenching Institute, and again in 1982–83 when he met with me on a weekly basis in Tokyo to share his vast knowledge of Saikaku with me. No student of Japanese literature could ask for a more competent and generous teacher, and I feel honored to have enjoyed his scholarly guidance. The year in Japan from 1982 to 1983 was made possible by a Fulbright Doctoral Dissertation Grant from the U.S. Department of Education for which I am grateful. My grasp of the literary discourse on male homosexual love, and on Japanese male love in particular, benefited tremendously from a faculty seminar I gave in the spring of 1987 entitled "Cross-Cultural Methodologies in the Study of Homosexuality: The Case of Premodern Japan" under the sponsorship of the Institute for Advanced Study in the Humanities at the University of Massachusetts-Amherst. The stimulating discussions that occurred in that seminar allowed me to make several breakthroughs in my conceptualization of Japanese male love. I want to express special thanks to the Institute's director, Dr. Jules Chametzky, for the professional integrity and personal kindness he showed in his dealings with me.

I will be forever indebted to him, and to participants from the University of Massachusetts, Wesleyan University, and Amherst College who attended the seminar and made it the once-in-a-lifetime experience it was for me. I am particularly thankful for the reduced teaching load that accompanied the Institute's fellowship, for it allowed me to put my thoughts down in writing. I want also to express my gratitude to Rutgers University for a Henry Rutgers Fellowship in the fall of 1988 that allowed me the time and resources to finish the final stages of preparing the translation for publication.

Several stories about male love from the first half of *Nanshoku ōkagami* and from other works by Saikaku were previously translated by Ken Sato, revised by E. Powys Mathers in 1928, and published as *Comrade Loves of the Samurai*.[73] These were the first of Saikaku's stories ever to appear in translation. Their publication was a direct result of the tremendous interest in turn-of-the-century Europe regarding the Japanese tradition of male love, motivated in part by efforts to decriminalize homosexuality in England and Germany. To those involved in the sexual reform movement, Japan served, like classical Greece, as a model of social tolerance that was profoundly inspirational. The first survey in English to discuss the literary traditions of Japan, *Japanese Literature* by William G. Aston, published in 1899, did little to satisfy their interest in this aspect of Japan, however. Aston describes *Mokuzu monogatari*—the story Saikaku retells in this translation in 3:4, "The Sickbed No Medicine Could Cure"—as "a highly melodramatic tale of love, jealousy, and revenge, the leading feature of which is of such a nature to debar more particular description."[74] Of Saikaku's works it says only that, "The very titles of some of them are too gross for quotation."[75] In an essay called "The Samurai of Japan" written in 1911, Edward Carpenter, a major mover in the sexual reform movement in England, quoted the comments made in 1906 by a German researcher, Ferdinand Karsch-Haack, regarding Saikaku's work and *Nanshoku ōkagami* in particular: "How is it possible to justify the complete neglect of this literature? Saikaku's work does not only belong to the history of literature generally, but is also a mine of information for the history of Japanese culture, such as can only be left out of consideration by wilful suppression of the truth."[76] Karsch-Haack and Carpenter shared a belief that male love had a rightful place in discussions of Japanese culture and literature. This translation ought to contribute, if belatedly, to their vision of integrating the topic into scholarly discussion of Japan. If it does so, my job as translator will have been worth the effort.

The Great Mirror of Male Love,
or
The Custom of Boy Love in Our Land

Preface

According to my humble reading of *The Chronicles of Japan*,[1] when heaven and earth were first formed, a single living thing appeared. It was shaped like a sprouting reed and became a god, the august Kuni-toko-tachi. From that time forth the male force existed alone for three generations. This represents the historical origins of boy love.[2]

From the fourth generation of the heavenly gods, male and female forces were in licentious communion. Only then did pairs of male and female gods appear.[3] Since that time, alas! women have managed to capture the attention of men, whether with hair tied back and hanging loose as of old, or coiffured in a "hanging Shimada" and reeking of plum blossom oil in the latest fashion of this floating world, their slender willow waists wrapped in scarlet underskirts.

Women may serve a purpose for the amusement of retired old men in lands lacking handsome youths, but in a man's lusty prime they are not worthy companions even for conversation. Our entry into the gateway of boy love has been delayed long enough!

New Year's Day
Jōkyō 4 [1687], Fourth Cyclical Sign, Year of the Hare
Kakuei
Shōju

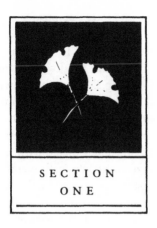

== I : I ==

Love: The Contest Between Two Forces

In the beginning was boy love.
Famous woman-haters of Japan.
Lectures on *The Record of the Origins of Male Love.*

In the beginning when gods illuminated the heavens, Kuni-toko-tachi was taught the love of boys by a wagtail bird[1] living on the dry riverbed below the floating bridge of heaven. From this sprang his love for Hi-no-chimaru.[2] Even the myriad insects preferred the position of boy love. As a result, Japan was called "The Land of Dragonflies." The god Susa-no-wo, no longer able to enjoy the love of boys in his old age, turned to the princess Inada for comfort.[3] Since then the cries of wailing infants have echoed throughout the world. Midwives and go-betweens have made their appearance; parents suffer with the burden of their daughters' dowries. Why, when there is no form of amusement more elegant than male love, do people nowadays remain unaware of its subtle pleasures?

Boy love is a profound thing. Similar cases in both Chinese and Japanese history attest to this. Wei Ling-kung entrusted his life to Mi Tzu-hsia, Kao Tsu gave his whole heart to Chi Ju, and Wu Ti pillowed only with Li Yen-nien.[4] In our country, too, the "man of old"[5] was for over five years the lover of Ise's younger brother, Daimon no Chūjō.[6] During that time there were springs in which he took no notice of the blossoms, and autumns when he did not see the harvest moon. For the sake of his overpowering love, he bore the weight of snows and filled his sleeves with stormy gusts. He crossed frozen streams and quieted barking dogs with handfuls of rice. When gateways in earthen walls were tightly locked to him, he entered with a pass key. Even in the darkness of night he damned the milky way and cursed the glow of fireflies lest their meager light betray him. On a bench where servants relaxed in the cool of evening he sat all night with his beloved until his legs were red with the blood of mosquitos. Still, his ardor did not cool, and when dawn broke he grieved that they should bid each other farewell for another day. The fierce wind parched his once glossy forelocks; to the distant crowing of roosters he stole away home. The tears that spilled from his eyes he caught in an inkstone and with his writing brush he unburdened his heart. The slender volume that preserves the memories of those days is called *The Collection of Nightly Visits.* How is it that he later turned his back on male love to write a tale about women?[7]

After coming of age, he abandoned his would-be lover[8] and set off for the Nara capital.[9] The cap of young purple that he wore surely makes him the father of all kabuki actors.[10] From behind, his figure was like a lovely peach blossom languishing in spring or a willow swaying drowsily in the breeze; he put even Mao Ch'iang and Hsi Shih to shame.[11] As an adult, Narihira still preferred the company of handsome youths to that of women. The fact that he is remembered in this floating world as the god of *yin* and *yang*[12] must cause him no end of vexation in the grave.

Another example is the priest Yoshida Kenkō,[13] who sent thousands of love letters to a nephew of Sei Shōnagon named Kiyowakamaru.[14] People did not reproach him for this, only for the single love letter that he wrote to a woman as a favor for a friend.[15] His sullied reputation remains with us to this very day. Truly, female love is something that all men should fear. When I was born, if I had known what I now know about women, I would never have suckled at my mother's breast. There are, after all, any number of instances in which children have been raised on gruel and sweet broth.

In any case, I took my bachelor's household and established a residence at a rented property in a remote corner of Asakusa in Edo, Musashi Province. Oblivious to the world's joys and sorrows and the strife that afflicts humankind, I remained sequestered behind my locked gate and expounded on *The Record of the Origins of Boy Love* before breakfast each morning. I wrote down in it everything I had ever seen, heard, felt, or learned about the rare pleasures of boy love in my 42 years of travel throughout the land.

First, let us examine the differences between male and female love.

Which is to be preferred: A girl of eleven or twelve scrutinizing herself in a mirror, or a boy of the same age cleaning his teeth?

Lying rejected next to a courtesan, or conversing intimately with a kabuki boy who is suffering from hemorrhoids?

Caring for a wife with tuberculosis, or keeping a youth who constantly demands spending money?

Having lightning strike the room where you are enjoying a boy actor you bought, or being handed a razor by a courtesan you hardly know who asks you to die with her?

Buying a *kakoi* courtesan[16] the day after suffering a gambling loss, or procuring a boy on the streets after a market collapse affecting goods in which you have just invested?

Marrying the master's daughter and going to bed early every evening until you gradually waste away, or falling in love with the master's son and seeing his face only in the daytime?

A widow over 60 wearing a scarlet underskirt and counting her silver, or a boy with shaved temples in a simple cotton sash who is leafing through his past oaths of love?

Visiting Shimabara[17] too often and losing your house to foreclosure, or spending all your money at Dōtombori[18] and discovering that the due date for the castle rice you borrowed is fast approaching?

Having the ghost of a youth appear after telling "100 scary tales," or having your ex-wife appear demanding money?

Peeking at the faces of actors under their sedge hats as they
return from the theater, or asking a young apprentice her mistress's
rank on their way to meet a customer?

Becoming a priest's attendant at Mt. Kōya,[19] or becoming the
mistress of a retired gentleman?

A shrine dancing girl who makes her rounds to bless the rice
pot and secretly hopes to come upon a household of men,[20] or a boy
peddling aloeswood oil who dreads the central chambers of a daimyo's residence?[21]

The mouth of a woman as she blackens her teeth,[22] or the hand
of a youth as he plucks his whiskers?

Seeking shelter from a storm in the gateway of a house of assig-
nation[23] where you have no connections, or being refused a lantern

for the trip home in the middle of the night after visiting a boy actor in his lodgings?

Becoming intimate with a bathhouse girl, or secretly visiting a youth who is on a 30-day contract to another man? [24]

Ransoming a courtesan, or setting up a kabuki actor in a house of his own?

Lending your jacket to a Yoshiwara jester, [25] or giving your pocket money to an actor's attendant on the dry riverbed for safe keeping? [26]

Going to Shinmachi before the Bon Festival and falling in love with a courtesan, [27] or becoming enamored of an actor just before the annual presentation on stage? [28]

A teahouse girl chomping on nuts, or a youth selling fragrance who double-checks his scales?

Watching from behind the head of a kabuki *tayū*[29] as he entertains on a riverboat, or glimpsing the hem of a dappled robe trailing from a maid's carriage on its way back from cherry blossom viewing?

A youth attired in skirt and jacket who has his attendant carry his books on an outing, or a sumptuously dressed female attendant who has her helper carry a period lacquer letter box?

A daimyo's favorite page seated in the great reception chamber, or the unseemly figure of a standing female courtier?

Being laughed at for sending a love letter to a boy whose sleeve vents are already sewn shut,[30] or being looked at askance when a girl in a long-sleeved robe takes a liking to you?[31]

In each case above, even if the woman were a beauty of gentle disposition and the youth a repulsive pug-nosed fellow, it is a sacrilege to speak of female love in the same breath with boy love. A woman's heart can be likened to the wisteria vine: though bearing lovely blossoms, it is twisted and bent. A youth may have a thorn or two, but he is like the first plum blossom of the new year exuding an indescribable fragrance. The only sensible choice is to dispense with women and turn instead to men.

Kōbō Daishi[32] did not preach the profound pleasures of this love outside the monasteries because he feared the extinction of humankind. No doubt he foresaw the popularity of boy love in these last days of the law. Where it flourishes, a man must sometimes sacrifice his life for the one he loves. Why in the world did "the man who loved love"[33] waste such vast quantities of gold and silver on his myriad women, when the only pleasure and excitement to be found is in male love?

I have attempted to reflect in this "great mirror" all of the varied manifestations of male love. Like someone gathering seaweed among the reeds in the shallow inlet of Naniwa,[34] I gathered my material for the leaves of this book. It will no doubt soon be forgotten by those who read it. Such is the way of the world.

The ABCs of Boy Love

Writing the copybook of boy love.
Country forelocks surpass capital flowers.
The priest who fell in love and then disappeared.

He turned everything over to his younger half-brother, even his six corner properties and his right to transact business with daimyo.[1] The echo of freight carts in the capital and the clanging of scales had become more than he could bear, and he was especially tired of hearing the voices of women hawking charcoal all day.

From this place near the base of Mt. Kamo he could look down to the north on a stand of white cedars. To the east were caverns choked with vines in vibrant fall colors. From a natural outcropping of rocks to the west flowed sparkling spring water, and pines towered to the south. He loved this place and the way the moon's light filtered through the pine needles at night. He had chosen this site to build a secluded hut for himself. To be sure, no clouds cast their shadow on his mind here, but he was on occasion subject to sudden showers of nostalgia for the love he tried to, but could not, forget. He yearned for a visit from a handsome youth. He had long ago resigned himself to the solitude of his nights, yet the calls of plovers that greeted him when he woke stirred up feelings of deep sadness.

The sound of the stream was busy to his ears. The lay priest Ishikawa Jōzan,[2] who wrote, "its waters reflect my shame; waves of old age rising," had also lived on this stream.[3] Soon its banks were treacherous with ice and even the myriad grasses, left behind by grazing cattle, withered away. The path to his hut disappeared under snow, and before long he was feeling the scarcity of bean curd and soy sauce.

He closed his lattice doors and thought back to the stages of Shijō-gawara where the annual presentations would just be starting.[4] He could only imagine what wonderful new young actors would be taking their places on the stage this year. Shortly even that season passed, and it was the depths of winter. The urgent footsteps of passersby, the cries of fern hawkers selling their fronds, the pounding of rice cakes, the last minute settling of debts;[5] his new way of life made it possible for him to avoid it all. Then, even the darkest night of the year was past, and with the song of the harbinger bird of spring the plum blossoms on branches facing south began to open. With them opened his lattice doors. Inspired by the spring mists, he applied fragrant oils to his hair and coiffured it with his own hands, but there was no one to appreciate the handsome man that he was.

Spring deepened and cherry trees flowered in the hills, inconveniently attracting to his remote corner of the world a hodgepodge of widows and new brides who, perhaps not satisfied with viewing blossoms at Kiyomizu and Ninna-ji, came to drown these green groves in sake. As if that fact alone were not distasteful enough, one of these enticing ladies came to borrow some salt. He told her he had none. A short time later she returned to ask for chopsticks. This time he just glared at her without answering. When at long last the sun sank in the west, a manservant attending to these unwelcome visitors dumped what sake remained in their kegs, emptied the hot water kettles, and expertly put everything away. The ladies, meanwhile, hurriedly prepared for departure. They removed their cotton stockings and stuffed them into their sleeves. Their silver hairpins were replaced with toothpicks, and hair combs went into tissue holders for safe keeping. Scarlet underskirts were hitched up and tucked in at the waist, and their sadly soiled collars were pulled back in a decolletage. Pell-mell they grabbed their hemp hats, left hanging on tree branches. The sight of these ladies in their mad rush to leave at the end of the day was an ugly change from their appearance that morning. He had been forced to witness the worst possible behavior of townswomen.[6] One of them peered through his hedge on her way home and noticed a peg for hanging fish.[7] She scolded him in a loud voice, "You are not even a priest, yet you have ignored us all day!"

And why not? If he had been interested in women, he could

have married into an old and distinguished family in Tsukiboko intent on having him, but he had refused. In addition, he had painted all of the windows to the north black because he was tired of seeing ladies seated in imperial carriages accompanying her highness to the detached palace at Shūgaku-ji[8] wearing robes of royal purple and sashes knotted behind with their black hair done up in the "jewel" style. Like a plant which prefers shade, he lived a forlorn and useless existence.

But even a useless existence has its pleasures. He opened a classroom for boys from surrounding villages and taught them penmanship using *The Schoolboy's Primer*.[9] They called him "Ichidō, the Penmaster."

Thus, he passed his days.

It was the fourteenth day of the third month. The sky was growing hazy when, toward dusk, the boys began to gather for their evening lessons. Each was determined to outdo the others in his penmanship practice for the next day's lesson. If a boy missed a word, he would suffer a blow from Ichidō's pointing stick or was sometimes made to carry his writing table outside the front gate on his back. How amusing it looked!

That day, two samurai boys from Shimogamo[10] had been assigned to get the room ready for class. One was Shino'oka Daikichi, age nine. Ono Shinnosuke, also age nine, was the other. They arrived together ahead of the rest of the class. On the way, they had come to a shaky bridge that Daikichi thought too dangerous to cross at dusk, so he hitched up the hem of his robe and solicitously carried Shinnosuke across the river on his back. Once at school, Daikichi insisted on carrying water from spigot to teahouse all by himself. Alone, he built a fire of dry leaves and braved the billowing smoke. He even swept the classroom himself, not allowing his partner to lift a finger. Shinnosuke merely scrutinized his face in a pocket mirror and smoothed a few stray hairs of his forelocks. The way he primped struck Ichidō as strangely sophisticated. Feigning sleep, he observed the two from a nearby vantage point.

Shinnosuke took Daikichi's hand in his. "Is that spot still painful?" he asked.

Daikichi scoffed. "A little thing like this?" He pulled back his robe and bared his shoulder for Shinnosuke to see. A welt, symbol of their pact of boy love, stood purple and swollen where he had pierced and cut himself.

"And to think that you did it for my sake," Shinnosuke said tearfully.

Ichidō imagined that this was how China's Duke Chuang of Cheng must have looked when he held Tzu Tu's lovely hand in his, causing the royal carriage to halt its progress.[11] They say that after King Ai of Wei took Lung Yang-chun as his lover, civil chaos caused by the subversive influence of women ceased and the entire nation was convinced of the virtue of boy love.[12]

Since he was himself such a devotee of this way of love, Ichidō thought, perhaps his young charges had unconsciously learned it

from him. That would explain the show of affection between the
two boys. Afterwards, he took careful notice of them and discovered that, indeed, they were always side by side, inseparable as two
trees grafted together or a pair of one-winged birds.[13] When the
two boys later reached their peak of youthful beauty, men and
women, clergy and layman alike were all smitten with the handsome youths. The two were the cause of a thousand sorrows, a
hundred illnesses, and untold deaths from lovesickness.

At about this time, there lived in the far reaches of Shishigatani
a Buddhist ascetic who was over 80 years old. They say that from
the moment he chanced to see these two splendid boys, his concentration on future salvation failed him and the good deeds he had
accumulated in previous incarnations went to naught. News of the
priest's feelings reached the boys. Not sure which of them the old
gentleman had his heart set on, both went to his rude abode for a
visit. Predictably, he found it impossible to dispense with either
cherry blossoms or fall foliage. Thus, he satisfied with both of them
the love he had harbored from spring through autumn.

The next day, both boys paid another visit to the priest, for there
was something they had neglected to tell him, but he was nowhere
to be found. They discovered only a poem, dated the previous day,
tied to a forked branch of bamboo:

> Here are travel weeds
> Tear-stained like my faithless heart
> Torn between the two;
> I shall cut my earthly ties
> And hide myself away in bamboo leaves.

Of what was this old priest ashamed? Long ago, the priest
Shinga Sōjō[14] wrote:

> Memories of love revive,
> Like rock azaleas bursting into bloom
> On Mount Tokiwa;
> My stony silence only shows
> How desperately I want you![15]

The boys took the bamboo branch and had a skilled artisan
make it into a pair of flutes. On cold winter nights when they

played together, heavenly beings were moved to peek down from the sky, and Taira no Atsumori[16] appeared along with our Morita Shōbei[17] to listen in awe.

There is nothing, however, more fleeting than human existence. Chinese poets called it "as brief as a dream at sunset," and our own poets liken it to "awakening in a temporary shelter at dawn." Ah, was it real or merely a dream? Had Shinnosuke but been frost he would have lasted until daybreak, but instead he awoke one night at the age of fourteen with the tolling of the seventh bell,[18] then closed his eyes forever. He left untouched the water of this stream,[19] offered to quench his dying thirst.

Daikichi was broken-hearted. "No one will ever be able to hear us play together again," he thought. He shattered the flutes and committed them, too, to the flames. He then secluded himself on Mt. Iwakura and took religious vows. With his own hand he picked up a razor and, alas! shaved off his lovely black hair.

Within the Fence: Pine, Maple, and a Willow Waist

Love revealed in a visitor's register.
A prayer said at Hachiman for his recovery.
Sad that he should enter manhood before putting in corners.[1]

"All men are beautiful, whereas women of beauty are rare." This was the orthodox opinion of Abe no Seimei.[2] Why? Because female beauty is completely artificial. Women bury their faces under a thick layer of powder, paint their lips red, blacken their teeth, reshape hairlines, and ink in eyebrows. Even the way they dress is designed to deceive.

There was a certain man who lived incognito in a village near Kazenomori, Ōsumi Province, where breezes cooled the sleeves of his silk summer kimono. Even there, in the province of his birth, his long years as a masterless samurai had taken their toll. Life was miserable, and his days of glory were nothing more than a distant memory. His name was Tachibana Jūzaemon, and he was a highly skilled practitioner of military arts. His lord of long ago deeply regretted releasing him from service, but because he had gotten embroiled in a dispute with a chief retainer, he was obliged to flee the castle under cover of night. He still waited for the day when he might once again resume service.

His wife was from remote Kurusu no Ono in Yamashiro Province. She had for many years served at the Murakumo imperial palace at Ichijō,[3] so her ears had grown more accustomed to the plucking of the jeweled koto than to the beating of the mortar and pestle from her birthplace. She had learned to call lighting a lamp, "bringing forth pine illumination"; even the paste used for pickling, called *nukamiso* in common homes, she referred to as "wine paste." She learned by imitation to do everything in a refined manner. Even her face and figure became those of a lovely woman of the capital.

While still in his lord's service, Jūzaemon had connections at this imperial palace. In the winter of the lady's 22nd year, on the first day of the boar,[4] he asked for and received her hand in marriage. They became husband and wife, and to them was born a remarkable child, a son so lovely he truly was deserving of a mother's pride. They gave him the name Tamanosuke.[5]

The boy was now fifteen years old. His beautifully coiffured hair was lovely from every angle, surely the object of covetous glances from the ocean palace of the dragon king.[6] People who saw him said, "Such beauty is wasted in this rustic place." Thus it was that early one morning Tamanosuke found himself preparing to leave for Musashi Province in the east to take up a long-hoped-for position in the service of a certain lord. He was under the guardianship of an old and trusted attendant to the family named Kanazawa Kakubei. At over 50 years of age, Kakubei was capable of sound judgement in all matters concerning the boy's welfare. Tamanosuke's father had only one piece of advice as he bid his son farewell. "Remember, a samurai must always be prepared to give up his life."

His mother moved over to Kakubei's side and whispered for a moment. "Be especially vigilant about that matter," she said in parting.

Those accompanying the boy were perplexed, but Tamanosuke beckoned to Kakubei and said, "I suppose my mother asked you not to deliver love letters from my male admirers. It would be heartless of you not to convey them to me, regardless of the station of their senders. I was blessed to be born into this world of humanity with looks that men find agreeable. It would be terrible to earn the reputation of a 'heartless youth,' as the Chinese boy Yu Hsin was called at Yang-chow in Tsung Wen's poem."[7]

Kakubei thought for a moment and answered, "If everyone were as concerned about the matter as your mother, I imagine that boy love would cease to exist in this floating world!" Laughing loudly, they set out on their way.

It was summer, and the sea was calm. They landed at Murotsu

and continued to the Suma barrier.[8] As they crossed it, Tamano-suke tried to imagine the pangs he would be feeling if he were in love. Later, when he heard that they would soon cross the Osaka barrier, he yearned to be on a lover's secret rendezvous. At Kanjū-ji he could see to the north the mountain that towered over his mother's birthplace. He no longer had kinfolk there, so they passed without stopping. He picked up some medicine for sale at an Ume-noki teahouse and gratefully cooled his sweaty brow with cold water. There, they met up with a man dispatched from Edo to serve as their guide. From him Tamanosuke learned the details of his service.

Tamanosuke was in high spirits when they finally arrived in Edo at the beginning of the sixth month. He soon completed his formal presentation to the lord and joined the lord's retinue on its way back to the domain in Aizu.[9] His unsurpassed attention to the lord's needs soon made him a favorite; his beauty made the hand-some youths of the province look like morning-glories at nightfall.

One evening, the wind died down and the willow and maple trees at the corners of the ball court were still. Iwakura Mondo, Yamada Shōshichi, Yokoi Hayato, and Tamanosuke began a game of kemari.[10] They were all skilled players, and the lord watched in great spirits. He was dismayed, however, to notice that Tamano-suke dropped the ball time and again. "He is normally the best player in the household," he thought, "worthy of being born into the Asukai family!"[11]

Just then, Tamanosuke's expression changed abruptly. His body convulsed, and his limbs turned blue. Before anyone could loosen his robes for him, he fell to the ground unconscious. Horrified, they brought him water and medicine and, when he had regained his senses, carried him inside. Doctors did everything in their power to help, but his condition only grew worse. It seemed that his earthly existence would soon end. The whole world hushed its clamor in sorrow.

There was a samurai named Sasamura Senzaemon in charge of guarding an outpost on the border of the lord's domain. He was a minor official whom few of his fellow samurai in the castle town could have identified. He had been in love with Tamanosuke for

some time and thought of the boy night and day. There was no way, however, for him to establish contact except perhaps to reveal his feelings in a letter. He had decided to do just that when this disaster struck. He felt he could not go on living if anything serious happened to the boy, so he went to the place where Tamanosuke lay ill. He asked after the boy's condition and signed his name in the guest register along with the other visitors. He returned home, but in the afternoon went once more to inquire after the boy's health. That evening he again visited to see if there had been any improvement. Thus, three times a day, every day for over six months, Senzaemon kept his vigil.

When Tamanosuke had recovered completely from his life-threatening illness, he purified himself, trimmed his hair, and made the rounds to pay his respects first to the lord and then to each member of the high council. When he had returned to his residence he asked Kakubei to show him the visitor's register. He looked it over and noticed that the signature of a gentleman named Sasamura Senzaemon appeared three times every day from the first day of his illness.

"Who could this person be?" he asked, but no one seemed to know.

"We assumed he had some connection with your family," Kakubei explained. "He asked anxiously about your condition each day. If you improved, he was overjoyed; whenever your condition grew worse, he was distraught. His grief was much more pronounced than anyone else's."

"He must be a remarkable man to have taken such an interest in my welfare without ever having met me," Tamanosuke commented. For the moment, he let the matter drop.

Senzaemon's residence was quite some distance away, but Tamanosuke decided to pay a visit. He sent in a message when he got there saying, "I happened to be in the area, and wanted to express my gratitude for your kind attention during my recent illness."

Senzaemon came rushing out immediately. "What an unexpected honor! Thank you for deigning to come to such a remote place, on a windy evening such as this, so soon after your recovery. The night is chill; please go home in safety."

"The world is like lightning that strikes in broad daylight. I dare not risk waiting until we meet again lest I die before that time. I must speak with you, for my heart will give me no peace. Shall we go inside?"

Tamanosuke walked ahead into the waiting room and sat on the veranda with Senzaemon. They were alone but for the pines in the garden.

"Allow me to tell you what is on my mind," he continued. "Your actions during my illness, and please pardon me if I am wrong, lead me to believe that you may be in love with me, unworthy though I am. If such is the case, allow me to give myself to you from this day forward. I came in secret today to tell you this, nothing more."

Senzaemon first blushed, then wept, looking very much like

autumn foliage buffeted by a sudden rainstorm. When he was finally able to speak, he opened his heart to the boy.

"But it is difficult to express these things in words," he said. "Come with me to the Hachiman Shrine.[12] There is something in the inner sanctuary that I want you to see."

Immediately, they went to the shrine. The head priest, Ukyō, told Tamanosuke all that had transpired.

"He came here every day to pray for your recovery and placed his petition to the gods in this box."

Tamanosuke looked inside and found a short Sadamune sword[13] and a letter in which Senzaemon pleaded for Tamanosuke's recovery.

"So, it was your prayers that allowed me to keep my fragile hold on life," he said. "Now I am determined more than ever not to abandon you."

News of their bond of love soon became public knowledge. After an inquiry by the administrator of legal affairs, they were both placed under house arrest.[14] They knew from the moment they made their vow of love that they were doomed to die, so the arrest caused them no special grief. They had prepared a secret channel of communication for just such an eventuality and were therefore able to exchange letters. The situation remained this way for quite some time.

Finally, Tamanosuke sent a petition to the lord.

"We are weary of life. If your lordship would but order us to commit seppuku on the ninth day of the third month, we would be most grateful."

They waited eagerly for the day to come, but a magistrate arrived to inform them that the lord had other wishes. Tamanosuke was ordered to undergo the coming-of-age ceremony,[15] and Senzaemon was forgiven unconditionally. In the future, they pledged to avoid contact of any kind until Tamanosuke reached the age of 25. Even if they were to meet by chance, they would not so much as greet each other. From that day forward they served the lord faithfully, never once forgetting his kind benevolence.

Or, so the story goes.

Love Letter Sent in a Sea Bass

Gods of the Great Shrine also ordain bonds of boy love.
His tale of three years of devotion makes people weep.
He wrote down his complaints in a final testament.

It is said that, "Cherry blossoms forever bloom the same, but people change with every passing year."[1] This is especially true of a boy in the bloom of youth. It is as if he were hit by a rain squall when the sleeve vents in his robe are sewn shut. He shudders under a rising wind when his temples are shaved. When at last he comes of age, his blossom of youth falls cruelly to the ground. All told, loving a boy can be likened to a dream that we are not even given time to have.

Jinnosuke was the second son of the Mashida family[2] in service to the lord of the province where "eight clouds rise."[3] He was a handsome boy from birth. By the spring of his eleventh year he had mastered the skills of both pen and sword. Everyone who saw him fell immediately in love. When the gods assembled at the Great Shrine, this boy was the main topic of conversation.[4] "There will never be another like him in all the provinces of Japan," they said.

The gods had matched Jinnosuke in a vow of love with a man also in the daimyo's service. He was Moriwaki Gonkurō, aged 28 that year, a samurai of reliable and trustworthy character. Gonkurō had first been smitten with the boy in the autumn of Jinnosuke's thirteenth year. Thereafter he made a point of becoming friendly with the boy's attendant, Dengorō. Through him he sent a love letter to the boy. In order to avoid discovery, he had it delivered to the attendant's quarters in the mouth of a sea bass. While combing the boy's hair the following morning, Dengorō slipped the letter into Jinnosuke's robe. The boy's lovely face reflected calmly in the mirror.

"He seems in such good spirits," Dengorō thought. "Now may be my chance to mention the letter."

He explained at great length the extent of Gonkurō's passionate feelings for Jinnosuke and how much the man suffered with love for him. Without even opening the letter, Jinnosuke hurriedly took out an inkstone to write a reply.

As he considered what Dengorō had just told him, he felt overwhelmed with joy and affection for his suitor. He decided to ally himself with the man from that day forward and ignore whatever condemnation the world might have regarding his conduct.[5]

Without writing his reply, he returned Gonkurō's letter still sealed and said to Dengorō, "The path of love will not tolerate a moment's delay. Go tell him immediately of my decision."

Touched by the boy's sensitivity, Dengorō put down the comb and left straight away.

Gonkurō wept when he heard of the boy's decision. "I can never thank you enough." He had not even met the boy, and he was already crying into his sleeves!

On a summer's night in his fourteenth year, like the long-awaited song of the nightingale, Jinnosuke first made love to Gonkurō. They met in strictest secrecy, fearful lest news of their love become known. Except for the moon, not a soul knew what was going on through the autumn of his fifteenth and sixteenth years.

Fate determines whom we love. There was a minor retainer named Hanzawa Ihei who fell in love with Jinnosuke. He used a guard named Shinzaemon as his unwilling intermediary to send letter after letter to the boy. Jinnosuke, however, refused to answer a single one. Having once revealed his feelings, Ihei now found it impossible to retreat. He sent one final letter:

"No doubt you do not deign to respond because of my lowly status. If you already belong to someone, let me know. If not, I shall clear up my resentment as soon as we have a chance to meet."

This was a challenge to fight to the death.

Thus far, Jinnosuke had kept the entire matter to himself, but he now spoke to Gonkurō, thinking that he should know what was going on.

"Just because he is a samurai of low rank does not mean you should treat his plea lightly," Gonkurō advised. "What if we were to get ourselves killed? That would be the end of our enjoyment together. Try to think of a response that will somehow satisfy him."

Jinnosuke's eyes turned red with fury when he heard this. "We made an eternal vow of love," he thought bitterly to himself. "Should the lord himself desire me, am I to surrender myself? I have a mind to kill Gonkurō and be done with him. But first I must duel with Ihei. If it is my destiny as a samurai, I will succeed in dispatching him. Then, with the same blade, I shall slay Gonkurō."

His mind made up, Jinnosuke headed home. There, he wrote his challenge to Ihei.

"You will have a chance to relieve your rancor tonight. Meet me at the pine grove at Tenjin."

He called Shinzaemon and had him deliver the letter to Ihei immediately.

It was already late in the day, the 26th of the third month. Jinnosuke listened dispassionately to the tolling of the sunset bell. He was sure that this would be the last time he ever heard its sound, but the thought did not alarm him, for he was familiar with the idea of life's uncertainty. He spent a few quiet moments with his parents, acting more solicitous of them than ever. Alone again, he wrote letters of farewell to all of his relatives and close friends. In his final letter, addressed to Gonkurō, he poured out all of the resentment stored in his heart. He was determined to make Gonkurō understand the righteousness of his anger.

"From the very beginning, when I first said, 'this body is no longer my own,' I understood that I would have to die if the nature of our relationship were ever revealed. Now that this situation has come about, I feel no particular sorrow. Tonight, I shall fight to the finish at a mountain temple.

"In view of our years of intimacy, I am deeply hurt that you should hesitate to die with me. Lest it prove to be a barrier to my salvation in the next life, I decided to include in this final testament all of the grudges against you that have accumulated in me since we first met.

"First: I made my way at night to your distant residence a total
of 327 times over the past three years. Not once did I fail to encounter trouble of some kind. To avoid detection by patrols making their nightly rounds, I disguised myself as a servant and hid
my face behind my sleeve, or hobbled along with a cane and lantern dressed like a priest. No one knows the lengths I went to in
order to meet you!

"Remember last year, the twentieth day of the eleventh month?
I was gravely ill (with worry about you, I am sure), and my mother
stayed at my bedside all evening. I was convinced that I would not
see morning, but the thought of dying without one last meeting
with you was unbearable. I cursed the light of the rising moon and
made my way in disarray to your door. Surely you recognized my
footsteps, but my only welcome was to have you extinguish the
lamp and hush your conversation. How cruel you were to me! I
would love to know who your companion was that night.

"Next: Last spring, I casually wrote the poem 'My sleeves rot,
soaked with tears of jealous rage'[6] on the back of a fan painted by
Kano no Uneme[7] in the pattern of a 'riot of flowers.'[8] You took it
and said, 'The cool breeze from this fan will help me bear the
flames of our love this summer.' How happy you made me! But
shortly it came to my attention that you gave the fan to your attendant Kichisuke with a note across the poem that said, 'This calligraphy is terrible.'

"Again, when I asked you for your favorite lark as a gift (the
one you got from the birdcatcher Jūbei), you refused and gave it to
Kitamura Shōhachi instead. He is, of course, the most handsome
boy in the household. My jealousy has not abated yet.

"Next: On the eleventh day of the fourth month past, the lord
ordered all of his young attendants from the inner chamber to
practice horseback riding. Setsubara Tarōzaemon was kind enough
to tell me that the back of my skirt was soiled and brushed it off
for me. You were standing directly behind me, but did not tell me
about it. In fact, I saw you exchange amused glances with Kozawa
Kurōjirō. After our years of love together, such a thing should
never happen.

"Next: On the eighteenth of the fifth month, you were angry

with me for talking well into the night with Ogasawara Han'ya. As I explained to you that night, he came for recitation practice along with Ogaki Magosaburō and Matsuhara Tomoya. There were no other visitors. Han'ya is still a mere child, Magosaburō is my age, and Tomoya you know. There should be no problem with our getting together to practice every night if we wish, yet you are still full of suspicions. I find your frequent insinuating remarks very upsetting. By the gods of Japan, I swear that I still cannot forget my anger at your distrust.

"Next: Since the time when we first became lovers, you never once saw me to my house when we bid each other farewell in the morning. In fact, in all these years, you only twice saw me as far as the bridge in front of Uneme's. If you love someone, you should be willing to see him safely home through wilds filled with wolves and tigers.

"Though I hold this and that grudge against you, the fact that I cannot bring myself to stop loving you must be the work of some strange fate. To weep is my only comfort. For the sake of our friendship up to now, I ask you to pray, even if but once, for my rebirth in paradise. How strange to think that the impermanence of this world should also affect me."

He closed the letter with a poem: "While yet in full bloom, it is buffeted by an unexpected gale; the morning glory falls with the dew, ere evening draws nigh." [9]

It ended, "These are the thoughts I wanted to leave with you. Evening, my last, is drawing nigh, so I shall bid farewell. Kambun 7 [1667], third month, 26th day."

He gave the letter to Dengorō with instructions to take it to Moriwaki Gonkurō that night at the fourth bell. [10] As the beat of the sunset drum began to echo in the dusk, Jinnosuke rushed to his rendezvous.

He had dressed with some flair, knowing that he would be saying farewell to this floating world in the robes he wore. Against his skin was a lined garment; over that he wore a pale blue robe blending into white at the waist. It was handsomely decorated with a cherry blossom pattern embroidered in multicolored thread. It also bore a circular ginkgo-leaf crest. Faintly visible were autumn leaves

dyed on the reverse side of his sleeves. His sash was gray, done in
a heavy eight-layered weave. He carried a matching set of long and
short swords made by Tadayoshi of Hizen.[11] In preparation for the
fight, he discarded his knife and checked to see that the rivet on
his sword hilt was secure.

He made his way to the pine grove at Tenjin about one *li*[12]
distant from the castle. There was a large boulder completely hidden by ivy with a giant laurel tree behind it where he sat in wait
for his foe. Dusk deepened, and soon it grew too dark to distinguish faces. Suddenly, who should appear but Gonkurō, gasping
for breath.

"Is it you, Jinnosuke?"

"A coward is no friend of mine," he answered.

Moriwaki wept. "I won't make apologies here. I shall prove my
love to you as we cross the river to the next world."[13]

"I don't need your help," Jinnosuke retorted.

In the midst of this argument, Hanzawa Ihei appeared with
fifteen of his roughest men.

The four of them[14] drew at the same instant and wielded their
swords in the chaotic fray, determined to die manfully in the on-
slaught. Jinnosuke cut two of them down, and four fell under
Gonkurō's sword. Of the sixteen men, six died outright, seven were
injured, and the others escaped. On their side, the attendant Kichisuke died on the spot, Gonkurō received a light wound above his
eye, and Jinnosuke suffered a slight gash where a sword grazed his
shoulder.

Their task completed, they crept in secret to a nearby temple
called Eiun-ji. They requested the resident priest to bury them
properly after their seppuku, but the priest insisted that they wait.

"You have made it this far alive. Why not first explain the reason for the duel to the elders and authorities in charge? Then, if
you commit seppuku for them to see, you can preserve your reputations unblemished in the world."

Convinced, the two went immediately to the nearest guard station and explained the sequence of events as recorded above.[15] After verifying the facts and reporting them to the lord, the two were
ordered to refrain from committing seppuku and taken that night

to the castle town where they were turned over to their respective families and told to nurse their wounds.

The lord ordered that those who had escaped the fight be cut down on sight. The province's ports were closed, and after an inquiry the injured were summarily executed. Later, the following favorable decision was handed down:

"In the matter concerning Jinnosuke, we find him guilty of grave negligence in breaking the law of his lord. Nevertheless, his father Jimbei is a loyal retainer and pious son, and Jinnosuke himself had served well previous to the event. Moreover, his valorous deeds during this incident we find most remarkable for one of his tender years. Therefore, we have decided not to punish the boy. Likewise, Gonkurō shall be forgiven unconditionally."

Jinnosuke was reinstated into his former position as a castle guard and ordered to begin service on the fifteenth of the month.

People flocked to Eiun-ji to see the wonders that Jinnosuke's sword had wrought that night. They counted 73 nicks on his blade and 18 cuts in his sheath. His robes were completely stained with blood. His left sleeve had been cut off entirely. In the midst of such violent fighting, he himself had escaped serious injury. No young samurai had ever performed such a feat. Those who saw it wept in awe. Later, when Jinnosuke came to properly mourn Ihei and his fallen comrades, his reputation for remarkable thoughtfulness was enhanced still further.

The likes of this handsome boy should be a model for future generations. I, for one, would like to take Jinnosuke's letter to Gonkurō, burn it, and make the tea brewed from the ashes required drinking for the faint-hearted young men of our day.

Someone posted a rhyme on the central gate designating Jinnosuke as the precious incense of boy love. "Ten times the love of Moriwaki, more fragrant than aloeswood: Mashida Jinnosuke." It became the topic of widespread conversation.

With him as their example, all the sons of samurai strove to emulate Jinnosuke. Even the sons of merchants sweating over their scales, farm boys slaving in the fields, and salt makers' sons burnt black on the beaches, no matter how rude their appearance or menial their task, all yearned to sacrifice their lives for the sake of male love. Boys without male lovers, like women without husbands, were thought of with pity. Boy love became the fashion, and the love between men and women went into precipitous decline.

Implicated by His Diamond Crest

Medicine that takes lives.
A woman's handwriting leads him to his lover.
Struck by an arrow at a river forded in secret.

The man announced that he could fit a collapsible boat into a portable chest. When reassembled, the boat was capable of carrying three men across a large river in safety. Such a boat would be very useful in wartime. He also claimed to be skilled at making flotation devices and guns that could shoot flaming arrows. As a result, he was granted a yearly stipend of 200 *koku*.[1]

He had been a masterless samurai for many years and utilized his skills with weaponry only as a means to keep himself fed. He hoped someday to realize his desire for proper employment in the service of a daimyo, but he had reached the age of 27 and was still waiting for such a position to materialize.

His younger sister used to live in the town of Sasayama in Tamba, but after her husband's death she left the world behind to live at Dōmyō-ji, a temple in Kawachi Province.[2] There, she put on the black robe of a nun in the summer of her nineteenth year. He had no word of her situation until the fifth month of this year when a letter arrived. Enclosed in it was some *hanako*,[3] a local specialty of Kawachi. Her thoughtfulness seemed to reach out to him across the many miles as he sprinkled the powdered *hanako* into a cup of Kagoshima water for a cool drink. It would help him fend off the summer's heat, he thought, but soon his sweat turned to tears. Sadly, he remembered his sister in the days of her youth so long ago and how she used to love wearing her red summer kimono.

His other sister was fourteen years old. Arrangements had not yet been made for her marriage, so she had accompanied her old mother to live with him in this unfamiliar place. The life of a samurai is full of such trials. His father had died when he was still a boy, and the fact that he was now known in the world as Shimamura Daiemon he attributed entirely to his mother's efforts. He was extremely grateful to her. Whenever the morning breezes were chill, he solicitously looked in to see that she was warm. He spread her bed himself in the evening rather than allow a servant to do it. His little sister and the others learned from his example. They would quit their task of stretching new cotton wadding in order to bring her a pillow for her nap, or see to it that her narrow sash or rosary purse were put away in their proper places. They religiously carried out their filial duty. This is the way all parents should be treated.

One evening, Daiemon was hurrying on his way to a place called Fukazawa for a firefly-viewing party. In a field on the outskirts of town was a dense growth of pampas grass and irises. Not far from the path was an underground spring from which fresh water bubbled up, and right beside it stood a stone Buddha said to have been carved by Kōbō Daishi himself. On feast days when ancestors were remembered, people came here to worship and sprinkle the figure with water. As Daiemon passed by this place, he observed a man, apparently a samurai's attendant, remove a new letter box from his robe and place it in front of the stone figure. The man glanced around furtively and then walked away, deliberately leaving the letter box behind. Daiemon wondered what this strange behavior meant, so he pursued the man.

"Why did you leave that box in front of the stone figure?" he demanded.

The man was frightened and tried to escape without answering, but Daiemon's suspicions were aroused. He captured the man and took him by force to a remote temple where he interrogated him. The man would reveal nothing. Ignoring his repeated pleas for mercy, Daiemon bound him with a length of rope and left him in the reluctant keeping of the priest in residence there. He then returned to pick up the letter box mentioned above. When he got there, however, local people had already discovered it and sent it off to the authorities.

The officials assembled that night in a special session. The box bore no address, so they opened it and found a letter inside.

"Here is the poison of which I spoke to you in private. It should be administered to the said parties as soon as possible. After you have read this letter, burn it." The message was unsigned; the only mark it bore was a diamond crest enclosed in a circle at the bottom of the page. With the letter was a small pouch that had been sealed with obvious care.

The entire assembly of officials was aghast. They discovered after an inquiry that the crest belonged to a young samurai named Haruta Tannosuke. He was summoned in secret and questioned about the matter, but he denied any knowledge of it. Nevertheless, because of the gravity of the charges, he was placed under house arrest. When Daiemon heard this, he took the man he had captured earlier to Tannosuke's house and tied him to a horse-hitch outside the gate. Before leaving, he wrote a message that said, "This man knows the truth about the letter box."

In the morning the man was dead. He had bitten his tongue and bled to death. But there was no concealing the fact of his identity. He was the attendant of Kishioka Ryūemon. The authorities finally thought they had their man, but when they went to arrest Ryūemon, he had already fled his house for parts unknown. Tannosuke was summoned once again and asked if he had any recollection of the matter, but he again insisted that he knew nothing. The authorities had reached a dead end in their investigation and could only assume that Ryūemon's flight was an admission of guilt. He would be punished when captured. As for Tannosuke, he was declared innocent of any wrongdoing and allowed to return to the lord's service.

Some time passed, and one day a close friend of Tannosuke's questioned him about the incident. Tannosuke then revealed everything.

"Ryūemon had for a long time been sending me letters expressing his affection, but I recognized him as the sort of man capable of this underhanded deed and refused his advances. Out of spite, he plotted that evil scheme against me. It was a crime of the heart, however, so I lied to protect him."

The friend was so impressed with Tannosuke's kindness in protecting his enemy that the story seemed to spread of its own volition. People called him unique in the annals of boy love, but even that characterization did not do him justice. As a boy of seven his graceful beauty "that with one smile triggered a hundred lusts"[4] was such that few people who saw him realized he was not a girl. The fact that now, at the age of fifteen, he was still without a male lover was only further proof of his outstanding beauty. As Li Tai-po said in a poem, "No one breaks blossoms from a tree at a distant house."[5]

Tannosuke had been able to avoid catastrophe in the letter-box incident because Ryūemon's attendant had appeared tied up at his gate. He tried to discover the identity of the man who left the note, but to no avail. He could only hope that if he prayed to the gods earnestly enough, they would reveal the man to him. Fall and winter passed with the matter still weighing on his mind.

A new year dawned and, with spring, the snow on the hills melted to reveal evergreens beneath. Streams swelled with the run-off, and waterfalls appeared once again in the valley. For diversion, Tannosuke went one day with some friends to the mouth of a stream to catch *ayu*. In each hand he held a fan-shaped fish net. On the way, he noticed an attractive girl in the company of her mother picking reed blossoms, horsetail shoots, and aster buds. They were with a group of servant women in the fields near a remote village. Something in their manner suggested that they were people from the capital. Tannosuke paused to watch them for a while and noticed that the young lady was staring his way. She whispered something to her mother, then took out a small ink-stone, added some water, and wrote a note on some paper that she carried in her kimono. She tied the note to the tip of a branch and walked far into the shadows of a path below a rocky cliff. Fascinated with what she might have written, Tannosuke went up and read the note:

"This field is thick with people, so I have gone further up the hill to the plateau south of the wisteria temple."

It was addressed to one "Daiemon" and was apparently meant to let the man know that she had gone ahead. When he looked at the message again, he realized with a shock that, though written in a woman's hand, the style bore a striking resemblance to the note left at his gate on that day last summer. He was still gazing at it in amazement when Daiemon came up, took the message, and started to walk away. Tannosuke called after him.

"Are you the gentleman called Daiemon? My name is Haruta Tannosuke. Though we serve in the same household, I do not believe we have ever had the opportunity to meet. There is something I would like to inquire of you. In the fifth month last year, was it you who kindly captured and bound Ryūemon's attendant at my gate?"

"Yes, it was," Daiemon said. "It is a pleasure to meet you at last."

"I am extremely grateful for your kind handling of the matter. I was unable to express my thanks earlier because I did not know your identity. You must have thought me lacking in feelings of any kind. I owe you an apology." Tannosuke wept as he spoke.

"No, it was entirely my fault for not revealing myself," Daiemon protested, deeply touched. "I hesitated because I was new in his lordship's service and did not want to cause trouble. I see that all I succeeded in doing was causing you a great deal of worry."

As they wept there together, a strong attraction developed between them. Without ever exchanging formal vows of love, they began meeting as lovers. To avoid discovery, Daiemon crossed the big river behind Tannosuke's house and visited him in secret. This continued for some time without incident.

Until one night.

The residence next to Tannosuke's had a teahouse built on piers over the river. A group of samurai had been playing a game of middle *shōgi*[6] since early evening and, after a great deal of drinking, their activities turned to Noh recitation, which they practiced until their voices were hoarse. It was the fourteenth day of the tenth month. One moment the moon's light would fill the sky and the next moment be obscured by clouds, not unlike our unpredictable human lives.

Daiemon crept to the river's bank and stripped naked in the shadow of a clump of reeds. With only a short sword at his waist, he entered the river. Its current flowed deep like his love for Tannosuke. Waves of love swept over his shoulders in the swift-flowing shallows. His hopes of ever reaching the other side seemed dashed several times, but at last he clung to the stone wall on the opposite shore and pulled himself up, using the rope Tannosuke had prepared. This was a sign that he was on the right path to love. Daiemon approached a low door in the garden wall and found it slightly ajar as Tannosuke had promised. Except for the light of a distant torch, there were no other signs of life. The silence struck him as unusual, so he paused, straining for some sound.

Suddenly, Tannosuke threw open the sliding doors with a crash. He was crying uncontrollably. "Even for a dream, that was too sad to bear," he said aloud to himself.

"Tannosuke, it's me, Daiemon."

Tannosuke was overjoyed. He pressed Daiemon's wet body against his and took him inside. Daiemon had soon forgotten all his sorrows. Later, he asked Tannosuke what it was that upset him earlier.

"For some reason, time seemed to go more slowly than ever as I waited for you tonight," he said. "I finally fell asleep after hearing the midnight bell and almost immediately had a dream. You were in the middle of fording the river when a log struck your leg and dragged you to the bottom. Your precious life was lost. I have no idea who first invented such sad dreams or when, but I find them hard to bear. It reminded me of the old legend of the buck crossing the sea."[7] Just recalling the dream made Tannosuke start weeping again.

To humor him, Daiemon said, "When we cannot see each other for a long time, at least we can meet in our dreams. Nothing could be better as far as I am concerned."

Tannosuke was cheered by the thought. After promising that they would meet again, Daiemon got up and left. For the sake of love, he willingly stripped himself naked a second time. Tannosuke followed him with his eyes for as long as he could. Daiemon's figure finally disappeared into the distant waves.

The party of young samurai next door noticed something in the river just then. "It is a large bird!" they cried excitedly. They drew their bows in archery practice and vied with each other to hit the distant target with their arrows. Daiemon was struck in the side but managed to make it home nevertheless. He deliberately wrote

down a garbled final message that made it sound as if he had lost
his mind and then manfully committed suicide.[8] The following
morning, news of his death spread throughout the province.

Tannosuke rushed to Daiemon's house the moment he heard it.
He could hardly bear to see the sorrow of Daiemon's mother and
sister. "It is because we have life that we experience such sadness,"
he thought bitterly. He clung to Daiemon's dead body and two or
three times put his hand to his sword, but he forced himself to
remain calm.

"Show me the arrow," he asked.

He scrutinized it and discovered that it bore the name of Fujii
Buzaemon.

"So this is the man from whom I must exact revenge," he thought. Weighed with grief, he stood and returned home. Without further ado, Daiemon's body was sent to his family temple, Shōrin-ji, and his ashes were committed to the ground. That day receded into the past, but Tannosuke made daily visits to the grave and promised to join Daiemon there shortly. He thought that the 49th day would be ideal[9] and invited Buzaemon to visit the grave with him, but the man was busy that day. Tannosuke had no choice but to postpone his plans.

Finally, on the 52nd day, the two walked the path to Shōrin-ji together, taking in the sight of the surrounding hills and stream. When they arrived in front of Daiemon's grave, there were two stupas erected on either side of it, one bearing the name Fujii Buzaemon, the other Haruta Tannosuke.

"What does this mean?" Buzaemon protested.

"I understand your bewilderment," Tannosuke answered. He then told his story from the beginning.

"This will come as a shock to you, but I want you to fight me to the finish here," he said in closing.

With these words of challenge, they drew their swords. Both were soon dead. The head priest of the temple was stunned when he discovered their bodies and immediately notified the authorities. After an inquiry, their remains were laid to rest in Daiemon's tomb.

There will never be another heart as true as Tannosuke's.

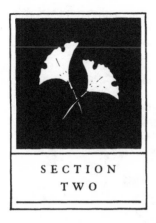

= 2 : 1 =

A Sword His Only Memento

Nakai Katsuya reads his mother's final testament.
As an outcast, Kataoka Gensuke finally consummates his love.
Vendetta in Yanagawa, Chikugo Province.

There will never be another invention quite like Enshū's standing lamp.[1] Likewise, had a man called Matajirō not discovered how to twist paper into Kanze rope, we would not possess that cherished process today.[2]

While preparing to dispose of some old papers, I came across a letter addressed to me in my mother's hand. On the outside it read, "Katsuya should read this letter when he reaches the age of thirteen." With tears in my eyes, I looked inside. This is what it said:

"Your father, Gemba, was killed by a man named Takeshita Shingoemon. This man changed his name to Yoshimura Ansai and now lives incognito in Yanagawa, in the Province of Chikugo. To society he presents himself as a children's doctor, but in truth he supports himself by teaching military tactics to the samurai of the domain. I sought out this information intending to avenge your father myself, though I am a mere woman, but my heartfelt desire

is coming to naught even as I lie here dying. I beg you, Katsuya: when you reach manhood, avenge your father in my stead. It will gladden the hearts of your dead father and mother in their graves."

The letter continued, but the handwriting was impossible to read clearly toward the end. She must have written it on her deathbed.

I turned eighteen this year. Six years had gone by wasted before I discovered my mother's final testament. But that was beyond my control; I had no idea such a letter existed. At the age of fourteen I had taken up residence in the house of a certain lord as his page. This is how it came about.

It was the seventeenth day of the fourth month. I was living near Kuromon at Ueno in Musashi in the care of an aunt who was my mother's sister. That day, as he passed, the lord noticed me

from the window of his palanquin. "Who is that boy?" I heard
him say. He sent a trusted samurai to inquire in detail about my
lineage. From that very day, I was taken by the lord's spare horse
to live at his main residence. I rarely left his side. Birds would fall
from the morning sky at my whim, and if I chose to call a crow a
heron, no one dared challenge me. I resented the moon's light
when it diverted the lord's attention from myself at night. If there
were someone I disliked, I could afford to ignore him completely.
All of this was possible because of the lord's favor, which I gratefully enjoyed.

Sometimes, when I fell asleep in disarray, my lord would slip a
pillow under my head or, if I became uncovered during the night,
would cover me with his underrobe of white cotton lest a breeze

stir and I catch cold. His kind attentions came to me as I slept, reality impinging on a dream. I feared divine retribution for receiving such favor. When I awoke from my dreams, the lord would say, "Now we are alone and there is no one to overhear our conversation." He spoke to me of grave matters concerning the entire household, matters of which he would not speak even to his own son. We swore our faithfulness to each other, like the pine that remains forever green; once, with a pine needle, the lord himself removed a tiny mole on my temple that he said bothered him, though it went unnoticed by anyone else. Thus, I spent my days and nights enjoying the lord's special favors.

The least I could do to repay the lord's kindness, I thought, was to manfully follow him in death if anything should ever happen to him. Though I knew that this practice had been forbidden by official edict,[3] in preparation for just such a contingency I placed a plain skirt and jacket and a small short sword in a chest for safekeeping, along with my determination to die if need be.

But the world is an unpredictable place. Just when I was thinking proudly that my looks had reached their peak, I was given cause to regret my pride. From the beginning of last month, my lord shifted his affections to a boy named Chikawa Morinojō. My tears at this betrayal were as long and dreary as a late-autumn drizzle. I decided to end my life on the third day of the tenth month, but a certain matter prevented my suicide on that day, so I was obliged to postpone it until the seventh. In the interim, I discovered my mother's letter and learned the identity of my father's murderer.

My destiny as a samurai had not run out after all. If I had killed myself for the sake of this petty grudge against the lord, my regret would surely have proved an obstacle to my rebirth in the next world. Had I requested time off to carry out the vendetta at the height of my favor with the lord which Morinojō now enjoyed, permission most likely would not have been granted. Now was my chance to make an appeal.

I submitted my request one day when the lord seemed to be in especially good spirits, and he granted it without hesitation. He not only presented me with a cup of sake in farewell, but urged me to avenge myself on Ansai and hurry home to a hero's welcome. He gave me a sealed deed for a yearly stipend of 500 *koku* redeemable on my return. I even received a traveling allowance from the lord's keeper of supplies.

Thus it was that Katsuya set out from Tatsunokuchi[4] in the ninth year of Kan'ei [1632], tenth month, twelfth day. He was accompanied by five of his most trusted attendants. They stopped first at the Mita Hachiman Shrine to pray for success in their venture.[5] Days passed, and on the nineteenth day of the same month they arrived in Kyoto.

Katsuya knew someone in town at Sanjō Koiyama. He had hardly dismounted from his horse when he went in secret, his sedge hat pulled low over his brow, to the area of the Great Buddha.[6] A man skilled at making chain-mail garments named Kojima Yamashiro lived there. Happily, the chain-mail shirt that Katsuya wanted was available.

On his way back, Katsuya encountered a strange man at Mimizuka.[7] Traces of the morning's frost had settled on the bamboo bark raincoat the man used as a windbreak, but he seemed unconcerned by it. The man spoke meekly, in a way strangely incongruous with his large stature.

"Excuse me sire, could you spare me a coin?"

When they saw each other face to face, the beggar crouched low and covered his face with his sleeve. Perplexed, Katsuya looked at the man more closely. It was an old compatriot of his, Kataoka Gensuke!

"You look terrible!" Katsuya gasped. "Tell me, what happened?"

Gensuke wept as he told his tale.

"I had ambitions and rashly asked for permission from our lord to go to Murakami in Echigo Province to take up a new position. Just when I got there, the man on whom I was dependent for making the final arrangements, Kataoka Genki, died very suddenly. To make matters worse, I have been suffering from an eye ailment since the end of the sixth month last year. I came to Yoshimine for treatment, but there was no improvement. My attendants all deserted me, but that was to be expected. They were only temporary hirelings. A man's fate certainly is unpredictable.

"I thought that I would rather die than continue this useless existence, but then I recalled Pien Ho who wept over his jade[8] and Ning Ch'i who beat the bull's horn,[9] and I decided that there was still hope for me. Leaving a disgraced name in the world would be far worse than death itself.

"At this point I am thinking of returning to the place of my birth in Nambu where I still have a few connections. After all, I am only 26 years old, and my eyesight has improved enough that I can see your face clearly.

"By the way, what brings you to the capital? It has me a little worried."

The vendors of rice-cakes and tobacco nearby had come out of their shops as he spoke. Pack-horse drivers and travelers, in a rush to catch the Fushimi ferry before it left at dusk, stopped to stare at the odd pair. Before long, a huge crowd had gathered.

"I will tell you all about it after dark," Katsuya said. "Until then, please wait for me here." With tears in his eyes, he said goodbye.

Katsuya waited impatiently for nightfall. As soon as the sun had set he went back without his attendants to the place, but the man was gone. Katsuya had no idea where to find him. Distraught, he spoke to some outcasts[10] on the dry riverbed.

"Is Gensuke there among you?"

"No," they answered. "We do not know the man. The only ones here are the lockpick Sankichi, shifty-eyed Torazō, and Gon, the escape artist."

Under their lean-to of rushes, they had lit a fire and in low voices were saying something about "hoping for a four and a nine." He could hear the sound of something small being tossed, but he had no idea what it was.[11]

Katsuya walked further along the stony river bank and came to a willow tree. Its dry, brittle leaves rattled in the wind, and in its shadow stood an old white-haired woman, so decrepit her immediate departure for paradise would have given no cause for regret. She was muttering something to herself.

"I have run out of food for tomorrow, so I think I will go out after midnight and try to sell the clothes of that abandoned baby I found in front of the temple gate at Seigan-ji." Everywhere he turned, Katsuya was surrounded with the world's misery.

The river was the only sound to be heard in the deep stillness of the night. Though it was past the time most people had turned in for the night, there were still a few men nearby gathering drift-wood for a fire. They set up stones as a hearth and put an earth-enware pot on it to heat water for a mock drinking bout with tea. Someone rinsed out his tea cup and chanted, "I shall return to conquer again and erase my shame at Kuai Chi."[12] He then began to boast of his knowledge of the esoteric. "The reeds of Udono are the only ones suitable for the mouthpiece of the *shō*;[13] the purple

corolla of the famed irises at Asazawa and Yatsuhashi are beyond
compare; and, by the way, that splendid Chinese robe of 'the man
of old' has now turned to a robe of paper!"[14] With this, the man
burst into laughter. Katsuya looked at him more closely.

It was Gensuke.

Gensuke recognized him but showed no embarrassment whatsoever. He simply said, "What a pleasure to see you again."

Katsuya hid his tears.

"I am on my way to the western provinces," Katsuya began. "I
have discovered the whereabouts of my father's murderer, and am
going by way of the Chikugo Road to avenge him. I have no way
of knowing what the outcome will be. If I am cut down in the fray,
we may never meet again.

"Remember when we were both in service at Edo? You sent me
many letters expressing your love for me. I was very grateful for
them. Unfortunately, I was sharing the lord's bed at that time.
Though I wanted to respond, I was unable to. Those days are gone
now. I can only rejoice that we have met again. At last we can
spend the night together, conversing to our hearts' content."

With these words, he pillowed his head in Gensuke's lap and
fell asleep. In his joy, Gensuke forgot all about love-making. As he
recalled those lonely days when he was barracked in the east,[15] the
resentment that he had harbored toward Katsuya in his heart since
those days was swept away. Like a doting husband, he gave Katsuya most of his crude bed, keeping watch over his beloved
through the long, cold night.

White clouds drifted across the capital's Mt. Fuji[16] as the bell at
Kurodani tolled the approach of daybreak. Soon, the faces of boat-
men poling their Takase barges[17] up and down the river became
visible. When it was time for the two to bid farewell, Gensuke
picked up a torn bag of straw and from inside withdrew a sword
disguised as a cane.

"This is a sword made by Sanemori of Ōhara."[18] (Though he
had fallen low in the world, he had not relinquished his sword. He
was a dependable man after all.) "My forefathers were in the service of Takeda Shingen, and this sword is said to have distin-

guished itself at the battle of Kawanakajima in Shinshū.[19] Use it to accomplish your vendetta."

He handed the sword to Katsuya, who accepted it without hesitation.

"When I have killed Ansai, we shall meet again. Until then, take this as a keepsake," Katsuya said, and presented his own sword to Gensuke.

As he left, Katsuya took from his left sleeve a package containing 100 *ryō* of gold. He whispered to the cripples and blind men crowded near his pillow, "I have something to ask of you. Take this money and use it to pay for travel expenses to take Gensuke back to his homeland."

On the twentieth day of the tenth month, Katsuya and his entourage boarded the noon boat for Naniwa. They arrived there toward dusk and set off on their journey the next day in a rented boat. They stepped ashore at Yanagawa on the 28th and quietly found lodgings. Dressed as traveling merchants, Katsuya and his men began to search the neighboring area as inconspicuously as possible, looking for their enemy.

The year soon came to an end.

About the time the wild horsetails and violets were in bloom, Katsuya was at last able to locate Ansai's residence. They set the night of the 28th day of the third month for their attack. Katsuya and his five retainers steeled themselves for the fray. After a last meal together, they set out at dusk for the village and attempted to devise an escape route. There was a valley to the south and a river spanned by a single earthen bridge. Waves crashed against the rocks below like a writhing white dragon. Behind the village was a high mountain, and to the north a swamp traversed only by animals. It would be a difficult place to leave alive. They crept in secret to a wayside shrine about eight *chō*[20] this side of the house. There, they waited for nightfall.

Behind them came Gensuke. He cut two *ken*[21] out of the middle of the bridge and readied the oars of a small boat that had been left tied on the east bank of the river. As he waited for Katsuya to finish his task, it grew dark. A farmer on his way back to the village fell through the break in the bridge and sank into the raging torrent below. Another followed, leading his ox with him. Four or five people died this way without even a chance to cry out for help, but Gensuke only crouched lower and waited.

Finally, at what must have been the early part of the hour of the tiger,[22] Katsuya and his men cut through the spiked bamboo fence surrounding the house and set up torches at the eaves on both sides of the straw roof, east and west.

"I am Nakai Katsuya, come to avenge my father Gemba," he shouted. "Shingoemon, come out and fight!"

Katsuya and his men pushed their way to the entrance of their enemy's bed chamber. He was given a chance to fight like a man, but they succeeded in cutting him down in the fray. They had come with a container for his head, an indication of the efficiency of their preparations.

The vendetta was now complete.[23]

They opened the front gate and proceeded about two *chō* in their escape. Then, the whole village seemed to light up the sky with its torches in pursuit. "Don't let them get away!" the villagers shouted. Katsuya and his men knew that their end was near.

Suddenly, from out of the darkness, there came a voice.

"Katsuya, your escape route is this way."

Katsuya did not recognize the voice.

"Who is it?" he demanded.

"It is me, Gensuke. Have you forgotten? Come this way, quickly!"

Gensuke helped them board the boat and pushed off into the powerful current. Their pursuers, numbering in the hundreds by now, were unable to proceed beyond the break in the bridge and returned to the village in an uproar.

Once the boat reached open sea, Gensuke guided it along the coast. They traveled three and a half *li*[24] that night and arrived at a cove called Wakinohama shortly before dawn. Katsuya and Gensuke were able to look at each other at last. Holding back his tears, Katsuya said, "Last night, you appeared in my hour of greatest need and saved us from certain death. How fortunate we were!"

Gensuke laughed. "You foolishly call it fortune, but I have been following you like a shadow from morning to night ever since we parted at Sanjō-gawara. Why, I was spending my nights right under the eaves of your lodge until last night! During the day I took care not to attract attention, and at night kept strict vigil outside.

"One time, I followed you on your visit to the castle town of Kurume. You were unable to make your way through the heavy snowfall at the foot of Mt. Nuresenu and lay down with your attendants. You lost consciousness in the cold, and your breathing grew so weak that I was sure you were gone. But I put some ginseng in your mouth and in my hands caught water for you to drink that was dripping from a rock. Then I held you against my bare skin until you were restored to your senses. The first thing you said to me was, 'Who are you? Thank you for your aid.' I almost revealed myself to you then. Fortunately, you did not recognize me, so I just said I was a passerby and left.

"I hid myself in a dense bamboo grove nearby and watched you for some time. You revived your attendants one by one and told them about the man who had helped you. 'Surely, he was the god of my clan, appearing in human form to lend me protection,' you said. You then tried to proceed on your way, but it was the ninth day of the twelfth month and it was too dark to follow the path. I took straw from haystacks in the fields and marked the way for you with bonfires. Do you remember?"

Gensuke reported everything they had done since the tenth month of the previous year and afterwards returned the bundle of coins Katsuya had left with him when they parted in Kyoto. Its seal was still intact. The entire boatload of men wept, overwhelmed with the depth of Gensuke's loyalty and love.

"Never has there been such a man," they exclaimed, their voices rising in unison.

"May I ask a favor of you?" Katsuya asked. "Please accompany me back to Edo."

Thus, they set out joyfully for home.

They crossed the Ashigara Pass at Mt. Fuji in the fourth month when the snow-like sunflowers were in bloom and reached Edo on the eleventh day. Katsuya explained the details of his successful vendetta to the lord as recorded above.[25] Both the lord and his son were so impressed with Gensuke's role in the affair that they summoned him for an audience. He was awarded his old position with an increase in stipend of 300 *koku* per year; he was also relieved of routine guard duty. Moreover, the lord relinquished his claims on Katsuya and yielded him to Gensuke. Katsuya celebrated the coming-of-age ceremony and took the name Genshichi. Thus, the two became true brothers.

Such treatment was unheard of in previous ages. Young men would do well to follow Katsuya's example in male love.

Though Bearing an Umbrella, He Was Rained Upon

How Nagasaka Korin, a filial son, made a living.
He killed a creature in the cherry-viewing teahouse.
He traded his life for a secret lover.

The sea at Urano Hatsushima grew rough and the winds blew strong on Mt. Muko.[1] Thunderheads billowed up in layers, as if the ghost of Tomomori[2] might appear at any moment. Shortly, rain began to fall. Travelers on the road found themselves in unforeseen distress.

An envoy named Horikoshi Sakon, who was on his way back to Amagasaki from Akashi, took shelter from the rain under some hackberry trees in a field by the Ikuta Shrine. Just then, a handsome boy of twelve or thirteen came running up with an unopened umbrella of the type called "fall foliage" (though it was summer).

The boy noticed Sakon. "Allow me to lend you this umbrella," he said, and handed it to an attendant.

"I am most grateful," Sakon responded. "But it strikes me as odd that you let yourself get rained on, though you had an umbrella."

At this, the boy began to cry.

"Now, now. There must be some reason for this. Tell me what it is," Sakon coaxed.

"I am the son of Nagasaka Shuzen," the boy said. "My name is Korin. My father became a masterless samurai and had to leave Kōshū for Buzen to take up a new position, but he took sick and died on board ship. My mother and I had no choice but to bury him in this coastal town. The local people were kind enough to help us build a crude hut on the beach. The black bamboo outside our window became our only means of making a living. We watched the artisans making umbrellas and learned to do it ourselves. When I think of my mother doing a man's work with her own hands, I cannot bring myself to use an umbrella for fear of inviting the wrath of heaven, even if it means getting wet."

So, that was it. Not unlike an old lady selling fans who would rather shade the sun with her hand, or the winnow seller who prefers to do his winnowing with a hat! Sakon was much impressed with the boy's filial sense, and sent one of his attendants to accompany the boy back to the village where he lived with his mother.

When Sakon returned to Akashi, he immediately presented himself at the lord's castle and delivered the other daimyo's reply. Since the lord seemed to be in a good mood, Sakon mentioned Korin and told him the boy's story. The lord was very impressed, and ordered the boy brought to him. It was Sakon's joyful task to fetch Korin. Obediently, the boy came to the lord's castle with his mother.

When he appeared before the lord, his lordship was smitten immediately with the boy's unadorned beauty, like a first glimpse of the moon rising above a distant mountain. The boy's hair gleamed like the feathers of a raven perched silently on a tree, and his eyes were lovely as lotus flowers. One by one his other qualities became apparent, from his nightingale voice to his gentle disposition, as obedient and true as a plum blossom. The lord increasingly had the boy attend to him, and soon Korin was sharing his bed at night.

The night guard stationed next to the lord's bed chamber listened carefully for signs of trouble, but all he heard were the unrestrained sounds of the lord amusing himself with the boy. When it was over, the lord could be heard to say, "I would gladly give my life for you."

Korin's response showed none of the gratitude one would expect from a boy receiving the lord's favor. "Forcing me to yield to your authority is not true love. My heart remains my own, and if one day someone should tell me he truly loves me, I will give my life for him. As a memento of this floating world, I want a lover upon whom I can lavish real affection."

The lord was slightly irritated with the boy but dismissed what he said as a joke. Korin insisted, however, that he was serious.

"I swear by the gods of Japan that I meant every word of it." The lord was astonished, but he could not help but admire even this stubborn streak in the boy.

One evening, the lord assembled a large group of his pages to enjoy the breeze at a teahouse in the garden. There, they sampled several varieties of sake from throughout the domain. After several rounds, the party was becoming quite lively. Suddenly, the stars disappeared from the sky and the pines at Hitomaru's shrine[3] began to shake noisily. The air stank of death. Clouds spread swiftly overhead, and from inside them leapt a one-eyed goblin. It landed on the eaves nearby and tweaked the noses of everyone there, stretching its hand over twenty feet. The boys stopped their amusement and immediately stationed themselves around their lord to protect him. They then rushed him to his chambers. Later, the ground shook violently with the sound of a mountain being rent asunder.

Shortly after midnight, word was sent to the lord that an old badger had broken down a cedar door in the teahouse used for cherry-blossom viewing west of the man-made hill in the garden. Though it had been decapitated, the head was still gnashing its tusks and screeching in an unearthly manner.

"Well then, the quake earlier must have been the badger's doing. Who killed the beast?" the lord asked. Everyone in the household was questioned, but no one came forward to claim merit for the feat.

One night seven days later, at the hour of the ox,[4] the voice of a young girl was heard coming from the box-like ridge of the great assembly hall. "Korin's life is in danger; it is he who murdered my blameless father." The voice screamed the words three times, then disappeared.

So, it was Korin who performed the deed, everyone thought in awe.

Sometime afterward, the magistrate in charge of buildings and grounds spoke to the lord about fixing the door damaged by the badger. The lord had other plans, however.

"Long ago," he said, "Marquis Wen of Wei got boastful and bragged, 'No one dares oppose a single word I say.' But the blind musician Shih Ching struck a wall with his harp and made him realize his arrogance. Marquis Wen left the damaged south wall as a reminder of his faithful subject.[5] I command that the broken door be left as it is so that all may see the evidence of Korin's brave warrior spirit."

The lord rewarded Korin generously, and his love for the boy grew even stronger.

A man named Sōhachirō, second son of Captain of the Standard Bearers, Kan'o Gyōbu, had for some time perceived Korin's true feelings. He told Korin of his love by letter, and they were soon in constant communication. They waited for an opportunity to consummate their love, and the year drew to a close.

On the night of the thirteenth,[6] a day set aside for house cleaning, the lord's presentation of silk for New Year's garments was to take place. One of Korin's attendants had the idea of concealing Sōhachirō inside the basket for worn-out clothing to be sent to Korin's mother for wash and repair. In this way, Sōhachirō was able to make his way to the room next to the lord's bedchamber.

Toward evening, Korin complained of stomach pains and secluded himself in his room. When the lord retired, he could not sleep at first because of the constant opening and closing of the door and creaking of the wheels,[7] but soon he was snoring. Able to make love at last, Korin embraced Sōhachi. In their passion, Korin gave himself to the man without even undoing his square-knotted sash. They pledged to love each other in this life and the next.

The sound of their voices woke the lord from his sleep. He removed the sheath from a spear he kept near his pillow and shouted, "I hear voices. Whoever it is, do not let him escape!" As he rushed out in pursuit, Korin clung to the lord's sleeve.

"There is no need to be alarmed. No one is here. It was merely a demon that came in the agony of my illness and threatened to kill me. Please forgive me."

The boy spoke calmly, giving Sōhachi time to climb an oak tree and jump across the spiked fence surrounding the mansion. The lord spotted him, however, and demanded an explanation, but Korin insisted that he knew nothing.

"Well then," the lord said, "perhaps it was just another of that badger's tricks."

The lord was willing to let the matter rest there, but a secret agent[8] named Kanai Shimpei came up just then with some information.

"The sound of footsteps just now was made by a man with loose hair tied by a head band. That much I could tell for sure. Without a doubt, he was someone's lover."

The lord's interrogation of Korin suddenly changed. Deadly earnest now, he commanded the boy to confess.

The boy said, "He is someone who swore his life to me. I would not identify him even if you tore me limb from limb. I told you from the beginning that you were not the one I loved." Korin's expression showed no trace of regret as he spoke.

Three days later, on the morning of the fifteenth, the lord summoned Korin to the hall where martial arts were practiced. He assembled his attendants to watch as a lesson to the entire household. Lifting a halberd, he said to the boy, "Korin, you have reached your end."

Korin smiled brightly. "I have enjoyed your favor for so long, to die at your hands would be one more honor. I have no regrets."

As the boy attempted to stand, the lord cut off Korin's left arm. "Still no regrets?" he taunted.

Korin stretched out his right arm. "I stroked my lover's body with this hand. Surely, that must anger you terribly."

Enraged, the lord slashed it off.

Korin spun around and cried out to the people assembled there. "Take one last look at the figure of this handsome youth. The world will never see his likes again."[9] His voice grew weaker and weaker.

The lord then cut off the child's head.

The lord's sleeve became a sea of tears, like the sea of Akashi visible before him, and the weeping of the assembled retainers echoed like waves upon the shore.

Korin's corpse was sent to Myōfuku-ji for burial. His brief life had evaporated like the dew. At this temple is Morning-Glory Pond,[10] named for the flower whose life, if it survives the morning frost, spans but a single day. In olden times there was a man ban-

ished to Suma for his seductive mischief in the capital.[11] He did
not learn his lesson, but fell in love with the daughter of a lay priest
there. On one of his visits to her, he wrote a poem:

> Braving autumn wind and waves
> I came each night
> By the light of the moon
> On Akashi's hill:
> Morning-glories![12]

If this poem had been composed for the sake of boy love, it
would surely be remembered today. Unfortunately, it was written
for a woman and naturally has been forgotten.

Korin's unknown lover became the subject of severe criticism.
"Korin died for his sake, yet he does not come forward and

announce himself like a man. He could not possibly be a samurai, just a stray dog who happened to be reincarnated into human form."

In the New Year, on the night of the fifteenth, Sōhachi attacked
Shimpei and cut off both of his arms. He then administered the
coup de grace and made a clean escape. After hiding Korin's
mother where no one would find her, he fled to Morning-Glory
Temple. In front of Korin's tomb he set up a signboard and wrote
on it a detailed account of his love for the boy. There, at the age of
21, he ended his life, a dream within a dream; like one gone to
sleep, he cut open his belly and died.

At dawn the next day, the morning of the sixteenth, people
found the body. The wound was distinctly cut in the shape of a

diamond with three cross-cuts inside. This was Korin's family crest. "If one is going to fall that deeply in love," people said approvingly, "then this is exactly the way to show it."

Within seven days, the *shikimi* branches[13] that people gathered from hills throughout the province filled the entire pond.

His Head Shaved on the Path of Dreams

Brocade in daylight at fireside Noh.
A youth stealthily follows a chrysanthemum-crested lantern.
Forced to stand in for his lover.

The man rushed to reach the Great South Gate in the southern capital before nightfall and took a seat in the stands.[1] The Komparu Noh master was performing a dance, accompanied by Seigorō on the hand drum and Mataemon drumming with a single stick.[2] Each was a master of his craft, but the man hardly noticed them. His attention was directed to the young temple pages from Kōfuku-ji and Saidai-ji seated in the gallery.[3] As the sun set, he bade them a sad farewell. "Like brocade at night, their beauty is wasted,"[4] he said aloud, not caring who might hear.

The man looked to be under 30. The pate of his head was shaved well back with a short topknot. Both inner and outer robes were made of a black dragon-patterned weave bearing the chrysanthemum-leaf crest on the back, sleeves, and chest. He wore a plain sash of braided silk and sported two swords, long and short, in the foppish Yoshiya style.[5] In short, he appeared to epitomize the connoisseur of boy love.

His name was Maruo Kan'emon. He was a well-known master of martial arts and an appreciator of boys without rival in past or present history. Boys found it impossible to resist his wily love letters. He waited impatiently to see the boys at fireside Noh each evening. Performances at the shrine began the following day.[6] When Ōkura Otome[7] appeared on stage as Kagetsu, not a person there remained unsmitten. "Such is love's ability to deceive."[8]

The sky clouded over the next day. The umbrella-shaped peak of Mt. Kasuga was desolate. In the afternoon, Kan'emon had an attendant bring some fish hooks and flies to go fishing on the banks of the Iwai River. The fishing was good, and he was busily pulling in willow dace and other fish when a lovely youth in the service of the Kōriyama clan appeared further upstream. His name was Tamura Sannojō.

The boy spit into the river. Downstream, Kan'emon scooped up the water in his hands and gulped it down without spilling a single drop.

Sannojō noticed this and came over to apologize.

"I had no idea you would be drinking from the river. It was rude of me to spit into it. Please forgive me."

"The truth is, I so hated to see your precious saliva disperse and disappear in the water's flow that I scooped it up and swallowed it," Kan'emon confessed.

"I won't forget your flattery," Sannojō laughed, and went on his way.

Kan'emon watched him walk along the edge of the rocky bank. The boy's natural, unadorned beauty was impossible to describe. He murmured to himself, "When the witch of Wushan spit in the face of the first Emperor of Ch'in, her saliva left pockmarks where it touched.[9] May this saliva I just drank remain in my mouth forever, so that I can always enjoy its nectar-like flavor!"

He set out after the boy, but the sun set in the west behind distant mountains in Akishino and soon it was too dark to discern people's faces.

It was the night of the twelfth day, second month, so the boy was expecting to enjoy the aid of the moon to light his way home, but he was disappointed. Though already spring, winter rainclouds billowed threateningly around the peaks of Mt. Ikoma and Kazuraki. He hurried on his way to Kōriyama, worried that it might start to rain at any moment. Passing a remote village, he crossed a bridge of shaky planks placed over flooded ground. He picked his way carefully across the stubble of last year's harvest of reeds in a burned-over field and walked on a path used by strange-looking deer shorn of their antlers.[10] He passed the dens of badgers and wolves. None of this frightened the boy, not even the rising smoke that normally startles the people of this floating world.[11] He stopped to gaze at the hut where a recluse priest lived and then passed by.

He was nearing the village at Daian-ji when a smartly dressed servant with a towel tied around his head emerged from a side street, carrying a lantern. Sannojō followed the light gratefully. His companion, the acupuncturist Dōjin, was elated by their good fortune.

"It is like enjoying a neighbor's singing with your own sake at a springtime blossom-viewing party," he exclaimed happily.

Shortly, they reached Kōriyama. The man with the lantern saw them safely to the boy's house, which was at the very end of a block of samurai houses. He watched the boy go inside and then turned back in the direction from which he came.

Until then, Sannojō had not thought anything of it, but now he found the man's behavior most peculiar. First, however, he went to greet his parents.

"I went to see the fireside Noh and just returned home," he told them.

Then, in secret, he went back out to follow the man. At last he got close enough to the lantern to see that it bore a chrysanthemum-leaf crest. He realized that it must be the same man he met earlier in the day. He decided to see him to his home in secret, but as they neared Nara the lantern's candle burned out. Their hearts were left in darkness.

"Since I was dressed in this disguise, I am sure he did not realize who it was that saw him to his door," Kan'emon said to his attendant.

The boy overheard this and decided to break his silence.

"On the contrary," Sannojō replied. "It is exactly because I recognized your intentions that I have come all this way to return the favor." He took Kan'emon's hand and squeezed it tight.

Kan'emon felt sure he was dreaming. He stood rooted to the spot, unable to speak for some time. "Do you really mean that?" he finally asked. "I must thank you for your kindness."

"Promise me that your love will never change."

"It will never change."

"Promise never to forget me."

"I will never forget you."

As they spoke, the bell in Nishinokyō began to toll. They counted eight strokes, which meant it was near dawn.

"Let us talk for a while, and I will leave when it begins to grow light," Sannojō suggested. He was already upset at the idea of saying farewell.

"This is not the last time we will meet. Your parents must be concerned at your absence. If you truly love me, let us save our loving for next time."

Without satisfying their desires, Kan'emon saw the boy back to Kōriyama once again. On the way, he told him, "Human life is unpredictable, but I hope to see you again before the double cherry blossoms open. I always go to view the early blossoms when they first come out. I promise to pay you a visit on the first or second day of the third month."

But Kan'emon was unaccustomed to wearing a servant's thin cotton robe and got chilled in the morning breeze. A slight stuffy nose grew progressively worse, and he died on the 27th day of the second month.

Sannojō came looking for him unaware of what had happened. When he found out, his grief was unbearable. He hoped at least to meet the relatives and family, but apparently Kan'emon was from a distant province and had no one to mourn him.

"Well then, where was he living?" the boy asked.

The place was the site of the old *renga* master Jōha's hut.[12] The boy went there, to a remote area called South Market. The house was surrounded by a deutzia hedge. He looked into the waiting room through a bamboo-slat window and was shocked to see a group of attendants gathered there, though hardly seven days had passed since their master's death, playing cards and chanting loudly to the tapping of fans, "Emperor Yung Ming pined for the Princess Yu Tai's love."[13] He could even smell dried sardines from Uwa-nokōri being toasted over a fire.

"I do not care how insignificant they may be in rank," he thought. "Don't they realize that their master has died?" Without a word, he opened the door and went in.

In one corner of the alcove was an earthen vessel from which rose a continuous stream of incense smoke. There were some fresh *shikimi* branches placed upright by a plaque inscribed with the posthumous name, Shunsetsu Dōsen. So this was the man he met, he thought, and pressed his sleeve to his face.

He sat there with his head bowed for quite some time.

Then, an attractive young man came into the room. He had apparently just recently undergone the capping ceremony. He was dressed entirely in mourning white, except for an outer robe of pale blue. His sleeves were damp with tears. He bowed before the Buddha altar and then moved to a distant corner of the room where he sat alone, overwhelmed with grief.

Sannojō went over to introduce himself. "Pardon me, my name is . . ."

But before he could finish, the young man interrupted him.

"Sannojō. Am I correct? Kan'emon remembered you with his last breath. 'I saw him home to Kōriyama, and he saw me home in turn.' Now I have seen him to the cremation fields.

"Am I dreaming? It must be a dream. Do you think it is a dream?"

The young man's grief made Sannojō feel even more desolate. Together they raised their voices and wept for over an hour. Their tears were like raindrops dripping from the eaves. Eventually, the spring day came to an end. Sannojō was startled to hear the sound of rain shutters being wheeled shut.

"I was aware of life's transience, but this brutal display of man's mortality is too much to bear. I will try to catch up with him at the base of death's mountain by the 49th day."

Sannojō drew his sword and turned to the young man. "Please take care of my remains."

Sanai[14] rushed forward to prevent Sannojō from killing himself.

"If anyone, I am the one who should kill himself. From the time I was just a boy, he loved me faithfully for five years. Even after I came of age he backed me reliably, as solid as Mt. Mikasa. Now I have lost him to cruel fate. How do you think your grief compares to mine? The last thing he said to me was, 'I have no one but you to place incense and flowers at my tomb. If you love me, keep on living.' I cannot turn my back on those words. I fully intend to take religious vows and devote the rest of my days to praying for him. But you, you only exchanged a few words with him. Why not just forget him and pretend you never met?"

"You can say that because you spent many satisfying years sharing his bed. I, however, must suffer the grief of never having spent a single night with him. I will end this brief life here and now."

Only after considerable persuasion from Sanai did Sannojō agree to abandon the idea of killing himself.

"If I am to go on living," Sannojō said, "I want you to take the place of Kan'emon and make a vow of love with me."

Sanai resisted. "It is not necessary to go that far. I will continue to be your good friend."

"That is not enough," Sannojō insisted. "I want you to be my lover."

Unable to protest further, Sanai made his vow of love with Sannojō. That night, he told Sannojō all about his years with Kan'emon.

"He was having a copy of the temple garden at Shōun-ji in Sakai built here.[15] On the day when the Sago palms were being transplanted, I was sitting on that rock over there. I cupped some water from the spring in my hands for a drink and threw the extra water on the ground behind me. I had no idea anyone was standing there.

"A low voice behind me said, 'I was hoping to be rained on by you one of these days.[16] I am grateful.'

"It was Kan'emon.

"I was thrilled, and soon after that we started sleeping together. To me, society's censure meant nothing. He arranged to visit me when my father was on night duty at the shrine and came secretly all the way to distant Takabatake just to see me.

"There was one happy moment I shall never forget. It was a windy, snowy night. I sent him a letter in the afternoon assuring him that I would be coming that night. He came to pick me up not far from my house and gave me a ride on his shoulders. From inside his robe he produced a little Kimpira doll dressed in helmet and armor[17] and gave it to me. On the way, we pretended to duel with it.

"That night, when I mounted Kan'emon in bed like a horse, he called me a Great General!"

Sanai grew drowsier and drowsier as he spoke. Soon he was asleep, with his listener joining him in a battle of snores.

Just then, the figure of Kan'emon appeared as real as life.

"I am happy that you two have made a vow of love to ease your grief. There is no one in the 190,000-*koku* realm of Kōriyama who even resembles Sannojō in beauty. However, there is something about the Kōriyama style of wearing the hair too low on the sides that I dislike. Sanai, what do you think? Let's bring the topknot up a bit in the back."

Kan'emon turned the boy to face the mirror.

"Is this just about right?" he asked, and disappeared.

Sannojō awoke from his dream. There was no washbasin nearby, not even a razor, but the pate of his head was cleanly shaved. Dreams are dreams, of course, but this was most remarkable.

Aloeswood Boy of the East

Girls mistaken for boys in spring fields.
Seed of a child they requested falls from a branch.
Proof his soul leapt into the man's sleeve.

Bush clover once bloomed at Miyagino, but not a single plant can be found there now.[1] Old poems are all that remain to testify to their existence.[2] Perhaps that food chest brought here on an outing was one left behind from among the twelve chests taken to the capital laden with bush clover.[3] In the fields, green with new growth, there were two youngsters gathering lovely dandelion and horsetail shoots. They wore sedge hats that hid their faces and long-sleeved robes with sashes tied in the back. They looked for all the world like boys deserving of male lovers.

A man stopped to admire them. Just then, an old woman stepped from inside a picnic tent and called, "Here, little Fuji, little Yoshi."

"Why, they are someone's little girls!" he realized with disgust. He spat on the ground and went on his way.

He reached the castle town of Sendai. At the edge of town was a place called Bashō's crossing where he passed the shop of a herbalist named Konishi no Jūnosuke. An incense of aloeswood wafted through the curtains over the doorway leading into the shop. The man paused to savor the fragrance. It had a penetrating quality in no way inferior to the White Chrysanthemum incense treasured by the lord of this province.[4] Curious as to whose sleeve bore the fragrance, the man entered the shop.

"I would like to purchase some fragrance for my clothing," he said. "Is the aloeswood available that I smell wafting through the room?"

"That fragrance is my son's favorite," the old man replied. "Selling it would be impossible, I am afraid."

It was a disappointing reply, but he could feel desire for the boy burning in him without even lighting the incense. He rested there for a moment and then went on his way.

The man's name was Ban no Ichikurō, a merchant from Tsugaru who was fond of boys to the point of obsession. He was on his way to Edo for the sole purpose of visiting a remarkable young actor by the name of Dekijima Kozarashi, popular of late in Sakaichō.[5] He had fallen in love with the boy sight unseen. A friend of his had sent a letter of introduction to the boy's attendant, Sakubei. Everything was now arranged. For someone from the country, he had quite sophisticated tastes.

Jūnosuke's son, Jūtarō, fell in love with the man the moment he saw him.

"Though I may be at the peak of youthful beauty, my bloom of youth will not last another five years. First they will take a tweezer to my hairline, and before long my forelocks will fall. I have left unopened the hundreds of love letters from my suitors and gained a reputation for being cold-hearted only because I have never found a man to my liking. This man is different, though. If he would but take pity on me and love me, I would gladly give myself to him in a vow of love."

He continued with this unexpected outburst, and his eyes took on a crazed look. With one arm he held his pet Pekinese, while with the other he waved an unsheathed spear menacingly. No one dared go near him.

At last, risking her life, his old nursemaid clung to him and said, "We will call back the traveler who just passed through, and you can love him as you wish."

At this, his raving calmed down somewhat.

The family called an ascetic named Kakudembō from Zenken'in to perform exorcising rites. He set up an altar where he chanted Buddhist incantations, accompanied by the noisy ringing of a bell and the rattling of his priestly staff.

These were the circumstances of the boy's birth. His father, Jūnosuke, had married into the Konishi family as an adopted son. Thirty-five years later, when he was over 60 years old, he had still failed to produce an heir. Grieved over this matter, he and his wife

secluded themselves in the Tenjin Shrine at Tsutsuji-ga-oka to pray for a son.

One night in a dream, a length of scarlet silk crepe used as a loincloth came falling from the branches of a red plum tree in front of the shrine and made its home in her womb. From the very next day, his wife developed a craving for sour plums. When the allotted time had elapsed, she gave birth to this boy.

Remarkably, he began at the age of five writing large letters he had never learned. These were hung in temples and shrines as votive offerings to the gods. His ability to write was identical to Sayo's of Izumiya.

When he reached the age of thirteen, he wrote a story called "Short Tale for a Summer's Night"[6] in which he depicted love's joyful meetings and sad partings. Even then he showed a remarkable grasp of the fleeting ways of love.

The fact that the sight of this man triggered in him such uncontrollable emotions must have been due to a very powerful karmic bond.

The boy's longing for the man grew stronger and stronger. Those around him did their best to nurse him back to health, but each morning his pulse was slightly weaker and his evening dosage of medicine had less and less effect. It seemed that his life in this floating world had reached its end. They prepared a shroud for his body and ordered a coffin, expecting him to die that evening.

As they waited for the end, Jūtarō feebly lifted his head.

"How happy I am!" he said. "The man I yearn for will pass here tomorrow when the sun is in the west. I beg you, please stop him and bring him to me."

They were sure that his words were the product of delirium, but they placed someone at the town gate of Biwakubi to keep watch. Just as the boy predicted, the man appeared. He was led to the Konishi home immediately. Jūnosuke quietly told him the story from beginning to end.

Ichikurō wept.

"If anything happens to Jūtarō, I will be the first to join you in taking religious vows to mourn him. First, though, let me see the sick boy and bid him farewell in this life."

He approached the boy's pillow and immediately the boy regained his former health. He poured out his heart to Ichikurō.

"My body remained at home, but my soul was with you the entire time. Did you know I spent a mystical night in your arms? It was after you visited the Takadachi ruins at Hiraizumi.[7] You spent the night at the Hikaridō Sanctuary in a temple there. I burned with passion as we made love in your traveler's bed and wordlessly vowed myself to you. As a sign, I broke a stick of aloeswood incense and placed half of it in your sleeve. Is it still there?"

Ichikurō reached into his sleeve and withdrew the incense. "How remarkable! Here it is! My doubts are dispelled, but your story is all the more puzzling."

"Allow me to show you something that will put your suspicions to rest forever," the boy said.

Producing a piece of aloeswood, he joined it to the piece that Ichikurō had taken from his sleeve. It matched perfectly to form one stick. When burned, both halves produced the identical fragrance.

Convinced, Ichikurō pledged himself to the boy in this life and the next and received Jūtarō for his own.

The hoofbeats of their two brave steeds echoed over the five-span bridge of Sendai on their way to Tsugaru.

Or, so the story goes.

Nightingale in the Snow

The errant priest who was a woman-hater.
He promised his life to them rashly.
One body, two youths.

At Yuno-o Pass in Echizen Province is a teahouse with a curtain under the eaves bearing the picture of a large ladle. There, they sell charms called "grandchild ladles" to protect children from smallpox. At a place dedicated to Kannon, called Kishinodō, in Kawachi Province, they bury roasted beans and say prayers in order to ward off the pox. Truly, there is not a parent alive who relishes the prospect of having a child with a pockmarked face.

For girls, pockmarks may not be so bad. In this world motivated as it is by greed, no girl need go unmarried so long as she brings with her a generous dowry. The unfortunate ones are the boys. Their figures are no different from those of other boys, yet because of a few facial scars they are doomed to go through life unloved by men. No one invites them on visits to shrines and temples, or laments when they put away their boy's garb for the clothes of a man before even reaching the age of fifteen. Like the blossoms of the *kusagi* tree,[1] their bloom of youth falls unnoticed and unappreciated. Parents nowadays take great pains to raise their children protected from the rough winds of life. As a result, one sees more and more attractive boys around.

The son of a certain daimyo in the Sakurada section of Edo contracted smallpox at the age of six. His complexion was once as fair as the new-fallen snows of Mt. Fuji, but after a curative bath in sake and water the change was painfully evident, as if his snow-white skin had been blocked from view by a lavender cloud cover. The entire household waited all night in tearful anguish.

"If the scars are stroked with the feather of a nightingale, they will heal completely," someone reported.

The lord immediately ordered a search for the bird. The people of the house divided into groups and scoured the area, but it was the wrong time of year for nightingales. The trees were bare and ponds were iced over. All they found were a few waterfowl.

In desperation, someone had a skilled artisan attach feathers to a brown-eared bulbul to make it look like a nightingale. Just when he was about to show it to the lord, a certain fishmonger named Kyūzō from Odawara-chō, who had daily business at the house of the lord's chief retainer, happened to overhear a discussion of the matter.

"By good fortune, I know of someone who keeps birds. Would you like me to ask him for a nightingale?" Kyūzō offered.

"Please do!" he urgently requested. The retainer then went to report the good news to the lord. "In a moment, a real nightingale will be forthcoming," he promised.

The lord was overjoyed.

People who heard the news remarked, "It is amazing that the bird was found."

The fishmonger went straight to the house of a masterless samurai who loved birds, taking along some fishmeal as birdfood. In the course of their conversation, Kyūzō brought up the subject of the nightingale.

"I know it is a big favor to ask, but would it be possible for you to give me one of your nightingales? You see, my son wants it as a charm to ward off the pox."

"Both of us know how charming boys are," the samurai said warmly and handed him the bird.

Kyūzō thanked him profusely and left, but returned a moment later.

"What I just told you was a lie. The bird is for a certain daimyo. There will almost certainly be a substantial reward coming to me. Allow me to present you with half of it."

The moment the samurai heard this, his mood seemed to change completely and he took back the bird. When Kyūzō saw him prepare to draw his sword, he beat a hasty retreat.

Kyūzō went back and told the lord's retainers what had happened. They were amazed, especially the chief retainer who had promised the lord that a nightingale would soon be found. Greatly distressed, he sent a stream of smooth-talking messengers to the samurai's residence in hopes of bridging the rift, but the man closed his gate and refused to discuss the matter. The household waited helplessly as days went by until, in desperation, the lord's young son finally called out for a nightingale. When his voice reached the lord's ears, the lord assembled his advisers to figure out a way to get hold of the bird.

After some discussion, they decided to send a worldly-wise female attendant named Akashi to see what she could do. She dressed four or five lovely girls from the capital in finery and rushed them by palanquin to the samurai's residence, located quite some distance down Shitaya Street near a field of honey-locust trees. They walked through a bamboo hedge and entered the gate to the house. On the left was a thatched hut bearing a weathered sign that read, "Women's Hall of Worship."[2] They looked inside through a window and were amazed to see a tall priest standing there disrobed, plucking a chicken! Further ahead was another gate with a sign that read, "New Mt. Kōya."[3] A steady wind blew through the pine trees, making things perfectly clear to Akashi.

A boy of fourteen or fifteen suddenly appeared. He looked like one of those street urchins who sells hair pomade and aloeswood oil.[4] His face was flushed and he had sweat on his forehead. He hastily knotted his sash behind him and fled with a look of disgust on his face. Akashi called after him, "Where can I find the master of the house?" but he made no reply.

She explained the situation to the lay priest in charge of the gate, but when she asked to be shown inside, he refused.

"All women, even drawings of them, are absolutely forbidden inside. The master especially dislikes those awful front-knotted sashes, painted lips, and blackened teeth. Even his old mother who comes all by herself to visit him is not allowed to come in. He comes out to the gate to meet her instead. Let you see him? Impossible!"

He turned a deaf ear to all her arguments.

It was rare for Akashi to find herself bested by a man this way.

"If only I could get inside, I am sure we could sweet-talk him

into something," she thought. "I have never in my life encountered such a woman-hater." She had no choice but to take the girls back home.

Among the lord's pages were two handsome youths, ages sixteen and seventeen, named Kanazawa Naiki and Shimokawa Danno-suke. They could not bear to see the chief retainer fail in his prom-ise to get the nightingale, so they agreed on a plan. First, they galloped to the samurai's house on their horses and left their atten-dants two blocks this side of the place. They then made their way to the inner gate alone, pounded the door open, and leapt noisily onto the bamboo veranda.

"Are you Shimamura Tōnai?" they demanded. "Pardon our in-trusion, but we have come for your life."

Tōnai did not understand what they were talking about, but when he looked at them he saw a perfect cherry blossom and a lovely autumn leaf.

"Yes, boys. Death comes but once. Let me die defending you. No need to give me the details. Put your minds at ease." He took out three suits of chain mail and unsheathed his long-bladed spear.

"Your pursuers should be here at any moment," he warned. "Be on your guard." But neither of the young men made any effort to ready himself. They just grinned at each other. This dampened Tōnai's fiery spirit.

"Well now," he said. "Tell me what is going on."

The two boys spoke simultaneously. "It is not at all what you think. We are here to take your life. Then everything in the house will be ours to do with as we please."

"I suppose you are after the birds, too," he replied. "A moment ago I promised to die defending you. I guess I no longer have anything to lose. Here, take them." He handed them two nightingales in a round cage fringed with multicolored tassles.

The boys thanked him and left.

At the gate, they summoned their attendants and instructed them to leave a large chest with Tōnai. They then returned to Sakurada. Thus, the problem of the nightingale was successfully resolved.

That night, Dannosuke and Naiki went again in secret to the samurai's house to properly express their thanks for his help that day. "We feel that this little episode was fate's way of allowing us to get to know you. Although you undoubtedly find us unappealing, we would like to ask you to be our lover and teach us the way of boy love."

"Normally, I should make the advances," he replied. "Your request is kind, but I am not worthy of it and cannot accept. For one, I would have a hard time choosing between the two of you, and besides, I have no way of knowing how sincere your love for me really is."

Naiki and Dannosuke's faces flushed with anger. "As proof of the depth of our love ..." they began, and together bared their shoulders. On his left arm Dannosuke had tattooed the name Shimamura, and on Naiki's arm was the name Tōnai.

"We did this in good faith even before consummating our love with you," they said.

"That is something women do," the samurai scoffed. "I will not make a vow of this sort unless I am convinced first that you are willing to die like men for my sake."

"Do you think that we are the type who would hesitate to give our lives for you? Give us that chest," they said. They immediately threw it open, and inside were two low tables and a pair of small short swords wrapped in paper, placed there in preparation for committing seppuku.[5]

Tōnai was shocked. He jumped between them and asked for an explanation.

"This," they said, "was just in case we had failed earlier to get the nightingale. We would not have returned home alive. If we were willing to die manfully for the sake of a bird, don't you think we would be all the more willing to give our lives for you?" They were weeping.

At this, Tōnai relented and made profuse apologies to the boys. "From now on, you will be the only ones I love." So saying, he bit off the last joint of each of his little fingers and gave one to each of the young men. In this way their destinies were joined.

In the annals of boy love, this surely ranks as one of the most unusual troths.

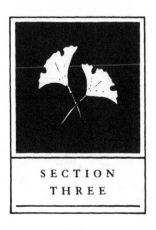

= 3:1 =

Grudge Provoked by a Sedge Hat

A topheavy set of pans.
Excitement in the temple's central sanctuary.
A first-class hairdresser.

Tradition says that women born in the third cyclical sign, year of the horse, are man-eaters. They are not the only ones, however. I once went to see a festival in Ōmi Province at a place called Tsukuma. It is the custom there for beautiful women of the village who were divorced, widowed, or caught in adultery during the past year to parade to the local shrine wearing pans on their heads equal to the number of men they have had. Among them was one older lady with a slender figure and pretty face who wore a single pan on her head, yet for her even this seemed an unbearable humiliation.

In complete contrast was a girl still wearing a vented sleeve kimono, her teeth not blackened and eyebrows unplucked,[1] with seven large pans on her head. She teetered along top-heavily, followed close behind by her mother who tried to support the pans with one hand while carrying a grandchild each on her back and

at her bosom, with a third child tugging at her free hand. It seemed
that the girl already had three youngsters of her own! She did not
pay the slightest heed to everyone's laughter, however, as we
watched her disappear beyond the twin pillars of the shrine gate.

Each with his own thoughts, we headed home when the festival
was over. Our path wound through fields where pale purple irises
bloomed in the clear waters of the marsh on either side. Bindweed
growing on the banks had lost the luster of its blossoms in the
oppressive late afternoon sun. We complained bitterly about the
heat. With us was a group of young pages from Eizan wearing
"Mt. Fuji" sedge hats, a style just becoming popular in the capital.
The boys were surely the source of love in the temple's central
sanctuary, for they served as night companions to the high priests

there. One of them was Rammaru, who hardly looked his fourteen years. He was a beautiful youth, and every monk in the entire mountain complex was in love with him.

In the same temple compound with Rammaru lived a hanger-on by the name of Iseki Sadasuke who was accompanying the pages on their way home. He took off his sedge hat and put it on top of Rammaru's, making the lovely boy look ridiculous. Rammaru decided to take it in the spirit of fun and continued on his way, but Sadasuke pointed at him from behind and mocked him.

"Just like the ladies, let's make the boys wear as many hats as they have lovers!" he laughed loudly.

Rammaru stopped in his tracks. "Are you suggesting that I have many lovers? If so, let me hear more."

"You do not need to hear it from me," Sadasuke replied. "Your own ugly heart can tell you all you want to know."

Rammaru smiled bitterly. "When priests use me as their plaything, that is not love. I have but one lover, the man who comes to visit me from the capital each day. He is on my mind even now...." He wept as he spoke.

To some, Rammaru's reaction seemed unmanly, but others praised him for his maturity and quickly changed the subject. Skirting the shore at Katada no Iso, they busily handled the rudder and sails and reached their temple home just as the evening bells reverberated across the mountain. Thus, the argument earlier ended without incident.

Rammaru was born in Komatsu, Kaga Province, the last son of a samurai named Hasegawa Hayato. This man had twelve children, all boys. His thriving household was considered auspicious and was frequently chosen to be the first to cross new bridges in the province.[2] When death struck, however, it struck in succession, and one spring his sons started to fall like blossoms. By autumn the branches were quite bare. By the eleventh month of that year, nine of them were dead, gone up in bitter smoke. The father went into retirement and turned his position over to his third-born son, Kimbei. Unfortunately, this son was asked shortly afterwards to join some colleagues in a vendetta. Unable to refuse, he joined in the fight on the night of the 23rd of the twelfth month and got himself killed. His mother, unable to bear this last blow, collapsed from the shock and herself died less than seven days later.

The father now decided to give up all earthly pleasures and leave the world of the bow and sword. He turned the household over to his remaining son Kindayū and prepared to have the youngest brother, Rammaru, enter the priesthood. They say that one person taking the tonsure saves nine generations from the sins of attachment and desire. He had his youngest son climb the mountain to this temple in the autumn of his twelfth year. The father himself went to live in seclusion at the foot of Mt. Hakusan. His only desire was to have one last look at his son wearing the black robes of a monk, but a year went by and the head priest still insisted that Rammaru wait until the spring of his fifteenth year.

Thus, the boy was heartlessly prevented from taking the tonsure by the priest's love for him.

If he were to kill Sadasuke that night, it would be the worst possible violation of his filial duty to his father, but Rammaru could not control his resentment at what had happened earlier in the day. When everyone had settled in for the night and only snores could be heard, he took out the love letters he had received over the years from his lover and looked at them longingly once again. None was written in the same hand and each employed different turns of phrase. The man was unable to write and had to ask others to put his feelings down for him. What lengths he went to! The thought made Rammaru love him all the more.

"When I am gone, his grief and anger will be terrible," he thought. "I am determined to kill Sadasuke, and my resolve will not falter should I postpone it a day. At dawn I shall go to the capital and show myself one last time to the man I love. We can lie together for a moment, but I will not tell him of my plans, just bid him farewell in this world of sorrow. . . ." His tears fell uncontrollably, unknown to anyone.

The young pages living on this mountain used to have their hair combed and tied by the clumsy fingers of woodcutters, since there was no one else to do it for them. The boys were never satisfied, however, and had begun going all the way to the Sanjō Bridge in the capital to get their hair done, a distance of four *li* on the steep mountain road called Kiraragoe.[3] Among the hairdressers was one so quick and skillful he finished even before the water used in dressing their hair had dried. His name was Shirasagi no Seihachi. Everyone said he was too good a man to be doing such menial work. He was a lifelong devotee of boy love, and his fingers were remarkably adroit. One time, he invented a new hairstyle that he called the "folded willow" because of the double fold in the top-knot. It was so popular that all of the temple pages had flocked to the hairdresser's one morning at daybreak, fighting to be the first in line. When Seihachi noticed that Rammaru was there, he took out a special comb and began working on the boy's hair immediately, not caring what the others, waiting impatiently in line for their turn, might think.

Another time, Rammaru had left with the others after getting his hair done and walked over one *li* on the mountain road home when the god-sending sky[4] suddenly grew dark with a tumult of multicolored clouds. Rain fell gently and a strong wind began to blow, burying their shoulders in leaves and drying out the oils used to dress their hair. Trying desperately to prevent their hairdos from being ruined completely, they huddled on the east side of a clump of cedars with their sleeves over their heads, pressing their hair down with their hands. As they waited impatiently for the sky to clear over the mountain peak, Seihachi appeared. He had followed Rammaru all the way from Sanjō.

He produced some combs from inside his robe and said, "I came because I was worried that your hair may have become undone." He scooped up some water in his hands from a stream flowing down the side of a nearby rock and returned each of the page's hairdos to its former condition. This act of kindness made it obvious to everyone that Seihachi was secretly in love with Rammaru. Afterwards, Rammaru's feelings for Seihachi began to grow and he gave himself to the man shortly thereafter. They had every reason to expect a long and secure future together.

Seihachi could not have imagined in his wildest dreams that today would be their last farewell. He was in a bad mood, something unusual for him, because he had not heard from Rammaru for four or five days and was suspicious. Rammaru was hurt by Seihachi's accusations, but invited him to a rest house where they drank together comfortably. When the wine had begun to take effect they lay down side by side, and Rammaru listened to Seihachi's complaints until dark. By the time they parted, it was with their usual tearful farewells.

Rammaru had brought with him a loyal servant from the temple, and on their way home they entered the shop of an artisan named Takeya. In a while they came out again and continued on their way. Seihachi, watching in secret, was upset by what he saw. He went into the sword furbisher's shop and questioned the man about Rammaru's visit.

"I do not know his purpose," the man said, "but he had me

replace the rivet on his sword hilt and put a cutting edge on the blade."

Seihachi found this very peculiar.

Immediately, he got himself ready for a fight and followed after Rammaru, taking a shortcut to Nishidani. He scratched his legs on the brambles and vines on the way and was exhausted and out of breath when darkness set in. It was so dark that even tree branches and the mountain peak were completely invisible, but he made his way at last to the lights of the temple of Gansan Daishi.[5] There, he rested. Thoughts of the past filled him once again with suspicion about the sincerity of Rammaru's love.

Long ago, the high priest Jichin[6] spoke of this holy mountain in a poem.

> To think that another
> Might love you as I do;
> My sleeves grow damp.[7]

When the mountain appeared as a lovely youth to Jichin, he must have wondered jealously if it had appeared to others in the same guise.[8] Since the boy whom Seihachi loved was in no way inferior to Teng T'ung[9] of China or Yoshiharu[10] of our land, it was only natural that other men should fall in love with him. That was the source of his nagging doubts.

Suddenly, the light of torches appeared throughout the temple.

"Rammaru has killed Sadasuke and fled!"

The temple bell was struck in rapid succession and the conch shell was blown in alarm. A group of rough monks who had accumulated grudges against the boy divided up to search for him. Seihachi followed them down the mountain towards the east. There, six or seven sturdy monks captured Rammaru and prevented him from manfully ending his life.

"There is no way he can escape beheading for what he did," one of them said. "He won't care what we do to him now. All this time we begged him to share some sake with us, but he always refused. This is our chance to get what we wanted. Let's have some sake with this boy as our side dish!"

The monks pounded on the door of a wineshop on the slope

and awoke the owners. They were soon shaking their near-empty jugs, chipped on the rim, to see how much remained. Someone filled a peeling lacquer bowl with sake and forced it to Rammaru's mouth.

"To everything there is a season! Now I can enjoy you just as I have always wanted," he said, slipping his hand under Rammaru's robe.

Someone else played with his ears and said, "Didn't you hear us when we begged you for favors before?"

They loosened his sash, put a piece of torn paper on his head,[11] and subjected him to all sorts of torments, but since they were holding him down by both arms he could do nothing to resist the terrible things they put him through.

One of the monks brought the tip of his tongue to Rammaru's lips, and all the boy could do was clench his teeth and weep bitter tears of frustration.

Suddenly, Seihachi attacked and scattered the monks with his sword. He comforted the boy and together they fled to parts unknown. All that remained behind was the fame of what they had done.

Three years later, someone reported, "I saw them at Tsurugaoka in Kamakura. They were dressed as wandering monks and playing a duet on bamboo flutes. It was the old, familiar tune, 'Nesting Cranes' that they played."

Or, so the story goes.

Tortured to Death with Snow on His Sleeve

A dream of Mt. Fuji and a hanging scroll.
His flower of youthful beauty blooms in winter.
Death comes suddenly.

Voices of hawkers selling charcoal, leather stockings for sale in shops, and the deers' full coats of fur all announced the approach of winter. In the light of dawn, the lord of Iga Province saw the pure white winter mountains and exclaimed, "I dreamed of the year's first snowfall, and indeed it has fallen!" One of the young men in the lord's service, Yamawaki Sasanosuke, went immediately to the storeroom, took out a scroll painting of Mt. Fuji by Tan'yū,[1] and placed it in the great alcove. The boy's ready wit put the lord in a splendid mood.

One morning after a snowfall in the Emperor Ichijō's reign,[2] the empress said, "I wish that I could see the beauty of Mt. Hsiang Lu's peaks." In reply, Sei Shōnagon rolled up the bamboo blinds hanging from the eaves on the north side of her chambers. They say that the empress was greatly moved by her ability to evoke the spirit of Po Chü-i's poem: "One may hear the bells of I-ai Temple by propping oneself on one's pillow, but to see the snows of Mt. Hsiang Lu's peaks one must raise the blinds."[3]

The lord of Iga was similarly impressed with Sasanosuke's apt association of Mt. Fuji with his dream of the first snowfall. From that day forward, he kept Sasanosuke close at hand in his service.

Sasanosuke was not yet required to accompany his lord for the year-long residence in Edo, so after the lord's departure Sasanosuke remained behind, living in relative freedom. One day he went to hunt fowl with three other young samurai in the foothills of the lord's land. Trail blazes on the pine trees were buried in snow and the path through dry fields of grass disappeared altogether, so they

wandered in circles chasing after stumps and stones they mistook
for birds. Soon they were feeling quite discouraged. Not even the
sparrows that lived at a tiny shrine in the woods could be found.

Just when they were ready to give up and go home, a pheasant
came flying out of a farmer's blind, built for guarding his melon
patch, deep in the shadows of a bamboo thicket. The boys chased
the bird with their wooden staves and bamboo poles and were
overjoyed to catch it. Immediately afterwards several more cock-
birds followed. The boys were wild with excitement, but one attendant grew suspicious and went over to investigate the blind.
He found two unknown men hiding inside with a cage full of
pheasants.

"Hunting birds on the lord's land is strictly forbidden. Don't
you know that?"

Even as he scolded them, one ran off holding a bamboo branch
to disguise his face. The attendant grabbed the other and was ready
to kill him when Sasanosuke came running up.

"Let him go," he commanded, and apologized for the man. "It
is only his way of making a living."

Since it was getting toward dusk, the attendant broke off the
branch of a plum tree waiting for spring and tied the pheasants to
it to take them home.

"Well, at least we got some birds for free," he said as the group
of young men headed home. How insensitive to feelings of love
and pity was this seasonally employed samurai!

Sasanosuke trailed behind, feigning a sore foot. He asked the
bird snatcher, "Why did you come here today in secret? Tell me
the truth, or I will make sure you never see home again."

The man was so terrified by Sasanosuke's threat that he lost all
composure.

"I am Haemon's servant," he blurted out. "He is the one
who fled."

"But everyone knows Haemon," said Sasanosuke. "Why should
he run away and hide? It makes no sense."

"He said that someone by the name of Yamawaki Sasanosuke
went out hunting today without realizing that there would be no
birds around since other members of the household had been out

every day lately. Also, the snow would make walking difficult for the young man, so to please him he released some caged birds where he would be sure to see them."

The servant seemed to be speaking the truth.

"I see," said Sasanosuke. "I am sure that the young man's joy knew no bounds. Allow me to return the favor with this gift."

He removed his open-vented jacket and presented it to the servant. (Strangely, the servant seemed to think that a keg of sake would make a more appropriate gift!) From then on, this man carried letters between Sasanosuke and Haemon. They developed a deep relationship in the way of boy love that was noticed and tolerated by the household.

One time, cherry trees in the temple garden at Sainen-ji on Mt. Nagata were blooming out of season. The whole household went out in a spring-like mood to see the sight. "Captive of the lovely scene, a butterfly flits joyfully."[4] Those who saw the blossoms fell into a poetic mood and forgot completely the principle that beauty is destined to decay, and attached a spout to a keg of sake. Even the youngsters joined in the revelry.

The keg was almost half empty when Haemon came by to view the blossoms. Happy to see him, a young man named Igarashi Ichisaburō stopped him and handed him a full cup. Haemon thanked him perfunctorily and took it. Even after the sake began to take effect, he spoke of no one but Sasanosuke. Later, when he left, he remembered to take both his swords with him.

Someone had already reported the incident to Sasanosuke and he was burning with jealousy when Haemon returned. Ignoring the fierce wind, Sasanosuke stood impatiently outside the front gate and immediately took Haemon's hand. To torment him, he stood Haemon alone in the garden, locked the garden gate, and secured the wooden rain doors from inside. Haemon felt uneasy but said nothing for some time. It began to snow heavily. At first he brushed the snow off his shoulders with his sleeve and later sought shelter under a paulownia tree, but all its leaves had long since fallen and it offered no protection. Eventually the cold became unbearable. When he spoke, the voice that came out of his lungs was a strange shriek. "Hey! I am about to die out here!"

Sasanosuke was with a young monk inside, and when he heard Haemon's cry he laughed.

"Don't tell me the friendly warmth of the sake has worn off already!" He spoke looking down from the second-floor drawing room.

"I swear I meant no harm by taking the sake. I have learned my lesson; I will never go near another boy again." Haemon's apology only made Sasanosuke more angry.

"If you mean that, then hand me your two swords as proof."

Haemon did so, but Sasanosuke only continued to humiliate him.

"Take off your robes and skirt."

Reluctantly, Haemon stripped naked.

"Now, undo your hair."

Haemon had no choice but to comply. With difficulty, he was

finally able to get his hair down. Sasanosuke then threw down a piece of paper on which he had written Sanskrit characters.[5]

"Put this on your head," he commanded.

By now, Haemon's breath was coming out in gasps. His body started to tremble pitifully and his voice became a ghostly moan. Before long, he could do nothing but stand there, arms raised in supplication.

Sasanosuke meanwhile had started beating a hand drum and was chanting, "Ah, I sing a dreadful dirge."[6] When he looked down again shortly, he was horrified to see Haemon standing there blinking his eyes rapidly, on the verge of death. He reached for some medicine, but before he could even open the case Haemon's pulse had ceased entirely. Sasanosuke cut open his own belly on the bed next to Haemon and died.

In the midst of the terrible grief they were forced to bear, Sasanosuke's survivors looked in on the bedroom where he always slept. The bed was spread neatly with two pillows at the head. On it was a perfumed white robe and a set of sake cups ready for use nearby. All those who saw the care with which everything had been laid out clapped their hands in admiration at the depth of Sasanosuke's love for Haemon.

The Sword That Survived Love's Flames

Memories of a rice husker.
A woman-hater unto death.
Saving his birthplace from disaster.

Carrying two funeral urns wrapped in cloth kerchiefs, a young man hardly old enough to comprehend fully the impermanence of life asked the way to Mt. Kōya with tears in his eyes. He had stopped to rest at a teahouse called "Three Provinces" at the place where the provinces of Settsu, Izumi, and Kawachi converge. It was his good fortune that the man he asked was on his way to the same destination, so they agreed to become traveling companions. The two of them spoke as they walked.

It was the summer solstice, and in farm villages everywhere rice-planting songs they had never heard before were being sung by women in sedge hats. The young man looked at their figures with obvious interest, but his companion passed by looking in the opposite direction.

"No matter what they are doing, I see no reason for you to be looking at women," he said. "Handsome youths are the only thing of interest in this world."

"I agree completely," the young man replied, weeping despite himself as he cradled the urns in his arms. "It makes no sense for me to go on living in this world of sorrow."

He seemed overwhelmed with grief.

"Tell me what happened," his companion asked.

"He was the son of a shopkeeper in the town of Fuchū, Suruga Province, who dealt in goods from the capital. His name was Yorozuya no Kyūshirō, and there was no other boy as handsome. He knew of love from the age of thirteen when he gave himself to me, and we were together night and day, as inseparable as a fish is from water. But life is uncertain, and he passed away one day like froth on a stream. One hundred days have now elapsed, so I wanted to bury his remains in the inner temple complex and make him a part of this holy mountain."

"What about the ashes in the other urn?" his companion asked.

"I have brought them for the same purpose. A friend of mine was to take a wife, but on the night of the ceremony, when the pine and bamboo-decorated tray was brought out, she bowed her head as if to sleep, ceased breathing, and died. He asked me to take her remains with me on this trip."

His companion laughed.

"What a fool you are! Just because a woman has turned to ashes does not make it right for a lover of boys to hold her in his arms."

The young man immediately realized the error of his ways and threw the woman's ashes into a muddy creek where they sank beneath the plantain and lotus leaves.

"What a pair of woman-haters we are!"

After that their conversation became even more friendly.

Shortly, they reached the place called Mikkaichi. Just then a priest who looked as if he might be in charge of one of Mt. Kōya's temples came by with a young cowherd from one of the temple-owned farm villages.[1] He had obviously tried to disguise the boy as a temple acolyte, but dirt was plainly visible behind the boy's ears. His hair was properly bound up, but it looked reddish and dry. The sleeves of his plain, light-blue hemp robe were far too short; it seemed to be an adult's round-sleeved robe slit under the arms to make him look boyish. He sported a pair of long and short swords, no doubt consigned to the temple by a parishioner in mourning. The sword guards were too big for the small hilts. The boy slouched under their unaccustomed weight as he walked along in the priest's tow. The men watched them pass, impressed with the priest's ingenuity.

Up ahead, a sturdy-looking man was pounding rice in a mortar set up outside a gate. The rice was almost completely hulled, but when he saw the priest he threw down his pestle and hurriedly bent down to hide himself. His blackened buttocks were a revolt-

ing sight. The priest continued for quite some distance before halting to whisper something to his attendant, who promptly put down the chest he carried with agar and dried gourd shavings attached to it[2] and went back to give the man pounding rice a link of 200 coins.

"The priest says he has not forgotten what went on between you in the past. Why have you not visited the temple since then? Please come again soon, he says."

The attendant relayed this message and left.

The travelers were curious and later asked him what the message meant.

"For several years I was the recipient of that priest's affections, but look at me now." The rice pounder brushed the husks from his sleeve and wept into it. Since this was the path of love they preferred, they did not laugh at him but went on their way.

The travelers avoided the way-station called Kaburo because of its name.[3] They found it necessary to avert their eyes frequently as far as the Women's Hall of Worship.[4] Once past Hanatsumi, however, the way grew more pleasant. Night overtook them at the thousand-trunk black pine deep in the temple complex. The hooting of an owl could be heard in the distance.

Suddenly, a figure appeared in white before them. When the young man looked more closely, he realized that it was the boy separated from him in death! The figure stood there mournfully, holding a sword in one hand. Its voice could just barely be heard. The man was astonished to hear his name being called. He stood there for a moment staring, uncertain whether the figure was real or a dream.

"Seeing you again makes me long terribly for the past," the voice said. "When I died, my father placed this sword in my coffin to be burned because he said there was no further purpose in keeping it. He mistook it for a sword handed down in our family for generations. In fact, it was one a certain samurai secretly left with me for safekeeping. After my death, he returned to demand the sword. My family is suffering great distress as a result. Please, return it to them for me."

The voice disappeared, leaving only the man's own feelings of loneliness and the ancient sword. It was his only proof that what he had seen was real. He doubted his senses, as if he had heard the plucking of a jeweled harp by the Chinese Hsiang Fei consorts.[5] In a daze, he headed directly home instead of going to worship at the Kumano Shrine as he had originally planned.

Though 100 days had long since passed, the grief of the boy's parents had not abated one bit when he returned. They were being bombarded by messengers demanding that the sword left in their custody be returned immediately. The samurai owner would not accept apologies or offers of money. He wanted the original sword back exactly as he had left it.

In their desperation, the parents had even gone to the boy's grave and looked among the charred bones buried there,[6] but not a trace of the sword could be found. With no other recourse open to them, the old man and his wife were ready to flee the house where they had spent their years together when the boy's lover, Hansuke, returned from his pilgrimage to Mt. Kōya and handed them the very sword. When he explained to them Kyūshirō's miraculous appearance, they were utterly amazed.

"Who would think that in this uncertain world, the keepsake of a dead loved one could reappear for all to see!" they said.

The Sickbed No Medicine Could Cure

A go-between for love.
A spring night's battle in darkness.
Sixteen- and eighteen-year-old blossoms fall together.

It is for the beauty of their blossoms that branches are torn from the tree.

In the service of a certain chamberlain to the shogun was a boy named Itami Ukyō. He was skilled in poetry and song, and to look at him was almost blinding, he was such a lovely youth. Living in the same household was Mokawa Uneme, a fashionable but solid young man of eighteen. One day he was so taken with Ukyō's remarkable beauty that his emotions became confused, his soul seemed to leave him, and even his feet stumbled uncertainly.

He took to bed, something unheard of for him, and shut himself behind closed doors, aware of neither night nor day. There, he pined in secret for the boy. His friends were worried about his gradual decline and discussed what medication he should be given. Just then, a group of young colleagues paid a visit to express their condolences over his illness. Among them was the boy for whom he yearned. When Uneme saw him, his confusion grew even more acute. He tried to conceal it, but his feelings were apparent from the way he spoke. Everyone realized immediately what was wrong. Among them was Shiga Samanosuke who shared a strong vow of boy love with Uneme. Desiring to discuss it, he stayed behind when the others had gone and approached close to the pillow where Uneme lay ill.

"It is difficult for me to understand your condition," he whispered. "If there is something weighing on your mind, do not let me be the last to know. Is it true that among the visitors who just left is one whom you love? It would be cruel of you not to tell me so."

"That is not the case," Uneme replied evasively.

Samanosuke persisted with his questions, but Uneme lay there silent, as if asleep.

In time, they summoned an almanac master[1] for a diagnosis.

"This illness will not lead to death," he said. "It seems to be of the sort caused by an evil spirit or possessing demon. Holy men must be hired to drive the spirit out with prayers and incantations."

High priest Tenkai of Ueno[2] and priest Chūzon of Asakusa[3] were duly summoned and for three days and two nights burned incense and prayed. His mother, too, visited the great shrines throughout the province where she lived to make supplications for his recovery. Perhaps as a result, his illness seemed to improve slightly.

Hearing this, Samanosuke came in secret to see Uneme. "Are you ashamed of loving another because of me? If so, allow me to take a letter to him and bring you his reply. Rest assured, I will handle everything as you wish me to."

"Your offer makes me very happy," Uneme replied. "I feel encouraged by your love."

He then wrote down his feelings in a long letter to Ukyō and gave it to Samanosuke, who put it between the layers of his sleeves. Samanosuke went nonchalantly to the clock chamber and found Ukyō reciting a poem to the cherry blossoms outside.

When Ukyō saw him, he approached him and explained, "The other day I was with the lord all day listening to a lecture on 'The Chen Kuan Fundamentals of Government,'[4] and today he had me reading from the *Shinkokin*[5] until a moment ago. To give my mind a rest, I was spending some time with these cherry blossoms as my companions, since they at least keep silent."

"By chance," said Samanosuke, "I have here something else that has kept silent for some time." He removed the letter hidden deep within his sleeve and gave it to the boy.

"Are you sure it is not meant for someone else?" Ukyō said, laughing. He then moved into the shade of some trees in the garden, no doubt intending to read the letter there in private. He returned a short time later and said, "If he is ill for my sake, how can I abandon him?" He gave Samanosuke his reply right away. When Uneme read it, he was so overjoyed he arose from his sickbed and in a matter of days had entirely regained his former health.

In this world, however, good fortune is always followed by misfortune. A samurai by the name of Hosono Shuzen had recently entered into service in the household. He considered bravery the greatest virtue and spent from morning to night rattling the hilt of his sword, to the chagrin of everyone there. He, too, fell in love with Ukyō.

He was an unsophisticated man and did not know what to do about his feelings. Without utilizing a go-between as he should have, he approached the boy himself one day as he stood under a blossoming cherry tree. Like a locust buzzing noisily in the boy's ear, he wept and laughed and pleaded his case in various ways, but Ukyō refused to exchange a single word with him. This only served to make his feelings all the more urgent.

In desperation, he turned to a friend (there is a saying, "Birds of a feather flock together") named Fushiki Shōsai, a monk in charge of preparing the tea ceremony. He agreed to plead Shuzen's case to Ukyō.

When Shōsai spoke to the boy, he begged him to answer Shuzen's letter with a pledge of life-long affection, but Ukyō simply laughed in his face.

"You should stick to your task of sweeping ashes with your feather duster after the tea ceremony. Your services as go-between are not required. Here, use this letter as a cover for one of your tea kettles." So saying, he tossed the letter back at him.

Enraged, Shōsai returned and encouraged Shuzen to kill Ukyō and flee to another province. Shuzen decided he would do so that very night.

When Ukyō heard that Shuzen was making preparations for an attack that night, he realized that it was already too late to avoid a confrontation. He debated for a moment whether or not to tell Uneme. If he did not, Uneme would be angry when he found out later, but, if he did, it would be a betrayal of his own warrior spirit. He decided not to drag Uneme with him into the abyss of this affair.

It was the seventeenth year of Kan'ei [1640], fourth month, seventeenth day.

It rained heavily that night, creating an eerie silence throughout the household. Guards on night duty grew unaware of their surroundings and drifted off to sleep, their heads pillowed on their sleeves. Ukyō chose this moment to set out for the fight. His beauty just then was beyond description. He was crisply dressed in sheer silk robes worn one upon the other, each so white that even the snow had reason for envy. His brocade trousers, worn high, were perfumed with burnt incense and smelled more fragrant than ever. Clasping his sword close to his side, he stepped lightly past the guards. His fragrance, however, was impossible to disguise and several of the men woke up in surprise. Nevertheless, they allowed him to pass unchallenged.

Shuzen was on duty in the Great Hall, leaning against a folding screen that depicted hawks of every variety. He was looking down at a fan in his hands, tightening its linchpin. Just then, Ukyō ran up to him and with a shout slashed at him, inflicting a wound that ran from the top of his right shoulder to below his nipple. True to his rough and ready spirit that had so irritated the household, Shuzen managed to draw his sword with his left hand and engaged the boy sword to sword for a while, but the severity of his wound proved to be too much. With a curse, Shuzen fell to the floor. Ukyō pushed him flat on his back and ran him through twice with his sword.

He extinguished the lamp and stood there in a daze, thinking he should next go and slay the monk, but already night watchmen awakened by the sound of the fray were running in an uproar towards the central chamber, while guards attending the lord's chambers rushed out to meet them. This must surely be what the Kenkyū incident at the Fuji hunting grounds was like long ago.[6] Quickly, lamps were lighted. Ukyō was captured in the entrance by a certain man named Oda and by Takebe Shirō and taken into the lord's presence.

The lord was furious. "I do not care what sort of grudge you harbored. Such defiance of authority is unforgivable."

Tokumatsu Tonomo was ordered to investigate the matter. When he had presented his findings, the lord decided that Ukyō's actions were completely justified. The lord ordered that Ukyō be kept under guard and set up a room for him in the main residence where he received the best of care that night.

The father of the dead man, Hosono Mimbu, had been in service to the Ogasawara family for many years. He rushed to the
place where his son was killed and angrily demanded that the boy
be ordered to commit seppuku. The mother, who had found favor
in certain quarters[7] and was regularly invited to participate in poetry meets and the like, paced the floor in her bare feet all night,
distraught over the lord's decision.

"How dare they save a murderer for no reason whatsoever and
allow him to enjoy their sympathy. It is a disgrace!" she said weeping. Her sleeves could not absorb all of her tears. Those who saw
it were filled with pity for her. A certain lady-in-waiting's[8] son
(who originally began as the Primate of Tōfuku-ji and later returned to government service as Gotō something-or-other) jumped
on his horse and urged it on with a whip to the lord chamberlain's
house. After he explained the circumstances affecting this matter,
the lord was persuaded to deal strictly with the boy and ordered
that Ukyō commit seppuku. Shōsai, who acted as go-between,
would also die by his own hand.

The day before Ukyō's attack, Uneme had requested relief from
his duties and gone to stay with his mother in Kanagawa. There
he received an urgent letter from Samanosuke describing in detail
what had happened. It ended with the words, "Ukyō must commit
seppuku at dawn at Keiyō-ji in Asakusa."[9]

Uneme dashed off a reply thanking Samanosuke for his prompt
letter. Then, without even bidding his mother farewell, he rented
a boat and went directly to Asakusa. The sky was just beginning
to grow light when he arrived at the temple. He waited at the gate
listening for news. Pages and priests were gathered and spoke excitedly together.

"A very handsome young samurai will be coming here at any
moment to commit seppuku."

"Parents will mourn any son, no matter how ugly. Just imagine
how distraught the parents of one so handsome must be."

"What a pity."

When Uneme heard these remarks, he wept bitterly.

Word spread of the coming seppuku and a crowd of spectators
gathered. Uneme mingled with them as they waited. Shortly, a
splendid palanquin appeared surrounded by a vast array of atten-

dants. It came to rest outside the temple gate, and Ukyō emerged
serenely from inside, looking lovely beyond compare. He wore a
pure white robe of Chinese twill embroidered throughout with the
blossom of the short-lived dewflower. He swept his eyes over the
scene before him with a look of clear-eyed resolve. There were
hundreds of graves marked by erect stupas, each representing the
grief of a household. On the left side of the temple grounds were
mountain cherries still bearing a few late blossoms. He gazed at
them and recited a Chinese poem:

> A Few Blossoms Linger
> On This Year's Branches,
> But They Are Ignored;
> People Look Forward Instead

To Next Year's Blossoms.
Such Is Human Nature.

Perhaps he recited it out of envy for Uneme, who would remain
behind to enjoy other springs.

Ukyō seated himself on the rush mat sewn with a border of
brocade. He cut off a sidelock of his lovely hair, wrapped it in
paper, folded it, and summoned his second, Kichikawa Kageyu.[10]

"Please see that my mother in the capital at Horikawa gets this.
Tell her it is my parting gift, something to remember me by." He
put the package aside.

Just then, the head priest appeared in a purple robe with his
sleeves rolled up and began to expound on the principle of death's
certainty for all living things. Ukyō interrupted him and said,

"Beautiful women who cling to life must suffer the disgrace of thinning white hair. To attain my innermost desire while my beauty is still fresh and die thus by my own hand, this is true Buddhahood."

He removed a strip of blue paper from his sleeve. Calmly, he smoothed it and asked for an inkstone. His last testament read, "Blossoms in spring and the moon in autumn enjoyed our admiring gaze; a dream within a dream."

He then cut open his belly. Kageyu cut off the boy's head and stepped back. Immediately, Uneme came running up.

"Do the same for me," he said. He plunged the blade into his own belly, and Kageyu beheaded him.

Thus, at the ages of sixteen and eighteen, two youths ended their lives one late spring day in the Kan'ei Era. Among the young men of the household in their service over the years were some so overcome with grief that they chose to follow them in death. Others cut off their topknots and entered the priesthood to pray for their dead masters' salvation.[11]

Even today their graves can be found at Keiyō-ji in Asakusa. Ukyō's final poem of farewell stands attached to a wooden post, preserving their reputations high in the eastern sky.[12] Shiga Samanosuke left behind a letter saying he could not go on living and ended his life seven days later.

Truly, people were forced to witness many unhappy events at this time.

＝ 3:5 ＝

He Fell in Love When the Mountain Rose
Was in Bloom

Exhausted by four years of following a lord's retinue.
Parting with life for love's sake.
A petition prompted by love.

Seeking relief from life in the barracks, he made his way from Toranomon[1] to a village called Shibuya at the edge of the endless plain of Musashi. The Konnō cherry tree[2] was at its peak of bloom, not unlike this spirited young samurai named Tagawa Gizaemon. Years ago in his youth he had been the most handsome young man in all four provinces of Shikoku and enjoyed considerable fame in Matsuyama. Due to certain circumstances he became a masterless samurai but before long was fortunate enough to get a new position at his original stipend of 600 *koku*. Grateful that things had gone smoothly for him this spring, he decided to visit the temple in Meguro dedicated to Fudō.[3]

There, at the base of the waterfall where people wash to purify themselves, stood a handsome youth wearing a jewel-rimmed sedge hat tied with a pale blue cord. Below the hat his hair gleamed rich and black. His long-sleeved robe was dyed in a morning-glory pattern, and at his slender hips he sported two swords, long and short, sheathed in polished shark skin. He held a lovely branch of mountain rose in his left hand. His quiet, untroubled beauty made it hard for Gizaemon to believe that he was human. Surely he was like the holy men of Mt. Ku She who could transform themselves into peonies at will.[4] In a daze, Gizaemon followed after him. It appeared that the boy was a treasured possesion of some great daimyo, for he led a horse behind him and was attended by a host of young samurai and two watchmen-monks. Gizaemon knew that this was no ordinary personage. He forgot everything else and fol-

lowed after him. The two monks had enjoyed some wine on the
outing and began singing songs. Shortly, at the edge of Koroku's
Shrine,[5] they entered a gate bearing the paulownia crest.[6]

At the crossroads nearby was a daimyo guard post. There Gizaemon asked about the boy and learned that his name was Oku-
kawa Shume, a page in personal attendance to the lord. Gizaemon
went home and that night could think of nothing but those lovely
forelocks parted in the middle. Early the next morning he went
back to the gate where he had last seen the boy and stood there for
the rest of the day. He lost all interest in his official duties, so he
claimed sudden illness and received permission to take a leave of
absence. He rented lodgings in an alley south of Kojima Ni-chōme
and lived there without employment, going every day from the
24th day of the third month to the beginning of the tenth month
in the same year to wait outside the gate. He never glimpsed the
boy's face again, however. To plead his case by letter was out of
the question, so he was condemned to suffer from dawn to dusk
the torments of unrequited love.

In the midst of his torment came word that the boy's lord had
been granted leave to return to his domain. He and his retinue
would depart from Edo on the 25th day of the tenth month. Gizaemon decided that he would follow the boy no matter where he
might go and immediately gave up his rented lodgings. He sold off
his belongings, settled his debts with the sake shop and the fishmonger, and dismissed his servant. Completely alone now, he set
out in secret after the daimyo's retinue.

That night, the lord and his entourage stopped at Kanagawa.
The following day darkness overtook them at Ōiso. At the edge of
a marsh where sandpipers rose, the lovely boy he so longed for
brought his palanquin to a halt and partially opened the door facing the cove. He recited an old poem, "Even the heartless soul feels
moved. . . ."[7] Intently, Gizaemon looked at him, and the boy returned his glance. They parted there and Gizaemon had no opportunity to see him again. Though wide awake, he walked the path
of dreams.

Later, on the road cut through Mt. Utsu, he hid himself among
some low boulders and peeked into the window of the palanquin

as it passed. His eyes filled with tears despite himself. Perhaps the boy he loved had begun to take note of him, for Shume looked back with a gentle expression of sympathy on his lovely face. This increased Gizaemon's ardor for the boy even more, but days passed and he failed to catch another glimpse of him. He finally saw the boy one last time at Toyama in Mimasaka and then entered Izumo Province where he painfully shouldered a carrying pole in order to make a living. Thus the year came to an end.

In the beginning of the fourth month of the following year, the lord was again required in attendance at Edo. Gizaemon saw the boy three times on the way to Musashi, first at the Kuwana River crossing, again at Shimozaka, and last at Suzunomori. During the year-long residence in Edo, Gizaemon went every day to yearn for him outside the mansion compound. By now Gizaemon's appearance was quite strange. He was in love, to be sure, but no samurai should so disgrace himself in society. That he should have allowed himself to fall so low could only be attributed to a remarkable karmic bond.

The following year he once again followed the boy to his native province. Three years had now passed since he first saw the boy and gave up his position as a samurai. By now his sleeves were torn, his collar threadbare, and his only remaining possession was a single short sword. Outside the waystation at Kanaya, Gizaemon was watching the boy mounted on a horse in the distance when Shume noticed him and suddenly seemed to realize how much Gizaemon loved him. His heart went out to the man in compassion.

"Perhaps I can speak to him when the guards are not looking. If we could but exchange a few words, it might relieve his yearning," the boy thought, and secretly waited for him in the shadow of some pines at Nakayama Pass. Yet Gizaemon never appeared. Soon afterwards, the boy lost track of him completely. At odd moments when at rest he would sometimes wonder what had become of the man. He was indeed a tender-hearted youth.

Ten days after the daimyo returned to his province, Gizaemon straggled into Izumo. He had injured his foot and was now totally unrecognizable as his former self and apparently on the verge of death. His yearning for the boy, however, made him cling to his useless life, and for survival he turned to begging. He warded off the morning frosts with his straw hat and tucked his legs under him against the fierce wind at night. During the day he avoided notice by staying in the far-off corners of fields, appearing late at night to wait outside the castle gate for the pleasure of seeing Shume on his way home from night duty.

One cold and rainy winter night Shume spoke sadly to Kyūzaemon, a young samurai assigned to his service.

"I was born a warrior but have yet to kill a man with my own blade. If I should ever have to do so, I am not confident I could succeed. Please, allow me to try out my swordsmanship on someone tonight."

"From what I have seen in your regular practice, your skill with the sword is excellent," Kyūzaemon replied. "To kill without purpose would invite heaven's displeasure. Please wait until the right opportunity presents itself."

"I am not talking about killing someone for no reason. Earlier, I was looking at the big drainage ditch outside the mansion facing ours. There was a filthy beggar there who looked like he would be better off dead. Do you think if I fed and clothed him for a time he would then let me kill him? Go and ask him, please."

"I don't know. All he has left is life, and he may want to keep it," Kyūzaemon remarked dubiously, but he went anyway to where the beggar lay.

"Excuse me. I have something to ask," he began. "It is impossible to guarantee that a person's life will last until the rain, now falling, clears. Look at yourself, debased and without any purpose in life. It is the desire of the young master I serve to satisfy your wishes for thirty days, and after that to practice his swordsmanship on you in exchange. If you agree, he will see that you are properly mourned afterwards," Kyūzaemon explained.

To his surprise, the man replied without a hint of sadness. "I know I will not last till spring; I am completely worn out trying to survive the freezing nights. I have no family. Therefore, no complaints could arise after my death. Yes, I think it would be a splendid way to die." So saying, he rose and was led into the house.

After Kyūzaemon had reported this to his master, the man was made to wash and given a change of clothes. He lived in the central chamber for ten days, the period shortened by his own request. During that time he received good food and was well cared for in every way. The promised day arrived, and after midnight the man was led to a large garden.

"When you said you would give me your life, was it the truth?" the boy asked.

The beggar thrust out his neck and said, "I beg the honor of death at your hands."

The boy hitched up his trousers and jumped down to where the beggar sat, slashing at him with his sword. The man did not even wince, however. The sword had no edge on the blade!

The boy's attendants were all amazed to see this, but he chased them beyond the middle gate and locked them out. Seating himself in the waiting room, he asked the man to show his face.

"I recognize you," the boy said. "You were once a samurai, were you not?"

Gizaemon denied it, insisting that he came from a long line of merchants.

"Come now, do not hide it. I know that you love me deeply. If you do not tell me now, when will you have another chance? Or, am I mistaken?"

When the boy said this, the man reached inside his robe and from against his skin took out a package wrapped in bamboo bark. It was a persimmon weave purse of brocade. He presented it to the boy and said, "I beg you to look inside. It contains the proof of my love." Even as he spoke, tears like a string of jewels streamed from his eyes.

The boy untied the purple cord binding the purse and looked inside. It was a scroll made of 70 sheets of thin paper glued end to end. In it, the man had written every detail of his love for the boy from the day he first saw him standing in the field at Meguro up to the present. Shume was able to read only four or five pages of the scroll before he rolled it up again. Asking Kyūzaemon to look after the man, Shume went at dawn directly to the castle and appeared before the lord.

"A certain man has fallen in love with me," he said. "If I refuse him, I betray my honor as a follower of the way of boy love. If I act freely, it means breaking my lord's laws and is tantamount to rejecting your long-standing benevolence toward me. Please kill me so that I may escape this quandary."

"Explain yourself," the lord demanded.

Shume produced the scroll mentioned above and gave it to him. In private, the lord spent over one hour reading the scroll from beginning to end. When he finished, he called Shume to him.

"First, I order you to return home," the lord said. "I will discuss the matter with my advisers, and when we reach a decision you will be informed."

"If you send me home now, I will act improperly with the man,"

Shume protested. "Allow me to commit seppuku here instead."
This was his second request to die.

The lord thought for a moment and then called his chief agent,
ordering him to place the boy under house arrest.

Shume returned home and from that day the masterless samurai
was presented with two swords and given new clothes befitting
his rank. They spent their nights together, knowing full well it
would cost them their lives. Never in previous ages was there
boy love like this. Shume meanwhile made preparations for his funeral. Waiting in this way for death, however, must have had its
pleasures.

Twenty days later Shume's house arrest was lifted. In addition,
he received five sets of robes with rounded sleeves[8] and a gift of 30
ryō of gold. It was a most unexpected conclusion to the affair.

As for the masterless samurai, he was ordered to leave for Edo
at an appropriate hour the next day. The man was overwhelmed
with gratitude.

"How can I ever repay the lord's kindness?" he said.

That very night he reluctantly parted from Shume and set out
on the trip home by horse. It was the 27th day of the twelfth
month. At Hyōgo he sent those who were to accompany him back
to their province and, instead of proceeding to Edo, secretly went
to live in Izumi near Mt. Katsuraki, in the town where the Enohai
well[9] is found. He cut off his hair and took the monk's name of
Mugen. There he lived, saying nothing and going nowhere. He
took comfort in the flow of water that never ceased pouring from
a pipe buried deep within the rocks beyond his bamboo fence and
found pleasure in the words of the Chinese sages.

Without even fanning himself with one of the gaudy fans so
popular nowadays, his heart grew pure and cool.

**SECTION
FOUR**

$= 4 : 1 =$

Drowned by Love in Winecups of Pearly Nautilus Shells

A collection of ancient calligraphy by courtesans.
A verbal battle of erotic words.
The midwife affected by life's impermanence.

In the present-day capital is a house facing Muromachi-dōri. It is of rather modest stature and built with Chinese black pine, whole logs of cryptomeria, bark-covered evergreen columns, octagonal zelkova, and even imported ebonies from China. Each pillar is of a different variety of costly wood and each rafter sports a distinctive decorative cap at the tip. Even the walls are of variegated colors, and the lattice-work windows employ every type of bamboo known to man. People point out the house to their friends and say, "That belongs to Shimano Kanzaemon, the expert appraiser of old calligraphy."

In the same capital, there was one man who had never heard of this famous person. The reason lay in his daily pilgrimages west on Matsubara-dōri in the direction of Ōmiya and Tambaguchi, which convinced him that the holiest of earthly pleasures were obtainable there alone. He did not know or care that the temple at Kurodani belonged to the Pure Land sect, or that the main sanctuary of the Gion Shrine faced south; he was dedicated to a single path, the pursuit of prostitutes in the quarter. Like everyone else, he had over the years collected samples of calligraphy from courtesans.

"Some of the love letters date from before my time," he said, "so I would like to have an expert verify their authenticity."

Everyone who heard it was amazed at the absurdity of the idea.

This man was the foremost patron of the Shimabara in those days and was called by the name, "Sir Nagayoshi of the Shinzaike District."[1] He had ransomed the courtesan Yoshino, lovely as a cherry blossom just bursting into flower, and later took up with another cherry-like beauty farther down the mountain range, the *tayū* Kazuraki.[2]

These dalliances soon came to an end, however, for he now abandoned himself to the true love of a certain lady in service at the imperial court. Night and day he had eyes only for her. The moon's light appeared but dimly, and the glow of fireflies was wasted on him. Leaves on the branches turned red without his notice, and snow drifted forgotten under his eaves. They took steamy daytime naps under a covered charcoal brazier with a tassled pillow for two; their nights they spent in love-making.

This lovely court attendant, now in the spring of her sixteenth year, was born the illegitimate child of a well-known noble lady by the name of Fujihime (or something of that sort). Her beauty, the very image of a cherry blossom, far surpassed even painted likenesses of Komachi.[3] She was well versed in the poetic style of her house and regularly entertained with music on her jeweled koto. When she sang popular songs in the modern style, her sound was remarkably different from the crude Nagebushi and Ise mode variations being mouthed by plebeian types. Since even her musical skills were so rich and pleasing, it was no wonder that her love too was guileless and true. Time passed, and their repeated vows of love led to a mutual meeting of hearts that was quite unlike the usual relationship between husband and wife.

She and the other numerous handmaidens and hairdressers, attendants and ladies-in-waiting were unequaled anywhere in following the latest fashions of the imperial court in their manners and dress. She was like a lovely cotton rose blooming before a garden stairway, its eight-petaled buds hidden amidst the leaves on fragile twigs and ready to burst into bloom at the first hint of rain. Her beauty was there for everyone to see, but no one dared pluck this blossom for it already belonged to someone. He called her his own and took pleasure in her night and day.

In the shadow of the mountains at Saga, he built himself a mansion from which he had a view of the capital stretched below. He constructed a garden framed by Mt. Arashi looming in the distance and formed a miniature lake by diverting waters of the Ōi River. Here they spent the third day of the third month enjoying themselves uproariously. Unfortunately, the peach blossoms were not yet in bloom that year. The day would be no fun without flowers, they thought, so he sent for several paper craftsmen from Kitano and quickly had them make artificial peach blossoms for their pleasure.

One of their games that day was to line up beautiful women left and right on both banks of the stream and have them set afloat winecups made of pearly nautilus shells. But instead of reciting poems, which they deemed a bit tired and old-fashioned, they proceeded to prove their skill in words of love-making. The women stood facing each other in pairs and, without regard for the shame they might bring upon themselves, bandied about lewd phrases in a verbal battle of undisguised eroticism. The woman whose words were lacking in rhetorical flourish was the loser and declared insufficiently trained in the ways of love. In punishment, she was stripped completely naked in front of the mistress of the house (even her underskirt was removed!) and then chased in circles around the entire garden by the other women. Even though they were her companions in fun, it must have been a dreadful experience nonetheless.

Meanwhile, in the drawing room a group had gathered that included a retired gentleman, several family intimates, and the family doctor, all of whom clapped their hands and howled with laughter. Truly, the sight of a naked woman can cause any man to make a fool of himself, no matter what his station in life.

After dark, the men and women went to bathe together. Except

for the mistress of the house, each man was allowed to corrupt
himself with any woman there who struck his fancy. Surely this
was one of life's fondest memories, like the pleasures of Hua
Ch'ing Villa where Yang Kuei Fei's gentle fingers soothed the emperor's moxa burns with ointment.[4] Rarely are men able to enjoy
such pleasures.

The one thing in the world that all men want is money. What
set this gentleman apart from you and me is that he knew the
freedom that hard cash allows. He was wealthy enough to live for
the rest of his life on the interest accrued from loans, an ideal way
to spend one's life! He could enjoy all of life's pleasures in the
privacy of his own home, even riding in an imperial carriage, without fear of rebuke.[5] He made love wearing a nobleman's cap à la
Ushiwakamaru[6] and imitated Michimori[7] making frantic love in a

coat of chainmail. Other times he enjoyed the peculiar pleasures of making love seated on a go board, or supported by a sash looped around their necks as depicted in erotic pictures. Since she was his wife, it did not matter that her hair became tousled during daylight hours or that she screamed out loud; he could enjoy her as he pleased.

Eventually, their love bore fruit; she developed a taste for sour plums and began to evidence her unusual condition. Soon it was time to celebrate the ceremonial putting on of the sash. The days and months passed, and when her time drew near he had a birthing room readied for her and scrupulously performed services according to the prescribed rituals. The family was overjoyed at the prospect of an heir and even sent a woman in his wife's stead to a distant temple to pray for her safe delivery. He hired a nursemaid and chose a wet-nurse for the child after verifying their good pedigree. He also prepared a wide-sleeved garment that was richly appliqued with a golden crane for longevity and embroidered with auspicious pines and bamboo. Even the child's diapers were readied before it was born.

Finally the time arrived and labor pains began in earnest. The midwife tucked up her sleeves with a sash and held the lady around her waist. One of the assistants placed a shell for easy delivery in her right hand. Another had her grip a sea horse in her left hand. In the next room a doctor, expert in both pre- and post-natal care, in a silver bowl prepared medicine to help speed childbirth. In the front room were a monk from Mt. Hiei known for the efficacy of his devotions and the head priest of Fushimi Inari Shrine, praying that their request for safe delivery be granted.

He waited impatiently, wondering why the baby had not appeared yet. Suddenly (was it a dream?), her breathing halted as if in a slumber and her pulse ceased. The attendants burst into tears and those in the kitchen were stunned. They did everything possible to help her, but it was useless. She was dead.

He bitterly mourned her passage from life to death. Even so, he knew that her body could hardly be left as it was and sent it to Mt. Toribe that night. She was cremated immediately, and the next morning all that remained of her were ashes. This is the nature of human flesh.

Others may grieve by muttering an obligatory prayer and shed a few tears on the sleeve of the garment they receive as a memento of the deceased, but before long the person is forgotten. Such is the way of the world. The bond between husband and wife, however, is different. His grief was inconsolable. He desired only to leave everything behind and take the tonsure, but when his family discovered his intentions they begged him not to and he finally gave up the idea.

One hundred days passed quickly.

When the period of abstinence was over, the family summoned without his knowledge a woman even more beautiful than his first wife and presented her to him. He did not want to disappoint them, knowing how concerned they were about him, so he kept the woman by his side. But he never spoke a single intimate word with her, so the poor young lady became a widow with a living husband.

He found it impossible to abstain completely from sex, however, and since he was utterly bored with women he kept a boy at his side from then on. This apparently served as a perfectly satisfactory replacement.

The Boy Who Sacrificed His Life in the Robes of His Lover

A boy in a Kaga sedge hat puts the moon's beauty to shame.
The leaf of a banana palm stirred by love's breeze.
A world in which we have no choice but to die.

Whose lovely figure is that, his face concealed beneath a sedge hat? There are many handsome youths in Kanazawa, but it is this one, Nozaki Senjūrō, of whom women say with envy, "How is it possible for a boy of such natural beauty to be born into this world?" But do not be deceived by his frail appearance, for he is a stout-hearted fellow indeed.

A sensualist of broad experience had the following to say on the topic of love: "In general, I prefer strong women to ones possessed of a normal feminine nature. It goes without saying that I like my boys bold and masculine." As a connoisseur of young men, he considered those blessed with maturity and a cool head particularly high-class items.

Senjūrō was an article *par excellence*, surpassing even Fuwano Mansaku[1] in beauty, destined surely to become the possession of some great daimyo. It was a shame to expose him to the gaze of men lacking in discrimination. He should rightfully have been hidden in a purse of rich brocade to be shown only to those capable of appreciating his rare beauty.

This boy had but a single flaw: he was by nature careless of his life, like someone who watches dispassionately as cherry blossoms scatter in the wind. Aware of this flaw, men feared to approach the mountain of his love lest it cost them their lives. Thus, Senjūrō reached the spring of his seventeenth year unloved. People pitied him; he seemed to them like a mountain rose that blooms and falls unseen in remote hills, or like a spray of wisteria that withers, unplucked, on the vine.

What they did not realize was that deep in the valley, Senjūrō had for several years been on intimate terms with a man named Takeshima Sazen. It was understandable that society at large not be aware of the situation, for he was a government official in charge of administering many towns and villages in the shadow of a mountain four or five *li* distant from the daimyo's castle.

This is how the two first met.

In the house next to Sazen's lived a woman who was Senjūrō's aunt. The trees had lost their leaves and with the arrival of autumn Senjūrō was feeling even more sad and lonely than usual, so he decided to pay her a visit and enjoy the view of the harvest moon on the way. Unfortunately, pine trees towered darkly on the ridge to the east, and all he could see during the early part of the evening was the moon's light poking through the trees. To the south, however, there were no obstructions. Drifting clouds obligingly departed as if aware of the beauty of the scene, allowing him to view the moon in the clear sky to his heart's content later in the evening.

The distant beating of silk—tap, tap, tap—(no doubt the work of some country girl) triggered in him gentle musings. Mingled with the sounds of the locale were the faint voices of grasshoppers and bell crickets. Before long, they too would be silenced by the frost he mused, warding off with the sleeve of his robe the breeze that rustled the tips of the blades of grass as he passed. He alone was there to appreciate the sight of the wild chrysanthemums, but surely by daybreak they would be catching the admiring glances of passersby, he thought feelingly, overcome with sad thoughts of the ways of this world. Truly, this handsome youth was a boy of rare emotional sensitivity.

That night, Takeshima Sazen was on his way to visit a priest in charge of the Kannon Sanctuary at a temple in the outskirts of town. The priest was his regular companion in *haikai* poetry composition, and Sazen was wondering how he might be enjoying the moon that evening. Sazen needed an opening phrase for a poem and hoped that the man could provide him with one; he would try to compose an interesting second line on the spot. But when he arrived at the door it was firmly shut and the priest nowhere in sight.

Sazen shone his lamp through the paper window on the north side of the hut and peered inside. Dimly, he could see a book lying open on the table, as if the man had been reading it until a moment ago. It was called "A Study of Poetic Place Names."[2] On the edge of the table was a mouse trap. It seemed that rampaging mice were vexing even to priests who had renounced this world. "Mice in the house mean thieves abroad in the land." So the proverb goes, but the entrance of the hut was unlocked, indicative perhaps of the peaceful times in which we live.

Sazen had his attendant trim the wick of the sputtering lamp. He placed a few drops of water into his portable inkstone and wrote the following note on the broad leaf of a banana palm growing against the eaves of the hut:

"I listen to the murmuring pines, but they tell me not where their master has gone. I bid farewell to the moon before the temple gate and go on my weary way.

"Perhaps I shall enjoy a cup of sake before retiring. When I awake from my dreams in the morn, allow me to offer you a simple meal at my home.

"The matter of Moemon's widow has been commodiously concluded. You are no doubt satisfied with the arrangements.

"The morning-glory seeds you so generously bestowed on me began blooming splendidly this morning.

"In your next letter to Echizen, please remember to include my order for 30 sheets of patterned *torinoko* paper.

"Thank you kindly for the boiled plums the other day.

"It seems that Yata Nisaburō of whom you spoke to me in private is not a believer in boy love. He was not interested in the idea of having a male lover and so, though only seventeen and in the flower of youth, has foolishly cut off his forelocks. I found his profuse apologies rather absurd but have decided to let the matter drop. Last night everyone came over and we spent the whole night laughing about it . . . ."

The note was a hodge-podge of things on Sazen's mind, written spontaneously as they occurred to him.

Just then, Senjūrō happened to come by and noticed something written on the·banana leaf. At first he thought it was a poem about

the full moon that night and went to take a closer look, but he was wrong. It was not a poem. He was intrigued nevertheless by the part at the end about boy love.

Sazen proceeded ahead, but Senjūrō spoke to one of the attendants in a voice loud enough for Sazen to hear.

"This must be what people refer to as 'unrequited love.' Any youth who would put a gentleman's overtures to naught knows nothing of love, but if the gentleman is sincere he should not hesitate to give even his life to obtain him. True, I have no beauty of form to recommend me, but at least I am capable of love. Yet I receive no offers. As the gods are my witness, I swear my willingness to suffer any hardship for the sake of boy love."

With these words, he removed the sedge hat and revealed his face.

Sazen took one look and his soul seemed to leap out at the boy. Unconsciously, he reached for the boy's hand.

"If the words you just spoke are true, let me be the one to worship you, oh Boddhisattva, come to lead this man to salvation." He made his plea in a daze, completely unaware of his surroundings.

Senjūrō was deeply moved. The man had a certain masculine charm and besides, Senjūrō could hardly claim that he was joking. Standing there just as he was, he pledged himself firmly to love Sazen in this world and the next.

On their way home, they passed a country farmhouse facing south in which the harvest moon was being rudely celebrated with boiled yams and sake served from a chipped flask. The sake was a local mountain brew with a superb chrysanthemum bouquet. Noticing the fragrance, Sazen and Senjūrō forced themselves on their unknown hosts and joined the revelry. Even in the midst of their cups they could hardly wait to get back to their lodgings. When they did, they frantically consummated their troth of brotherly love. From that day forward Senjūrō gave himself completely to Sazen, who soon came to occupy even the boy's dreams.

Senjūrō's innate grace and youthful good looks caught the eye of a well-known devotee of boy love named Imamura Rokunoshin, a samurai who lived in the castle town. He sent the boy several letters, but Senjūrō steadfastly refused to look at them. A warrior's pride does not allow him to retract his words, and Rokunoshin soon reached his limit of frustration. Then he found out about Senjūrō's bond with Sazen, and swore he would make Sazen relinquish the boy, by force if necessary.

Senjūrō heard of this and pondered what to do.

"I am prepared to fight Rokunoshin to the finish," he thought, "but Sazen will be heartbroken if I go ahead without telling him. Yet that is what I must do so that he may go on living."

His decision made, Senjūrō went in secret to the residence of Rokunoshin where he met and spoke with the man.

"It was not my intention to ignore your recent attentions," Senjūrō said. "Unfortunately, Takeshima Sazen has made some very unreasonable demands of me that I am bound by duty to honor. Moreover, he is a man completely lacking in emotional sincerity. I was searching for a way to escape this dilemma when I received your letters. You may be the man I had hoped would appear, to provide me with the strong backing I need. If you but murder Sazen for me in secret, I will make myself yours."

Rokunoshin was delighted. "Why not tonight?" he proposed eagerly.

"There is a seldom-used road that runs through a field of hack-berry trees," Senjūrō explained. "Sazen travels it every night at ten o'clock. This will be the sign: he will be wearing a sedge hat at night.³ Cut him down when he reaches the roadside shrine."

Rokunoshin agreed to the task and, when his preparations for battle were complete, he set out for his rendezvous on the country road. Such is the compelling nature of this floating world.

Meanwhile, Senjūrō returned home to bathe and groom. He put on a half-coat with rounded cuffs⁴ and placed a sedge hat low on his brow as a disguise. He was the very image of Sazen. Carefully avoiding notice, he then set out for the appointed country road.

He walked stealthily in the shadows of the tree-lined path to the place where Rokunoshin lay in wait. Rokunoshin attacked and cut him down from behind. The victim did not utter a sound. Nor did he even attempt to draw his sword. It was truly an ignominious end.

Rokunoshin gave him the coup de grace with a stab to the neck. Unsure where to go now that his harried task was accomplished, Rokunoshin slipped into the thick undergrowth of jewelweed. He was startled, however, to hear a faint voice behind him.

"Though I have come to this, at least my lord Sazen is safe," it said feebly.

Rokunoshin quietly had an attendant strike a flint and once again approached the body. He could not believe his eyes.

It was Senjūrō.

For a moment Rokunoshin was stunned by the magnitude of Senjūrō's act of love; even in the world to come, one would be unlikely to find another like it. He recalled the old "Lover's Tomb" at Koizuka⁵ and wept bitterly into the sleeves of his robe, but no amount of weeping could undo what he had done.

"I could go on living as if nothing had happened, and no one would be the wiser for it," he thought. "But there would be no joy in such a life."

He decided that he, too, would die.

After explaining his plan in detail to an attendant, he changed quickly into Senjūrō's long-sleeved robe. He placed the sedge hat on his head and, carefully avoiding notice, they went to the village where Takeshima Sazen lived. His attendant ran up to Sazen's gate and pounded on it wildly.

"I have urgent news!" he shouted.

Sazen sat up in bed. He ignored the voice for as long as he could, but finally dressed and woke his retainers. They readied their spears and carefully checked the situation outside the gate from the observation deck. When they were convinced that it was safe, they opened the gate for Rokunoshin's attendant to come in. He immediately relinquished his sword to them.

"I am Manshichi, in the service of Imamura Rokunoshin," he said. "My master and Nozaki Senjūrō recently established a bond of boy love, complete with written vows. They were concerned, however, about Takeshima Sazen and secretly developed a scheme to kill him. I was one of the men chosen to carry out their plan, but when it was explained to me, I refused. My master accused me of ingratitude for his years of support and struck me in full view of the others. He was ready to put me to the sword, but somehow I managed to escape and make my way here.

"I beg you, please save me. I am a mere attendant and know that it is wrong to refuse to obey my master's orders. Still, I cannot take part in a plot unbecoming to the tenets of the warrior's code. You, too, are a samurai. My master should challenge you to a duel in daylight and settle his differences with you that way. Instead, he plots a night raid. That is why I have forsaken him and come running to this place for shelter. Please, I beg your protection."

Sazen heard him through but remained skeptical.

"We shall look into the matter in the morning. Until then," he said turning to his retainers, "I leave this man in your custody."

Sazen got up to leave, but Rokunoshin's attendant called out to him.

"As proof that what I say is true, Senjūrō will appear soon, in advance of the others."

When he heard this, Sazen decided that it would be safest if he made the first move. He went out to the road with a large group of retainers and hid in the shadow of some trees. Just as Rokuno-shin's attendant had predicted, someone in a long-sleeved robe was stealthily approaching.

It was Senjūrō.

Sazen was overwhelmed with anger. "You faithless scoundrel!" he shouted. The next moment Sazen had swung his sword, cutting Senjūrō down with one blow. The boy fell in the shade of some withered trees.

"Did you think you could betray our vows of brotherly love and still escape the wrath of heaven?"

With these words, he finished off Senjūrō with a stab to the throat.

When Sazen had a beacon brought forward, he was amazed to find that the man he had slain was Imamura Rokunoshin. He immediately had Rokunoshin's attendant brought out and demanded an explanation. When he heard the entire story from beginning to end, Sazen wept so copiously that his garments were soaked to the skin.

"Senjūrō loved me so much he was willing to die in my stead. Rokunoshin so regretted what he had done, he too gave up his life. In the face of such example, it would be profitless for me to go on living."

He sat on the corpse and there, in the autumn of his 28th year, dyed his blade the color of autumn leaves and ended his brief life.

The example of these three was without precedent in antiquity. Rumors of their intense love continued to be voiced long after the proverbial 75 days. Those who recounted the story wept as they told it; those who heard it wept as they listened. Not only people of sensitivity but even unfeeling peasants and horse drivers reverently avoided walking on the spot where Senjūrō spilled his life-blood, a lingering testimony to the way of boy love.

Were one to walk all the provinces of the land in sandals of iron, one would not be likely to find another such example.

They Waited Three Years to Die

Clearing up doubts about a Chinese love poem.
The samurai quandary: love or honor.
They exchanged memorial tablets and died.

The "cloth-pulling" pines of Wakanoura are models of longevity.[1] Forever green, they emerged from seed in a bygone age to flourish and grow, like this lasting age of peace in which we live. Each year on the night of the tenth day, seventh month, dragon torches from the ocean king's palace appear without fail in the sea at this spot.[2]

One year on this night, a group of people prepared pleasure boats and embarked together from Shimbori, swept up in the excitement of the evening. Female attendants rivaling women from the capital in beauty offered glimpses of themselves through gaps in their curtained chambers as they viewed the sights. The sound of the waves harmonized with the murmuring of the pines, like the little tunes being sung to koto and samisen accompaniment. Demizu sake flowed freely as the revelers descended to the mouth of the river. Even the mountain looked like a pair of lovers in embrace. The boats pushed through the tangled reeds. People could hardly take in the variety of sights before the day came to an end and the sun set over windless, waveless Naruto to the west. The calm in their hearts and the sense of life's richness they enjoyed was proof that the sword had been sheathed and peace prevailed in the land.

At that moment they noticed a small boat near the shore being poled by obviously inexperienced hands. Inside was a handsome boy, his face hidden intriguingly beneath a low-brimmed sedge hat. A slight breeze off the river lifted the hat, revealing the boy's face. It was Kikui Matsusaburō, a youth known to all for his remarkable beauty. Normally he was never seen without his "elder brother" Segawa Uhei, with whom he shared a deep vow of love. On this day, however, not only was Matsusaburō alone, but he seemed to be trying to avoid notice. Those who knew him had a hard time dispelling their amazement at seeing him there.

He guided his craft towards the cove at Tamatsushima where a gaudy boat with seven or eight youths on board was anchored. Unlike the other boats, there was no sound of Noh chanting or hand drums being struck. Instead, the boys were clumped intimately in pairs with men who seemed to be their lovers. Some of them whispered with their heads held close together or just lay there side by side. Others played drawing games or wrestled with fans. There is nothing as enviable as a boatful of boys in love.

Among them was a handsome youth who stood alone, apart from the rest. He was perched in a turret at the stern and held a fan decorated with a persimmon pattern. On it was a poem written in Chinese that he read over and over until he could recite it from memory. Matsusaburō stealthily poled his little craft closer and listened.

> No Pen Can Describe Your Blossom-Like Face
> Trothed by Fate One Bed to Share
> Night After Night I Dream of Your Grace
> Twenty-Four Hours, Never Once Unaware.

Matsusaburō's face immediately flushed with anger.

"I am not unaware of that poem either," he thought. "My partner in a bond of brotherly love, Uhei, gave it to me just last month. It was the night of the seventeenth, and we had spent an unusually wonderful evening together. When he left, he composed that poem and wrote it down for me on a towel by the wash basin. No one else could have known about that poem. How could it have fallen into the hands of this young man? And why should he recite it with such deep feeling? Something must be going on here."

He asked a servant on the kitchen boat what the young man's name might be and discovered that it was Iwahashi Torakichi. The servant also told him other details about the youth, including where he lived. When Matsusaburō had heard it all, he left for home, arriving there with the tolling of the sunset bell at Kimii-dera. From there he went straight to Uhei's place for a visit.

"You seem to be in a bad humor," Uhei said when he saw him.

"Is it because I did not accompany you on the boat?" He tried to explain the unavoidable business that had prevented him from going, but Matsusaburō was in no mood to listen.

"You should be ashamed to call yourself a samurai," Matsusaburō said bitterly. "I was so happy when you wrote that poem about how much you loved me, but you are such a man about town, it seems that you later sent the same poem to someone else. In fact, I would not be surprised if you gave it to him first." He could hardly finish speaking before he melted into tears of mortification.

Matsusaburō seemed ready to end his life, so Uhei did his best to calm him down. "Of course, of course. I know what the problem is now. It's all a misunderstanding caused by your youthfulness. You see, for every poem there is always another that sounds almost identical.[3] For example, Li Po wrote this one while thinking of his wife back home:[4]

> When You Look at the Moon in Wu-chow
> Think of Me One Thousand Li Distant.

"Likewise, the poet Tu Fu wrote,

> Alone in Bed, You Must Be Looking
> At the Moon in Wu-chow Tonight.

"The Chinese often have related poems of this sort that express an identical sentiment. In Japan, someone composed this poem:

> We promised to look
> at the moon and remember;
> back home, does she weep
> into her sleeves
> again tonight?[5]

"What sort of young man was it who recited the poem?" Uhei asked calmly.

Matsusaburō refused to tell him.

"I hardly need tell you who he is. I am sure you know already. Try hard, maybe you will remember his name."

But Uhei had no way of knowing who it was.

"Just tell me his name," he begged.

"Your feigned innocence I find very disappointing," Matsusaburō said. "The lovely young man to whom you gave the poem goes by the name of Iwahashi Torakichi."

Uhei laughed uproariously when he heard the name.

"Torakichi? Didn't you know? That is my sister's son!"

Matsusaburō felt better immediately when he heard this. "Then my suspicions were groundless," he said. "I am terribly ashamed of myself."

"It is only because you love me so deeply," Uhei replied solicitously.

After this incident, they became extremely careful of each other's honor, and their love grew even stronger. Most people admired the relationship, but there was one fellow ignorant of love named Yokoyama Seizō who became smitten with Matsusaburō. He was a friend of Uhei's, but sent him a letter anyway demanding he relinquish the boy. It was a heartless proposal, and Uhei was put in an extremely awkward position.

His reply was brief and to the point.

"My love for Matsusaburō is eternal; your request is out of the question."

Seizō could not simply abandon his claim to the boy, so he readied himself for a fight and went to Uhei's residence to request a duel to the death.

Uhei was expecting him, and was prepared to see the matter to its end. "There is no point in postponing it. Meet me tonight at the pine grove at Wakanoura and together let us take the road to the next world." They agreed on a time, and Seizō left the house.

He returned almost immediately, however. "I have had second thoughts," he said. "Matsusaburō will be sixteen this year, just entering the flower of youth. It can hardly be your true desire to die and leave him behind just now. If we were to wait three years, he will have shorn his forelocks and become a man. At that point you should have no regrets about bidding this world farewell. Let us wait three years. The solemn promise of two warriors cannot be abrogated. Three years from now, on this month and this day, I swear to relieve this yearning in my breast."

Uhei was satisfied. "By then, what further pleasures could this

floating world hold for me? I told you how I love him. In three year's time, let us conclude this matter manfully with the points of our swords." They made firm their pledge and Seizō returned to his own home.

No one else was aware of the matter. Uhei hid it carefully from Matsusaburō; their love continued unchanged.

Subsequently, Uhei and Seizō found themselves strangely drawn to each other by their common fate and spent more and more time together. Days and months passed, and almost before they knew it three years had elapsed.

Uhei spoke to Matsusaburō about his coming-of-age ceremony. Matsusaburō wanted to wait until the spring of the following year, but Uhei insisted that he go through with it right away. Thus, Matsusaburō became a man.

Uhei was overjoyed that everything had gone smoothly. On the seventeenth day of the tenth month he spoke to Seizō. "This is the day several years ago when we swore to die."

Early in the morning, the two of them went to a remote temple in the fields. They sadly shared a few last words. Neither the head priest nor their attendants were aware of what was about to happen. In this world, what seems real soon proves to be illusion.

When the end was near, Uhei had one of his attendants open his carrying case and removed two memorial tablets, carved with the common names of the two men and the date. Each holding the other's tablet, they made offerings of flowers and incense at the altar. They sat for a moment in silence, savoring each other's manly resolve. Their sleeves grew moist, as if in the early winter rain. Then they unsheathed their blades, sharp and true as the mind of Buddha.

Uhei was 23 and Seizō 24 when they died. Blossoms fell and the moon clouded over in sorrow. Matsusaburō was left behind, his mind lost in darkness. When the news reached him toward midnight, he rushed immediately to the temple.

Everyone had advice for him.

"You are only nineteen."

"Take holy orders and pray for their repose."

But he would not listen. Rather, he too chose to vanish with the dew on the dry grasses of that same wasted field. Thus do those born in the lineage of the bow and horse die valorous deaths, their honor to be sung by future generations.

The details of this case were written down so that the example of these men would be more widely known, but their great love and strict adherence to honor have overwhelmed my heart with sadness. I shall put down my writing brush and leave the story, imperfect though it be, to pine for their memory.

Two Old Cherry Trees Still in Bloom

Age advances, but the heart remains young.
The eccentric who kept his natural hairline from birth.
Women, viewing cherry blossoms, scattered with a broom.

"Hemorrhoid Medicine Sold Here; Cures All Woes." This hand-written sign hung outside a tiny shop with a sliding paper door and hanging reed blinds. The owner sold calligraphy manuals done in the style of the Ōhashi school, but his was an old-fashioned hand that few admired, so it proved to be an undependable source of income.

The meager dwelling where he had quietly lived for many years was situated before a temple gate in Yanaka. There was a twisted pine under the eaves and trumpet vines bloomed there in lovely profusion. In the yard he grew summer chrysanthemums in pots. The well water was fresh and clear. A crow perched on one end of the dipping stick, a strange sight indeed with its faded tail and wing feathers!

Living there was this masterless samurai who in his youth had lost hope of ever regaining official status in a lord's service and now lived day to day selling his various personal belongings. His only companion day in and day out was an old man of about the same age, his partner in games of go. A spotted Pekinese was his only other companion. No one ever came by even for brief visits.

One day, his hemp kimono was soaked with sweat and he felt too listless even to stir up a breeze with his fan, so the old man hurried the arrival of evening with an early bath and began washing the sweat from his body. His old companion watched him and thought, "Ah, the ravages of time!" Affectionately, he massaged the man's bony spine. He was grieved by the wrinkles below the man's waist and soon sank into tearful sobs.

"Sing the Tune Loudly, Hide the Mirror Bright
Yesterday, Youth; Today, a Head of White [1]

"Seeing how this body of yours has changed reminded me of
that poem. How sad to think that not so long ago we sang songs
and played games together ...." They held hands and lamented
until the bath water turned cold.

At first glance, one would have taken them for a couple of holy
religious companions praying together for salvation, but the truth
was somewhat different. It seems that they were samurai born long
ago in the castle town of Chikuzen. One was called Tamashima
Mondo. In his youth, his beauty could kill birds on the wing and
was so remarkable that people who saw him took him for one of
the famed Hakata courtesans. The other was Toyoda Han'emon, a
man skilled in swordsmanship. He fell in love with Mondo in his
youth, and the boy responded to his attentions. Mondo was sixteen,
Han'emon nineteen when they made fast their bond of love, like
the connecting strand of Umi-no-nakamichi.

In the midst of their ever-increasing love, another man became
enamored of Mondo and was unable to cease his yearning for the
boy. Like the "fire cherries" of Mt. Kamado, there were those who
fanned the flames of this man's passion. The two sides finally
agreed to a duel. They met at the Bridge of Happiness (happily, it
was a dark night) where Mondo and Han'emon cleanly dispatched
the suitor and his entire entourage of swordsmen. That night, they
stole through the Konomaru checkpoint, boarded a boat at the
"Bay of Floating Fortunes," and shrank from the eyes of society to
seclude themselves here.

Mondo was now 63 and Han'emon 66. Their love for each other
had not changed since the days of their youth; neither of them had
ever gazed at a woman's face in his life. Having lived together all
these years, they truly deserved to be emulated as models of the
way of love for all who love boys.

Han'emon still thought of Mondo as a boy of sixteen. Though
his hair was thinning and had turned completely white, Mondo
sprinkled it with "Blossom Dew" hair oil and bound it up in a
double-folded topknot anyway. (A strange sight, indeed!) There

was no sign that he had ever shaved his temples; he still had the rounded hairline he was born with.[2] He followed the daily rituals of his youth, polishing his teeth with a tufted toothpick and carefully plucking his whiskers. Someone unaware of Mondo's reasons for doing this could hardly have imagined the truth.

Sometimes, a daimyo will love one of his pages deeply and, even after the boy has grown up and established a family, will be unable to forget his youthful charms. This is praiseworthy. It makes one realize what a distinctly different flavor the way of boy love possesses compared to the love of women. A woman is a creature of temporary interest to men, whereas the attraction of a youth is impossible to comprehend unless one experiences this way of love oneself.

Repulsed by the vulgar ways of women, these two old men refused even to exchange coals with the neighbor lady to the east, although they ostensibly remained part of the society around them. When in the normal course of things quarrels erupted between the husband and wife next door and even pots and pans were being thrown around, the two old men made it none of their business to step in and attempt to reconcile them. On the contrary, they would encourage the husband by pressing their faces against the wall and shouting, "Beat her to death, mister, and replace her with a sandal boy!"[3] It was most amusing.

Cherry blossoms bring people to the hills of Ueno in the third month. At this time the fine sake from Ikeda, Itami, and Kōnoike is always sold out. The heavens themselves are inebriated, and the ground echoes with drunken footsteps. From inside their house the two old men could distinguish between footsteps of men and women. If it sounded like a man, they rushed out to get a look in hopes that it would be a handsome youth. If it sounded like a woman, however, they locked the door and sat inside, silent and depressed.

Spring showers are unpredictable, and one spring day it suddenly grew dark and began to rain. Beautifully garbed young women scattered like blossoms. Loath to part so soon with the day, a noisy group of them took shelter under the eaves of this masterless samurai's house.

"I wish we had friends in the area," one said. "We could have

them prepare some tea for us and visit until evening, then borrow umbrellas and go home. Or, depending on how things went, maybe we could stay for dinner. But I cannot think of anyone here I know."

She was a cocky sort and pushed the door open slightly to peek inside.

The moment he saw her face, Han'emon grabbed a nearby broom and rushed out in a fury.

"Such filth! Disgusting! Get out of here!"

Roughly, he chased them out into the rain.

Afterwards, he spread dry sand where they stepped and swept the area clean four or five times. Then he scattered salt water to purify the ground.

They say a big city like Edo has everything, but I had never seen such a woman-hater.

Handsome Youths Having Fun Cause Trouble for a Temple

The tip of a real sword and its terrible consequences.
Risking his life to save Geki's.
An unknown beauty determined to die.

Rain on the night of the harvest moon and wind when the blossoms are at their peak epitomize life's tragedies. But there will be other springs, other autumns when these things can be enjoyed once again. Nothing in the world is as tragic as a life sacrificed for honor. Who knows, after all, what awaits us in the afterworld? Far better that we enjoy long life and spend our days contentedly eating the sweet fruits of this Wormwood Isle.[1]

In Atsuta, Owari Province, in the outskirts of the station stop called Miya, stands a wooden image of the old hag of the River of Three Crossings.[2] Many travelers pass by this spot, but none are on their final journey of death, so this old hag cannot strip them of their clothes. There are advantages after all to extending one's life in this floating world.

There was a boy whose life was so brief, it made one wonder if his bloom of youthful beauty had been born from the seed of a morning-glory. His name was Ōkura, son of Onakai Hyōbunotayū, the high-ranking priest of Atsuta Shrine who lived by its western gateway. In the service of the same shrine was one Takaokagawa Rintayū whose son, Geki, had just turned eighteen that year. Although still in the prime of youthful beauty, his forelocks shaved into corners, he had already made a vow with Ōkura as his male lover. Over two years had passed since they pledged their lives to each other before the gods at Yatsuragi, and each had remained faithful to his vows. Like clinging shadows, they were never seen alone from morning to dusk.

One day, a large group of youths and their friends got together for some fun at a pleasure temple[3] deep in some woods. They were overjoyed to find that the head priest was absent. "Now we can do whatever we want," they said gleefully and immediately began to make an incredible rumpus. They let loose with imitations of Kataoka Izumi[4] doing acrobatic tricks and crawling through narrow hoops. Beating gongs and cymbals, they marched through the temple's main sanctuary and reception vestibule. Even the holy Buddha figure fell over, and its halo and lotus pedestal were trampled underfoot. The candle holders with their turtles and cranes, far from lasting "a thousand ages, ten thousand generations," were smashed instead into a thousand pieces. The boys laid waste to the carefully tended garden and gave the neighborhood a shock by rapidly tolling the temple bell.[5]

Afterwards, they turned to theater imitations, beginning with the three-act performance of "Revenge of the Outcasts."[6] Geki staggered from the shadow of a stone monument acting as if he had sustained a wound. He was so swept up in the excitement that he forgot what he was doing and threw down the wooden sword in his hand. Drawing his real sword, he brandished it over his head with eyes closed. It looked as if he were about to stumble, so Ōkura ran up to help.

"What is the matter?" Ōkura cried, attempting to support him. Without realizing what he was doing, Geki swung the blade.

Ōkura's head fell to the ground with a thud.

No amount of sorrow could undo what he had done. The other boys wept uncontrollably. For a while no one spoke. Geki quickly came to a decision.

"There is no sense in prolonging my life. Ōkura! Here I come."

With these words, he knelt beside the lifeless form and prepared to commit seppuku, but the others subdued him and cruelly postponed his day of reckoning.

Just then, the head priest returned and was informed of the tragedy. He spoke to Geki, exhorting him on the proper course to take.

"Your life is no longer yours to live," he said. "You must explain to Ōkura's parents the karma that led to today's events and try to alleviate their suffering. Then you should ask leave of your parents in this floating world of sorrow and immediately end your life.

Only that way can you hope to leave behind a good name for yourself."

"You are right. My life is no longer mine to do with as I please," Geki answered. "I shall do as you suggest."

As he waited for his opportunity to commit seppuku, Geki's companions wept into their sleeves and moaned, "How awful!" His resolve was both beautiful and heart-rending to observe. All of the handsome youths there would gladly have given their lives to save his.

Relatives, both close and distant, came to the temple and wept over Ōkura's lifeless form. Their tears were enough to drown the pines and oaks at the temple entrance. Hyōbu accepted his son's death but was distraught over Geki's fate. He asked the head priest to intervene and allow Geki to replace Ōkura and become his

adopted son to continue the family line. The priest conveyed this
request to the authorities, but after an inquiry the request was
deemed impossible to grant and Geki was ordered to commit seppuku. When the news was conveyed accordingly, Geki was not
particularly perturbed since he had anticipated their decision.

He began his preparations immediately.

"Since this is the place where Ōkura met his end, I ought by
rights to die here at this temple," he told those around him. "But I
have a special request: allow me to die at Jōren-ji where I have
worshipped all these years."

They agreed, and took him there as he requested.

He rode in a palanquin open on both sides and wore a white
robe and plain blue trousers. His forelocks were dressed handsomely, giving him today in particular an almost royal air of splen-
dor. Bystanders who had come to see him off were dazed with

grief. Soon their cries of farewell faded into the distance as Geki was taken away. In the palanquin he took out his inkstone and some paper, writing to Ōkura's parents at unusual length to apologize for what he had done. Shortly, they arrived at the temple where he calmly received the last rites and instructions for salvation. Kneeling on the reed mat spread before him, he bowed to each of those present and then took up the short sword in his hands.

Just as he was about to plunge the blade into his belly, a beautiful girl of fourteen or fifteen wearing white robes came rushing forward. She clung to Geki and said with a determination that was apparent to everyone, "I refuse to survive you."

Geki had never seen her before, and here she was disrupting his final moments.

"What are you talking about?" he said angrily, demanding an explanation.

Suppressing his tears, Geki's father Rintayū explained it all.

"You know nothing of the girl. She is the daughter of Tsukahara Seizaemon, a masterless samurai to whom I owed a debt of gratitude. Unfortunately, your mother and he did not get along, so I had been visiting him all these years without her knowledge. I was frequently impressed with the girl's maturity and promised to take her into our home as your bride, if that should be at all possible. Sometime next spring I had hoped to get your mother's permission and make her your wife. But all that has come to naught. What a sad place is this unpredictable world!"

Those who heard the explanation began weeping anew. "One rarely finds such strength of character in a woman. They can hardly ask Geki to take his life now." Many voices expressed such sentiments.

Ōkura's father, Hyōbutayū, risked his life to make a second request to the authorities that Geki's life be spared. This time the plea was granted. He took Geki as his son and without delay made the girl Geki's wife. When the celebrations were over, he retired as head of the household and they lived together as parent and child.

= 5:1 =

Tears in a Paper Shop

Boys onstage go for one piece of silver.
Violence against cherry blossoms even in the capital.
Hanasaki Hatsudayū[1] takes the tonsure.

"What is the latest craze in the capital?" someone asked.

"Everyone is being frugal and piling up money," was the reply.
But there is nothing new about that!

After the prohibition of Grand Kabuki,[2] Murayama Matabei[3]
opened a mime and dance show for which he gathered together a
large troupe of handsome young actors. Until that time it was uncommon even in the capital for men to take pleasure with boy
actors. Each went for the same sum, one *bu* of gold,[4] and took on
customers much the way street boys do nowadays. At some point,
it became the custom to celebrate a boy's promotion as a full-
fledged actor of female roles by inviting the entire cast to Higashiyama for a tremendous feast. After that, his fee increased to five
ryō of silver.

In those days, having fun was easy. For two *momme* of small cash to the sandal carrier and a payment of two *ryō* of silver to the teahouse, you could have a boy of your own to play with from the final curtain call until daybreak the following morning. Boys in those days were real boys. Though you might visit them night after night for love, they never demanded spending money. A toy doll, a colorfully dyed towel, or some tooth powder, none of which cost more than four or five *fun* of silver, would delight them.

Then one year wealthy priests assembled in the capital from all over the country to commemorate the 350th anniversary of the death of Zen Master Kanzan,[5] first rector of Myōshin-ji. After the religious services were over, they went sight-seeing at the pleasure quarter on the dry riverbed. They fell in love with the handsome youths there, the likes of which they had never seen in the countryside, and began buying them up indiscriminately without a thought for their priestly duties. Any boy with forelocks who had eyes and a nose on his face was guaranteed to be busy all day.

Since that time, boy actors have continued to sell themselves in two shifts, daytime and nighttime. The fee for a boy who was appearing onstage rose to one piece of silver. The priests did not care about the cost, since they had only a short time to amuse themselves in the capital. But their extravagance continues to cause untold hardship for the pleasure-seekers of our day.

The pride of Murayama's theater in those days was a young actor in the full bloom of youth named Fujimura Hatsudayū[6] who excelled in the latest dance styles. None who saw his lovely figure onstage remained unsmitten. One day he went on an outing to view the cherry blossoms at Higashiyama, and on his way home plucked a branch of Shiogama blossoms nearing full bloom for those who waited his return. He was a thoughtful, gentle-hearted youth.

In the vicinity of Kaguraoka he encountered a group of smartly dressed men who, it seemed, had been drinking all day. The curtains surrounding their picnic site were furled and their faces glowed brightly in the setting sun, plainly visible to passersby. Unconcerned, the revelers drank round after round of sake from their deep-tiered picnic boxes with quarrels on the side to accompany the wine. One of the heartless dandies noticed the cherry branch in Hatsudayū's hand and approached him.

"Give me those blossoms," he said. "I will enjoy them dipped in miso for a make-shift snack with my sake."

It is cruel enough that blossoms are scattered by stormy winds and even plucked by the hand of man, but this request was the ultimate sacrilege. Still, it was not regret over the fate of the blossoms but disdain for the way the request was worded that provoked Hatsudayū to refuse.

"Impossible," he said briskly and continued on his way.

"You insult my manly pride. I will have to take the branch from you by force," the man insisted.

If Hatsudayū were to relinquish the blossoms, his youthful pride would also suffer. He was confronted here with a major crisis.

Travelers on the road were amazed at what was going on. "Are such unreasonable demands made even in the capital?" they wondered. Cart drivers pulled their oxen to a halt and people stopped their palanquins until soon a veritable mountain of onlookers had assembled, all waiting nervously to see how the incident would resolve itself. Hatsudayū's attendant, "Lightning" Kyūzō, was ready to fight the man to the finish, but concern for the boy's safety made him reluctantly suppress the impulse.

"If only I could put him in someone's safekeeping," he thought, "I would gladly take on this entire pack of rogues."

Just then, a strikingly handsome man chanced upon the scene. He wore a double-lined black robe decorated with a Kaga pattern of tiny dolls over a lined underrobe of purple silk crepe. His sash was a seamless folded affair of brown material dyed in the manner of Sōden,[7] and from it hung two lustrous coral beads. His sword was sheathed in polished shark skin, and on his bare feet he wore sandals of straw. A clean-shaven servant followed behind carrying an extra pair of leather-soled sandals and a cane of square oak.

The newcomer approached quietly and, when he heard the cause for the tension, said, "Allow me to settle the quarrel. Have the youth relinquish the blossoms to the fellow who requested them. I will take responsibility for the consequences."

Hatsudayū was slightly irritated but relinquished the cherry branch as he was told. The ruffian took the blossoms to eat as a snack with miso and prepared to go, but the handsome stranger grabbed his sleeve and stopped him.

"Hand me that cherry branch right now."

"Don't be unreasonable," the fellow said, his temper up. "You just now gave them to me, didn't you?"

The stranger remained as calm as possible. "Unreasonable demands seem to be on the rise in the capital these days. Hand over the cherry blossoms. Or would you prefer I take your head in exchange?"

At this, the fellow was thoroughly intimidated and relinquished the branch. The abrupt change made him look quite foolish.

The stranger first returned the cherry branch to Hatsudayū, then grabbed the other fellow.

"I want to have a few words with you, but I can see that you are drunk. Some day when you are sober, pay me a visit and let me get it off my chest." He took a lead pencil from his robe and carefully wrote down his name—ABC Jūrōemon—and address, and handed it to the fellow.

Not one of the bystanders who watched the incident to its conclusion failed to offer words of praise for the mature way he handled the affair.

It was but a passing incident, but for the joyful Hatsudayū it was unforgettable. From that night on he ceased taking customers and made his way in secret to Jūrōemon's residence in Higashi-no-tōin. "If those awful men decide to attack," he vowed to himself,

"I will meet them in advance and sacrifice my life, lest any harm befall this man." Before long, Jūrōemon became aware of this determination and his own feelings for the boy began to grow.

The gang of fools never did return for revenge.

Presently, Jūrōemon relaxed his watchful stance and developed a bond of love with the boy. They devoted themselves completely to each other. In the more than two years of their vow, they amused themselves repeatedly with almost unheard-of feats of love-making. Jūrōemon stopped seeking other forms of sexual pleasure[8] and thought only of Hatsudayū. The whole household was extremely resentful as a result, and Jūrōemon soon found himself no longer welcome at home. With nowhere to go and his stepmother making life impossible for him, he disappeared one day leaving behind only a letter briefly expressing his bitterness.

Hatsudayū was broken-hearted. He prayed fervently to the gods and searched everywhere for him, but he was unable to learn anything of Jūrōemon's whereabouts. In his grief, he could not bring himself to appear onstage and simply remained in seclusion at home. Eventually his good looks began to suffer. He explained the reason for this to his theater proprietor and received permission to take leave from the stage. He found lodgings in a back alley in Naniwa and gradually his spirits improved. He did not want to appear entirely idle in society's eyes, so he opened a tiny shop where he sold paper. Thus, the year passed.

One day, one of his old actor friends came to visit. "Why did you quit work on the dry riverbed without taking the tonsure?" his friend asked.

"It was not attachment to my black hair, but love of a man that kept me in this world," he answered. "Should he desire to see me this way again, I thought I would show myself to him one last time and then shave off my hair. But I have waited for him in vain. I am ashamed that you had to ask."

Right there, he cut off his topknot and at the tender age of nineteen fulfilled his desire to become a monk. Thereafter, he secluded himself at Mt. Kōya and refused all visitors from the capital. He practiced his religious austerities faithfully, fetching water from the valley in the morning and raking leaves in the evening.

Over one year had passed when he heard that, quite some time ago, the man he loved had been overtaken by nightfall at a place called Ama-no-hashi-date in Tango Province and died on a point of land jutting into the sea, his passing known only to the pines. Though much time had elapsed, the boy immediately went down to the place and prayed seven days for the repose of the man's soul. Afterwards, he turned his back on this floating world and was never heard from again.

He Pleaded for His Life at Mitsudera Hachiman

Hirai Shizuma digresses from boy love.
A silver-hoarding old man visits a theater for the first time.
Meeting a girl from Sakai, he abandons his love of men.

It seems that the world is forever changing. The female kabuki of Tayū Kurōzu and Okuni[1] so popular in Naniwa long ago came to an end to be replaced by troupes of boys, their dancing the finest the world had ever seen. In the theater of Shioya Kurōemon[2] one could see actors like Iwai Utanosuke and Hirai Shizuma;[3] two such handsome youths will never be seen again in future ages. There were 45 other dancers in the troupe, and not a single unattractive one could be found among them.

Up until that time, actors did not divide their time between acting during the day and selling themselves at night. You could summon one anytime and he would gladly accept your invitation and spend the day drinking with you. If you fell in love with him, he would give you his love just as boys do throughout society,[4] and no one ever complained about it.

Even the theater proprietors showed a remarkable lack of greed. They carelessly let their boys entertain guests unable to pay for services rendered. And yet, if at year's end they received a gift of yellowtail fish from Tango Province and a lacquered three-*jō* keg of sake, or before the Bon Festival received ten packages of Miwa noodles, they would politely send out notes expressing their gratitude.

In addition, when first making advances to a young actor, it was possible to simply meet him at a teahouse on the riverbank on your way home from the theater, having had him called there by the mistress of the establishment. Over sake you could ask him to sing little songs (if he had a voice) and entertain yourself with him exactly as you pleased. Afterwards, if you sent him one *ryō* of silver collected from your circle of companions in pleasure, a servant with a drooping mustache would come with greetings from the theater proprietor. "He wishes to express his profoundest gratitude for your kind attentions," he would say, bowing deeply with three fingers pressed to the floor. How we would laugh at his long-windedness and exaggerated politeness!

Nowadays, you can give an actor's attendants two *bu* of gold apiece and it hardly elicits a smile. If you should delay slightly in paying your bill, you may find the long autumn night interrupted about ten o'clock by pounding at the door. "He's got to appear onstage tomorrow. It is time he came home." What a depressing thing to hear in the middle of love-making.

Be that as it may, there is in present-day society a glut of both stray puppy dogs[5] and ready cash, a state that results in widespread ostentation and wasteful spending. It used to be that actors wore stage costumes of imported cotton printed with simple designs paper-screened in ink, and for everyday dress they made do with robes of Kaga silk lined in material dyed an inexpensive sappan-wood red. If an actor wore a robe of Asakusa weave with a purple lining, it was considered quite shocking, so much so that he would be accused of outrageous extravagance. The use in recent years of Chinese weave, spun gold, and imported furs is in no way justified by the fact that they are actors, and only shows how ignorant they are of their proper position in society.

Thus, it has become common these days for actors to sink into an abyss of debt despite the fact that they are earning fantastic sums of money. In the old days, when income was meager, an actor never had trouble making ends meet. True, things were not very exciting in those days. After all, excitement and titillation belong to the here and now. But in terms of generosity and emotional sincerity befitting a youngster, Hirai Shizuma and the boys of his day deserve to be remembered by future generations.

At one time there was a man living on the main artery through Sakai whose household prospered on the Nagasaki trade.[6] This gentleman was old-fashioned and set in his ways. Not once in his 70-odd years had he caught a cold or taken medicine. His only concern in life was collecting his rents and computing the interest on loans. Never once in his life had he visited the pleasure quarter. He took no interest in how the maids looked who worked in his kitchen. So long as they were capable of weaving cloth in their spare time, he hired whoever would accept the lowest wages. It never once occurred to him to fall in love. He never stepped outside his gate and was totally lacking in social graces.

It was natural then that people were amazed when this man went to see a play for the first time one day. Unfortunately, it began to rain in the middle. The other theater-goers jumped to their feet and scrambled for shelter, but the old man stayed where he was without moving.

"Shizuma is supposed to appear in the third play, 'Sakuragawa,' isn't he? I cannot go home until I have seen him," he said. While the hubbub of voices continued, he shouted, "Everyone, please!"

Though the sleeves of his robe were soaked through, he watched "Sakuragawa" to the end and afterwards went around to the stage entrance to wait.

Shizuma emerged unmindful of the drops of rain that fell on his sleeves from the overhanging eaves. An attendant held out an umbrella for him, and as he proceeded on his way the old man thought his figure was surely the most captivating he had ever seen. He followed after the boy as far as the graveyard at the temple. Shizuma noticed him there standing silently, deep in thought, and felt an immediate sympathy for him.

"Sir, may I ask where you are from?" he ventured, but received no reply.

The old man only muttered to himself, "This thing called love—when and by whom was such a painful emotion invented?"

Shizuma took out a book of six or seven theater tickets from a packet of tissues he carried.

"Please come again soon," he said.

The old man was so overwhelmed with gratitude that he forgot completely the words of love he had prepared in advance for the occasion, thus wasting his opportunity.

The sun sets early in winter, and a rainbow that had formed was fading fast. The old man crossed Tazaemon's Bridge where the wind blew cruelly off the river and stood there for a while gazing bleakly after the boy. When Shizuma entered the proprietor's house where he lived, the man had no choice but to go into a nearby teahouse. He pretended only that he was there to sit out the rain and positioned himself to keep an eye on Shioya's house, giving no hint of the real reason for his visit.

The owner of the teahouse noticed the man's thoughtful expression, however, and asked what was bothering him. The old man was unable to ignore the question and told all about his life-threatening love for Shizuma. The owner felt very sorry for him and secretly reported it to Shizuma, who immediately responded with sympathy.

"I cannot refuse this man's love for me just because he is old," he thought. He quickly changed into his favorite outfit, perfumed his robes with a rare burnt incense called "Dawn to Dusk," and went to the teahouse. The man he found waiting there had not a single strand of black hair on his head. He wore a striped Takijima kimono and a red-lined halfcoat fastened high on his chest with a cord, and carried a short sword with a removable hilt ornament made from a walnut shell. From his sash hung an old-fashioned medicine box and a money pouch of tanned leather held in place with an ancient coin. It was amazing that an old man of such uncouth appearance should lose his heart for the love of a youth.

Shizuma went to the further of two rooms and called the man to him. "The teahouse owner did not have to tell me that you loved me," he whispered. "I already realized it when I saw you on my way home from the theater earlier. It was on my mind all the while. Fate is strange, isn't it?"

He poured the man some sake and got him mildly drunk before beginning love-making. He pressed his body against the man's and worked hard to please him, but instead of showing any gratitude the old man simply mumbled sutras to himself. After some skillful cajoling on Shizuma's part, he finally started talking.

"I will never forget your kindness," he began, "but I am not the one in love with you. It is my only child. You are all he talks about lately, and he is so distraught he seems ready to expire. As a parent concerned for his life, I have come to ask a favor of you. Kindly agree to see him, even if just for a moment."

Shizuma's sympathy for the man grew even stronger when he heard this. "Having come this far, I would not refuse you now. I will do exactly as you wish."

The old man was overjoyed to hear this.

"Then I shall bring him here this evening after dark. I beg you, please speak of this matter to no one. He is waiting at a rented house in Nagamichi," he explained and left immediately to fetch him.

Shizuma waited for quite some time and wearily pillowed his head on his arm. Just as he was falling asleep, a palanquin of the type used by sick people was quietly brought up to the house. Shizuma was awakened by the sound of footsteps. He opened his eyes to find a beautiful girl of fourteen or fifteen standing there before him. She had on a pure white singlet and another robe of light pink under her pale blue lined kimono, appliquéd with pieces of colored material on which poetic phrases were written. Her sash of persimmon weave was decorated with a double diamond pattern and tucked, untied, around her waist. Her hair fell loosely down her shoulders, tied with studied carelessness about halfway down her back with a piece of twisted paper. Suffice it to say, she was an incredible beauty.

She seemed unembarrassed to be standing there in front of him and quietly approached him where he lay.

"How lovely," she said, the words unconsciously escaping her lips. They smiled as they looked at each other. Shizuma was thrilled; he could hardly believe that she belonged to this floating world. For a moment, neither spoke.

Suddenly, Shizuma came to his senses. He had made a promise of boy love for the night! This was totally unexpected, and he was worried what others would say if they found out. (His quandary showed how sincerely devoted he was to the way of male love. Nowadays, boys do not even refuse propositions from widows.) Shizuma struggled with himself.

"If I heartlessly insist on maintaining my exclusive devotion to

men, her illness will only grow more grave," he thought. Reluctantly, he made up his mind to sleep with her.

He was in utter disarray when they parted. Despite the brevity
of their encounter, their words of farewell were spoken with great
depth of feeling.

"From now on I will think of myself as yours," he told her.
"When you have regained your health, let us meet again. I am sure
we will never forget each other, even in the world to come."

More fleeting than dew is life. The next day dawned to find the
poor girl of sixteen asleep in death. Death spares no one, but hers
was all the more moving because of her youth.

After the seven days of mourning were past, the girl's mother
thought, "The least I can do is to go and see the young man for
whom she yearned and died. Perhaps it will dispel my grief."

She went to Osaka and paid Shizuma a visit. When she presented him with some keepsakes to remember the child by, he once again sank into tears.

Afterwards, he grew depressed. "Without even meaning to, I have taken someone's life," he thought. Afraid of divine retribution, he prayed to Buddha and the gods pleading for his life. Then, a most amazing thing happened, something never heard of before.

One day, on his way home from worship at Mitsudera, people who saw him insisted that he looked different, though he was wearing regular dress.

"He had on a thin white robe and his face looked pale and distant. Could it be that he lost his mind?" they asked.

That very evening he passed away to become another of Naniwa's long forgotten dreams. Like a bud rudely torn from the snowy branch of a plum tree waiting for spring, he became a topic for moonlit talks about days gone by.

Love's Flame Kindled by a Flint Seller

Tamagawa Sennojō's secret papers.
A small heating pot staves off cold winds.
A new "Tomb of Love" is erected in the capital.

In addition to the seven rivers that bear the name Tamagawa, there is Tamagawa Sennojō,[1] renowned for his singing of ballads long ago. His shrill voice rose in song like waves rising from the wind-blown sea, and when the reed blinds rose for him to make his appearance onstage, his beauty surpassed even that of the Izutsu girl.[2]

Sennojō first stepped onto the stages of the capital in the spring of his fourteenth year and continued to wear the long-sleeved robes of a young girl until his year of misfortune at age 42.[3] Not for a single day did the audiences tire of seeing him perform. Youthful actors of female roles in future generations have much to learn from his example. In Edo he starred in the play "Nightly Visits to Kawachi"[4] for three years running and won the hearts of theatergoers there, too. His lavish praises even appeared in *Yarō mushi*.[5]

It was a desolate night in the autumn of the first year of Jō-ō [1652]. Clouds obstructed the light of the moon when, toward evening, from the south-facing parlor at a certain nobleman's house, came the sound of a reed mouth organ. As the night deepened, the revelers turned to other forms of entertainment. In those days, a merchant named Ichiheiji had come from Nagasaki and introduced bamboo castanets. They were the rage throughout the capital. Even street urchins who did nothing but strike dogs all day had learned the beat, but of course it was not something an aristocrat would bother his hands with.

The noble gentleman quieted the ruckus in the room and turned to a painter famed for his depictions of the entertainment world. "I know by report of young kabuki actors on the dry riverbed, but I have never seen them myself. I want you to depict them for me exactly as they are."

The painter, named Hanada Takumi, exercised all of his skill with the brush to accomplish the assignment. Unimportant though it was, established young stars of female roles and budding actors alike vied with each other to ply him with gifts of aloeswood incense, heirloom swords, and favorite halfcoats. The world is such that he conveniently grew blind to their faults; with his brush he straightened the crooked noses of boys he liked and even smoothed the jutting brows of those he disliked. As a result, they came out looking uniformly attractive.

Sennojō was justifiably proud of his good looks and thought it beneath him to ask for special favors. But of all the actors, Sennojō alone was depicted with a horribly bent back. (This is reminiscent of the T'ang Emperor's concubine Wang Chao Chun who similarly neglected to present a certain court painter with gifts.)[6] Later, when the completed pictures of the actors were ranked, Tamagawa took last place. No one even saw fit to eulogize him with a poem,[7] so Sennojō's name was sadly lost to posterity.

Since the beginning of that autumn a disease of the joints had been raging throughout the capital, and Sennojō was severely afflicted. His hips grew heavy and unsightly, and even after he had recuperated completely he was left with a protruding rear end. Strangely, that is exactly how he was depicted in the picture! Nevertheless, Sennojō was a boy of many talents and never lacked for work at night. His patrons, in fact, vied with each other to be first. He was in such demand that it was not unusual to wait ten days for an appointment. It was impossible to share even a drink with him without advance notice.

At his appointments, Sennojō entertained with a slight flush of wine on his cheeks, pale red like maple leaves in autumn. One look could drive a man mad with desire. Wayward priests from Takao, Nanzen-ji, and Tōfuku-ji, not to mention myriad other temples, sometimes sold entire collections of calligraphy passed down for generations in their temples, whereas others cut down and sold whole forests of trees and bamboo under temple jurisdiction, all for the sake of acquiring the love of this boy. Afterwards they were invariably thrown out of their temples with nothing but an umbrella to hide their shame. There were also sales clerks who out-smarted their merchant bosses and embezzled incredible sums of money that they spent on the boy. No one knows the number of men who lost their families and fortunes for the fleeting pleasures of Sennojō's love.

One time I had the opportunity to open Sennojō's private letter box. Inside was a loosely bound sheef of papers that looked like a diary. On the cover were the words "First Pillow." Intrigued, I opened it and began reading. As I suspected, it was a record of Sennojō's liasons with a variety of patrons from New Year's Day to the close of the year, detailing how he slept with brawny samurai, turning devilish rogues into purring pussycats, breathed sophistication into earthy farmers, made Shinto priests cut their thick hair more stylishly, and put *hakama* on Buddhist abbots.[8] At each appointment he entertained without restraint and yet maintained all the while complete control over his patrons, using them for his own personal pleasure.

The story grew more fascinating the further I read, but I finally put the diary down. Sennojō was so perfect in everything he did, what fault could one find with him? Perhaps his one weakness was this: if a man, no matter how low his rank, expressed his love for the boy, Sennojō would meet him on the sly. In time he frequently developed deep attachments this way. He did not care if these relationships became public knowledge. Like waves in the ever-flowing tide, Sennojō's name was forever coming up as a topic of rumor.

One day toward dusk the wind blew fiercely and snow threatened to fall. Already the pines at distant Mt. Kitayama formed a panorama of white. Under the well-traveled bridge at Gojō was a man who slept at night on the dry riverbed. He was making his way through this dreamlike existence by the light of sparks from flint stones. Each morning he gathered flints from the banks of the Kurama River and made his rounds through the capital selling them. At the end of each day he threw away those that remained unsold. He enjoyed his day-to-day existence, and as a result people in the capital began calling him a "modern-day holy man."

Even this saint had difficulty abandoning the way of male love, however, and wrote a four-volume work describing Sennojō's activities through each of the four seasons. The book was called "The Abyss of Tamagawa's Heart" and should be required reading for anyone with an interest in boy love. (The account is especially amusing when it records minute details like the number of moxa burns or flea bites on the boy's body.)

This man was once a prominent connoisseur of boys from the province of Owari. He had shared deep vows of love with Sennojō from the time the boy was first promoted to being an actor of female roles. He found it necessary to go into hiding, and for a long time his whereabouts remained unknown to Sennojō, who was broken-hearted by the man's disappearance. Finally someone reported to Sennojō that the man had been seen in a wretched state at the dry riverbed near Gojō. Tears came to Sennojō's eyes when he heard the news.

"Nothing is so precarious as man's fortune. If I had been told sooner perhaps I could have prevented his being humiliated in this way. But since I did not know where he was, I could do nothing for him. Such is the way of the world. I never imagined he would be right here in the capital. I sent letters to his native province several times but never got any response. I began to wonder if perhaps he had cast me out of his heart altogether. Such bitter frustration he made me suffer . . . ."

Sennojō paused to pull himself together and then continued more dispassionately. "I suppose in this line of work one must be prepared to suffer not just this but many such heartbreaks. What's done is done, and nothing will change it."

That night, Sennojō worked especially hard to make his patron happy and spent an intimate night in bed. By the time Sennojō got up to leave, the man was completely satisfied. It was almost dawn and the frosty night pierced him to the quick. He recalled how cold the wind was on the riverbed and placed a sake cup inside his sleeve. With him, he carried a small heating pot. He made his way alone across the stony shore, setting to flight the waterfowl that pillowed for the night in the swirling waves. He made his way to the base of the distant bridge and there called out that name from long ago, "Master Samboku of Owari." But the man was nowhere to be found.

It was the 24th day of the eleventh month, just before dawn, and

still too dark to distinguish faces clearly. There seemed to be a myriad of wretched figures sleeping all around him. Sennojō went from form to form, searching for the man. He suddenly recalled something he had noticed long ago, a knife wound that the man bore on his left temple. Sennojō continued on his rounds, looking carefully for the scar on the face of each vagabond there. Just as he expected, he finally found the man.

"I called your name for some time," he said weeping. "Why didn't you respond? You grieve me so."

His tears were so copious it was as if flood waters had suddenly risen in the riverbed. For a while he talked of the past and served sake with his own hands to fend off the chill of the early morning wind. The sky to the east began to turn white.

"Looking at you now," Sennojō said, "I see hardly a trace of your former self. It does not seem possible that someone could be changed so completely."

As he spoke, he massaged the man's feet. Blood oozed from the dry, cracked skin. Sennojō's grief grew even more unbearable. He cared as best he could for the man's needs and then lay down beside him. Travelers getting an early start were already pounding the bridge overhead. The time was rapidly approaching for the drum roll to announce the opening of the day's theater events.[9] Sadly, and fearing discovery, Sennojō decided that it was time he had to go.

"Please wait for me tonight," he begged. "I will come to meet you here." The echo of his voice soon disappeared without a trace.

This man, having abandoned the world, was not at all pleased by the unexpected visit. "I want nothing to do with him. He will end up destroying the pleasures of my simple life," he thought with disgust. Abruptly, he left the place and set out for an unknown destination in another province.

Sennojō was distraught when he found the man gone. He scoured the capital for news of him, but it was useless. Finally, in despair, he gathered all the leftover flints he could find and had them transported to a remote corner of Imagumano Temple at Higashiyama. There, deep in a thicket of dry bamboo grass, he built a tomb. Next to it he planted a single paulownia, since the gentleman's family crest was patterned after the leaf of that tree. Sennojō built a hut of grass next to the tomb and hired a priest of the Nichiren sect to intone the lotus sutra and keep watch over the monument, just as if he were mourning a dead man. Someone gave the place a name: the "New Tomb of Love."[10]

Visiting from Edo, Suddenly a Monk

Living in a pathless hut of grass.
Tamagawa Shuzen dips from the well of his heart.
A country girl goes mad with love.

The broad-billed roller sings only at Mt. Kōya, Matsuno-o, and
Kōki-ji here in Kawachi Province,[1] and even then only in the utter
darkness of midsummer religious retreat. Priests who chance to
hear its song find their hearts suddenly purified, especially on this
holy ground where Kōbō Daishi founded his temple.

Farther along the same mountain range is another ancient temple in a grove near the village of Tamade. An abbot who was an
expert in the sutras lived there, and among his many disciples was
handsome monk by the name of Kaken. I inquired about his past
and discovered that he was once the actor Tamamura Shuzen,[2]
whose name appeared prominently on billboards throughout Edo.
When he played female roles he drove men mad with desire, and
his dancing would surely never be seen again, even in the world to
come. He was especially skilled in the ways of boy love; no one
remained unaffected by his charms.

Time passed, however, and soon people were lamenting the
change in his once beautiful figure. At the age of twenty, gazing
one night at a moon also on the wane, he decided to hide himself
in a certain temple, something he had been considering for a long
time. There he shaved off his topknot and changed into the robes
of a monk. For a time he traveled the provinces as a pilgrim, but
he had now settled here in a grass hut of his own making. Vines
strangled his scraggly hedge of bush clover, and the window of his
hut opened south toward the moon, his only companion. He pursued his devotions morning and night without break. For three
years he lived this way without telling anyone of his whereabouts,
and soon even thoughts of his birthplace were forgotten.

There was a boy named Asanojō,[3] who was both beautiful and deeply affectionate, whom he had supported while still in the world of the theater. He was the object of innumerable men's desires, but when Shuzen acquired him he won the boy's heart completely. Of his own accord, Asanojō stopped entertaining other men. Although they had promised each other that their feelings would never change, when Shuzen put on the black robes of a monk he did not inform the boy of his plans. Bitter and distraught, Asanojō had traveled the roads from distant Musashino to pay Shuzen a visit.

The moment Asanojō saw him, he felt as if the Shuzen of old had vanished like foam on the water, for with his own hands Shuzen was drawing water from a well using a weighted pole. Asanojō's tears alone were enough to fill the bucket to overflowing.

"What have you done?" the boy cried, clinging to Shuzen's robe. (The fact that he wept shamelessly into the man's sleeve in full view of others showed the extent of his love for Shuzen.)

"Yes, I have taken the tonsure," Shuzen said. "Though still in the world, my abode was unsettled. I feared that we would never meet again. I am grateful you came to visit me here for the sake of our past love. I will always treasure it. But you are after all still in the bloom of youth, of the age that the blossom-viewing public in Edo most appreciates. It would be a shame to turn your back on them. Your parents in Kumagaya would miss you terribly. In light of all this, I think it would be best if you immediately returned east."

Knowing that at the end of this night they would be bidding each other farewell, Shuzen entertained Asanojō by building a fire of dried leaves under a tea kettle, but its meager flame did little to warm his welcome. Aside from two tea bowls, there were no other utensils. He had hung an unmounted piece of paper bearing six words of the sutra above a Buddha shelf made of split bamboo stalks, and on the shelf was a chipped sake bottle filled with summer chrysanthemums. The cool breeze that blew through the hut was their sole source of pleasure. Since Shuzen had no netting to protect them during the night, they stayed awake swatting mosquitos with their fans and spoke of the past until the sound of their voices finally ceased and only their tears remained. The ringing of

the pre-dawn bell found them thus, caught between slumber and wakefulness.

"When the first cock crows, turn your steps toward the east. In the future, I do not expect to receive any news from you, not even a letter announcing your safe return home. If you should hear word of me, ignore it. Go now, and take this to remember me by." He handed Asanojō a Pure Land rosary, one that he used constantly in his devotions. Asanojō's tears flowed again like a string of jewels.

Clouds lifted at daybreak and the summer mountains became clearly visible in the distance. Asanojō spoke. "I will do as you wish and return home."

Shuzen watched the boy's figure disappear into the shadows of the lush mountain forest.

It took many days for Shuzen's former peace of mind to return.

He secluded himself in his rude hut and turned his attention to intoning the sutras in hopes of forgetting his sorrow. One day, he was startled from his devotions by a knock at the door. He went out to see who it was, and there stood Asanojō shorn of his lovely locks.

"I did as you said and returned east," the boy explained. "Now I have come back to you."

Shuzen regretted the loss of Asanojō's youthful beauty, but there was nothing he could do about it now. He went to speak to the abbot, who agreed to accept the boy as his disciple. "He has realized that life is a mere dream. The world's pleasures no longer hold any fascination for him." Without a trace of regret, Asanojō dyed his robes black and thereafter concentrated his thoughts completely on the world to come. He was a true seeker of enlightenment. Each morning he drew water from the mountain spring and in the evening gathered brushwood for the fire. It was truly rare to see such pleasure as Asanojō evinced performing his ascetic tasks.

In a neighboring village, at a place called Old Market, lived a farmer's daughter of unusual beauty. She chanced to see Asanojō pass by in traveling dress and immediately fell passionately in love with him. Half crazed, she started after him on his way to the temple, but the maidservants dragged her back home. They scolded the girl for her behavior, but she was hopelessly in love and that night crept in secret to the temple. She peered through a window into the hut, illuminated only faintly by a pine torch. Lo and behold, the one she loved had shaved his head and become a monk!

She raised her voice in an anguished cry. "What could have caused that youth to renounce the world?" She wept and wailed as if she would die.

The uproar outside was completely unexpected and Asanojō tried at first to ignore it, but the girl's crazed shrieks soon roused the entire monastery. Many of the monks who gathered around the girl recognized her.

"What a vulgar display," they said in rebuke, but she paid them no heed.

She continued to scream, "Who cut off the boy's hair? Whoever it was, I hate him! I hate him!" She had unmistakably gone mad.

Word was sent to her parents, and soon a close relation arrived to talk to her. "Think how people will criticize you for this. He is a monk. Your desires for him cannot be satisfied. Perhaps someday the time will come when you can meet him once again."

These words seemed to calm her.

"I suppose you are right," she responded. "I was blinded by my own wicked desire when he had no feelings for me at all. It must have been fate that led me to love him in this way. My black hair, which I have treasured each of my fourteen years, I will now abandon as grass on the path towards enlightenment."

With those words, she herself cut off her hair.

Her family had no choice but to allow her to become a nun. A cottage was built for her in the western reaches of the hills. From that time on, the sounding of the morning and evening bells was all that anyone heard of her, for no one ever laid eyes on the girl again. Enlightened by love, she completely turned her back on love.

The two monks, once actors, also completely abandoned the floating world and its ways. They never once strayed from their mountain hideaway, but lived there in total devotion to the performance of their religious duties. Friends from their days of glory in Edo frequently came to visit, nostalgic for the past, but their door was closed to them. The gateway eventually became overgrown with honeysuckle and the path to their door disappeared under a thick growth of bamboo grass.

Some years later, a handsome young actor named Yamamoto Kantarō[4] came to admire the autumn leaves at Tatsuta. He enjoyed the colors immensely. On his way home, he stopped to pay them a visit and was deeply moved by what he observed. Realizing that life was truly but a dream within a dream, he too took the tonsure. His decision was no doubt arrived at after much careful thought, but it was a pity nevertheless to lose him at the peak of youthful beauty.

= 5:5 =

Votive Picture of Kichiya Riding a Horse

A man selling wolf meat before winter gives his life for love.
Tamamura Kichiya, unsurpassed in the knowledge of love.
Lack of forelocks turns to society's advantage.

A certain craftsman began selling toothpicks carefully engraved with actor's crests, and soon they were the rage of the capital. There was one crest, unmatched by any other, that used the word "world" of "floating world." It belonged to Tamamura Kichiya,[1] an actor in the troupe of Ebisuya.[2] He was the cause of unfulfilled desires not only for the men of the capital in those days but also for their wives and daughters. Many of them ended up turning to smoke on the funeral biers at Funaoka and Mt. Toribe. When Kichiya appeared as Yang Kuei Fei with a sprig of blossoms decorating his hair, he surpassed even the beautiful Chinese women depicted in paintings, although that may be because no one has been to China to see the real thing. It would have been wonderful indeed if he could have remained a boy forever. Enshū, a connoisseur in such matters, said it best: "I only wish that handsome youths and trees in gardens never grew old."[3]

There is no reason to bemoan change, however. Such is the way of the world.

One year, there was a riot among samurai guards at a theater in Naniwa over a certain actor's affections.[4] As a result, kabuki came under legal restriction. All boy actors were required to shave off their forelocks in the manner of adult men. It was like seeing unopened blossoms being torn from the branch. Theater proprietors and the boys' managers alike were upset at the effect it might have on business, but looking back on it now the law was probably the best thing that ever happened to them. It used to be that no matter how splendid the boy, it was impossible for him to keep his forelocks and take on patrons beyond the age of twenty. Now, since everyone wore the hairstyle of adult men, it was still possible at age 34 or 35 for youthful-looking actors to get under a man's robe. How strange are the ways of love!

These actors hid their years from others and reduced the number of beans they ate at the Setsubun Festival, rectifying the discrepancy later in private.[5] The more observant theater-goers, however, realized to their great shock that actors whose stage debuts had come at the same time were now playing villains and old hags opposite them. If skill is what the audience is looking for, there should be no problem in having a 70-year-old perform as a youth in long-sleeved robes. So long as he can continue to find patrons willing to spend the night with him, he can then enter the New Year without pawning his belongings.

Tamamura Kichiya was on his way to rehearse the first play of the year. As he crossed the crumbling bridge at Shijō,[6] he was spotted by a most unusual-looking man who could not have been more unmistakably from the north country if he had worn a sign around his neck announcing the fact. He wore a crude cotton robe and hemp cap and carried a heavy lumberman's sword with a rucksack on his back. He had come to the capital selling charred wolf meat for people to fortify themselves against the cold winter months ahead. The moment he saw this unbelievably lovely youth, he stood stock still in amazement. Kichiya noticed the man staring at him and, thinking to give the fellow a bit of innocent pleasure, tossed a toothpick he was holding into a sleeve of the man's robe as he passed. The man seemed to lose his senses; he abandoned the goods he was selling in front of Kinai's puppet theater[7] and immediately returned to his homeland, Sado Island. Night and day, he worked to save money. Interestingly, he seemed to believe that money was the only means for him to consummate his love for the boy.

"Faith can move mountains," they say. Well, the man located a mountain containing gold and began mining it, and he was soon an unexpectedly wealthy man. A little over five years later he returned to the capital and went immediately to the dry riverbed where he halted his pack horse and asked for Tamamura Kichiya.

He was told that, as actors often do, the boy had gone to Edo four years earlier.

Undaunted, the man immediately set out again on the road east without spending a single night in Kyoto. There were no gatekeepers at Osaka Pass to stay his lovelorn rush, and he proceeded on his way unhindered. In the past he used to linger with the made-up ladies at way stations like Goyu, Akasaka, and Kanagawa, but this time he paid them no heed and hurried on his way from Shinagawa to the heart of Edo. He went straight to Sakai-chō to enquire about Kichiya. He was told that, after displaying his beauty on the stages of Edo, the boy had shaved off his forelocks and become an adult at a fairly early age. When the man heard this, he was overcome with nostalgia for the boy.

He asked for a guide and was led to the studio of Bandō Mata-

kurō.[8] Inside, actors were still making up. Even without powder
on their faces, they looked uniformly lovely. The stars Yoshida
Iori,[9] Nogawa Kichijūrō,[10] and Kagawa Ukon[11] were all boys
famed for their beauty, but none could compare to the boy from
the capital, Kichiya, for whom he yearned. Trying to recall the
boy's image in his mind, he looked around at all the lovely youths.
He was irritated that he could not distinguish him from the rest.
Finally, a big man pointed the boy out to him.

"This is the way Tamamura looks now," he said.

Startled, the man took a closer look. He had seen the boy only
once before, but sure enough, his figure, the beauty of the nape of
his neck, was just as he remembered it. Even now he found the
boy irresistible.

Later, in private, they talked about their first meeting in Kyoto.

Kichiya once again thought with nostalgia of the capital. "In those days, I would gladly have satisfied your love for me," he said, reflecting in words the sincerity in his heart.

The man was overjoyed, grateful that the boy had spoken from the heart rather than treating him like a customer. He then told Kichiya the entire story of his good fortune and presented him with enough money to live comfortably for the rest of his life. With that, the man returned to Sado, the land of his birth.

This whole affair stemmed from a single toothpick. All boy actors should learn from this to be friendly and let men hold their hands whenever they wish. After all, hands do not wear away with use.

No one knows how many men gave up their lives for the sake of Tamamura Kichiya's love. He appeared on many votive pictures [12] offered to temples and shrines throughout Edo. In one, he appeared riding a horse led by a horse driver, played by Bōzu Kohei. [13] It is said that one man fell in love with Kichiya just by looking at the picture. People are still talking about it to this day.

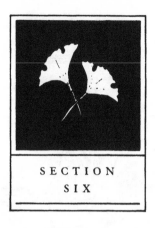

= 6:1 =

A Huge Winecup Overflowing with Love

Itō Kodayū, exactly like a girl.
The secret go-between of boy love.
Yesterday's robe becomes today's memento.

They say that Buddhist priests are "scraps of wood" purged of all feeling,[1] but there is no occupation more pleasant in the world. They can hold parties in their temples whenever they please, their only duties to intone the sutras of their sects and don robes when meeting parishioners. Rather than waste the offerings of the faithful on things without meaning, they use the money to buy the love of young actors, entertainment well suited to the priest's lot.

Even when entertaining boys in their rooms, they never once forget the gravity of their vows and adhere religiously to their vegetarian diet of stewed dumplings and mushrooms, chilled chestnuts with silvervine pickled in miso, and clear soup of sweet seaweed and salted plums. With these delicacies they extend their drinking bouts through the long nights. (How they can drink!) Such sincere devotion to their vows is highly commendable. Just because they do not suffer Buddha's immediate divine punishment

does not mean chief priests can go ahead and enjoy the meat of fish
and fowl. After all, if priests could indulge in fish and women to
their hearts' content, it would be foolish for a man not to take the
tonsure!

A certain chief priest with unusual tastes amused himself by
dressing Itō Kodayū[2] in stage costume and a female wig so the boy
looked exactly like a lovely girl. He was simply satisfying his natural curiousity about women; therefore, no one condemned him for
it. (Shōjō no Gembei, a man who happened to be included in the
wild revelry that night, told me all about it.)

When it came to entertaining at parties, Itō was unequaled in
past or present. The same group of fellows could be in the place
they always gathered, and this actor would singlehandedly trans-

port them to a completely different world. The moon over Higa-shiyama would look as if it were wearing a purple kerchief, and even the feathers of crows in the trees at Gion took on the color of Sōden's burnt-tea dye-work. All were buoyed up by the charms of this much-sought-after boy, and not only his patron but everyone there regretted the arrival of dawn. "Autumn nights are a mere dream, pillowed in your arms."[3] The long autumn night felt brief as a spring night, leading someone to misquote the old poem. By then they were no longer aware anyway of where they were or what they were doing. In the "Ode of A-Fang Kung," Tu Mu wrote, "The heart of one man is the heart of all men."[4] No one could resist sinking into the abyss of Itō's heart. Even practiced connoisseurs were swept away and made to suffer helplessly for love of the boy.

Although there were many young actors like him, this Itō was by birth soft-spoken and endowed with a calm, untroubled de-meanor that made him a natural actor of female roles. The way he dressed established fashions, and his grooming was impeccable. He spoke in a soft and soothing voice, excelled at dance, and could follow any rhythm perfectly. The stunt that Somekawa Rinnosuke[5] first performed using two ropes, he could cross on one, causing great excitement even among the jaded theater-goers of the capital. His feats seemed superhuman. In "Ransom of Yoshino,"[6] he played the courtesan promenading to meet her patron. The audience said that his wisteria-like beauty left the real Yoshino looking like a faded cherry blossom in comparison.

But to go on and on like this becomes tedious. Is anyone un-aware of the ultimate proof of his superiority? A lover of boys whose passion for Itō burned ceaselessly began calling this hand-some youth a "burial ground" because his fee for a single night was three pieces of silver.[7] It is amazing that merchants from the capital so precise with their weighing scales were willing to spend 129 *momme*[8] for a night of dreams on his pillow. No matter how much they loved him, it must have taken tremendous resolve to pay the fee. But then, merchants are well aware that you get what you pay for.

Women throughout the capital regardless of rank or station also developed overwhelming desires for this actor. No one knows how many of them died, lovelorn, having never told him their feelings. Some sent love letters, hoping against hope for a response, but he ignored them completely, not out of cold-heartedness but because he was devoted to the way of male love.

"Actors nowadays resign themselves while on the job to wearing long-sleeved robes with side vents, but when night comes they put on their round-sleeved robes and go off in search of ladies at tea-houses in Gion-machi, Ishigaki, Kami-hachiken, Koppori, Yasaka, and Kiyomizu. In secret they visit Dotemachi streetwalkers or go home and make it necessary for the live-in seamstresses to take naps the following afternoon. As if that were not enough, their activities in the evil place[9] erupt as blemishes on their faces. (So much for their youthful beauty!) How sad that they, due to such behavior, should be rejected by their patrons while still at the peak of youth. All working boys[10] should assiduously avoid this one pitfall. In three or four years' time, when they are no longer young and in demand, they can pick up ladies all day and all night if they wish without a word of protest from anyone. Even a Chinaman[11] should be able to figure that out!"

This was greeted with laughter by all of the boy actors at the party, but each was guilty of exactly such behavior at one time or another. Soon the revelry ceased and the partiers decided to go wash off their sweat with cool water. In a noisy group, they went off to the adjoining bath.

One spring day toward dusk a light rain began to fall, inaudible on the shingle roof. It would be good for viewing the blossoms tomorrow, they thought to themselves. Quietly, they listened to a chorus of frogs on the riverbank. Peering outside the bamboo fence, someone noticed a beautiful woman standing there who appeared to be 31 or 32 years of age. Her lovely black hair, with its natural hairline, showed no sign of ever having been parted by a comb. They could detect no scent of hair oil on her tresses, which were folded carelessly and tied with nothing more than a scrap of old almanac paper wound into a cord. Her short-sleeved robe was a reddish-brown color and bore a painted pattern of famous mountains, so faded and worn that the scenes were barely visible. The view of Mt. Yoshino on her shoulder was gone, and in its place was a patch of pale blue cotton cloth. Matsuyama on the hem had been mended with a piece of striped material. She wore a man's sash of Kokura weave lengthened with a piece of cotton cloth and tied over her left hip. The scarlet color of her silk crepe underskirt was faded, but something still lingered of its former beauty. They wondered what sort of person she was to have ended up that way.

She had with her a boy of three or four dressed in a paper robe with wide sleeves. She broke off two or three stalks of rapeseed blossoms growing untended on the riverbank and was comforting her crying son.

"Your Papa fell madly in love with a young actor far beyond his means. That is him over there, the one with the crest of wisteria circling the letter "I" on his great-sleeved purple robe. They say that purple is best seen in the morning,[12] but in the evening it is even more lovely. Look!"

She put the child on her shoulders and held him up so he could peek through the green leaves of the tree where they hid. The child put his tiny hands together as if in worship and asked, "Is that the holy one?" staring all the while at the young actor. It was most amusing.

The men inside could no longer bear to simply listen through the fence, so they opened the cedar door and went out to speak to the woman. She panicked when she saw them and tried to walk away, but the men stopped her and asked for details of her story. She only hung her head and said, "I am ashamed to tell it." Looking at her closely for the first time, they realized how stunningly beautiful she really was.

"Forget your shame, and tell us what brought you all this way in secret," they pressed.

Her tears fell like a string of jewels that she caught in her sleeves, and she began the story of her husband's love for Itō. Almost immediately the men found themselves weeping, even the more stout-hearted among them, but that was to be expected.

"I suppose I no longer have anything to fear," she began. "In fact, I am grateful to you for asking. You see, my husband was well known in the capital for his infatuations with handsome youths.

While in his lord's service, he became intimate with the plum of Naniwa, Matsumoto Saizaburō.[13] Later he took his pleasure with Hanai Saizaburō,[14] whose beauty even the moon over the plain of Musashi envied. Here on this dry riverbed he lost his mind over Murayama Kumenosuke[15] and spent his nights in dreams at Gobō Shōzaemon's lodgings[16] where the boy lived. During a recent fight at the dance performing place in Kamisuki-chō[17] my husband risked his life for him and fought like a man.

"But there is nothing more unpredictable than this world in which we live. Now we are no longer able to continue living in his family home in Muromachi and have moved to a remote corner of Kitano where people only wander on the 25th day of the month.[18] We live there in utter poverty, and he makes ear cleaners from twigs of the deutzia tree to sustain our day-to-day existence. Even so, he is unable to forget his love of youths.'

"For some time he suffered in silence for the boy and has now taken to bed. I am afraid he does not have long to live. Today he cried out to me in a heart-rending voice, 'Must I die, never having seen Itō Kodayū?' and wept despite himself. As his wife I was distraught, all the more so because of our poverty, but I thought the least I could do was to convey his words to Kodayū and perhaps take back a quick note so that my husband might die in peace."

When she finished her story, all she could do was weep. The men were all sensitive types and for a moment simply savored the woman's love for her husband in silent admiration. Then, without telling Kodayū, they gave her one of the unlined robes he always wore against his skin.

"Show this to your husband, and when he has regained his health, we will see that he is able to satisfy his love for the boy."

At this, the woman's weeping only increased. "Thank you so much. I must go to tell him right away."

After she left, they told Itō about her. "Where did she go, that woman?" he asked and rushed outside. He searched after her for two or three blocks but had no idea which direction she went.

"For my sake a man's life is in danger," he said bitterly. "I must meet him to relieve his yearning." The boy seemed to go mad with grief.

Finally, that day ended and a new day dawned. When it was just light enough to distinguish people's faces, the woman reappeared to return the robe.

"I cremated my husband at dawn," she said weeping. "When he saw this robe of Kodayū's he cried out, 'Oh, joy! I feel as if I have seen him with my own eyes. Now I can die in peace.' His body shuddered and his words ceased. Now all that remains is my grief."

Everyone there was stunned. They asked about the details of his death and were considering going to his grave to mourn him when suddenly a crowd of men and women came rushing up. Without a word of explanation, they dragged the woman away and put her in a palanquin.

"You should not be here," they scolded. "Think of your parents' reputation." With their lanterns still lighted, though it was broad daylight, they left in a great flurry of confusion.

Kozakura's Figure: Grafted Branches of a Cherry Tree

Sennosuke's love revealed in a prayer petition.
The words that bind husband and wife.
A secret night of love at Sasanoya.

In India the lotus, in China the peony, and in Japan the cherry are considered the most beautiful of flowers, the source of both viewing pleasure and poetic inspiration. Cherry trees do not speak, however; neither can they walk with their limbs. When storms strike the blossoms at Yoshino or it rains at Hatsuse, the falling petals shock us into a realization of spring's passing and serve to impress us with the impermanence of our lives. In contrast, the blossom-like figure of a youth in full flower is something one can gaze at forever without tiring.

One such figure belonged to Kozakura Sennosuke,[1] who stood out as the finest among a thousand lovely actors. Onstage he was so like a woman that women themselves were overwhelmed by his beauty. No one could gaze at his face and remain unaffected. He spoke his lines distinctly but hardly moved his lips, something rare in modern times. His words were full of warm emotion. His smile was irresistible. Theater-goers let smoke rise unnoticed from their sleeves where tobacco embers fell, just like the empress of long ago for whose sake fires were kindled,[2] giving further proof of his ability to captivate an audience.

He was particularly strict about his personal conduct. He never stepped out at night unless to entertain a patron and was careful never to show his disheveled face to anyone in the morning, not even to lowly servants in the house where he lived. Unless one met him in person, it was hard to imagine his many attractive qualities. Kozakura's natural charm and courtesy extended to everyone, regardless of rank, due no doubt to the benefits of praying regularly to Aizen Myō-ō,[3] deified at the Great Temple in Naniwa and worshipped by all actors. They presented lighted lanterns bearing their actor's crests in hopes that the Buddha's gentle light might likewise illuminate their lives. Only full-fledged actors were allowed to do so. The paulownia-head crest belonged to Matsumoto Kodayū,[4] the double-cap crest to Sodeoka Ima-Masanosuke,[5] and the crest with overlapping oak leaves and three commas to Suzuki Heishichi.[6] Each actor hung his hopes for success together with his lantern before the image of the Buddha.

A certain priest who specialized in purification rituals and the driving-out of evil spirits was tidying the temple's central sanctuary where the Buddha image was kept and discovered a sealed letter of petition placed there. Sadly, it had been chewed to shreds by rats. (What troublesome creatures they are!) The petitioner was none other than Kozakura Sennosuke. Piecing the letter together, he was able to read the contents.

"It is my prayer to be united with the man I love. I swear to deny myself certain pleasures and keep myself pure until my wish is granted."

After reading it, the priest quickly disposed of the torn pieces. A worshiper came to the sanctuary just then and, learning of the petition's contents, was deeply impressed with Sennosuke's sincerity. From that moment, the worshiper was overcome with fascination for the young man.

It happened to be the first day of the second month, when the New Year's play was to be replaced with a new one, so the man went immediately to the theater of Araki Yojibei[7] to get a glimpse of the youth. Matsumoto Bunzaemon[8] came out to announce the three-act play, and after reading the title from the theater bill he rattled off the names of those appearing in each role.

"Well spoken!" someone shouted in praise.

At that instant, the curtain parted to reveal the young *onnagata*, his face as lovely and fragrant as a cherry blossom.

"At last!"

"Master Sen!"

"Master Sennosuke!"

"There will never be another like you!"

"You mankiller!"

"You'll send me to my grave alive!"

Immediately, the cheers of his fans echoed to the farthest corners of the stage. The musical accompanist finally had to lift his half-closed fan to quiet the crowd. Sennosuke approached center stage walking on bird-like stilts. He wore a paper patchwork robe of varied colors in an eye-catching pattern.

("Only he could wear such an outfit. The other actors of female roles would look terrible in it." A group of theater sophisticates in the second tier of the west gallery had already begun discoursing about him.)

Even the sound of the bell hanging from his neck seemed in character. He faced forward and smiled slightly to quiet the crowd.

Then, summoning all the charm at his disposal, he began speaking his lines; the words flowed from his lovely lips.

("Listen to him!" "Be quiet!")

"I, who stand before you now, am a wandering priestess making temple membership solicitations. Having abandoned the world of love, I now bring men and women together to make them husband and wife. Since the gods enshrined at Ashigara, Hakone, Tamatsushima, Kibune, and Miwa are all gods who protect the bond of love between husband and wife, I am spending a whole night every other night at each of these shrines in fervent prayer for the fulfillment of my heartfelt wish. The desire to do so came about in this manner: I once loved someone deeply, but, just as the moon is sometimes blocked from view by clouds, our love was never consummated. How cruel is this world! Though I never tired of him, nor he of me, we were forced to part. The grief I felt was enough to make me die.

"To be sure, it was my misdeeds in a previous existence that doomed me to suffer such sadness, but I decided that I could at least act as a guardian for those in this world who enjoy love's fulfillment. Thus I have dedicated myself body and soul to praying to the great gods of these five shrines for the sake of people throughout all generations who have loved.

"The gods have graciously heard my prayer and granted me a divine revelation by bestowing this grafted cherry branch[9] on me. This was the august revelation of the gods: 'Encourage many to love, and when their numbers reach one thousand, hold a service for them. May those who make the marriage vow, men and women alike, be pleasing to behold, of refined and comely figure. Above all may they be good-hearted, living their entire lives without bickering. We will guard over their love in this world, in the world to come, and again in the world following.'

"Ladies and gentlemen, if you desire in your hearts a good husband or wife, then tie your hopes to this cherry branch. No matter who the object of your love may be, your desires will surely be fulfilled."

He finished his long speech without any difficulty, and immediately hordes of excited men came up to tie their wishes to the branch. Among them was one who appeared to be 24 or 25 years old. He removed his large sedge hat as he came up, but his cheeks were covered with a purple face mask so it was impossible to identify him. He calmly tied his letter to the branch, and though no one knew the contents, on the outside were the words, "My feelings lie herein." The way he looked at the boy's figure made it obvious that his feelings were far deeper than anyone else's.

When Sennosuke returned to the dressing room, everyone surrounded him to read the notes tied to the branch. Most of the letters read "I'm in love" or "My life is yours," nothing more. But as soon as they opened the letter mentioned earlier, they realized that this one would have to be taken seriously. It was written in the Kōzei style of calligraphy, and this is what it said:

"Love is mere vanity, so I need not go into the story of Izanagi and Izanami[10] in detail. In spring, everything in this land of Japan looks lovely, even the figures of spiritless grasses and trees. Time passes and returns each year to this month and this day, and the buds emerge once again. Those actors who carry this spirit of spring in their hearts are lovely as young leaves, but those who lack it find it impossible to perform their feats onstage. Some say that the theater is nothing more than entertainment for the masses, but I view it differently. It is a place where spiritual beauty is revealed to the audience through the grafted cherry branch and Kozakura's own youthful beauty.

"Since the path of religious discipline makes no distinction between prince and pauper, how could the sincere request of any man be denied? I have prayed single-mindedly, convinced that you, oh living Buddha, would not refuse me. Though many people collapse in laughter at my foolishness, I bear the shame gladly for your sake.

"I express myself clumsily, but if you would show me your true beauty and let me roost featherless in the branches of your grafted cherry tree or allow me to approach as close to you as the one-winged Hiyoku,[11] I would gladly receive your love for seven generations. If, however, you should refuse me, my vengeful spirit will surely haunt you through seven rebirths.

"On the tenth day of this month, I will return wearing the same robes to receive your reply. Please, please favor me with an answer."

People drew near to read the letter and were greatly impressed with the depth of the man's feelings. Just then Kitahōgaku no Kurōsuke, who also had designs on the boy, took the letter and slipped it into his sleeve. Sennosuke walked up to him, however, and took the letter back with a stern look on his face.

"I do not intend to ignore this love letter," he said.

Kurōsuke was disappointed but produced some ink and managed at least to copy the letter before going home.

Later, Sennosuke asked where the man was living and learned that he lodged at the Sasanoya in Uemachi. He came from Bizen where he had been a man of no mean rank, but certain circumstances made it necessary for him to now live incognito. Without looking further into details, Sennosuke secretly invited him to his quarters for a visit.[12]

Darkness on a moonless night in spring is always disappointing because you cannot see the cherry blossoms, but the man far preferred scattering Kozakura's petals in bed than viewing his blossom-like beauty in daylight. Sennosuke allowed the man to have his pleasure with him over and over again.

"How I hate the sound of crows at daybreak," the man said when it came time to leave.

Sennosuke went out to see him off and handed him something as a memento of his love.

"Do not make this the last time. Come again," he said.

The man was so overjoyed, he drew his sword and said, "It may seem old-fashioned, but this is the least I can do to prove my love for you." Immediately, he drew the blade twice, then three times, across his hand. It was as if autumn leaves had appeared out of season.

Then the man went home.

Sennosuke later inquired about the man, but he had disappeared. The boy spoke of it to no one, however, for he knew love's ways all too well.

Some time later, a group of men including Kurōsuke held a party early one evening at the house of Tanakaya Jiei.[13] By good fortune, Kozakura's attendant, a man named Kagonosaku, happened to be there. After getting him drunk, Kurōsuke asked, "Whatever happened about that letter a while back?"

Kagonosaku told the entire story from beginning to end. Those who heard it were amazed. This young man, deeply rooted in the way of boy love, was a mountain cherry at its peak of bloom growing on the mountaintop of love. There were none who did not regret the thought that its petals would soon fall.

= 6:3 =

The Man Who Resented Another's Shouts

A smoldering in his breast led him to sell tobacco pouches.
Cut by his words, a masterless samurai slew him.
Sanzaburō: Love's confusion like threads of a waterfall.

Although they say that the priest of Murasakino[1] considered paintings on fans among the deceptions forbidden by Buddhist law, some paintings are so life-like that crows fly off the page and crabs (if painted with ten legs) edge into the water. Takuma's[2] water buffaloes and Tong P'o's[3] snow-covered bamboo and banana palms turned deceptions into reality.

A volume of life-like prints of the lovely figures of kabuki actors carved onto blocks of cherry wood made it possible for a certain man to enjoy the pleasures of these lovely boys all day in the privacy of his own home. All of them surpassed the peony and lotus in beauty. Among the exquisitely painted figures was one he particularly loved. Like the peaks of Tsukubane where the waterfalls flow, his name was Takii Sanzaburō.[4] Surely the special beauty with which he alone was depicted was real, and not the result of a bribe. (Chao Chun herself said, "Gold cannot buy the face of a Han Empress."[5] But what an unspeakable shock the resulting picture must have been!)

The man had once seen a woman holding a lovely fan and fallen in love with her. It was on his way home from Tadasu. Intrigued by the sound of a lute, he had peered over the earthen wall surrounding a certain house, curious who might be living there. He saw a woman sitting all alone, weeping. Her figure looked like the bending branches of a willow at twilight. In comparison to her, prints seemed not so interesting after all. He felt something for her he had never felt before.

It was a different form of love, but this yearning for Sanzaburō somehow seemed to him more attainable. And yet, because he suffered the tribulations of being a masterless samurai, it was all he could do to pay for the cramped rented quarters that protected him from the morning breezes and evening rains. Gazing out of his window, he realized how greatly his feelings for Sanzaburō had grown. His breast smoldered like the plume of smoke at Mt. Fuji's crater, and his tears flowed into the waves of the Fukagawa River. He wrung out his sleeves, always wet lately, and began making tobacco pouches of tie-dyed cloth. This was his means of livelihood. He walked around the boat docks selling his wares so that he could afford to pay the entrance fee to see Sanzaburō perform every day.

This particular day, he went into the theater as they announced, "Takii Sanzaburō will be appearing in the next play." He leaned against the *shite* column[6] near center stage to view the one-act play with a humorous monologue by the jester Bandō Matajirō[7] and jokes by Mannōgan Gorōbei.[8] That day, they were given a different routine at the last minute and confused some of their lines. Sanzaburō also stumbled slightly on his words at a certain point.

From the bottom of the stands on the south side of the theater came a voice. "Get off the stage!"

Immediately, the masterless samurai shot back, "Shut up!"

"No, I won't shut up!" the voice answered. "Take Sanzaburō off the stage!"

The audience was furious at the man for making such a terrible fuss at the best part of the play. With his dark complexion and full beard, they recognized him instantly as Niō Dansuke, a perennial troublemaker well known throughout the Kantō region. He swept his eyes belligerently over the crowd. Since people feared him, he felt encouraged to increase his tirade of abuse against the boy. Sanzaburō's face flushed slightly during the play as he stared angrily at the man. In his entire stage career, this was the first time he had ever been told to leave the stage.

Shortly, the play came to an end and the audience filed out of the theater. The masterless samurai followed stealthily after the man who had insulted Sanzaburō, and when they reached a fairly deserted section of Hamamachi, he wheeled around in front of him and shouted, "Was it you who demanded that Sanzaburō leave the stage?"

Without even giving the man a chance to put his hand to the hilt of his sword, the masterless samurai cut him down with one swift stroke. Merchants and farmers, fearful of the blade, pulled their pack horses out of the way and unwittingly cooperated in his escape. He sought shelter in a house on a side alley where, as fate would have it, Sanzaburō's personal attendant was living. Naturally the attendant hid him there, though doing so meant certain death if discovered.

After nightfall, Sanzaburō came in secret to thank the man.

"You risked much for my sake," he said. "It makes me very happy." Then, dressed just as he was, the boy gave himself to him in a bond of love.

Later, he satisfied the man's wishes by exchanging written vows. The man grew to be very dear to him, and before long Sanzaburō lost all interest in the work he did for a living. Eventually, he gave it all up for the masterless samurai.

Nothing is as unpredictable as human life. The man was a native of Hamada in Iwami where his widowed mother still lived. One day he received a letter written in another person's hand saying that she was near death. The minute he read it, he spoke to Sanzaburō and convinced the boy that, under the circumstances, he had no choice but to go visit her. They bid each other a tearful farewell.

Sanzaburō never heard from him again.

The boy grieved and grew despondent. During the day he yearned for the man, and at night he merely tried to survive his loneliness until morning. His face grew thin and his figure lost its former beauty. Soon, he took to bed. As so often happens in this floating world, like a blossom in full bloom pummeled by cruel rain, or the moon blocked from view by clouds and mist, he parted this life at the age of nineteen.

"His healthy complexion grew gaunt on his sickbed; his lovely body, as if in slumber, became the figure of one now dead. The pallor of his lovely flesh darkened, like petals falling in the wind."[9]

Those who saw it wrung the tears from their sleeves, while those who heard about it wept into their cuffs. "Weeds will grow in Kobiki,[10] and the forests turn white with grief.[11] Negi-chō[12] will become a den for wild boars." Thus they were left, bereft, to grieve.

A Secret Visit Leads to the Wrong Bed

An actor opens a face-powder shop.
Modern ladies imitate the actor Kichiya.
Her elder brother's unexpected pleasure.

"High-Quality Kichiya Face-Powder at Honest Prices." This sign appeared outside a new shop near the bridge where Shijō-dōri crosses the Takase River, and women of the capital with even the slightest blemish lined up to buy some on their way home.

"How does that shop manage to attract all of you lovely women without advertising?" someone asked.

"Why, that's the home of the Great Kichiya,[1] father of all actors of female roles. Business is flourishing because he is perfectly suited to such a job," they explained.

(Actually, it was because the only way that women can attain beauty is by painting their plain faces!)

Male actors of female roles in the old days of Ukon[2] and Sakon[3] were not particularly concerned about looking like women. They simply placed towels on their heads and applied some rough makeup, and theater-goers used their imaginations to fill in the rest. The scenarios, too, were terrible by today's standards.

Nowadays, provincial ladies try to imitate women of the capital in their manner and hide their natural defects by means of careful grooming. Only the mirrors they use every day from morning to dusk are aware of the truth.

Kichiya had been stunningly beautiful as a boy. Then, as a young actor, he polished his natural beauty with all the good things money could buy and effortlessly reached the rank of *tayū*. His skin seemed to cast off the sheen of a silver piece. There was no use in hunting on the dry riverbed at Shijō anymore, for everyone had grown bored with cheap thrills and went instead to spend time with this lovely youth.

As a result, Kichiya began to pay even more attention to his appearance. On the eighteenth day of the month when cherries bloom, he went to a certain house in Gion-machi where he sat behind a bamboo blind to observe in secret how real women of the capital dressed, hoping to find something interesting he could introduce into his own wardrobe. He was enthralled with the dappled robes and free-falling hair that women let show from the windows of their palanquins as they passed. His spirit all but leapt out at them. Perhaps not all were great beauties, but he doubted that any were truly ugly. (The rich have an advantage over the poor because they can afford such tantalizing displays. Thank goodness for Yang Kuei Fei face-powder!)

He spotted one woman who seemed very attractive from a distance, but on closer inspection her face looked as if it were the repository for all the pockmarks in the world. Of all the ugly faces he had ever seen, hers was remarkable in that it lacked a single redeeming feature. Her figure, however, and the style of her knotted sash, were incomparable.

"Who is she?" he asked.

There was a man who regularly went outside the capital selling salt door-to-door, and he recalled having seen her once before.

"She's the daughter of a popular dye-works merchant in Higashi-no-tōin. She's famous for her figure; they call her 'Shapely Oshun,' " he said.

Kichiya, in imitation, took an eight-foot sash and sewed lead weights into the corners, thus introducing to the world the "Kichiya knot," a style that remains popular to this day.

One time, Kichiya received word from the house of a certain noble personage to come dressed in his stage costume. Work was work, he told himself, and when it grew dark he secretly boarded a palanquin sent to take him there. When they neared the main gate of the house, the palanquin bearers extinguished the lamps they carried, emblazoned with the house's crest.

Security was strict. A lady whose love-making days were obviously long since past came out to meet him. She took Kichiya's hand to show him the way. He felt uneasy at first but realized that love took many guises and so allowed her to lead him inside. To the gatekeeper's drowsy question, the old lady replied, "One woman," and her answer was duly noted in the ledger. Once past the gate, they walked about a hundred *ken* on a sand path lined with trees until they reached the middle gate. Colorful pebbles covered the banks of a man-made stream to the left and glistened like a seashore of jewels in the light of stone lanterns placed between the trees. Several birds were kept there in cages, and though it was night, some were singing. Kichiya looked closely and could see a white Chinese pheasant sleeping under a dead tree, an owl puffed up wide awake on a branch, and a parrot perched asleep nearby.

Quietly, they climbed a stairway and came to a pair of doors made of precious wood. The doors were painted with bush clover so realistic that it looked as if Miyagino[4] had been transported there. They opened the doors and proceeded on tip-toe down a long hallway. Kichiya could hear the laughter of female voices, sounds of a *sugoroku* game,[5] and in the distance the gentle echo of koto and flute. His excitement mounted uncontrollably as they walked quietly through an unlighted reception hall and came out onto a plank-board veranda. They passed through several curtained doorways and finally came to a sliding door covered with silk. Nearby hung a red tassled cord. The old lady tugged at it. Kichiya could hear the pretty ringing of a bell on the other side.

Suddenly, there was a clatter of many footsteps, along with the crash of a folding screen and the sound of an incense box being kicked over.

"He's here!"

"It's Kichiya!"

The ladies rushed forward, curious, to look at him. It had been a long time since most of them had seen a man, and they seemed to go suddenly and uncontrollably mad. Some of them were so excited that they turned pale with desire. It was truly vulgar behavior. A lady-in-waiting who seemed to be in charge managed to calm them and then led Kichiya into the innermost room, where he found a stunningly lovely princess sitting all by herself. It was impossible for him to think of words to describe her beauty.

Cups made of gold and silver were brought out, and the princess excitedly began entertaining him with sake. Just then, a female servant came rushing in.

"Look out! He has just returned!" she cried, extinguishing the candles and darkening the room. There was nowhere for Kichiya to hide, so they tried to smuggle him out with a group of women, but the nobleman noticed him.

"Who is she?"

"My dance and singing teacher," the princess said.

"She is unusually attractive for a commoner." He decided to make her his own for the night.

He did not hesitate to begin love-making immediately. Kichiya, unable to reject his advances, was in a quandary. Having no other recourse, he removed his lady's wig and showed himself to the nobleman.

"Why, this is even better!" the gentleman said when he saw him, and proceeded to give Kichiya the full measure of his affection. The boy remained in the gentleman's bed until dawn the next morning, much to the chagrin (one would suspect) of his younger sister, the princess.

A Terrible Shame He Never Performed in the Capital

The young star Heihachi, unequaled in ancient and modern times.
He calls out his own name in a drunken dream.
Female passion takes his life on the 30th day.

Kyoto may have mountains covered with cherries in bloom, but I would rather show you the sea in Osaka where Suzuki Heihachi's[1] lively performances brought the beauty of boy love to the theater stage. One might travel the entire land and never see another actor like him. Could such beauty have existed even in China? They say that Su Shih[2] went on an outing to the Red Cliffs[3] at dusk and caught some fish there in his net. They reminded him of Sung-kiang sea bass, though not half as good, and he ate them and drank wine until dawn. Surely, if Su Shih had spent that night with Suzuki Heihachi as his drinking companion, he would never have written, "In the East, Day Begins to Break," but would have called it moonlight and made the night last forever. What a terrible shame the boy never performed in China, either.

There was no one who matched Heihachi in beauty. With a single glance, wisemen and fools, noblemen and commoners, all fell in love and became like children again, swinging their arms and jumping with glee. Those who shared his bed lost interest in their wives and children, such was his power over men. Suffice it to say, he was everything people said he was, and more. He had a remarkable ability to play any role to perfection and excelled especially in warrior roles, something to be expected since he bore the same name as the famed Fujishiro elder.[4]

One spring day in this Jōkyō Era,[5] Heihachi starred in a wildly popular play called "Tariki Honganki."[6] It attracted huge crowds of spectators who fell into the abyss of his love. They reached out to grasp the cord extending from his holy hand as if he were Amitabha come to welcome their eager souls to paradise.[7] Even his lines echoed like the golden words of the Buddha in their ears.

In those days, it was impossible to find a single palanquin bearer in the vicinity of Nipponbashi after two in the afternoon because theater-goers from remote villages in Yamato, Kawachi, and Izumi were on their way home. Among them were farmers' wives in short-sleeved robes of barley-husk weave proudly wearing gaudy appliquéd sashes tied around their waists. They had abandoned their farm chores and prettied themselves up for a day at the moat.[8] Now, on their way home, they chattered about the day's play with a studied shake of their hips. It had been years since such huge crowds gathered from villages outside the city, and it was all due to the infatuating beauty of this one actor, Suzuki Heihachi. They suffered and yearned for his love. No one knows how many brokenhearted men and women ultimately passed away like the evening dew.

On the third day of the third month,[9] even the boys from the blacksmith shop were dismissed to enjoy themselves at Tennō-ji, Kiyomizu, and Shioi. The upper classes, too, dressed up in their finery and set out ostensibly for Sumiyoshi Shrine, but actually to go to the theater to see Heihachi. Their drooling raised the water level of the moat, and their noses so perked up when they caught his scent that they could have flown kites from their long nostril hairs. They were so gripped by his acting that their tobacco pipes seemed to melt in their steamy hands. Ignoring the crook in their necks, they strained for a better look and shouted noisy words of praise. The place was filled to capacity with men in love with the boy. There were also women, among them an old lady one year short of a hundred with newly cut hair, and a nun in black robes with her hair shaved to the roots. Their inner passion for the boy was plainly visible on their faces, a laughable (if disconcerting) thing to see.

There was one other woman in the gallery, in the third box on the east side, who was surrounded with screens and attendants. She seemed to be from a well-placed family and was just past the age when girls wear their hair rolled up on their heads. Her figure and

face were quite attractive. She seemed to have reached that time in
life when young women acquire a natural interest in men and are
eager to learn about love. (Perhaps she already had plenty of experience of that sort, I don't know.) She watched Heihachi steadily
with a smile of rapture on her lips from the beginning of the two-
act play. Her love for him seemed so intense, if the theater had
been empty she would surely have run up and embraced him. I
watched her with mixed feelings of amusement and pity.

Time passed, and soon it was time for the play to end. The girl's
face took on a pained expression, as if she were overwhelmed with
grief at the thought of bidding Heihachi farewell. The play ended,
and she watched intently as he exited via the walkway. In her
excess of passion, she fainted dead away. Her attendants' frantic
cries for water and medicine were muffled by the drumbeat signaling the end of the day's performance and the noisy crush of
people getting up to leave. Being the man I am and well acquainted
with the ways of love, I half expected something of the sort to
happen. Sympathizing with the girl's plight, I leapt up to the gallery with my medicine pouch a-dangling and proceeded to play the
doctor. I gave her some *enreitan* [10] that I had received as a New
Year's gift and she soon resumed breathing. They put her in a
carriage and took her home immediately. (I learned her address,
but will refrain from including it here.)

She turned out to be the daughter of a certain couple who treasured her as if she were cherry blossoms and the moon combined.
When this strange disease began tormenting her in her waking and
sleeping hours, her parents exhausted the medical arts for a cure,
but since the source of her problem was in the theater there was no
help for her. She grew weak and gradually lost her beauty until no
one could bear to look at her anymore. If she had been able to talk
about what was bothering her, perhaps she could have kept her life
(if not her reputation), but instead she stubbornly refused to reveal
the cause of her heartbreak. On the eighth day of the third month,
like a blossom that falls before flowering, she passed away. The
grief and sorrow of her parents was terrible.

That day, Heihachi had gone to Sakata Gin'emon's [11] to hear
Takemoto Gidayū, [12] Iori, [13] and others recite *jōruri*. Toward eve-

ning, he quietly returned home. Although it was already spring, an autumn-like wind was blowing that chilled him to the bone. In the morning he felt ill and weak, and by evening he was writhing in agony. We gradually accepted that he might not have long to live. Among those who came to visit him at his sickbed was Sakura-yama Rinnosuke,[14] who was especially grieved. Remembering their years of love together, he swore that if Heihachi should die, they would die together. Uemura Kichiya[15] happened to be in Osaka from Kyoto and went to bid Heihachi farewell. Though gaunt and breathing with difficulty, Heihachi properly thanked him for coming and shared a tearful cup of sake with him in parting.

People were not aware of it, but Heihachi had frequently given himself for love, not pay, to men who yearned for him. On many occasions he had slashed his arms and cut his thighs to prove the sincerity of his love. Once, when a farmer cut off his finger and threw it onto the stage, Heihachi had handled the matter magnificently, increasing the good repute of boy love by his actions. His heart was always prepared for any eventuality; such a youth seemed too good to be an actor. In the course of his stage career, he must have received hundreds of offers of love. Once, in his youth, he had written down the names of five men in a formal contract that read, "I swear to give myself once to each of the above stated men, at a time of their choosing." Strange that he should make such a promise. (That group of fault-finders must have discovered something that he wanted kept quiet.)

Heihachi was pleasing in every way. His equal will never be found even in the world to come. His acting skill in the arts of war and love were unsurpassed by any actor, ancient or modern. He was a worthy model for all the boys of Japan to emulate. If they were to follow his example, they could not go wrong.

Alas, days passed and his strength left him. It was just as the old poem said:

> The Body Grows Cold,
> Emptied of Its Spirit,
> And Is Sent to the Barren Field.[16]

Seeing this happen before our very eyes, our sorrow grew unbearable. Even life-restoring drugs were powerless. When it seemed the end was near, we prayed in desperation for his salvation, fingering the beads of a long rosary, and had priests read 1,000 volumes of Dharani.[17] But the sutra's power to extend his fated lifespan was unequal to the power of love's desire.

Heihachi's only words at the end were, "I can see a phantom, the figure of an exquisitely lovely girl." On the eighth day of the intercalary third month,[18] his breathing finally ceased.

They say that a single unfulfilled desire lasts through 500 rebirths. It was then that we realized he had been possessed by a spirit of passion. In his 23rd year, like the moon just rising over the mountain's edge at Higashiyama, his sudden setting in the west grieved us all.

**SECTION
SEVEN**

$== 7:1 ==$

Fireflies Also Work Their Asses at Night

The capital's moon and blossoms: Yoshida Iori
and Fujimura Handayū.
A stealthy visitor questioned on a rainy night makes no reply.
Someone places new flowers at the altar of Buddha.

There is nothing in this world more painful than making a living.
To do any job well requires hard work, but the most difficult I
have ever seen (and I have seen many) is that of the drum-holder[1]
in the pleasure quarter, for his success depends on patience and
forbearance in the face of impossible provocation.

One time I had the opportunity to see the actors Yoshida Iori[2]
and Fujimura Handayū[3] of Murayama Matabei's troupe together
side by side at a party at Ōtsuruya in Ishigaki-machi.[4] My immediate reaction was that they are unequaled in the present-day world
of theater. Their figures were just like those of famous beauties of
ancient times preserved for us in paintings. All those who saw them
dance in the latest style went mad with desire.

The skill of these two in entertaining patrons was especially
remarkable. Playful and affectionate, they were pliant without be-

ing weak. Even while seeming to follow the patron's lead, they continued to make sure that everything was going smoothly. Once in bed, Iori would say all sorts of pleasing things to his adversary,[5] and before long the gentleman on the pillow would forget both life and fortune in his frenzied excitement. Handayū used a different approach, however. He said not a word after getting into bed and refused to snuggle up close, always making the gentleman wonder uncomfortably what he had done wrong. Just when the man's discomfort began to turn to annoyance, Handayū would whisper a single happy suggestion, one the man would remember for the rest of his life. If you were to teach this method to any other boy, he could never learn to do it right. These two could flatter and seduce even the pros with their lies, they were so utterly convincing.

"There are 31 boy actors in the capital today and they all go for the same price, so you'd be a fool not to ask for these two."

"If you have any gold or silver saved up, you should spend it on a boy. Leave it to your son and he may prove to be a thrifty dolt who would live his whole life without ever buying a kabuki actor. Imagine your hard-earned money lying in the corner of a safe, never to experience life's pleasures. Why, even money itself would regret being left to rot away like that."

"Why is it that men like us who have the proper perspective on things and know how to use money are always without it? Life is certainly unfair."

Thus, entertainers[6] from Gion-machi could be heard complaining among themselves.

Before long, Kagura Shōzaemon[7] began whistling a melody from night *kagura*.[8] To this accompaniment, each of the other drum-holders performed in turn whatever feat of skill struck his fancy. Their antics surpassed even those of actors onstage. Our laughter could not wait until later; we held our sides and howled uproariously.

One of the drum-holders at this party was Muraoka Tannyū, once the respected son of a certain man of importance. He was talented, lived well, and was liked for his generous nature, but as so often happens in this floating world he squandered the family fortune and was reduced to selling calligraphy manuals in the

Ōhashi style near the intersection of Shita-tachi-uri and Horikawa. The business failed to prosper, however. Next, he put out a sign advertising himself as an acupuncturist, but no one called for his services. In dire straits and desperate for money, he took to entertaining wealthy patrons in the pleasure quarter. On that day, he had been summoned to this party.

Tannyū was annoyed that the table for his meal was the last to be brought out. To compound the offense, the gentleman hosting the party shed his outer robe and kicked it into the next room, ordering him to fold it. Tannyū was in no position to refuse, so he did as he was told. Then the man sent him to empty an ashtray. Having no other recourse, he was about to oblige when suddenly the other drum-holders jumped on him and tied him up. They pretended he was the "thief from Narutaki"⁹ and dragged him around the room. Tannyū knew that they were doing it to entertain the gentleman, but he could not control his anger. He swore that when they untied the rope he would kill two or three of them and then show how nobly he could die.

Just then, the gentleman took four or five Chōtoku-ji coins¹⁰ from his packet of tissues and scattered them on the floor. This was Tannyū's reward for the teasing he had just suffered. When he saw the glittering objects thrown at him, his mood changed completely.

"Really sir, you are too generous!" he said shamelessly, his greed making him forget the humiliation he had just experienced. From that moment he hid his talent and intelligence and simply played the idiot, slavishly pandering to the foolish gentleman's every whim. He exhausted every word of flattery in the language until he himself could hardly bear it anymore. Even the young actor who had been bought to be Tannyū's bed-fellow for the night made his contempt for him obvious. No one knew it, but later poor Tannyū had to all but worship the boy before he was allowed to untie the youngster's sash.

Because Tannyū was without influential friends at the party, he had been treated brusquely when he checked his sandals at the entrance. Later, on his way out, he found one sandal here, one sandal over there, and had to rush on foot to keep up with the gentleman in his fast palanquin. It is strange that even among res-

idents of the capital there should be such a variety of ways to make
a living.

Though the wares he sold were different, a working boy like
Handayū was in an equally painful occupation. The previous day,
for example, he was forced to drink from sunset to late at night
with a stubborn country samurai who took a liking to him, and
today he had to work again, this time bought by a group of seven
or eight pilgrims on their way to Ise. Sleeping partners were decided in secret by drawing straws, and as luck would have it he
was assigned to a repulsive old man, even though there were others
among them he actually found attractive.

From the start, the old man was leaning all over him and strok-
ing him with his long fingernails without a thought for how it
messed up his hair. He brought his mouth close to Handayū's for

a kiss. Obviously, the man had never used a toothbrush in his life.
The boy cowered from the coarse touch of the man's cotton underrobe and tried to plug his nose against the musty stench of deerskin
socks that clung to the man's feet. Then, without any sense of the
finer aspects of boy love, the man began to fumble with his own
loincloth. For the sake of money, the boy had no recourse but to
let the old man have his way, though he satisfied him with the
secret thigh technique.[11] Between nightfall and when they got up
and parted, the boy must have aged years with worry that his deception would be discovered.

And none of this effort brought him any financial gain; it all
went into his proprietor's coffers, which made the work even less
agreeable. What made it possible for him to forget the agony of the
job were those moments when he saw the love-lorn faces of men

and women gazing after him on his way home and could hear their countless cries of admiration. It filled him with a sense of pleasure and pride in his own beauty, and this alone made him willing to bear his bone-grinding regimen. When you think of it, he resembled a beautiful woman. His wares were different, but otherwise he was exactly like a courtesan.

One night, the faint sound of an early summer rain echoed on the shingled roof overhead where Handayū was entertaining a familiar group of patrons until dawn. They had downed a vast quantity of chilled sake in their second-floor room at the Ōtsuruya and were presently arguing among themselves whether the bell just now had tolled eight times or seven.[12]

"Well, shall we make an attempt to leave?" someone finally suggested.

Just then, two or three fireflies entered through a lattice-work window, rekindling excitement in the room. They seemed accustomed to people and flew around the room, their glow rivaling the lamplight. One of them came to rest on Handayū's sleeve.

"'I am just like the firefly,'" Handayū said, quoting from the *michiyuki* scene in the play "Heianjō."[13] The roomful of patrons was somewhat taken aback and laughed awkwardly.

"You may be right. This firefly's work also involves using its ass," someone said rudely.

"But it shines only at night and rests during daylight hours. I am envious. Here I am, working until dawn, and yet I must be on the stage all day again tomorrow. It's not fair." Handayū was blunt with his complaint.

More and more fireflies appeared in a frenzied tumult. Curious as to where they were coming from, someone went out to take a look. In cover of darkness, a priest wearing a sedge hat was releasing fireflies one by one from a thin paper package hidden inside the sleeve of his black-dyed robe. It was apparently meant to please someone there in the room. They were reminded of that incident long ago when fireflies were slipped into a certain lady's carriage.[14] It seemed suspiciously like a confession of love (done, I might add, with unusual refinement).

When the man came back and reported what he had seen, Handayū began to weep even as he listened.

"The same thing has happened before," he said. "A man of religion was coming in secret every night to my proprietor's house to release fireflies, or so I was told. Everyone wondered who they were intended for, and now I realize that they were meant for me. I am overjoyed. Please, allow me at least to share a cup of sake with him."

When the priest heard this, he fled. They could hear the clatter of his clogs on the stone wall as he rushed away; then, it seemed he lost his footing, for he fell with a splash into the normally shallow river. Swollen now with constant rains, it was a raging torrent. By the time they rushed out to the spot, he was gone without a trace. The men were left standing there, desolate and grief-stricken.

From that time on, Handayū suffered with thoughts of the priest he had never met. He lived each day in sorrow.

Some time later a certain gentleman fell deeply in love with Handayū and ransomed him from his contract at the theater. He set up residence in Kamisuki-chō near the Great Buddha, but Handayū still found it impossible to forget the love of that priest. Finally, he went into seclusion at Makino-o and took the tonsure.

His piety was admirable. Morning and evening he faithfully recited the sutras and purified his inner soul. He stayed up all night to build religious discipline in himself, but whenever he quietly drifted into a slumber the priest would appear to him and converse affectionately. It gave him the greatest joy. When he awoke, the figure faded, but as soon as he fell asleep it appeared again vividly, albeit in his dreams. To comfort the boy, the priest brought new flowers every day that he had plucked from among those that bloomed in each of the four seasons on the mountain paths, and placed them as an offering on the altar before the figure of the Buddha. Handayū told someone about this, but the man refused to believe him and insisted on spending a night in his bed at the temple.

Later, the man reported that although he had seen no priest, the flowers were indeed changed in the morning.

An Onnagata's Tosa Diary

That year's gossip: this amputated finger.
A wonderful party hunting for mushrooms at Mt. Chausu.
The fans Han'ya sells stir up more than a breeze.

A new fan shop called Izutsuya opened in the northwest corner of Tatamiya-chō in Dōtombori. It was run by the actor Matsushima Han'ya[1] who, like a flower in full bloom or the moon at its brightest, foolishly underwent the coming-of-age ceremony at his peak of youthful beauty and changed his name to Shichizaemon. His attendants in the quarter regretted it terribly.

When just a bud in the way of boy love, this youth was already as beautiful as the diving girls of Matsushima and Ojima islands. Moreover, he was deeply affectionate and sophisticated at entertaining his patrons; he excelled in the serving of sake. No other actor could even approach his love letters in style.

In winter, when daffodils were in forced bloom, he invited guests to his house for a private party and broke the seal on a jar of Yuki-mukashi tea. In spring he painted the falling cherry blossoms with his brush and composed poems in the ancient style. On quiet rainy nights in early summer he burned Hatsune incense, to the great pleasure of those waiting to hear the nightingale's call. In autumn he spent his time reading books and gazing all night at the moon. Thus, he cultivated each of the disciplines in himself and excelled in them all. He was, in particular, by birth so skilled in love-making that he could almost kill a man with pleasure. Even those who met him only infrequently found it impossible to forget those rare occasions. Great numbers of men, driven by relentless desire, visited him over and over again until they fell into a moat of debt.

A purple kerchief was the typical head gear for male actors of the day, but he was the first to wear one of pale-blue silk crepe. It made him all the more lovely. Offstage, he dressed in subdued colors, a black double-lined robe over a white underrobe of silk, something no other boy actor could have carried off successfully. But perhaps the boy's primary point of attraction was his generous nature. He never touched those heavy golden objects that most people craved, and he was completely lacking in vulgar greed.

I once went to visit an actor at the season of the Bon Festival to pay my mid-year debts and found him haggling with a fishmonger who accused him of cheating. He had paid for a mackerel with four silver *momme* that the man weighed and found short by two *bu* and five *rin*. As if such petty cheating were not ugly enough, the boy had come out to make his purchase wearing nothing but an old, soiled loincloth of the type woven in the village of Katsuma. Perhaps he thought no one would notice. I certainly wish it had been at night so that I could have been spared the sight.

When you compare such an actor with Han'ya, the vast differences that exist among working boys become readily apparent. Some are rushed, others calm and unhurried, as different as New Year's Eve and New Year's Day. The older one gets, the more unpleasantness one must witness through the passing years. (I told Hiragi Hyōshirō[2] about this, and we had a good laugh.)

One day, Han'ya was to entertain a gentleman named Doko and so requested that they go to Mt. Chausu in Naniwa, one of his favorite places. When the group arrived, they found it very different from when they had been there in the spring to view cherry blossoms. Autumn had its own special flavor, and the voices of myriad insects made them poignantly aware of life's sadness. Near a pond to the south they set up their curtains and soon their drunken faces vied with the color of sunset over the Sea of Nago. Full of sake, they argued about this and that and soon found that they had eaten all the food brought to accompany their drink.

"What can we do if we have nothing to eat?" someone said in disappointment.

Just then a group of four or five children from a nearby village appeared, each carrying a large bamboo basket.

"What are you doing?" the men asked them.

"Hunting for mushrooms," they replied.

"How could there be mushrooms in such a sparsely wooded place?" the men thought to themselves, but sure enough, when they parted the leaves of the dayflowers and looked among the colorful fallen leaves, they found mushrooms here and there, caps tilted to the side. They gathered as many as they could and immediately roasted them over a fire of pine needles. Dipping them into the fragrant juice of bitter lemon, they ate them with gasps of delight at the delicious flavor.

But wait! One year, they had taken Komatsu Handayū[3] mushroom-hunting to Amano where the same thing happened. It had been an exceptional party; bearded Han'emon had sung a verse from the still popular "mushroom song," and Utayama Harunojō[4] had joined in the revelry. This limitless supply of mushrooms was but a sign of the host, Han'ya's, remarkable perceptivity; he had sent people the night before to plant them in the fields! How clever of him, they thought with admiration.

Han'ya was an intelligent actor who thought out carefully each role he played. He made sure that onstage even the way he said a little word like "hello" was attractive. It would be no exaggeration to call him an actor of female roles without rival in past or present.

Early in the fourth month, when he was first taken on at the Araki Theater, Han'ya was performing in an unusual play dressed in a lovely orange-pattern robe with long sleeves. The audience was enraptured by his voice, like the song of a long-awaited nightingale, when halfway through the play a rustic-looking man climbed up onto the stage from one corner of the area where everyone sat.

"Master Han'ya," he called. "It is brazen of me to love you as I do, but please accept this as proof of my sincerity."

With these words he drew his sword, pressed the little finger of his left hand to the floor, and calmly cut it off with five or six strokes of his blade. He then wrapped it in a piece of paper and handed it to Han'ya, who quietly accepted it.

"I am honored by your love for me and promise not to disappoint you. Since we are in the middle of the play, please go backstage and wait for me there." But even as Han'ya spoke he lost sight of the man in the crowd. "Be sure to come visit me at my house later, then," he called out in parting.

Han'ya would not let anyone else touch the finger, but washed it himself until the bleeding stopped. He then wrapped it carefully and placed it in the breast of his robe. His sensitivity was obvious to all who saw it, and he met with nothing but praise wherever the story was spoken. An incident of this sort was unheard of in the history of kabuki.

Han'ya returned home and prepared his bed, perfumed his sleeves with burnt incense, and waited all that night for the man. Finally, at about the time the dawn bell tolled at Tetsugen, he fell into a light slumber. The morning sky gradually began to get brighter, and just when it was light enough to distinguish people's faces, the man of the day before came with a friend to visit. Han'ya greeted them warmly and said many things that should have made the man feel overjoyed, but he only trembled and expressed his gratitude over and over while hanging his head with embarrassment. Han'ya was very touched by his innocence.

The man's companion explained the extent of his feelings for the boy. Han'ya held back his tears and gave himself to the man, taking his hand in his. He attempted to start love-making, but the man would not even go to the small room Han'ya had prepared for them. They exchanged cups of sake, but the minute they finished he got up to leave, ignoring Han'ya's pleas for him to stay. Han'ya was full of lingering emotions.

"Until we meet again, this is something to remember me by," Han'ya said. He gave the man a pale-blue lined kimono of beaten silk and a medium-length short sword made by Kanemitsu in the richly ornamented style of a daimyo's sword.

Han'ya inquired in secret about the man's homeland and learned that he was from Tosa. "But you must say your farewells now. His boat is about to depart." The voice rose into the wind with the sails.

The boat set out from Ichinosu at the mouth of the river. The man's tears must have outnumbered the frothy jewels on the waves. That day, the wind changed direction at Ashinoura and they were forced to tie up at a place called Sangen'ya. Overwhelmed with loneliness that evening, the man filled the deep well of his inkstone and began to write down his thoughts of the boy in a diary.

It was the fifth day of the fourth month. The evening moon was shaped just like one of the ladies' hair combs that Master Han'ya wore. Before he could shake off the delusion, a passing shower drenched his sleeves. The tapping of the mud hen's mating call sounded to him like the beating of the drum in the theater turret. The place was Nambajima, to be sure, but his heart had not left Dōtombori. Even the fireflies reminded him of street boys, their lights reflecting on the surface of (strangely enough!) Shirinashi River.[5]

On the next day, the sixth, there was a strong morning breeze, so they lifted anchor and put the helm to port. Skirting the shore, they passed Amagasaki and reached open sea at Naruo, where they caught the wind in their sails once again. He spotted the shrine at

Hirota and felt as if he were crossing the bridge of dreams. The boat at last neared Cape Wada. For a while he managed to forget his sorrow, but when he saw Mt. Muko only half visible through the clouds he recalled Han'ya once again.[6] His feelings were more than he could bear and burned uncontrollably in his breast.

Paddle-wheel pleasure boats moved noisily through the water around them as they passed Tsuno-no-Matsubara and neared Susa Inlet. Toward dusk they went ashore at Hyōgo Bay and had a bath heated for their enjoyment. The man washed Han'ya's lingering fragrance from his hair and afterwards perfumed himself again with the famed incense called Hatsuse, a keepsake from the boy. But the fragrance only served to make him miss Han'ya more.

On the seventh they sailed all night after a hurried departure. He was upset because in the rush he had forgotten his traveling pipe at the rented lodgings. Smoke no longer rose over the salt-makers' huts on shore, making the night lonely and forlorn. He stared toward the coast line, wondering if they might be passing Ueno in Suma at that moment. As dawn broke feebly in the east, they all bowed in worship towards the shrine of Hitomaru. After tying up at Akashi they were caught in a sudden shower and had to cover themselves with matting against the rain. The man joy-fully took the downpour as a sign that he would soon hear the song of a nightingale and waited expectantly, wishing all the while that he might hear the voice of that boy instead. Everything seemed to remind him of Han'ya.

On the eighth day, they remained in the same place. His thoughts of the boy continued.

On the ninth and morning of the tenth they sailed past the stop at Karakoto Harbor in Bizen Province and reached Seto. As they passed Mushiake, the man thought of the poem left behind by Lady Asukai[7] on a fan, saying how dearly she missed the capital. It reminded him of the pattern of fans inscribed with old poems that Han'ya wore on his robe. The waves and breeze grew still.

On the eleventh they sailed all day and entered the cove at Tomo-no-ura in Bingo Province. Everyone aboard went ashore. He did not want to spend his time alone in the boat, so he accom-panied them. There was a pleasure quarter in the town, but the courtesans there did not look much better than common street-walkers. They were just now learning the songs like "Springtime Mountain Road" that had long since lost popularity in the capital. Their dancing, too, was ridiculous to watch. He finally had to get up and leave. Since he was utterly bored with even the shapeliest of courtesans, the thought of satisfying himself with one of these common creatures made his flesh crawl.

He reboarded the boat and was relieved when they were once again on their way west under clear skies.

At Kazabaya-ura, from late on the twelfth, the man grew restless and depressed. He lost all awareness of his surroundings and writhed in agony, obsessed with visions of Matsushima's face. Soon he was raving mad. The sailors feared for the boat's safety and decided that he should be put ashore. They asked the owner of a lean-to on the beach to look after him and left two of his companions with him. The men did everything they could to relieve his suffering, but it was no use. His condition grew progressively worse, as if his body were burning itself up.

Alas, perhaps he should never have accepted those mementos from the boy, for with the very sword that Han'ya had given him when they parted in Naniwa he now took his own life. His blood stained the grasses and weeds where his dead body fell at the wayside.

The feelings of this man who died for love remain behind, along with his fame, preserved in this diary. Like the well of a Tosa inkstone,[8] his love was deep indeed.

An Unworn Robe to Remember Him by

The Jizō of safe childbirth does not lie.
Putting the crested toothpick of their favorite actor to their lips.
Cremation at dawn on the second day of the first month.

A man dressed a monkey in trousers and displayed a sign near the intersection at Ebisu Bridge that read, "Original Floating-World Toothpicks." There, he sold toothpicks carved with the crests of young kabuki actors. Anyone who could not afford to pay for a night with the boy of his dreams could at least pick up one of these crested toothpicks to relieve the yearning in his breast. Unfortunately, when they cleaned their teeth with the toothpicks, they felt as if the lovely lips of the boy they loved were pressed to theirs, thus aggravating their frustration. A love so strong would normally cost a man his life; he would die like frost that disappears with the first rays of the morning sun. In this case, however, since working boys were available for the viewing pleasure of anyone who could pay the fee,[1] it was unnecessary for anyone to die of frustrated yearning.

Those fortunate enough to have been born in the three cities of Edo, Kyoto, and Osaka could see the faces of these boys every day and still never tire of them. For the people from distant provinces who rarely had the opportunity to see such boys, it was a miracle that they managed to return home alive afterwards. One of their rewards for traveling all the way to the capital district was to get hold of theater programs and actors' lists, which they would memorize and use later for spinning tales at night when they got back to their provinces.

In this world, there is nothing more painful than making a living. A man called Ningyōya no Shinroku lived at Shinsai-bashi in Dōtombori, where he made a variety of children's toys by hand, among them lion whistles, papier-mâché tigers, red demons with-

out loincloths, and thundergods lacking drums. All year long he
traveled to Tamba to sell his goods and on the way home shouldered a new burden of bamboo bark and coarse cloth. He never
observed holidays but was busy from New Year's Day straight
through to the last day of the year just keeping himself and his
wife fed. Just across the next bridge south of where he lived were
several permanent theaters,[2] but he had never once gone to see a
play there. He was a thrifty man who hated even to burn oil for
illumination.

One day, this man was overtaken by nightfall while still on the
road, far from any village. Clouds above Mt. Murakumo threatened rain and the wind blew noisily through the pines, making
him feel more and more forlorn. At last he reached a temple dedicated to Jizō,[3] guardian of safe childbirth, and spent the bitterly
cold night in the sanctuary. About midnight he was awakened by
the loud sound of a colt's bell. Thinking it might be a group of
travelers, he listened to what they were saying. He could see no
one, but the voices were clearly audible.

"Jizō. Jizō," it called out. "Aren't you coming to help with the
births tonight? It's me, Monjū,[4] from Kireto in Tango Province."

From behind the brocade curtain that housed the Jizō image
came a voice.

"I have an unexpected visitor staying with me tonight. Please
explain to the various gods and Bodhisattvas that I can't make it."

Then there was silence.

Toward dawn, the voice that identified itself as Monjū returned
once again.

"Last night, within the five provinces alone,[5] there were 12,116
safe births. Of these, 8,073 were baby girls. A hoped-for son was
delivered safely to the toothpick seller's wife in Dōtombori who is
under the protection of Mitsudera Hachiman in Settsu Province.
The mother is overjoyed and proudly eating miso soup and rice
cakes."

"How sad that she must remain unaware of her son's fate. This
child will grow up to be a lovely boy and later become an actor.
He will be a favorite with the theater-goers, but just when he
reaches his peak of popularity, on the second day of the first month

in his eighteenth year, he will end his brief life, like a dream at dawn, for the sake of his honor."

Shinroku clearly heard every word of the revelation. Before long the night sky grew light, so he got up and left the sanctuary of the New Six-Jizō[6] Temple.

When he returned home to Naniwa from Tamba he discovered that at the exact day and hour spoken by the voice, a son had been born to the toothpick seller who lived next door on the south side. Today was the sixth day after birth, so family members were gathered to celebrate the first shaving of the baby's head. Even then it was clear that the child had what it took to become an actor. His hair was already a deep black color and the shape of his neck and hairline were beautiful. They were sure that he would someday become a *tayū*[7] without peer.

He received the best of care throughout infancy and early childhood, and by the age of thirteen had acquired a knowledge of the ways of love. Men who saw him even briefly were immediately smitten, and because he was so skilled at love-making there were many who sought him. He went by the name of Togawa Hayanojō,[8] and appeared in Yamatoya Jimbei's[9] theater troupe. He was always much quicker than other actors when changing costumes between scenes in his youthful male roles. He was tutored in all of the various acting styles by Fujita Koheiji.[10] He so excelled in warrior pieces that people swore he would someday replace Onoe Gentarō.[11] Moreover, he was affectionate and well-trained in the subtleties of boy love. He never refused a proposition from an admirer, but no one knows the vast number of men he satisfied, since he always did so without stirring up gossip.

At some point, one of his fellow actors became his lover. It would be impossible to describe here every detail of their love for each other over the years and months, but this is the promise Hayanojō made: "I regret that I must continue to meet those wealthy patrons whose support for me is public knowledge, for it is my only means of livelihood. But I swear to you before the gods that I will never allow another man to so much as hold my hand, except when the script of a play requires it."

He never once strayed from this promise. In time, the patrons he took for pay began to abandon him one by one. He became increasingly devoted to his lover and this resulted in boring parties for them. Soon, not one remained. His accounts were in complete disorder, and though his attendant warned him that the bill-paying season was near, the boy continued without mending his ways. He just gazed at the moon, lost in his own thoughts, until the 22nd or 23rd day of the twelfth month. The moonlit nights turned into mornings, days passed, and soon the year came to a dark end.

Time for the first play of the New Year was already approaching, so he ordered beautiful stage costumes for the event, choosing the ones that would show off his best qualities.

"I'll wear these wonderful short-sleeved robes one on top of the other and give a private performance of my favorite play for my lover. I'll make sure that he weeps!" he thought excitedly. He could hardly wait for the New Year to dawn.

That night, the gifts from various quarters that his attendant had been counting on to help pay the bills failed to materialize. As a result, the accounts were completely off.

"How could those rich patrons who drank so greedily with him nineteen, twenty times fail to send him something now? I wish the demon of darkness who roams on the last night of the year would take a bite out of them. Since neither doctors nor actors are allowed to go out and collect their fees,[12] what am I to do?" At the last minute, Hayanojō's attendant found himself in a terrible quandary.

To the other bill collectors making their rounds, he claimed that the boy was not at home and thus postponed the problem until the morning, but the clothing merchant stubbornly refused to accept his excuses. But how could the attendant give something he did not have? The merchant rejected his promise to settle accounts by the middle of the month and cruelly insisted on taking everything, including the boy's everyday clothes, as collateral.

"What a heartless thing to do," the attendant said, but his angry words had no effect whatsoever. He was still wondering what to do next when he heard the sound of footsteps in new leather-soled sandals coming from the south. They belonged to boys from Imamiya selling New Year's talismans stamped with the figure of Ebisu. People's dress and manner had the feeling of spring. To the

east, the sun rose through the pines at Takatsu Shrine, looking
somehow different on this first day of the year. Hayanojō gazed
innocently at the scene and rinsed out his mouth with "water of
youth" at a stream from the moat in celebration of the New Year.
He was reciting a New Year's poem when Sakata Kodenji[13] and
Yamamoto Sagenda[14] appeared in lovely long-sleeved robes, looking like plum and cherry blossoms side by side.

"Hello!" they called out. "We are on our way to wish the theater
proprietor New Year's greetings. Care to join us?"

Overjoyed at the invitation, Hayanojō threw off the robe he
had been wearing all winter and said to his attendant, "Bring me
my pale-blue underrobe."

The attendant wanted to spare him the truth, so he said, "The sleeves were all measured wrong, so I sent them back for adjustment."

Quietly, the boy told his friends he would go later. It was painful for him to say so.

That day ended emptily.

The next day was the second, when the first play of the New Year would begin. The sound of the drum resounded, announcing the opening of the theater. Even before it was light enough to see faces clearly, apprentices from various artisan's shops were up preparing for a rare holiday at the theater. They all wore tattered five-crested robes, and their leather socks were far too small for their feet. Who cared if the seams were beginning to split? They walked hastily towards the theater, whispering to each other in urgent voices, "We're off to see Hayanojō onstage!"

When the three-part New Year's celebration was finished, a messenger came from the dressing room to say that the play would soon begin. Unfortunately, Hayanojō had no clothes. His attendant now had no choice but to tell him the truth. When he found out, the boy laughed and said, "Why is it that things never go as we wish in this floating world?"

The attendant watched him go up to the second floor. There, Hayanojō wrote a quick letter of farewell to his lover that hid the true reasons for his decision, and then ended his life. No matter how they grieved, the lovely youth would never return to them now.

He really need not have died. He was pushed to kill himself by an exaggerated sense of honor, something not even a samurai would have done in the circumstances. It will surely remain a topic of conversation for years to come.

One cannot defy fate. The boy died on the second day of the first month, just as the Jizō of safe childbirth had predicted.

Bamboo Clappers Strike the Hateful Number

A monk's hermitage papered with love letters.
Boy actors hide their age.
A pushy samurai loses his whiskers.

When being entertained by a kabuki boy actor, one must be careful never to ask his age.

It was late in autumn, and rain just light enough not to be unpleasant had been falling since early morning. It now lifted and the afternoon sun appeared below the clouds in the west, forming a rainbow over Higashiyama. Just then a group of boy actors appeared wearing wide-striped rainbow robes of satin. The most handsome among them was an actor in the Murayama theater troupe, a jewel that sparkled without need of polishing, named Tamamura Kichiya.[1] He was in the full flower of youth, and every person in the capital was in love with him.

On that particular day, a well-known lover of boys called Koromo-no-tana Shiroku had invited him to go mushroom-picking at Mt. Shiroyama in Fushimi, so a large group of actors and their spirited companions left Shijō-gawara and soon arrived at Hitsukawa. Leaves of the birch cherries, the subject of a long-ago poem,[2] had turned bright red, a sight more beautiful even than spring blossoms. After spending some time gazing at the scene, the group continued past the woods at Fuji-no-mori, where the tips of the leaves were just beginning to turn brown, and moved south up the mountain.

They parked their palanquins at the base and alighted, heads covered with colorful purple kerchiefs. Since pine trees were their only observers, they removed their sedge hats and revealed their lovely faces. Parting the tangled pampas grass, they walked on with sighs of admiration. The scene was reminiscent of the poem, "My sleeves grow damp since first entering the mountain of your love,"[3] for these were boys at the peak of physical beauty. An outsider looking at them could not but have felt envious of their gentleman companions. A certain man well acquainted with the ways of love once said, "In general, courtesans are a pleasure once in bed; with boys, the pleasure begins on the way there."

It was already close to dusk by the time they began hunting for mushrooms. They found only a few, which they carried like treasures back to an isolated thatched hut far from any village. Inside, the walls were papered at the base with letters from actors. Their signatures had been torn off and discarded. Curious, the boys looked more closely and discovered that each letter concerned matters of love. Each was written in a different hand, the parting messages of kabuki boy actors. The monk who lived there must once have been a man of some means, they thought. He apparently belonged to the Shingon sect, for when they opened the Buddhist altar they found a figure of Kōbō Daishi adorned with chrysanthemums and bush clover, and next to it a picture of a lovely young actor, the object no doubt of this monk's fervent devotion.

When they questioned him, the monk told them about his past. As they suspected, he was devoted body and soul to the way of boy love.

"I was unhappy with my strict father and decided to seclude myself in this mountain hermitage. More than two years have passed, but I have not been able to forget about boy love even in my dreams." The tears of grief he wept were enough to fade the black dye of his priestly robes. Those who heard it were filled with pity for him.

"How old are you?" someone asked.

"I am no longer a child," he said. "I just turned 22."

"Why then, you are still in the flower of youth!" they exclaimed. All of the actors in the room dutifully wrung the tears from their sleeves, but their expressions seemed strangely reticent. Not one of them was under 22 years of age!

Among them was one boy actor who, judging from the time he

worked the streets, must have been quite old. In the course of the conversation, someone asked him his age.

"I don't remember," he said, causing quite some amusement among the men.

Then, the monk who lived in the cottage spoke up.

"By good fortune, I have here a bamboo clapper that has the ability to tell exactly how old you are."

He gave the clapper to the boy actor and had him stand there while the monk himself gravely folded his hands in prayer. Shortly, the bamboo clappers began to sound. Everyone counted aloud with each strike.

At first, the actor stood there innocently as it struck seventeen, eighteen, nineteen, but beyond that he started to feel embarrassed. He tried with all his strength to separate his right hand from his left and stop the clappers from striking, but, strangely, they kept right on going. Only after striking 38 did the bamboo clappers separate. The boy actor's face was red with embarrassment.

"These bamboo clappers lie!" he said, throwing them down.

The monk was outraged.

"The Buddhas will attest that there is no deceit in them. If you still have doubts, try it again as many times as you like."

The other actors in the room were all afraid of being exposed, so no one was willing to try them out. They were beginning to lose their party mood.

When sake had been brought out and the mushrooms toasted and salted, they all lay back and began to entertain their patrons. One of the boy actors took the opportunity to request a new jacket, another was promised a house with an entrance six *ken* wide, and still another was presented right there with a short sword. (It was amusing to see how nimbly he took the sword and put it away!)

Into the midst of this merry-making came a rough samurai of the type rarely seen in the capital. He announced his arrival with the words, "Part, clouds, for here I am!" as if to boast of his bad reputation. He forced his way through the twig fence and into the garden, handed his long sword to an attendant, and went up to the bamboo veranda.

"Bring me the sake cup that Tamamura Kichiya is using," he demanded.

Kichiya at first pretended he had not heard, but finally he said, "There is already a gentleman here to share my cup."

The samurai would not tolerate such an answer.

"I will have it at once," he said angrily, "and you will be my snack!"

He took up his long sword mentioned earlier and waved it menacingly at the boy's companion. The poor man was terrified and apologized profusely, but the samurai refused to listen.

"What an awful fellow," Kichiya laughed. "I won't let him get away with this."

"Leave him to me," he told the others and sent them back home. When they had gone, Kichiya snuggled up to the foolish samurai. "Today was so uninteresting," he said. "I was just having a drink with those boring merchants because I had to. It would be a real pleasure to share a drink with a lord like yourself."

Kichiya poured cup after cup of sake for the man and flattered and charmed him expertly. Soon, the fool was in a state of waking sleep, unaware of anything but the boy. The man was ready to make love, but Kichiya told him, "I can't go any further because of your scratchy whiskers. It hurts when you kiss me."

"I wouldn't dream of keeping anything on my face not to your liking, my boy. Call my servant and have him shave it off," the samurai said.

"If you don't mind, please allow me to improve my lord's good looks with my own hands." Kichiya picked up a razor and quickly shaved off the whiskers on the left side of the samurai's face, leaving the mustache intact on his upper lip. He also left the right side as it was. The samurai just snored loudly, completely oblivious to what was going on.

Kichiya saw his opportunity and escaped from the place as quickly as possible. He took the man's whiskers with him as a memento. Everyone laughed uproariously when he showed them the hair.

"How in the world did you get hold of that! This deserves a celebration!" they said. Akita Hikosaburō[4] invented an impromptu "whisker dance" and had the men holding their sides with laughter.

Later, when the samurai awoke, he was furious at the loss of his whiskers. Without his beard he had no choice but to quit living by intimidation. Rather than seek revenge, he decided to act as if the whole thing had never happened.

When they saw him some time later, he was making his living as a marksman with his bow. Recalling how he had lost his beard, they could not help but laugh at the man.

Nails Hammered into an Amateur Painting

Kyoto has mountains, but in Naniwa fishnets catch a picture.
A bad reputation floats from Chikuzen to Sakai Bay.
Okada Samanosuke forgives all.

"Today, they must be drawing nets filled with cherry sea-bream at Sakai Bay; a memento of passing spring."[1] Thus wrote Lord Tameie in wide-eyed wonder after seeing harvest tuna and flying fish, not found in the capital, leaping in the sea off the coast of Sakai.

"The fish caught by net from shore in midsummer are far better than those caught in spring," a handsome actor named Okada Samanosuke[2] said in invitation. Yajūrō agreed to go with us, and the entertainer Gozaemon could hardly control his excitement. We set off for Sakai, urging the palanquin bearers in their boldly emblazoned summer robes to go as fast as their shoulders would allow.

Others seemed to have had the same idea, for on the way we met a certain gentleman from Nabaya in Kyoto. He was being entertained by Arashi San'emon,[3] who decided to take him to the sea he loved as a change of pace from the mountains in Kyoto. He planned to have nets put out at Hosoe Bay and show him some of Naniwa's famous scenery.

When both groups had alighted, there were eighteen palanquins on the shore. It looked as if a village had suddenly appeared. There were many actors with us, among them Arashi Monzaburō,[4] Sawamura Kodenji[5] and Fujita Tsurumatsu.[6]

"Ransan[7] is a great drinker, so tonight we'll have a fine time as usual until Matsu[8] nods off again and shows us how little he can take," someone said, pointing an accusing finger.

We then took our seats at Kichi's teahouse. From the bottom drawer of a chest she removed some Temmoku[9] cups patterned with morning-glories.

"Here, use these for your sake," she said.

We had been frequenting her establishment for so many years now, she knew exactly what we wanted without our saying a word. Looking closely, I noticed some paper and an inkstone she had put out for our use. This woman was a capable calligrapher and had a good grasp of poetics, I had been told.

We were drinking lightly when we happened to look north and notice the beckoning motion of pretty hands coming from a nearby teahouse run by a lady named Kuni. It turned out that the hands belonged to Uemura Tatsuya[10] and Arashi Ima-Kyōnosuke.[11] With them was Kuro no Ichizaemon. They said they had come to see the nets drawn at a place called Minato, brought there by a gentleman named Kigen.

It was already past noon, and we were unhappy to see the shadows lengthening at Awaji-shima. We watched several thick-haired men go into the shade of some nearby pines and begin playing *kemari*. The gentle tap of their feet against the ball sounded most elegant. Long ago, Hikaru Genji is said to have played on this strand when he came to worship at Sumiyoshi.[12] There is an old poem that reads, "As we count kicks, the ball becomes caught in flowering branches, until a light rain begins to fall."[13]

Yesterday was the 28th, and at Onda rain had fallen like Tora's tears of farewell.[14] Today, too, a misty rain was falling, so light it hardly wet our sleeves. Around us were some who came to this place every day on holiday, regardless of wind or rain. Most of them seemed to be people who made their living lending money and collecting rents.

There was a boldly striped curtain stretched in the shade of some trees to the west, and from behind it came the sound of a koto playing "Kumoi no Yadori."[15] Our interest was aroused by the elegance of the scene until two well-dressed women came out. This extinguished our excitement completely. Even a fat-thighed boy burnt black selling clams on the beaches would have looked more enticing, provided he still had his forelocks.

"In this wide world, you can still find women with their hair tied back and hanging loose down their shoulders like that. It is incredible," someone said in disgust.

Together, we made our way along the path of male love through the Arare pine grove and Enatsu, past villages of thatched huts, until we reached traveler's lodgings at the southern edge of Sakai. At one place, a girl came out whose job it was to stop passersby. She told us that the bath was hot and promised to provide mosquito netting if we spent the night there. We accepted, and summoned the owner of the lodging, Kajiya no Sōbei.

"We are on a pilgrimage to Mt. Kōya, so please don't serve us with utensils that smell of raw meat," we told him.

Dinner was served shortly. It consisted of bean curd, arum root noodles, and bamboo sprouts dressed with sauce.

"One has to expect poor fare such as this when traveling. Don't forget it," someone commented.

Afterwards, we went out to the beach at Nakahama. The rowboats that had been out since morning were drawing their nets toward shore so that the little fish could be caught by hand. A boat filled with live catch sat half-submerged below the waves and held 24 large sea bream. No sooner had we killed them than we salted and baked them over an open fire and poured ourselves plenty of sake. We begged the fishermen for a song, and they obliged with a shake of their reddish hair. Our uproarious mood must have been like that at Hsun Yang River.[16] Were Lo-t'ien to see us now, he would no doubt have laughed at our idiocy.[17]

Just then, from the direction of the open sea, a one-foot length of cedar board came floating towards us in the seaweed. On it was painted the figure of a young boy, covered from head to foot with nails hammered into the board. It was frightening just to look at. The painting was obviously the work of an amateur, for the robe was painted left-fold forward and the eyes and nose were not spaced right. The thumbs were slender, the little fingers fat, and the whole figure looked out of proportion. On the reverse side were written these words:

"In the second ward of Honmachi in the city of Fukuoka, Chikuzen Province, lives Mankichi of the soy sauce shop. He is fifteen years old and endowed by birth with great beauty, but he has no feelings. I told him of my great love for him, but it was useless. He claimed he had his reasons, and returned all of my letters unopened. My grudge demands relief. If there be gods in heaven, please see that he is dead within seven days." It was a petition addressed to the god Myōjin worshipped at Hakozaki, written in the Ōhashi style of calligraphy.

"This board was driven here by wind and waves across a distance of 10,000 *li*. Now the boy's disgrace has been brought all the way to the capital region," someone said, and threw it back into the sea.

Samanosuke retrieved it, however.

"It is from a distant province of which I know nothing," he said, "but I think this man's deed is very foolish. As all of you know, I have more than my share of experience in the way of male love, and yet I am careful never to frustrate the desires of any man deeply in love with me. If I can fulfill the desires of so many, cannot this inexperienced youth comprehend the urgency of a single man's feelings?"

He wept uncontrollably into his sleeve. One by one he removed all the nails hammered into the boy's body and hid them behind some boulders where no one would find them.

"Why should a guileless boy be made to suffer?" he said.

The fair manner in which he handled the matter made us think that his was the true spirit of boy love.

Not long ago, this Samanosuke was the subject of an illustrated broadside[18] claiming that a man by the name of Kagano Jūbei had murdered him, though it had no basis in fact. Everyone who heard it was heartbroken, and the whole world seemed to stop and grieve for a day or two. Later, when they realized it was a hoax, everyone was overjoyed.

At the end of the third month, on his way home from an outing by boat, Samanosuke injured his finger slightly on a pillar of the Naniwa Bridge. The injury was not serious enough to draw blood, but he bandaged it with paper anyway. When people noticed it, the rumor started that he had cut off his finger to prove his love for someone. He was always the topic of such rumors, for both men and women were always watching with fascination, wondering what would happen to him next. Others might cut off fingers

for patrons or burn their thighs with hot tobacco pipes to prove their love, and though they gladly bore such pain for their patrons' sakes, no one was ever aware of what they had done. Sama, on the other hand, had not a single mark on his body, yet he enjoyed a reputation for remarkable sensitivity to love.

Samanosuke's manners were those of the son of a rich merchant from Kamigyō-ku, the type who leaves business to his clerks in Edo and spends his days looking at blossoms on Higashiyama and his nights gazing at the moon over Hirosawa. His face showed no signs of ever having worried about paying bills at the end of the year, and his lips had never been used for scolding clerks. He was a boy who cared about people and made friends easily. (Once you begin describing his good points, it is impossible to do him justice.)

We finally abandoned the beach as the evening set in. We en-

tered Nanshū-ji through a Chinese gate and found the temple
compound remarkably quiet inside. To the south was a forest, and
beyond it the wide plain of Tama-yoko-no, a place mentioned in
Moshiogusa.[19] To the west was a long pond full of reeds spanned
by a bridge.

"What a beautiful spot this is!" someone remarked as we
crossed it. Just then, Kima Rokubei opened up the stacked lunch
boxes we had brought with us. By chance, the lacquer work on the
cover depicted three monks crossing the bridge at Tiger Gorge.[20]
The monks among us clapped our hands with pleasure at the
splendid coincidence. Before long we were drinking heavily and
had become oblivious to our surroundings.

One of the men in our group was a handsome fellow, and we

watched him remove a lady's hair comb from inside his robe. It was painted with the charming picture of a narrow vine-covered road in Suruga, and it bore the *kagezakura* crest.[21]

"Doesn't that belong to the courtesan Yoshida of Sadoshi-maya?"[22] someone asked.

"Indeed it does," he replied, lifting it reverently.

His companion took it from him and nonchalantly threw it into the pond. It sank into the muddy water without a trace.

"What a terrible waste!" the handsome man protested.

"If it were even an actor's toothpick, Aoto Zaemon[23] would gather a large group of people to search for it, but it was nothing but a courtesan's comb. Just to look at it made me sick. You really ought to quit going to that pleasure quarter." He spoke with utter seriousness.

We then caught some tiny crabs scuttling sideways in the shallows of the pond and ate them raw with our sake. By now we were drunk and had lost track of time. We ignored our guide who was telling us the temple's history and did not even laugh at his tale about the three-legged fox at Shōrin-ji, where Hakuzōsu used to live.[24] Without moistening our eyebrows,[25] we continued on our way.

We soon reached the courtesan's district at Chimori. It was evening, the time of night when the ladies stood outside their doorways in search of customers, so to avoid discovery we wore our sedge hats low over our faces. Remembering that there was some cool water at the corner of a teahouse run by Tennōjiya Rihei,[26] we went for a drink at the well.

We were spotted immediately by four well-known courtesans called the "Four Devas," who sent over their little attendants.

"Tell those nasty men from Osaka to come in," the ladies told them.

"We don't even like to speak to women anymore, much less sleep with them," we answered, laughing. Nevertheless, as the sun set we joined them for a few minutes of relaxation.

After leaving the women, we looked out over the wide beach and saw Tatsuya sitting in a small boat floating in the water. Kyō-nosuke stood on the shore, and Sama gazed across the waters towards Ebisu Island. Each seemed lost in his own thoughts. As the group headed home in darkness, the light of the oil lamps at Tōsato Ono was faintly visible in the distance. At Imamiya and Dōtombori, the smoke rising by the cremation grounds caused our spirits to sink with the realization of life's brevity, but that was all but forgotten as soon as we reached Tatamiya-chō.

That night, we attended rehearsal at the theater proprietor Yojibei's[27] house. Namie Kokan's[28] beauty, Yoshikawa Tamon's[29] singing, Ueda Saizaburō's[30] movements, Kozakura Sennosuke's[31] spectacular acting skills, Yoshikawa Gempachi[32] in his role as a young lord, Mitsue Kasen[33] as a young courtesan, Nakagawa Kinnojō[34] as a fallen samurai, and Namboku Sabu's[35] tongue-twisters: each and every role made us either weep or laugh, they were done with such skill.

It is truly a privilege to be able to see on a daily basis the simple, unadorned faces of these lovely young actors. We were fortunate enough to be born in a place where boys are available for us to do with as we please. As connoisseurs of boy love, we cannot help but pity the rich men of distant provinces who have nothing half as fine on which to spend their money.

= 8:1 =

A Verse Sung by a Goblin with a Beautiful Voice

A sorceress talks of a past that never was.
The handy portable screen of Fujita Minanojō.
A woman's spirit leaps over rooftops.

"Glad tidings! The crane lives a thousand years, the tortoise ten thousand, and Tung-fang Shuo[1] lived to the age of nine thousand." Beggars chanted these words in loud voices to exorcise evil spirits on the last night before crossing into the New Year. Old age overtakes us like white waves rising in the sea, and we realize with a shock that spring is upon us and it is time once again to spread the "boat of fortune"[2] beneath our pillows. The next morning dawns the same as always, yet we wash our faces with the "water of youth" in celebration of the New Year. But does this halt the advance of our years? The parents of unwed daughters and masters of kabuki boy actors share a special grief when they count the roasted beans[3] and realize, "Ah, another year has come to an end!"

No kabuki boy actor can earn money much beyond the four or five years he is at his peak of beauty. Just when you begin to appreciate his beauty, suddenly it is gone. Many people have been heard to say, "Female beauty is so much more durable. How we wish the *onnagata* Fujita Minanojō[4] could be turned into a real woman!"

But in this wide capital, every sort of woman imaginable can be found without turning a boy into one.

"Anyone who would even think of such a thing is perverted," someone retorted. "It is sacrilege to suggest that something as precious as a boy seek to imitate female beauty." All those devoted to the way of male love should respond in this way.

Minanojō was a real beauty. To see his face when he appeared onstage in costume was like glimpsing the moon through gaps in the clouds. His eyes were as lovely as lotus blossoms, and he spoke his lines with skill and deep feeling. There was not a single aspect of acting in which he failed to excel. Onstage he always assumed an air of innocence, like one of those naive court ladies unfamiliar with men who ride in front of and behind imperial carriages in Kamigyō. To theater-goers his deception was utterly convincing, and even those altogether lacking in feeling fell passionately in love with him. Upper-class ladies liked him almost as much as men did; how many times did they put the boy in difficult situations? But he never once allowed the unallowable to happen and strictly avoided their company his entire life.

Minanojō differed from the others in his manner and everyday dress. He wore a simple black-lined kimono over a padded white silk robe. One never tired of seeing him in it over and over again. When he ordered underrobes, he would have ten made at a time, something working boys in this day and age could never afford to do. This was possible because of Koheiji's[5] support and sober tastes, and it allowed Minanojō to stand out as one of the loveliest actors on the dry riverbed. This beautiful boy first appeared onstage when Matsumoto Nazaemon[6] was in his heyday in the great theaters of Naniwa. Minanojō was like an unopened plum blossom in those days, immature yet wonderfully fragrant.

One spring, drawn by the two-jointed bamboo ring the boy wore on his little finger, Nazaemon took him to worship at Tennō-ji at the time of the equinox. Accompanying them were Asaka

Shume[7] and a patron from the capital who shared in singing songs
and drinking wine. Inebriated, they decided to go to Miko-machi
and make contact with the spirit of Sawai Sakunosuke[8] through
Kosan of Umenoki. When they heard her speak with his voice,
they were both saddened and amused.

"How grateful I am that you came by," the voice concluded, and
they quietly left the place. It was impossible for them to shed tears
even out of a sense of obligation.

"In their youth, Uemura Monnojō[9] and Nishikawa Ichiya[10] said
that forcing tears in a kabuki performance was the hardest thing
about acting. That might be the only thing they ever said that was
not a lie!"

The comment was greeted with loud laughter.

Spring had passed like a dream. The summer breeze that blew
through the green reeds on the coast where they lived was so familiar that it no longer afforded them any relief. They thought
with nostalgia of the cool breezes in Kyoto.

"Let's go cool ourselves on the river," someone suggested, and
after a quick discussion at the widow's teahouse they set off for the
capital. Loose-lipped Shichijūrō and Stone Cart Iemon (who would
not budge once he had voiced his opinion) agreed to go along.

"We'll bring our drums and keep you entertained, but don't
expect any polite conversation from us," they warned as they left.

They boarded a boat in the shallows of the river south of Dōtombori and, beginning with the party's host, started the winecup
dancing. In the time it took the cup to pass once around from left
to right, they arrived at Ishigaki-machi. It was early in the evening.

From their second-floor perch in the Ōtsuruya, they looked
down on the scene below. So, this was the capital. People in Kyoto
had eyes and noses like everyone else it seemed, and even though
this group hailed from Osaka their arms and legs were attached in
much the same way. People here, too, would not fail to retrieve a
gold coin should they drop it. Nothing was strikingly different,
they thought. And yet, all around them were decks set out over
the water to catch the cooling breezes, and scattered among them
at their ease were women, every one of whom was exquisitely
dressed. The variety of patterns on their summer kimonos was a

treat to the eyes. The shapes of decorative New Year's braids dyed
into fabric, a pattern of scattered flowers in the courtly style, a
thousand-stripes, depictions of famous mountains, graduated bands
of color, bush clover by Yūzen[11] painted on the hem, and young
pines by Hakuen:[12] their beauty would have been wasted on someone with an untrained eye. Surely, the god of Gion would be feeling extremely pleased this evening.

To begin the party, Kagura arranged with Mokubei to move
their decks to where the ladies were as soon it grew dark. Minanojō
was led out by the light of an unmarked paper lantern with his
face hidden in shadow. All of the boy actors wore round-sleeved
jackets over their robes to disguise themselves, something the men
found most amusing. They hid their heads under cloth caps, like
brocade hidden in darkness, and disguised their voices so well that
not even the playwright Heibei[13] would have recognized them.

Soon the wine was flowing freely and the party grew quite
rowdy. In a fit of forgetfulness, Yozaemon[14] called Minanojō by his
name and revealed the boy's identity to everyone. With him were
Kawashima Kazuma,[15] lovely Tamamoto Kazuma,[16] and Utayama
Harunojō[17] who sang softly to the plucking of a samisen they
brought. One of them dozed off for a moment in the middle of the
entertainment and when he awoke recalled that it was a day of
abstinence in memory of his father. He realized with a shock that
he had eaten some sushi earlier in the evening and so washed his
mouth out thoroughly, much to everyone's amusement (including
his own).

"The next world seems so far away. What's interesting is the
here and now," someone was saying, when an odd fellow wearing
a sedge hat (at night, no less!) came up to their deck. He must have
decided that it was the most attractive spot on the river.

"May I have the ashes of your aloeswood incense?" he asked.
Only in the capital would you get such a sophisticated request from
a beggar. They took a closer look at him and discovered that it was
Hanasaki Sakichi.[18]

"Have you been making the rounds looking for a lovely lady?"
they asked.

Sakichi laughed uproariously. "So far, every girl I've seen here this evening has been ugly. It's unfortunate that the decks can be rented for the same price by those women, don't you think?"

"Surely you've overlooked someone really beautiful," they said.

To cheer him up, the entertainers immediately began imitating hawkers peddling their wares.

"Charcoal braziers, anyone?" (What a strange thing to be selling when people are cooling themselves by the river!)

"I'll play you a game of go for three *mon*, and play to lose!"

"I'll pluck out your mother's white hairs by the light of the moon."

"Doesn't one of you young men want to pick a fight with me?"

They made the rounds of the decks with a clamour of voices, but perhaps as proof of the peace that prevails in the world, not a single person offered to take them up on their wares. They just sat (daggers ready) and enjoyed the breeze from their fans. Such a contented sea of humanity could only exist here in the capital where those who have amassed fortunes come to retire.

The group took a walk farther up the river to see what was going on. Beyond the Sanjō Bridge were some men cooling themselves on decks set apart from the rest. They had only a Bizen-ware teapot and a Temmoku bowl; not a single sake cup was visible. Their faces had a look of intense concentration. They huddled in a group with their faded hemp kimonos hitched up over their thighs and worked figures on a 21-row abacus.

"Sake, side dishes, tea, tobacco; how much do you estimate it all comes to?" They were amusing themselves adding up the expenses of everyone cooling-off by the river!

"It's lazy fellows like these who ruin the many pleasures of the capital," someone said.

"Hey, kabuki actors' fees are expensive, too, you know. Aren't you going to include them in your calculations?" They pointed at the men and made fun of them.

By the time they turned back, it had grown late. With their sleeves they warded off the night dew and returned in two's and three's to their deck on the river. The crowds of people were now gone and only the lonely sound of flowing water remained. On the eastern bank they could hear the scattered voices of actors. Sakata

Tōjūrō[19] and his party, Fujikawa Buzaemon[20] with his drinking companions, and Arashi Saburōshirō[21] were all in a great mood, but when they heard the midnight bell they remembered that they had to appear onstage early the next day.

"We know our physical limitations. We don't want to lose our voices to the river breeze," they said, and returned home.

Afterwards, the moon of the thirteenth night had Higashiyama to itself and climbed, shining, up the pine branches. In its bright light, even a flea would have been clearly visible crossing Shijō-dōri.

"Now we can go to bed and enjoy ourselves," the rich patron said. He presented a boy to each of the men to enjoy for the rest of the evening. Those who were judged undeserving of partners could only regret their foolish words earlier in the evening, for there was no undoing it now. These poor fellows lay disappointed

side by side under the same piece of mosquito netting and wondered if perhaps there were still a few boys roaming about free this
evening, but there was little chance of that.

They gazed regretfully toward shore. By the light of lamps in
Ishigaki-machi, they could see the figures of boy actors casting
shadows on the shoji. They watched in envy, when suddenly the
figure of a lovely woman appeared on the peak of the roof of a
teahouse standing eave to eave with others on the bank. She wore
a wide-sleeved robe of silk crepe with a black satin sash knotted in
front. Her hair hung down her back and was tied casually in the
middle. In her hand she held a round fan decorated with gold
tassels. The sight was so unexpected that even the moon shining
brightly overhead could not dispel their sense of horror. They in-
toned the Kannon Sutra to themselves in terror, but the figure not

only refused to go away, it actually moved closer and beckoned to someone among them; who, they could not tell.

"How heartless," the woman said.

It was then they knew without a doubt that she was in love with one of them. No one was able to identify her. Their hearts beat with excitement amidst their fear as they thought how nice it would be to be loved by someone like her.

She rocked back and forth in anguish. "Please, can't you even respond with a few words?" she begged. Her tears fell to her sleeves like jewels and shattered into a thousand pieces. From her perch, she tossed them a letter. On the outside it read, "Fragrant are your sleeves at Tago Bay. . . ."[22] When they saw this, they realized that she must be in love with Minanojō.[23] They felt very sorry for her.

"At least exchange a cup of sake with her," they insisted, forcing Minanojō to drink a cupful. Then they tossed the cup up to her through a space in the eaves. She accepted it joyfully and tossed it back almost immediately.

"The cup is empty, but please have a sip," she told Minanojō. They could hear her singing a little song to accompany his drink.

"Why, that sounds very much like the voice of the daughter at Izutsuya. She's well known in the area for her singing," someone said.

No one criticized Minanojō for sharing a drink with her. Soon, the sky grew light and it was time for everyone to say farewell. The fact that both men and women fell in love with him in this way was one of Minanojō's most attractive traits.

Siamese Roosters and the Reluctant Farewell

The long pillow that sleeps eight[1] now becomes a dream.
A new theater season; this flower's beauty surpasses Yoshino's.
Mineno Kozarashi's wealthy conduct.

An old proverb passed down through the ages states, "The nose is a mountain on the human face." Among both men and women one will find high noses and flat noses, but few ever look the way their owners would wish. (Long ago, there was the Safflower Lady whose nose was remarkable for its ugliness, but she herself was considered a beauty nonetheless.)[2] Of course, if one must make a choice, a high nose is better than a flat one I suppose, but theater-goers forgave Kamakura Shinzō[3] his flat nose, perhaps because he played the role of jester. Then there was Matsumoto Nazaemon[4] in olden days, Miyazaki Denkichi[5] in more recent times, and in the present we have Mineno Kozarashi,[6] but each of them was considered handsome in his youth (despite his flat nose), and many men suffered for their love. Their patrons can still vividly recall them sitting at their sides sharing a cup of sake and dressed beautifully in their latest costumes. Kozarashi in particular wore clothes so splendid that he became a model for all boy actors to emulate. Word of his famous velvet tiger-skin jacket spread like wildfire to even the remotest villages.

"He was the first working boy to begin wearing imported fabrics and was the one everyone else tried to imitate with his stenciled letter prints and almanac patterns," reminisced Hirakawa Kichiroku.[7]

The famed Kojima Tsumanojō[8] of those days is now called Hikojūrō, and Onoyama Shume[9] is called Ujiemon. Their frightful faces are now the source of excitement for theater-goers in the present-day capital. And they are not the only ones. Mihara Jū-dayū,[10] Shibasaki Rinzaemon,[11] Sawada Tarōzaemon,[12] Sakurai Wahei[13] and others all play sturdy leading men now, though they once used to act boys' roles. It has not been that long since Iwakura Man'emon,[14] Matsumoto Bunzaemon,[15] and Yamamoto Hachi-rōji[16] wore ladies' wigs. Matsumoto Masaburō[17] used to be called Kozen, but now he and Tarōji[18] play old hags with cotton kerchiefs on their heads. Nothing goes through changes like a kabuki actor. Somenojō[19] is making a living now as Sōbei, Tsunezaemon[20] is unrecognizable as he was before, Umenosuke[21] has become Roku-zaemon, and Shuzen[22] is now a man named Rokurōemon. Shōda-yū's[23] samisen is no longer heard, for he is dead, and no one speaks of Okinosuke[24] anymore. Truly, each day we manage to extend our lives in this floating world is a blessing.

Through the years I have observed the many different ways actors amuse themselves. When the game of identifying scents lost popularity, it was replaced by short-bow archery that required little strength. The next rage was collecting bell crickets from distant Otowayama, giant katydids from Osaka, and pine crickets from Sumiyoshi that were kept in cages, but that too went out of fashion. From the end of autumn, the popular pastime was to spin tops made of shells. Finally, after enjoying all of the amusements available in Japan, it became the vogue among actors to collect fighting cocks from Siam.

One time Kozarashi sponsored a cockfight with all of the Siamese roosters he could gather. They constructed a fighting pit eight-feet square and appointed a judge to determine the victor of each bout. It was a fantastic spectacle. The huge roosters, lined up left and right on both sides, went by names like Iron-Stone, Fire-Spark, Riverside Warrior, Siamese Screw, Monster-Face, Mighty Wind, Fushimi Genius, Nakanoshima Number One, Devil I, Devil II, Powerful Demon, Modern Daredevil, Imamiya Alarm Bell, Spring-Water Mountain Cherry, Dream Black Ship, Bearded Hankai, Thunder Baby, Ripple Iron Anchor, Red Tatsuta, Modern Mount Fuji, Capital Earthcart, Hirano Boulder Smasher, Terashi-ma Weeping Willow, Wataya Fighting Hood, Zama White Neck, and Tail-less Kimpira. There were countless others besides. At the

tournament the actors looked for the fiercest birds they could find and willingly threw away huge sums of money to obtain them.

Kozarashi picked 37 of the ones he liked best and had them put in cages in his garden. Nowhere could there be more ferocious roosters than these, he thought proudly.

That evening, a patron of whom he was very fond stopped by. They spent an especially wonderful night together in bed, but the gentleman was worried about getting home too late the next morning. He spoke to one of the helpers in the kitchen.

"Even if I am asleep, be sure to wake me when the eighth bell tolls.[25] I want to get home before daybreak."

Although the man was a paying patron, the night seemed short to Kozarashi because he had deep feelings of love for him. All too soon, the long candle had burned out and the bell began to toll. Kozarashi tried to distract the man, but the gentleman listened carefully to each peal. They were still arguing whether it had rung nine times or eight[26] when all of a sudden the 37 huge roosters started crowing loudly.

"What did I tell you?" the man said.

He immediately got up and left as quickly as possible by his usual secret palanquin. Kozarashi hated to see him go, but there was nothing he could do.

"It's wrong of you to get in the way of love," he said to the roosters, weeping bitterly. Without even waiting until dawn, he released them and chased them all away. This was hardly something you would expect of a professional boy actor. It was well worth a patron's trouble to love such a boy.

One spring some years ago, a man from China who had become very devoted to Yoshikawa Tamon[27] had to leave and go back to his country. Tamon, weeping bitterly, went as far as the mouth of the river to see him off. The night was cold and it began to rain and storm, soaking him to the skin, but he bore it gladly. Like Kozarashi, he must have been loved even more by the man after this.

Long ago, when Risshi Kakuhan[28] sent a boy named Tamon the poem, "If you bore me no grudge...,"[29] it was no doubt from feelings similar to these.

Loved by a Man in a Box

Visitors to the capital ascend to Hishiya's second floor for love.
Love letters add up to 1,000 figures of Buddha.
One burden of love for both Takenaka Kichiza and
Fujita Kichiza.

Tashiro Jofū[1] killed 1,000 men with his sword and later set up a
stone monument at the Great Temple in Tsū Province to atone for
the sin. Likewise, in my 27 years as a devotee of male love I have
loved all sorts of boys, and when I wrote down their names from
memory the list came to 1,000. Of all these, it was with only a very
few that I shared a sense of honor and masculine pride; the others
were working boys who gave themselves to me against their will.
When you consider their suffering in aggregate, it must have been
considerable.

Therefore, I decided that the least I could do in atonement was
to make 1,000 papier-mâché figures of boys from soft tissues and
consign them to a temple in Saga. Someday those figures will be
recognized as the holy work of the founder of the Male Love Sect
and perhaps even be placed on view when this Way gains more
followers in future generations.

There were some men from Bizen who had grown thoroughly
familiar with the springtime sea on the shores of their province.
They could drink night and day and enjoy whitefish from Ushi-
mado, jellyfish from Seto, and clear shrimp from Koto-no-tomari
to accompany their Kojima wine, but it no longer gave them any
pleasure. Their faces had taken on the stern Confucian expression
typical of the province[2] and their lives (of whose inevitable demise
they were all too well acquainted) offered them little enjoyment.
Thus, they decided one day to visit the capital while the cherries
were still in bloom.

Fortunately for the boatful of men, there was a good wind. As soon as they arrived in the capital they went to Yasui to see the wisteria, which looked its best at twilight,[3] and were greeted there by the tolling of the evening bell. The following morning they went to the theater and stayed until the very last show. After nightfall they discussed which of the boy actors they liked the best, and those who made the deepest impression on them during the day were invited for the night.

There are many houses of entertainment, but none surpasses Hishiya Rokuzaemon's two-story lodging on the river. Directly to the east is the famous mountain,[4] and diagonally in front is Ishigaki-machi with Shijō Bridge visible directly below. When people in Kyoto say "Kyoto," this is the place they mean.

There was nothing ordinary about the party that evening. Among the rare boys gathered there were two whose lovely figures stood out even among a hundred handsome youths, Takenaka Kichisaburō[5] and Fujita Kichisaburō.[6] Nothing like them had been seen since the age of the gods, and the way they dressed was overwhelmingly beautiful. With them were Sodeoka Masanosuke,[7] whose clinging fragrance captured many a heart, and two boys whose voices caused men to fall in love after only one verse of a song, Mitsuse Sakon[8] and Toyama Sennosuke.[9] These five were the finest boy actors this world had to offer. The men entered the mountain where blossoms speak and spread their pillows side by side with them that spring night. The boys were so skilled in lovemaking, it was just like being with a woman.

"Professional boys are the finest. Others make vows of love from mutual feelings of affection and give their lives to their lovers in return for support in a crisis, but these boys have no such pleasures. They must make themselves available to their patrons from the very first meeting before they have even had time to get acquainted. Such love far surpasses the affection of other youths." A monk[10] who looked like a real man-about-town insisted on pointing out these subtleties, which most people try to avoid.

His words were perhaps too clever and caused some discomfort for the men, but these were smart actors doing the entertaining tonight and they did not let the spirit of the party falter for a minute. Soon the exchange of cups became even more animated.

When the pace began to slacken, they called out to the proprietor of the house.

"Yes, yes," was all he said.

He drank cup after cup of sake until he became genuinely drunk. He launched into a long speech about his cooking, of which he was very proud, but since he was already half asleep his servants led him away before he could finish. Nevertheless, he was still aware enough of reality to ask them, "Have you already served all six varieties of soup since the evening began? Well then, you'll have to serve something simple a second time. Why not serve Katsura willow dice garnished with pine weed in covered bowls? After that, float some cherry blossoms in a deep bowl of water, fill it with abalone cut into square pieces, and serve it with pointed chopsticks on the side. A party is nothing but appearances, remember. You can charge two *ryō* for food worth only 30 *mon* if you serve it up right. With my talents alone I have kept thirteen mouths fed for 40 years simply because I know how to keep customers happy. Since our guests are from another province and the actors with them tonight are the pride of the capital, I want you to make especially certain that their needs are met if they clap for service, even if it means getting a helping hand from the cat." After giving the servants these directions, he went straight to sleep.

Little did he know that everything he said could be heard on the second floor! So this is what it took to make a living, the men thought with amusement.

Afterwards, everyone began drinking more freely, and even the actors (who were accustomed to quantities of sake) grew red in the face. They then moved to the next room where red bedding was laid out.

This is how each of the boys was dressed.

First, Takenaka had on a lined robe of pale blue, over that a robe of dappled red, and finally an outer robe of gray satin that sported his crest on the sleeves. He wore a white woolen jacket lined in Chinese silk with a pattern of tiny birds. The eight-colored cord at his chest was untied. He had removed his long sword, the hilt of which was wound with white thread. He sat with his body twisted slightly to the left. The way his mouth turned up at one corner when he laughed was especially charming.

Fujita was wearing two silk crepe robes the color of his name[11] over a white padded silk underrobe. Both his jacket and sash were the same color, as was his cap. He sat there silent and correct, careful to control even his breathing, and seemed to effortlessly personify the perfect boy actor. If he had been born with the proper background he would surely have become the favored possession of some great daimyo. His looks were now at their peak, but I told Iwai Hanshirō[12] while we were still sober that I expected great things of the boy in the future, for his acting style was already greatly loved in Kyoto and swiftly becoming popular in Osaka.

Sodeoka wore a yellow underrobe with an outer robe of alternating bluish and reddish-brown stripes. His gorgeous manner of dress was just like a woman's. His voice was naturally high-pitched and sounded affected to people who heard it for the first time. He was appealing in every way, and every man there was enthralled with him.

Mitsuse wore a white underrobe and over that a light-purple, stencil-patterned robe with a ribbed sash of striped embroidery work. The hilt of his sword was wound with heavy pale-green thread and sported a square sword-guard of gold with rounded corners. His hairstyle made him stand out one notch above the rest. There was nothing lukewarm about him, and he had a figure that men loved.

Toyama wore a dark red underrobe and a white outer garment hand-painted with scenes from the Tōkaidō Road. Even low-born horse-cart drivers hitched their hopes on this boy, and river-forders sank into the abyss of his love, forgetting their proper station in life.[13]

Just then the voices of real travelers could be heard on Shira-kawa Bridge,[14] and the crowing of roosters signaled it was time for the men to rise. The bell of Chōmyō-ji seemed to toll end-lessly—could it be 108 times?[15] Frost had settled on the ground

for the last time as the 88th night, the third month, 28th day, came
to an end.[16] The morning breeze was chilly on their sleeves, but
these men had not yet tired of their pleasure. Who cared if people
labeled them hedonists? In this floating world, it made not the
slightest difference to them. After one thing or another, someone
finally suggested, "Why don't we have some more sake? We can
snack on fried miso on the side."

Just then, someone pounded on the door at the gate. A servant
went to see who it was and was handed a box.

"Please take this to the gentlemen on the second floor," the messenger said, and promptly disappeared.

The servant took the box up to the second-floor room, but no
one had any idea who it could be from. (The man had been clever
enough not to leave his name, and perhaps they had been smart
not to ask him for it.) The box was obviously made of cedar, which
meant only one thing: it contained cakes. Since no other actors had
been told about the party that night, they decided that someone
must have noticed them and sent a gift, but when they went over
the various possibilities they realized that not Fujimoto Heijūrō,[17]
Sakakibara Heiemon,[18] Sugiyama Kanzaemon,[19] nor Sakata Densai[20] could have known they were there.

"Well, the box must have fallen from heaven," someone said.
This was greeted with great laughter. They then put the box aside
just as it was, unopened.

Shortly, the actors' palanquins arrived to take them home.
There was a great deal of noise as they all said farewell and promised to meet again that evening. The men would miss them until
then. They returned to the empty room the boys had abandoned
and lay down. All five of them fell asleep immediately, their beds
in disarray. In the midst of their dreams, they heard a voice calling
from inside the box they had received earlier. "Kichiza, Kichiza,"
it said. They listened carefully. When they got up to take a look at
the box, it was still making sounds. They were terrified. There was
one man who was unfazed by such things, and he removed the lid.
Inside was the figure of a boy with his temples shaved. What sort
of man had made such a thing, they wondered? It looked alive,

from the expression of its eyes to the plump flesh of its arms and legs. Looking more closely still, they discovered a letter accompanying the gift.

"I am a doll-maker who lives in the vicinity. This figure is one I made with special care and set up for many years on a sign outside my shop. At some point, it began to move around as if it were alive and has gradually gotten more and more conceited. Lately, it shows an interest in boys and keeps its eyes on young kabuki actors returning home from the theater. As if that were not strange enough, it calls their names every night.

"I began to feel frightened and secretly threw it into the river at Shijō two or three times, but each time it somehow crawled back home. I have never heard of another case in which a piece of wood learned to talk. Although I made it myself, the doll has become more than I can handle. Just when I was at a loss about what to do

next, I happened to see both masters Fujita and Takenaka enter
this lodging house, so I am sending the doll to them. See for your-
selves if what I say is not true; it will make a tale that will last
through this world and into the next."

The letter was written with great care.

The man who usually remained unfazed went forward and
bowed to the figure as if it were a person.

"I am very impressed to hear that someone like yourself should
take an interest in boys. Are you in love with the two Kichisabu-
rōs?" he asked.

Immediately the doll nodded its head, "Yes."

The men were aghast; their feelings of amusement disappeared
and the evening's pleasures, instantly forgotten, all went to naught.

One logical-looking fellow put on a serious expression and said,

"It may be only a doll, but we mustn't make light of its feelings. After all, figurines date back to the eighth year of the Emperor Suinin's reign,[21] when they were first made by Nomi Otodo to serve in the place of human sacrifices. Even in China there is the story of a figurine that looked at an empress and smiled. Clearly, these two actors are outstandingly handsome. It is not at all strange that a doll should fall in love with them."

For a moment the men simply sat in awe. Then one of them picked up a full cup of sake still sitting by his pillow.

"This cup is something the boys' lips touched not long ago," he said, and gave it to the doll to drink. "You must realize that these two boys are loved by many theater-goers. There is no way your love for them can ever be fulfilled." He continued in a whisper, explaining to the doll just why its love was doomed to frustration.

Though a mere doll, it seemed to understand and from that day forward gave up its desire for the two boys. In this world where even dolls have enough sense to heed good advice, there are men who ignore their parents' objections and become obsessed with the love of boys. They lose their houses, flee their homes, and send away the wives and children whom they still love in order to leave the capital behind and go to Edo. No pot of buried gold awaits them there, however.

Nevertheless, if there were a pole made of gold that could be used for a lifetime and never wear away, the load I would love to carry on either end would be Takenaka Kichisaburō and Fujita Kichisaburō. Both boys are of equal value, each easily worth 1,000 pieces of gold.

= 8:4 =

The Koyama Barrier Keeper

Sharing a friendly cup on the way to and from worship.
The ransom of Yamamoto Sagenda.
Uemura Tatsuya proves himself a fine young actor.

The fifth of the 33 Kannon figures worshipped in the western provinces is at Fujii Temple in Kawachi Province.[1] It was placed on view in the fourth month of the Third Year of Tenna [1683]. A man named Shige came by and invited me to go worship there with him, so I quickly washed my still sleepy face. I did not have to bother dressing my hair, however (one of the advantages of being a monk!). We urged our palanquins on as quickly as possible and arrived at Naniwa Temple at the tolling of the fifth bell.[2]

It was the death day of Tokugawa Ieyasu,[3] so the sanctuary where his spirit was housed was bedecked like an earthly paradise. We passed the Eastern Gate of Paradise[4] and continued on our way. Since all music was forbidden on that day, kabuki actors had a theater holiday. They walked about freely in groups, but their dress was quite subdued in observance of the recently promulgated clothing regulations.[5] Still, their lovely figures and actor's hairstyles made it impossible for them to hide, like a hillside of cherry trees in bloom.

We finally reached the village of Hirano and rested at the main sanctuary of Dainembutsu.[6] There, as agreed the night before, we met up with a man named Mori.[7] He brought along Kyūko the masseuse, which made the group even more enjoyable. Spring still lingered in the fields as we happily made our way through the blooming grasses on our way to the temple. We worshipped, and on the way home stopped at a village called Koyama to ask a villager for a place to rest.

"Let's set up a checkpoint here and stop the young kabuki actors

who come to worship today. We can make them all share drinks with us!" someone suggested.

We spread a carpet under the eaves as a guardhouse and displayed a sign reading, "Wineshop Where We Stop the Handsome Ones." Gen'emon,[8] who plays leading men, was designated overseer of the operation, and someone else began playing the samisen and telling jokes. We waited expectantly for the young actors to begin to arrive. Soon we had Sawamura Kodenji[9] laughing; Takenaka Hanzaburō[10] we forced to share a drink; we made Komatsu Saizaburō[11] want to stay longer; and we even managed to lift the spirits of Onoe Gentarō,[12] who was feeling ill. Altogether, there were sixteen of us carrying on in high style until dusk. When we finally got up and left, the place immediately reverted to being a quiet country village.

As we made our way home we could see that water buffaloes

were black, cotton cloth was white, and our faces were so red that they rivaled the setting sun.[13] The *onnagata* brothers who were with us separated here, Kichiya[14] for Sakai and Tatsuya[15] to go, home to Osaka. Farmers selling refreshments at the side of the road tried to guess his name as he passed.

"That is the most handsome boy to pass all day. It must be Uemura Tatsuya." They were correct, of course.

"People know quality when they see it," a man from Mogami[16] commented, sounding like a merchant selling wares. "No matter what I buy, I always feel uneasy. That boy is the only thing I know of that is guaranteed to increase in value when you buy it."

"Are you sure your mental calculations are correct? If so, I'll take him," someone else said.

"Agreed!" the man answered with a hearty laugh, and they

made their plans to buy the boy for a night. If he had not been available for money, they would surely have died of frustration.

Among working boys there are vast differences in attitude. Some entertain their patrons in a daze, concentrating only on paying off their proprietors. Then there are those, full of feeling, who think, "Even these brief pangs of love for me must be deeply felt," and give the gentleman special treatment. They recognize that money is not something people give up easily even to family members.

In the old days working boys used to be genuinely affectionate, but at some point they started to act just like ladies in the pleasure quarter. Whether or not they really love a man, they will meet him at outside trysting spots to earn extra cash, or get him drunk and ask for spending money. Before long their proprietors will probably invent festival days when they can double the boys' fees: eighth month, twelfth day for Yakushi at Mitsudera, the fifteenth for Hachiman, and the eighteenth for Kannon at Kiyomizu. With regular festival days, it will be even more financially difficult to enjoy oneself each month.[17]

They say that it is best to meet both courtesans and kabuki actors when they are in greatest demand, since for the same price you can expect much more pleasure. It is heartless of me to say so, but I find it truly amazing that anyone would do such work. People experience enough pain from the slight swelling of a mosquito bite, yet to prove their love, for duty or for greed, courtesans and actors will cut off a precious finger, of which they have only a limited number and each of which has a specific function. How sad it makes me feel for them. In China, too, there is the story of a man who turned his own blood into wine and sold it to make a living.[18]

In a fit of passion, Yamamoto Sagenda[19] cut off his finger to prove his love for the owner of a certain wine shop. People thought that what he did was wonderful, and the fame of it remains to this day. If various stories about him are correct, he was a deeply affectionate boy from the time he was under Ukon Genzaemon's[20] care. Once, he looked up an old patron of his who had lost his fortune and gone into hiding, someone most actors would have abandoned without a second thought. Those who saw his example wept, and all who heard the story praised him. It would be wonderful if working boys today were like this. Such generosity would make them the talk of society forever.

One time, Uemura Tatsuya was entertaining an infrequent patron of his. He was very subdued and the winecups were moving slowly, so no one was having much fun. At some point, someone made the following innocent comment.

"I've heard lots of stories of actors trying to prove their love by cutting off a finger; it must take tremendous resolve to do such a thing."

Tatsuya heard it and laughed. "Depending on the situation, I could imagine giving up my life for love. A finger hardly seems impressive." No one challenged him to prove his boast, since he seemed to be speaking in jest, and they went back to singing songs.

Tatsuya stood up and quickly drew his sword. He pressed his thumb against a wooden pillow and, without a sound, pushed down on the blade, cutting off the thumb. He calmly adjusted his robes and threw it to the men.

"Have this to go with your wine," he said.

Everyone was flabbergasted and lost all sense of enjoyment. What would he do in the future, they wondered sadly? But Tatsuya only seemed more animated than ever, talking and playing a fan game. The men said nothing, but marveled at his seeming self-control. Apparently, his deed had nothing to do with greed. There might be some who would call him rash, but everyone there was extremely impressed. They were amazed that such a thing was even possible.

He was the finest actor, past or present, and all people everywhere were in love with him. It makes one wonder what sort of seeds he had sown in a previous life to bloom so beautifully now.

Who Wears the Incense Graph Dyed
in Her Heart?

The crest of Yamatoya Jimbei.
A boy actor in his prime, a patron in decline.
To a lover of boys, even a beautiful woman is ugly.

They say that when mandarin orange trees from south of the
Yangtze are transplanted to north of the Yangtze, they immediately
change to trifoliate orange trees. Such a transformation certainly
sounds plausible, for we have a similar phenomenon in Japan. If
you put a rusty-haired youngster from north of the river in the
hands of a theater attendant south of the river,[1] his hair will shortly
turn black and shiny like that of a *tayū*. The change is so dramatic,
it makes one wonder if the boys are not really two different people.
Appearances can certainly be improved with careful grooming.

   Some say, "Kabuki boy actors are uniformly good-looking these
days." Others counter, "There are few truly beautiful ones among
them." I have observed the outcome of several such boys who were
picked up by theater proprietors and actors. Those capable of acting on the present-day stage were perhaps one in a thousand. The
others were either good-looking and stupid, or smart and incapable
of entertaining people. No one knows how many proprietors suffered huge financial loss when it turned out that the boy they
groomed for stardom could not keep a simple beat, or when the
boy on whom they pinned their hopes for success suddenly took
sick. Surely, there is nothing more risky than trying to create a star
for the theater.

   Be that as it may, how could any man regret spending money
on boy actors? Actors' fees should be regarded as the cost of medicine to extend one's lifespan. Such boys provide a unique remedy.
They may look like ordinary boys, but emotionally they are exactly

like upper-class courtesans, with two exceptions: they have overcome their stiffness, and one never tires of their conversation.

In the old days, boy love was something rough and brawny. Men
swaggered when they spoke. They preferred big, husky boys, and
bore cuts on their bodies as a sign of male love. This spirit reached
even to boy actors, all of whom brandished swords. It goes without
saying that such behavior is no longer appreciated. Even the portable shrine of the San-ō Festival makes its rounds without drawing blood nowadays.[2] In an age when even warriors need no armor,
clearly it is best not to show knives while entertaining at parties.
Watermelon ought to be cut in the kitchen and brought out served
on plates. Boys these days are expected to be delicate, nothing more.
In Edo, a boy actor is called "Little Murasaki" or in Kyoto is given
the name "Kaoru," soft-sounding like the names of courtesans and
pleasing to the ear.[3]

Sodeshima Ichiya,[4] Kawashima Kazuma,[5] Sakurayama Rinnosuke,[6] Sodeoka Ima-Masanosuke,[7] Mitsue Kasen,[8] and others ac-
centuate their natural beauty by wearing women's red underskirts,
a habit men find very erotic. Hordes of men stop and stare, though
they have no intention of spending any money, just to memorize
the actors' crests and learn their names as they set out for the theater in the morning or head back home at dusk.

When Suzuki Heizaemon,[9] Yamashita Hanzaemon,[10] Naiki Hikozaemon,[11] and Kōzaemon[12] are on their way home, no one takes
much notice of them, despite the fact that they are excellent actors.
Instead, men already have their eyes on the apprentice boy actors
wearing wide-sleeved cotton robes with medicine pouches hanging
at their hips and sporting double-folded topknots. In addition, the
young brides and older wives of these men stand in noisy groups
in the vicinity of Sennichi Temple,[13] their excitement all the more
intense because they know their desires for the boys are doomed to
frustration.

Once, I invited Yamatoya Jimbei[14] to go and worship with me
at Kachiō-ji on the occasion of the unveiling of the holy image
there.[15] We crossed the Nakatsu River by ferry and parked our
palanquins by the shrine woods at Kita-nakajima.

"Tobacco and tea," we said, and rested for a while. Shortly after

us came a beautiful girl who looked about sixteen but was probably
fifteen. She wore a long-sleeved black satin robe appliquéd with
assorted precious treasures. Her sash was an unusual affair of
white-figured satin embroidered with swallows caught in a net of
purple threads, and tied in the back. She wore light-blue silk stockings and straw sandals with toe-cords of several slender threads.
With each step she took we caught a glimpse of her red diamond-
patterned underskirt. Her hair was tied low in a flaired chignon
and decorated with an open-work comb and a bodkin inlaid
with gold and silver. Her sedge hat was lined in light-blue material woven with threads of gold and tied by a cord made of
twisted letter paper. Everything she wore, her whole manner
in fact, reflected impeccable good taste. Moreover, she wore no
makeup. There was absolutely nothing one could say in complaint
about her.

Accompanying the girl on her left was a nun dressed in a black robe, and on her right was a woman who looked like her nurse-maid. She had a personal attendant with her, and a servant girl, both of whom were also beautifully attired. A palanquin was being carried behind them. An old man over 50 years old, who seemed to be in charge, and a younger man wearing a large sword walked in advance. It was obvious that they were from a wealthy merchant family.

The girl approached us innocently, but as soon as she saw Jimbei she became extremely agitated. She lifted her sleeve for him to see. His incense-graph crest[16] was clearly visible, dyed into her robe. Her feelings for him were no sudden impulse, then.

Afterwards she began to quiver with excitement and her legs could no longer support her. At the village where the Ebisu Shrine

is found she finally boarded her palanquin. We then lost sight of
her lovely figure and continued on our way.

Perhaps because of a karmic bond, we met her again later at the
temple. She came up from behind us with a lovelorn look in her
eyes. A priest was expertly explaining the history of each of the
treasures in the temple, but she showed interest only in Jimbei. Her
expression seemed to say, "What's so great about a wasp stinging
your unicorn's horn? I don't care if your stupid buffalo stone
breaks into a million pieces. Even your precious Buddha statue that
miraculously came down from heaven means nothing to me.[17] Just
give me Jimbei!" We could not but feel sorry for her, knowing that
her passion was doomed to frustration. (I pity the fellow who gets
this girl for a wife!) If she had been a boy none of us would have
thought twice about sacrificing our lives for her, but we were fashionable men, a group of woman-haters, so we ignored her and left
for home.

That night we entertained ourselves with some serious composition of comic linked verse at the Sinking Moon Hermitage in
Sakurazuka,[18] where we went to see fall colors. We were treated to
fine Itami and Kōnoike sake by the host.

"Now and then, we get wandering street boys in this town," the
host said.

Our pleasure destroyed by this comment,[19] we headed home. On
the way, we felt uneasy about having rubbed sleeves with that girl
who had taken a liking to Jimbei, so we purified ourselves in the
Temma River and rinsed out our eyes, sullied by the sight of her.
We then returned to Dōtombori. At the theater the next day, from
the opening love scene to the play's conclusion, we talked about
nothing but boy love.

This way of love is not exclusive to us; it is practiced throughout
the known world. In India, strangely enough, it is called the Mistaken Way.[20] In China, it is enjoyed as *hsia chuan*.[21] And here in
Japan, it flourishes as boy love. Because there is female love, the
foolish human race continues to thrive. Would that the love of boys
became the common form of love in the world, and that women
would die out and Japan become an Isle of Men.[22] Quarrels between husband and wife would cease, jealousy disappear, and the
world enter at last into an era of peace.

REFERENCE
MATTER

Notes

Introduction

1. This way of configuring male homosexuality has been observed in various cultures throughout the world, the best documented of which are classical Greece and modern Melanesia. See Dover, *Greek Homosexuality*, and Herdt, *Ritualized Homosexuality in Melanesia*.

2. Cf. "Cultures in which homosexual relations involve the sexual submission of the young to their elders (i.e., in which homosexual relations continue, but one's role in them changes) have been described more often than cultures in which homosexual relations are abandoned altogether with the attainment of age." Murray, *Social Theory, Homosexual Realities*, 46.

3. A detailed discussion in Japanese of male love up to the seventeenth century appears in Iwata, *Honchō nanshoku kō*. For an extensive bibliography of male love in Japan, see Iwata, *Nanshoku bunken shoshi*.

4. The rationale for the higher ranking of farmers was based on Confucian concepts of productivity; farmers produced rice from the elements of soil, water, and sunlight and were therefore deemed more productive than artisans, who required raw materials—such as bamboo and wood—to produce goods. Merchants ranked last since they merely profited from the sale of goods and their wealth derived entirely from the productivity of others.

5. Keene, *World Within Walls*, 189.

6. Callahan, *Tales of Samurai Honor*, 17.

7. See the introduction to Thornbury, *Sukeroku's Double Identity: The Dramatic Structure of Edo Kabuki*.

8. These seals appear in three other books by Saikaku: *Honchō nijū fukō*, 1686; *Budō denrai ki*, 1687; and *Buke giri monogatari*, 1688.

9. See McCullough, *Ōkagami: The Great Mirror*.

10. "Saikaku, however, went beyond his predecessors in his insistence that it was preferable to love a man, rather than a woman." Keene, *World Within Walls*, 188.

11. Keene, *Dawn to the West*, 1184.

12. This theory of masking and signaling as textual strategies is developed in Keilson-Lauritz, *Von der Liebe die Freundschaft heisst, Zur Ho-*

moerotik im Werk Stefan Georges. See also Strauss, *Persecution and the Art of Writing.*

13. In the Judeo-Christian west, homosexual love was stigmatized first as spiritual sin, then as a medical, social, or psychological abnormality. According to John Boswell, there was no significant Christian intolerance of male homosexuality until the twelfth century. See Boswell, *Christianity, Social Tolerance, and Homosexuality*, 269–302.

14. See Rivers, *Proust & the Art of Love*, 107–52.

15. *Mishima Yukio zenshū*, 25: 258–59. Quoted in Keene, *Dawn to the West*, 1185.

16. Ibid., emphasis added.

17. For further discussion of hyōbanki, see Brandon, Malm, and Shively, *Studies in Kabuki*, 49–50.

18. See Childs, "*Chigo monogatari*: Love Stories or Buddhist Sermons."

19. For a general analysis of the legends surrounding Kūkai, see Kitagawa, "Master and Savior," in *On Understanding Japanese Religion.* The legend of Kūkai as "divine boy" (*chigo daishi*) is discussed in Guth, "The Divine Boy in Japanese Art."

20. *Iwatsutsuji* can be found in Ōta, *Misonoya*, 1: 367–87.

21. *Kokinshū* poem 495. Cf. "My stony silence / recalls the rock azaleas / at Mount Tokiwa: / you cannot know of my love—/ but how I long to meet you!" McCullough, *Kokin Wakashū: The First Imperial Anthology of Japanese Poetry*, 115.

22. For a detailed discussion of Saikaku's use of irony and humor, see Schalow, "Literature and Legitimacy: Uses of Irony and Humor in 17th-Century Depictions of Male Love in Japan."

23. Schalow, "Saikaku on 'Manly Love,'" 6. Emphasis added.

24. Aston, *Nihongi*, 16–17.

25. Ibid., 13.

26. Ibid., 52.

27. *Ise monogatari* poem 1: "The fields of Kasuga are dressed in young-purple; the confused pattern of my robe reflects my troubled feelings!"

28. Keene, *World Within Walls*, 189.

29. For a discussion of the genre in English, see Hibbett, *The Floating World in Japanese Fiction.*

30. Munemasa, *Kinsei Kyōto shuppan bunka no kenkyū*, 182.

31. Callahan, *Tales of Samurai Honor*, 13.

32. Keene, *World Within Walls*, 189.

33. Danly, *In the Shade of Spring Leaves*, 110.

34. *Teihon Saikaku zenshū*, 1: 28. See Noma Kōshin's comments on the inclusion of *Shinyūki* in *Nihon shisō taikei*, 60: 377.

35. *Teihon Saikaku zenshū*, 1: 37–39.

36. Sargent, *The Japanese Family Storehouse*, 14.

37. I follow the dating in Noma, *Saikaku nenpu kōshō*, 17. The year 1681 is tentatively given in *Teihon Saikaku zenshū*, 9: 5. Danly dates it 1680, two years prior to *Ichidai otoko*. Cf. Danly, *In the Shade of Spring Leaves*, 303.

38. Danly, *In the Shade of Spring Leaves*, 303.

39. *Taiyaku Saikaku zenshū*, 6: 351.

40. *Teihon Saikaku zenshū*, 1: 239.

41. Ibid., 4: 29.

42. Ibid., 1: 471, 4: 259.

43. Pollack, *The Fracture of Meaning*, 194.

44. Walker, *The Japanese Novel of the Meiji Period and the Ideal of Individualism*, introduction.

45. The vision begins, "As I stood there gazing calmly at these 500 Buddhas, I found that every single one reminded me of some man with whom in the past I had been intimate." Morris, *The Life of an Amorous Woman*, 206–7.

46. Ibid., 187–88.

47. Miner, Odagiri, and Morell, *The Princeton Companion to Classical Japanese Literature*, 80.

48. See Hibbett, "The Role of the Ukiyo-zōshi Illustrator."

49. The stories are 6:5, 7:5, 8:4, and 8:5. *Taiyaku Saikaku zenshū*, 6: 355.

50. *Kinsei bungaku shiryō ruijū, Ihara Saikaku hen*, 7: 451–62.

51. This point and others in the following discussion are based on Teruoka, *Saikaku shinron*, 249–61.

52. Lane, "Postwar Japanese Studies of the Novelist Saikaku," 191.

53. For detailed discussions of the haikai style in Saikaku's prose, see Sargent, *The Japanese Family Storehouse*, introduction, and Danly, *In the Shade of Spring Leaves*, 109–32.

54. Keene, *World Within Walls*, 189–90.

55. This bias, held by the majority of Japanese critics, is summarized and apparently shared by Keene in *World Within Walls*, 189–90.

56. This was suggested to me by Maeda Kingorō.

57. *Nihon koten bungaku zenshū*, 39: 320.

58. Callahan, *Tales of Samurai Honor*, 18.

59. See Noma, *Saikaku shinshinkō*, 180–204.

60. For a detailed comparison of Saikaku's narrative and the historical accounts on which it is based, see Noma, *Saikaku shinshinkō*, 205–25.

61. Danly, *In the Shade of Spring Leaves*, 114.

62. The definitive study of vendettas is Hirade, *Katakiuchi*. See also Callahan, *Tales of Samurai Honor*, 14–16.

63. For a detailed discussion of kabuki's history, see Brandon, Malm, and Shively, *Studies in Kabuki*. See also Gunji, *Kabuki*, and Leiter, *Kabuki Encyclopedia*.

64. See Bolitho, *Treasures Among Men*, 171.

65. For a detailed discussion of the changes that were introduced with adult men's kabuki, see Ortolani, "Das Wakashu-kabuki und das Yarō-kabuki." See also Ortolani, *Das Kabukitheater*.

66. Danly, *In the Shade of Spring Leaves*, 131.

67. The nature of Saikaku's realism has received considerable attention. See, for example, Hibbett, "Saikaku as a Realist."

68. "As the laws became more strict, townsmen and farmers who were guilty of wounding or killing a dog were sometimes crucified or beheaded. Samurai also were severely punished. There were instances of a lower samurai being exiled for failure to care for a puppy abandoned by his gate, for not stopping a dog fight, or for injuring a dog that barked at him. One samurai who killed a dog that had bitten him was ordered to commit *seppuku*." Shively, "Tokugawa Tsunayoshi, the Genroku Shogun," 95.

69. Dunn and Torigoe, *The Actor's Analects*.

70. Ibid., 41–42.

71. Ibid., 42.

72. Ibid., 43.

73. Sato's original translation appeared as "*Quaint Stories of Samurais by Saikaku Ibara*" in 1928, printed by Dijon France in a limited edition (500 copies only) for "private distribution." A printer's prefatory note states that the book was printed exactly as translated because Sato's "foreign use of the language was thought to have peculiarly retained the primitive and quaint quality of the tales." Mathers's so-called translation is simply a literate reworking of Sato's language. See Mathers, *Comrade Loves of the Samurai*, introduction.

74. Aston, *Japanese Literature*, 268.

75. Ibid., 269.

76. Karsch-Haack, *Forschungen über gleichgeschlechtliche Liebe*, 117; quoted in Carpenter, *Intermediate Types Among Primitive Folk*, 159.

The Translation: Preface

1. *Nihongi*, or *Nihon shoki*, was Japan's first national history and completed in A.D. 720. It contains many of the same creation myths recorded in *Kojiki* (late sixth century; *Record of ancient matters*). Cf. Phillipi, *Kojiki*, and Aston, *Nihongi*.

2. Cf. "At this time a certain thing was produced between Heaven and Earth. It was in form like a reed-shoot. Now this became transformed into a God, and was called Kuni-toko-tachi no Mikoto. Next there was Kuni no sa-tsuchi no Mikoto, and next Toyo-kumu-nu no Mikoto, in all three deities. These were pure males spontaneously developed by the operation of the principle of Heaven." Aston, *Nihongi*, 2–4.

3. Cf. Aston, *Nihongi*, 6. The four generations of male and female pairs of gods were Uhiji-ni and Suiji-ni; Oho-to-nochi and Oho-to-mae; Omo-taru and Kashiko-ne; Izanagi and Izanami. Izanami gave birth to the islands of Japan and to the sun goddess Amaterasu who ruled them.

1 : 1 Love: Contest Between Two Forces

1. *Nihongi* recounts that a wagtail taught Izanagi and Izanami to copulate by shaking its tail at them.

2. "Boy of a thousand suns" is a humorous link to the sun goddess Amaterasu.

3. Cf. Aston, *Nihongi*, 52.

4. The relationship between the fifth-century-B.C. Wei Ling-kung and Mi Tzu-hsia is recorded in *Han Fei-tzu*. Cf. Giles, *A Chinese Biographical Dictionary*, 586. *Han shu* records that Chi Ju was a favorite minister of the first Han emperor Kao Tsu (Liu Pang) and that Li Yen-nien was a minister loved by the sixth Han emperor Wu Ti for his exceptional abilities in music and poetry.

5. The "man of old" (*mukashi otoko*) is Arihara no Narihira (825–880). For a detailed analysis of the Narihira legend, see McCullough, *Tales of Ise*, introduction.

6. The name signifies a court rank, "Middle Captain of the Great Gate," possibly Prince Koretaka (844–897), whose sister was the Ise virgin in chap. 69 of *Ise monogatari*. Narihira served Koretaka in an official capacity and addressed several affectionate poems to him.

7. A reference to *Ise monogatari*.

8. Kitamura Kigin (1624–1705) attributes the anonymous *Kokinshū* love poem 495 to Shinga Sōzu (801–879) in *Iwatsutsuji* (1667), alleging it was addressed to Narihira. Cf. Mitamura, *Saikaku rinkō*, 5: 19.

9. Nara was the capital of the Japanese Yamato state from 710 to 794; the phrase "Nara capital" echoes the opening lines of *Ise monogatari*.

10. "Young purple" (*wakamurasaki*) refers to the color of Narihira's robe in the first poem of *Ise monogatari*. Cf. McCullough, *Tales of Ise*, 69. Saikaku turns the robe into a cap in order to create a humorous link with the custom of kabuki wakashu who covered their shaved heads with purple kerchiefs.

11. Two famous Chinese beauties. The phrase appears in the *Taiheiki*,

where it describes Sanekane's daughter, chosen as Go-Daigo Tennō's consort in 1318. Cf. McCullough, *The Taiheiki*, 8. *Shin'yūki* (1643) uses the same passage to describe the beauty of Noritoki, son of Hino Dainagon Hirotoki.

12. That is, the god of love between men and women.

13. Yoshida Kenkō (1283–1352), author of *Tsurezuregusa*. Cf. Keene, *Essays in Idleness*.

14. Sei Shōnagon (late tenth century), author of *Makura no sōshi*. Cf. Morris, *The Pillow Book of Sei Shōnagon*. *Kiyo* is an alternate reading for the character *sei* in the name of the Kiyohara family, but Kiyo-wakamaru is Saikaku's invention.

15. The story of this love letter, which Kenkō wrote to the wife of En'ya Hangan (Hōgan) for Kōno Moronao, appears in *Taiheiki*, chap. 21. Saikaku does a parody of the story in 1:2, *Kōshoku ichidai otoko*. For examples of other appearances of the same story in Japanese literature, see Maeda, *Kōshoku ichidai otoko zenchūshaku*, 1:54.

16. Third in the hierarchy of high-class courtesans, after *tayū* and *tenjin*. Cf. Morris, *The Life of an Amorous Woman*, 295.

17. The Kyoto pleasure quarter.

18. The Osaka theater district.

19. Main temple of the Shingon sect of Esoteric Buddhism, founded by Kūkai (774–835; posthumous name: Kōbō Daishi) in 816. It is said to be the place where male homosexuality was first practiced in Japan between monks and their *chigo* attendants.

20. Shrine dancing girls (*miko*) sometimes engaged in prostitution. Saikaku describes one such liaison in 3:7, *Kōshoku ichidai otoko*.

21. Boys selling aloeswood hair oil were engaged by men as boy prostitutes, sometimes forcibly.

22. Courtesans and married women blackened their teeth as a mark of beauty.

23. A house where high-class courtesans met their customers.

24. A boy's services could be reserved for a one-month period for the exclusive use of one patron.

25. Jesters provided slapstick entertainment at parties in the pleasure quarters and theater districts. Yoshiwara probably refers to a corner of the Osaka pleasure quarter at Shinmachi that went by that name, not to the more famous pleasure quarter in Edo of the same name.

26. Cf. Keene, *World Within Walls*, 188.

27. Bon, celebrated in the middle of the seventh month, is the Buddhist All Soul's Day when the spirits of the dead are believed to return briefly to earth. In the pleasure quarters, higher rates applied during the Bon season, from the fourteenth to the seventeenth of the seventh month.

28. The annual face-showing presentation (*kaomise*) marked the beginning of a new theater year in the eleventh month. In order for the boy actors to look their best, patrons were expected to pay for new costumes and other theater finery.

29. A kabuki *tayū* was an actor of female roles who occupied the highest rank when entertaining at parties.

30. When a boy came of age and shaved off his forelocks in the manner of an adult male, he also exchanged his boy's robes with vents under the sleeves for an adult robe with no vents and short, rounded sleeves.

31. An unmarried girl in her early teens might wear such a robe.

32. The posthumous name of Kūkai (774–835), attributed with the introduction of male homosexual love to Japan from China.

33. Saikaku refers to Yonosuke, the hero of *Kōshoku ichidai otoko* (1682).

34. Osaka.

1 : 2 ABCs of Boy Love

1. Only the wealthiest merchants owned corner properties, valuable for their extra street frontage, or had the privilege of transacting business with daimyo.

2. Ishikawa Jōzan (1583–1672) was a retainer of Tokugawa Ieyasu and enjoyed a distinguished career until his resignation after the summer attack on Osaka castle in 1617 due to a breach of the military code. In his later years he secluded himself in Ichijō-ji (Shisendō), a temple north of Kyoto, and devoted himself to poetry and scholarly pursuits.

3. The stream is the Kamo River. The headnote to Jōzan's poem reads, "He wrote this poem to show his firm determination to not cross the Kamo River towards the capital." Another account states that the poem expressed Jōzan's excuse for rejecting the invitation of abdicated emperor Gomizuno-o (r. 1611–29). The poem is inspired by *Shinkokinshū* poem 1894 by Kamo no Chōmei.

4. In the eleventh month.

5. Activities in preparation for the New Year.

6. Ejima Kiseki (1667–1745) borrowed this passage to describe the uncouth behavior of townswomen in the introduction to *Seken musume katagi* (1717; *The character of worldly young women*). Cf. Hibbett, *The Floating World in Japanese Fiction*, 101–2.

7. Priests were vegetarians and not allowed to eat fish or meat.

8. Shūgakuin, the detached palace where the abdicated emperor Gomizuno-o established his residence in the northeastern environs of Kyoto.

9. *Dōji kyō*, a collection of simple Buddhist teachings and aphorisms of unknown authorship dating to the thirteenth century, published in the seventeenth century, and widely used in temple schools as a writing text.

10. The boys were probably children of the hereditary samurai guardians of the Shimogamo Shrine in Kyoto.

11. Tzu Tu was a minister of Duke Chuang of Cheng (Cheng Chuang-kung) during the Spring and Autumn Period (722–481 B.C.). This incident is mentioned in *Shih ching* and in *Meng-tzu* (*The Mencius*). In Japanese sources, it can be found in *Shin'yūki* (1643) and in *Shudō monogatari* (1661).

12. Civil chaos caused by the subversive influence of women (*nyoran*) is a Chinese term for the political turmoil that results when men in government allow themselves to be controlled by women, such as an emperor under the influence of a powerful concubine. King Ai of Wei (Wei Ai-wang) lived in the fourth century B.C. His relationship with Lung Yang-chun is recorded in *Chan kuo shih*. *Yodarekake* (1665) mentions the names and may have been Saikaku's source for them.

13. The mythical one-winged *hiyoku* required its mate to fly.

14. Also known as Shinga Sōzu (801–879), Sōjō was one of Kūkai's ten major disciples and served as rector of Tōji in Kyoto from 835 until his death.

15. Anonymous *Kokinshū* love poem 495. Legend attributes the poem to Shinga Sōzu, addressed to Arihara no Narihira. Cf. Kitamura, *Iwa-tsutsuji* (1667).

16. Taira no Atsumori (1168–84) died at age sixteen in the Gempei wars. His skill with the flute is immortalized in *Heike monogatari* and in the Noh play "Atsumori."

17. The greatest flute player of Saikaku's day, Morita Shōbei, lived in Kyoto and was known for his Noh accompaniment.

18. About 4:00 A.M.

19. The Kamo River, which has played an important unifying role throughout the narrative.

1:3 Within the Fence

TITLE: The title describes the fenced court used for playing *kemari*, a type of kickball. Pine, cherry, maple, and willow trees were planted in the four corners of the court, as depicted in the illustration accompanying the text. Here, the willow doubles to describe the boy's slender hips (*yanagigoshi*).

1. "Putting in corners" involved shaving the hair on a boy's temples

into right angles at approximately age sixteen-as an intermediate step towards adulthood.

2. Abe no Seimei was also known as Abe no Kiyoaki (921–1005). A distinguished scholar, he is attributed with definitive statements on a variety of subjects. Cf. Keene, *World Within Walls*, 189.

3. A Nichiren temple in Kyoto called Zuiryū-ji, it was founded in 1596 by Toyotomi Hidetsugu's mother as a haven for women of the imperial court and was later patronized by the Tokugawa family.

4. Marrying on the first day of the boar in the tenth month was believed to guarantee offspring.

5. *Tama*, "jewel," suggests the boy's gem-like beauty.

6. This may refer specifically to an incident in the Noh play "Ama," in which a precious stone is stolen from a fisherman by the dragon king of the sea, or more generally to the dragon king's preference for handsome boys. Cf. Seidensticker, *The Tale of Genji*, 246.

7. The original Chinese sources are unknown. *Shin'yūki* (1643) states that Yu Hsin was a boy of great beauty who rejected the advances of his suitors and died a lonely, miserable death. Tsung Wen, lord of Yangchow, wrote the poem describing Yu Hsin as a "heartless youth" after visiting the boy's grave. Cf. Noma, *Kinsei shikidō ron*, 9–10.

8. Suma was Genji's place of exile in *Genji monogatari* and had associations of separation and loss.

9. Aizu, modern Fukushima, was a large domain of 230,000 *koku* located east of Edo. The daimyo lord of Aizu at the time of Saikaku's account was Matsudaira Masanobu, who was in Edo as one of the shogun's trusted allies.

10. A type of kickball played by courtiers and aristocrats.

11. The Asukai family was known for producing skilled poets and *kemari* players.

12. Hachiman was originally the patron deity of the Minamoto clan but by the Edo Period was patronized by the samurai class in general. It was the logical place for Senzaemon to pray for Tamanosuke's recovery.

13. One swordsmith named Sadamune was from Ōmi (modern Shiga) and died in 1349, another was from Hizen (modern Nagasaki) and flourished in the Tenmon Era (1532–54); a Sadamune sword by either was an heirloom of great value.

14. It was a crime against the laws of the domain for a youth in the personal service of the daimyo lord to establish sexual relations with another samurai.

15. The coming-of-age ceremony signaled a boy's entrance into manhood and usually took place at age nineteen. Tamanosuke skipped the

intermediate stage of shaving his temples ("putting in corners") and was ordered to adopt the hairstyle of an adult samurai three or four years earlier than normal as a means of making him sexually inaccessible to Senzaemon, since sexual relations were not practiced between adult males.

1:4 Love Letter Sent in a Sea Bass

1. *Wakan rōeishū* poem 791 "on impermanence."

2. This story is based on an actual incident involving a young samurai named Mashida Toyonoshin that took place in Bizen Province in 1667.

3. "Eight clouds rising" (*yakumo tatsu*) is an ancient poetic epithet (pillow word, *makura kotoba*) for Izumo Province.

4. According to Shinto myth, the gods assembled annually at the Great Shrine in Izumo in the tenth month to arrange love matches for the coming year. Because the gods were busy in Izumo, the tenth month is traditionally called the godless month (*kannazuki*) in the rest of Japan.

5. Jinnosuke knows that the laws of Izumo strictly forbid boys in the lord's personal service from establishing sexual relationships outside.

6. From a poem by Sagami (*Hyakunin isshu*, 65): "My sleeves rot, soaked with tears of jealous rage, and with them, alas! rots my good reputation, ruined for the sake of love."

7. Uneme was the adolescent name of Kano Tan'yū (1602–74), official painter to the Tokugawa *bakufu*.

8. A pattern of white chrysanthemums and yellow *ominaeshi* vying with other flowers, said to be an adaptation of the elegant "flower battles" T'ang emperor T'ai Tzung used to entertain his consort, the legendary beauty Yang Kuei Fei.

9. The poem by Mashida Toyonoshin in the original account of the events reads, "The morning-glory has its moment of full flower, so it seems they say—yet it does not wait for twilight, this life that is but dew."

10. Approximately 10 P.M.

11. The swordsmith Tadayoshi was from Hizen Province and died in 1632.

12. One *li* equals about 2.5 miles.

13. The River of Three Crossings (*sanzu no kawa*) is the Buddhist equivalent of the River Styx and divides the world of the living from the world of the dead.

14. Jinnosuke and Gonkurō were aided by their attendants, Dengorō and Kichisuke.

15. This is an uncharacteristic phrase for Saikaku, who rarely makes

explicit references to the form of the text unless he is working from written sources.

1:5 Implicated by His Diamond Crest

1. A *koku* was equivalent to approximately five bushels of rice, the medium in which samurai stipends were paid. A 200 *koku* stipend was meager.

2. Dōmyō-ji is a nunnery of the Shingon sect located in Fujii-dera, Osaka, and is said to have been founded by Shōtoku Taishi (seventh century).

3. Made from dried steamed rice and used as a flavoring and sweetener in summer beverages.

4. A phrase from Po Chü-i's "Song of Eternal Sorrow" describing the beauty of Yang Kuei Fei.

5. That is, his beauty made him seem out of reach. The phrase does not appear in the collected works of Li Tai-po (Li Po, 701–762).

6. "Middle *shōgi*" was an early form of *shōgi*, a chess-like board game, that originated in the fourteenth century and was already considered old-fashioned in Saikaku's day.

7. A legend from the region of Kobe tells of a male deer from Tagano (or Yumeno) that visits its mate in nearby Noshima, an island in Awaji. The mate has a dream in which the male deer is shot and killed by an arrow, and the dream comes true on its next visit when it encounters a boat full of hunters in the middle of its crossing and is helpless to escape their arrows. Saikaku mentions the legend in his travel book, *Hitome tamaboko* (1689). Ironically, the way Daiemon actually dies is closer to the legend than to Tannosuke's dream.

8. Injuries were required to be reported to the authorities and would have led to an investigation. To protect Tannosuke, Daiemon left a final testament that would deflect an inquiry.

9. In Buddhist belief, the soul wandered for 49 days before crossing into the world of the dead. Tannosuke had hoped to die on the last day that Daiemon's spirit lingered in the world of the living.

2:1 A Sword His Only Memento

1. Kobori Enshū (d. 1647), a vassal of Toyotomi Hideyoshi and later of Tokugawa Ieyasu, invented a circular standing lamp with sliding panels that could be rotated or adjusted up or down to control the amount and direction of light.

2. Kanze rope was made by twisting paper into lengths of cord, used

by warriors to tie helmets and armor. There are several theories about who invented the process, but Saikaku suggests it was Kanze Matajirō.

3. The Tokugawa government forbade *junshi* (the samurai custom of a lord's closest retainers following him in death) in 1663 to strengthen its authority over regional daimyo. The ban was put to a test when retainers of Okudaira Tadamasa, lord of Utsunomiya, committed seppuku after his death. Tokugawa retribution was severe: Tadamasa's son was stripped of his fief and the sons and brothers of those who committed *junshi* were executed. A chronological discrepancy is revealed later in the narrative when we learn that the events on which the story is based took place in 1632, predating the *junshi* ban by 30 years.

4. This was an area of daimyo residences within the outer circle of Edo castle.

5. This was the Hachiman shrine closest to Edo castle.

6. In 1588, Toyotomi Hideyoshi built a great Buddha figure at Hōkō-ji in Kyoto in imitation of the Great Buddha at Tōdai-ji in Nara. It was made from melted-down weapons collected in Hideyoshi's campaign to disarm the populace. The figure was destroyed in an earthquake shortly afterwards, and the metal was then used to mint coins.

7. Mimizuka, meaning "ear tomb," was the place Toyotomi Hideyoshi buried the ears taken as proof of enemy dead during his brutal invasions of Korea in 1592 and 1597.

8. *Han Fei-tzu* records the story of Pien Ho (Ho Shi) as a model of persistence who presented a piece of precious jade to three kings. The first two rejected it as fake and punished him with amputation of his feet, but King Wen (Wen Wang) realized its authenticity and accepted the precious stone from his subject.

9. *Meng ch'iu*, a fourth-century Chinese collection of ancient moral tales, records the story of a persistent and ambitious cowherd named Ning Ch'i who beat time with a bull's horn and sang about his regret that he could not serve his sovereign as a government official. Duke Hung of Ch'i (Ch'i Hung-kung) heard him, realized the man's worth, and immediately made him his minister.

10. In the Edo Period, outcast beggars and criminals called *hinin* (literally, "not human") congregated along riverbeds and slept under bridges. Unlike members of the Eta pariah class, who were permanently excluded because of their hereditary association with occupations Buddhism declared unclean, such as burial of the dead, butchering of animals, and working with leather, *hinin* were regular people temporarily down on their luck and capable of returning to their former positions in society. Cf. Morris, *The Life of an Amorous Woman*, 378, note 744.

11. Katsuya, brought up in the comparative luxury of a daimyo residence, would not have recognized the sound of dice being cast.

12. The line is from the Noh play "Funa Benkei" and refers to a story in *Shih chi* about a Chinese king who was defeated at Mt. Kuai Chi but later regained the lost territory.

13. The *shō* is a Chinese reed instrument that works as a sort of mouth organ. Reeds from Udono in Osaka were prized for their high quality.

14. The man has fallen in the world, from wearing fine silk robes to ragged paper ones. "That splendid Chinese robe of 'the man of old'" is a reference to the Chinese robe (*karagoromo*) in the opening line of *Ise monogatari*, poem 10, about irises (*kakitsubata*) at Yatsuhashi, evoked in the previous line.

15. Edo.

16. Mt. Hiei, towering over Kyoto to the north, was called "the capital's Mt. Fuji" (*miyako no fuji*).

17. Takase barges were flat-bottomed boats with high sides used for hauling freight. The name comes from the Takase canal used for transporting goods from Fushimi to Osaka via the Yodo River.

18. Sanemori of Ōhara was a ninth-century swordsmith.

19. The most famous of several battles fought in the late sixteenth century between Takeda Shingen and the neighboring Uesugi clan in Shinano Province.

20. About a mile.

21. About twelve feet.

22. Between 4:00 and 4:40 A.M.

23. Katsuya has fulfilled the three requirements of a formally sanctioned vendetta: the announcement of name and grievance (*nanori*), the actual duel, and the taking of the head.

24. About ten miles.

25. This phrase indicates that Saikaku may have been working from a written account of the story.

2:2 He Was Rained Upon

1. Mt. Rokkō, in Kobe.

2. Taira no Tomomori, fourth son of Kiyomori, died in the Heike defeat at Dannoura in 1185 led by Minamoto no Yoshitsune. In the Noh play "Funa Benkei" his spirit tries to sink Yoshitsune's ship in a powerful storm, but the attempt is foiled by Benkei's fervent prayers.

3. A shrine in Akashi dedicated to the early-seventh-century poet Kakinomoto no Hitomaro, called Hitomaru in the Edo Period.

4. About 2 A.M.

5. The story is based on one in *Han Fei-tzu* in which Duke Ping of Chin (Chin Ping-kung) was admonished for his pride by the blind musician Shih K'uang. Saikaku's version may be from a Japanese *setsuwa* (legend) source.

6. Of the twelfth month.

7. Korin's feigned gastro-intestinal distress required frequent trips to the toilet, apparently located beyond wheeled doors that ran on a track.

8. Secret agents (*kakushi yokome*) were employed by daimyo lords to spy on members of the household in order to catch violators of house laws and protect against intrigue.

9. The implication is that these words were spoken by a possessing spirit, probably related to the murdered badger. Saikaku is drawing on a tradition in *setsuwa* literature of supernatural fantasy as a metaphor for psychological or social conflict.

10. The temple in Akashi famous for its "morning-glory pond" is actually Kōmyō-ji.

11. A reference to Genji, hero of *Genji monogatari*, who was banished from the capital for a time, first to Suma and then to Akashi. In Akashi, Genji was befriended by a lay priest, a former governor, whose daughter he loved; the offspring of their affair was the Akashi princess who, at the end of the tale, became consort of the reigning emperor.

12. Not recorded in *Genji monogatari*. Saikaku attributes the same poem to Genji in the Akashi section of his travel guide, *Hitome tamaboko* (1689).

13. Branches of the Japanese star anise, *Illicium religiosum*, are used as decorative greenery to mourn the dead.

2:3 His Head Shaved

1. Outdoor night performances of fireside Noh (*takigi nō*) were given annually at the south gate of Kōfuku-ji in the ancient capital of Nara, called the "southern capital" to distinguish it from Kyoto in the north. Performances ran for seven days, from the seventh to the thirteenth of the second month. Cf. Johnson, "Takigi Nō: Firelight Performances in Sacred Precincts."

2. The Komparu school, one of the four major schools of Noh performance, was founded late in the sixteenth century by Komparu Shigeie; the "Komparu Noh master" in Saikaku's narrative would be a descendant of his. Seigorō (later called Shōzaemon) died in Edo in 1649; the name Mataemon was used by several generations of Komparu performers.

3. The gallery was located close to the stage, directly behind the seats of the priests from Kōfuku-ji and neighboring Saidai-ji.

4. From *Kokinshū* poem 297 by Ki no Tsurayuki: "Autumn leaves have scattered unseen deep in the hills, like brocade worn at night."

5. The Yoshiya style got its name from a group of Hatamoto footmen in Edo called the *Yoshiya gumi* and was characterized by the way they wore their long-handled swords blade up, with the handle and sheath wound in white thread.

6. In conjunction with fireside Noh at Kōfuku-ji, Noh performances were also given at Wakamiya Shrine (Kasuga) for two days each year, usually the ninth and tenth of the second month.

7. Adopted into the Ōkura line of Noh actors by Ōkura Keiki (1636–98).

8. The line is from Zeami's Noh play "Kagetsu" and describes Saemon Ietsugu's reunion with his only son, Kagetsu, who disappeared as a child and whom he found years later dancing in a Noh performance at Kiyomizu-dera in Kyoto.

9. Perhaps a reference to a legend preserved in *Kao t'ang fu* describing a dream by King Huai of Ch'u (Ch'u Huai-wang) in which he met a witch on Mt. Wushan in Szech'uan Province.

10. The custom of cutting off the antlers of deer at the Kasuga Shrine in Nara began in the Kambun Era (1661–72) and continues to this day.

11. That is, the smoke of cremation biers.

12. Satomura Jōha (1524–1602) was one of the great sixteenth-century masters of linked verse (*renga*) and a native of Nara. His most famous student was Matsunaga Teitoku (1571–1653), one of the founders of the comic linked verse (*haikai no renga*) tradition in which Saikaku excelled.

13. From the puppet play "Yōmei Tennō," describing the legendary love affair between the Chinese emperor Yung Ming and the lady Yu Tai.

14. The young man's name is introduced here without explanation.

15. The temple garden at Shōun-ji, planted in 1625, was famous for its large Sago palms.

16. The word for "to be rained on" (*nureru*) also means "to make love." The pun is not lost on the boy.

17. Kimpira, samurai hero of a puppet play by the same name, was famous for his readiness with the sword. A simple Kimpira puppet allowed the sword to be manipulated by a stick from inside.

2:4 Aloeswood Boy of the East

1. The famous bush clover of Miyagino died out for a time in the Kambun Era (1661–72).

2. A reference to the anonymous *Kokinshū* love poem 694: "Just as the fragile bush clover waits for the wind to remove its burden of dew, so wait I for you."

3. According to the thirteenth-century *Mumyōshō*, Tachibana no Tamenaka returned to the capital from his administrative appointment in Sendai carrying twelve chests filled with bush clover.

4. The Date family of Sendai possessed a fragrant log of aloeswood imported to Japan via Nagasaki in the early years of the Edo Period. Incense made from the log was used to perfume the robes of the family for several generations. The Date called the fragrance *shibabune*, and a portion of the log acquired by the Hosokawa family was called *hatsune*. A piece presented to Emperor Gomizuno-o was named "White Chrysanthemum" (*shiragiku*) because its fragrance reminded him of autumn chrysanthemums.

5. Sakai-chō was the main kabuki theater district in Edo, equivalent to Dōtombori in Osaka and Shijō-gawara in Kyoto. Dekijima Kozarashi is mentioned in *Shin yarō hanagaki* (1674) as possessing "peony-like beauty, unsurpassed acting skill, and a bright, pleasant voice," but he left the stage in 1677 because he grew too big to attract patrons; Edo men apparently liked their boys petite.

6. The title is a parody of *Aki no yo no nagamonogatari* (*Long tale for an autumn night*), a fourteenth-century tale about a priest's love for his temple acolyte and the religious awakening it produced. See Childs, "*Chigo monogatari*: Love Stories or Buddhist Sermons."

7. The estate of the Fujiwara clan in Hiraizumi was destroyed late in the twelfth century by the forces of Minamoto no Yoritomo after his brother Yoshitsune, whom he wanted dead, took refuge there.

2:5 Nightingale in the Snow

1. The *kusagi*, or "stink tree," has attractive white blossoms, but they are ignored because of the tree's foul-smelling leaves.

2. Women were forbidden to enter the temple precincts of Mt. Kōya beyond the women's sanctuary at the foot of the mountain.

3. The reclusive samurai has created an all-male haven for himself in imitation of Mt. Kōya.

4. Such boys were often engaged as boy prostitutes.

5. The short sword used for disembowelment was placed on a low table. When the sword was taken up to begin seppuku, the table was placed as a brace behind the man to prevent his body from falling backwards.

3:1 Grudge Provoked by a Sedge Hat

1. These are characteristics of an unmarried woman.

2. The "first crossing" (*watarizome*) of a new bridge was usually performed by an old married couple with many children or by three genera-

tions of a single family as a way to ensure the bridge's safety and bless its future use.

3. Kiraragoe, also called Kirarazaka, was the shortest route between Enryaku-ji on Mt. Hiei and Kyoto; four *li* is approximately ten miles.

4. Stormy skies in the tenth month were attributed to the movement of the gods who assembled in Izumo at that time each year.

5. A building within the huge temple complex of Enryaku-ji. Gansan Daishi, whose priestly name was Ryōgen, was a tenth-century prelate of Enryaku-ji. His posthumous appellation "Gansan" came from the fact that he died on the third day of the New Year (*ganzan*).

6. Jichin was the posthumous name granted by the court to Jien (1155–1225), priest and scion of the Fujiwara family appointed abbot of Enryaku-ji in 1192.

7. The poem is not among Jichin's (Jien's) known works.

8. Saikaku may have had access to a now lost *setsuwa* source for this legend about Jichin (Jien).

9. Teng T'ung was a favorite of the Chinese emperor Han Wen-ti. Their relationship is recorded in *Han shu*.

10. Wakinoya Yoshiharu was a boy of legendary beauty from the twelfth century.

11. Priests placed a paper death-cap written with Sanskrit letters on the head of a corpse before cremation.

3:2 Tortured to Death

1. Kano Tan'yū (1602–74) was official painter to the Tokugawa shoguns.

2. Ichijō, r. 986–1010.

3. Sei Shōnagon records this self-flattering incident in *Makura no sōshi*.

4. The phrase is a Chinese rhyme, source unknown.

5. This represented a Buddhist death-cap.

6. A phrase used by the Noh chorus during death scenes.

3:3 Sword That Survived Love's Flames

1. Large temple complexes such as Mt. Kōya controlled surrounding villages as sources of income.

2. Ingredients of the vegetarian meals that priests and monks were required to eat.

3. The name "kaburo" means a courtesan's female apprentice and for that reason would have been distasteful to these woman-haters.

4. Women were forbidden to go beyond the sanctuary designated for women at the entrance of the main temple complex at Mt. Kōya.

5. Hsiang Fei, "fragrant concubines," were two concubines of legend-

ary Chinese emperor Shun who drowned themselves in order to follow him in death.

6. Kyūshirō's cremated remains had been divided between his parents and his lover, Hansuke, part to be buried in the family tomb and part to be buried on Mt. Kōya.

3:4 The Sickbed

1. A fortune-teller trained in Chinese astronomy and Taoist thought.
2. Tenkai founded the temple of Kan'ei-ji in Edo in 1624, first year of the Kan'ei Era, by order of the second Tokugawa shogun Hidetada (1579-1632).
3. Chūzon was head priest of Sensō-ji in Asakusa until his death in 1639.
4. *Jōgan seiyō*, a Chinese collection of questions and answers between T'ang emperor T'ai Tzung and his advisers about Confucian precepts used in governing. Tokugawa Ieyasu (1543-1616) made the book essential reading for the samurai administrative elite.
5. The imperial poetic anthology *Shinkokinshū*, compiled in 1205.
6. This refers to the Soga brothers' vendetta in 1193, the fourth year of the Kenkyū Era, to avenge their father's murder.
7. People close to the Tokugawa shogun.
8. In the personal service of the shogun's family.
9. Keiyō-ji was founded in 1620 and moved from Kuramae in Asakusa to its present site in Imado, Taitō-ku in the Jōkyō Era (1684-87).
10. The second (*kaishaku-nin*) was responsible for decapitating the condemned man from behind in order to hasten the end after he had disemboweled himself.
11. The accompanying illustration shows two samurai preparing to commit suicide by running each other through with swords, and another cutting off his topknot in preparation for assuming Buddhist vows.
12. The eastern sky (*azuma no sora*) of Edo, in eastern Japan.

3:5 He Fell in Love

1. "Tiger Gate," one of the gates that led out of Edo castle, where samurai in the shogun's service were confined to barracks (*nagaya*).
2. On the grounds of Shibuya Hachiman Shrine, the Konnō cherry tree is said to have been planted in the twelfth century by Minamoto no Yoritomo (1147-99) as a tribute to his vassal Shibuya no Konnōmaru. It would have been 500 years old at the time of this narrative.
3. Fudō Myō-ō (Sanskrit: *acala*) was the god of fire in the Buddhist pantheon.

4. Chinese legend recorded in *Chuang tzu* gives magical powers to ascetics living on this imaginary mountain.

5. This shrine in Akasaka was named for a local horse-driver named Kantō Koroku who funded the rebuilding of the shrine's main sanctuary in the Keichō Era (1596–1614). He was famous for his singing of popular songs, a link to the previous line of text.

6. One of several crests incorporating a stylized paulownia leaf belonged to the Izumo Matsudaira branch of the Tokugawa family.

7. From Saigyō's *Shinkokinshū* poem 362: "Even the heartless soul feels moved; sandpipers rise from a marsh one early evening in autumn."

8. These are the robes of an adult man, indicating that the lord was relinquishing his sexual claims to the boy and requiring him to undergo the coming-of-age ceremony.

9. This famous well is located in Nara on the site of the first Buddhist temple in Japan, Toyora-dera, founded in the middle of the sixth century by the courtier Soga family.

4:1 Drowned by Love

1. Shinzaike has since been absorbed into the Kyoto imperial palace grounds.

2. Yoshino and Kazuraki are mountains outside Kyoto famous for their cherry trees. *Tayū* was the highest rank a courtesan could attain.

3. Ono no Komachi (ninth century) was one of Japan's legendary "passionate poetesses," renowned for her beauty and, sometimes, for her cold-heartedness.

4. T'ang emperor T'ai Tzung dallied with Yang Kuei Fei at the Hua Ch'ing Villa in Po Chü-i's poem, "Song of Eternal Sorrow."

5. Public ostentation could result in the confiscation of a merchant's entire fortune by the Tokugawa authorities.

6. Ushiwakamaru, the childhood name of Minamoto no Yoshitsune (1159–89), is depicted making love in this manner to Princess Jōruri in *Jōruri gozen monogatari (Jūnidan)*.

7. The Noh play "Michimori" depicts Taira no Michimori in battle gear as he lingers in his wife Kozaishō's arms before the battle of Ichino-tani (1184) in which he died.

4:2 Boy Who Sacrificed His Life

1. Fuwano Mansaku (also, Bansaku; sixteenth century) was a boy famous for his beauty in the service of Toyotomi Hidetsugu, Hideyoshi's adopted heir.

2. *Karin meisho kō*, a reference book for place names used in haikai poetry, was compiled early in the seventeenth century and published in the Kambun Era (1661–72).

3. Sedge hats were worn during daylight hours to conceal one's identity; wearing one in the dark would be unusual.

4. Rounded cuffs identified the wearer as an adult male.

5. The tomb commemorates a similar incident in the Heian Period. A courtier named Moritō loved a woman, Kesa, and plotted to kill her husband, but on the night of the attack Kesa secretly took her husband's place out of loyalty to him and died by her lover Moritō's hand. Moritō killed himself when he discovered what he had done.

4:3 They Waited Three Years to Die

1. The "cloth-pulling" (*nunobiki*) pines derive their name from a local Wakayama legend of a priest who discovered a mirror in the sea and retrieved it with a rope made of cloth.

2. There was a major festival at Kimii-dera on this night. What people called dragon torches (*ryūtō*) was the natural phenomenon of underwater phosphorescence.

3. Saikaku borrowed this argument and the following examples from *Hyaku monogatari* (1659), a collection of 100 entertaining stories about Chinese and Japanese poets.

4. Actually addressed to a male friend, Chang She-jen.

5. *Shinkokinshū* poem 938, by Saigyō.

4:4 Two Old Cherry Trees

1. The third and fourth lines of a poem by T'ang poet Hsu Hun from *San t'i shih*.

2. Mondo kept the wakashu hairstyle his entire life and apparently never underwent the coming-of-age ceremony. To become a man, he would have shaved his head in the adult manner.

3. A young servant, so-named because among his duties was to carry a samurai's or actor's footwear.

4:5 Handsome Youths Having Fun

1. "Wormwood Isle," synonymous with Japan, is another name for the Atsuta Shrine. The name derives from the island of Hōraitō of Chinese legend where holy men were thought to live forever.

2. According to Buddhist legend, an old woman stands at the River of Three Crossings (*sanzu no kawa*) reviling sinners and robbing them of their clothes as they cross into the world of the dead.

3. Pleasure temples (*asobi dera*) were separate buildings within temple compounds rented for parties or poetry meets.

4. A trickster (*karuwaza shi*) from Nagasaki who performed in the Osaka region during the Empō Era (1673–80). Unlike kabuki, attendance at *karuwaza* performances was not restricted for samurai.

5. Rapid tolling of the temple bell (*hayagane*) was a signal of extreme emergency.

6. A two-act play by the kabuki playwright Yagozaemon called "Hinin katakiuchi" was first performed in Osaka in 1664 at the theater of Araki Yojibei.

5:1 Tears in a Paper Shop

1. Fujimura Hatsudayū, not Hanasaki Hatsudayū (as the headnote indicates), is the subject of the following narrative.

2. Also known as wakashu or boys' kabuki, Grand Kabuki (*ō-kabuki*) flourished from 1629 when women were banned from the stage until boys were banned in 1652. Cf. Shively, "Bakufu Versus Kabuki," 238, 242–43.

3. Kyoto theater proprietor and actor, fl. 1652–81. His grandfather, Matahachi, founded the Murayama kabuki dynasty. Matabei adopted Kozakura Sennosuke as his son and gave him the name Murayama Heiemon in 1686 (see 6:2 note 1). His legendary role in reopening Kyoto's theaters after the prohibition of boys' kabuki is recounted in *Yakusha rongo* (1776). See Dunn and Torigoe, *The Actor's Analects*, 44–45, 183. See also Shively, "Bakufu Versus Kabuki," 243.

4. Four *bu* equaled one *ryō* of gold, the most valuable unit of currency. For more on gold and silver values, see Morris, *The Life of an Amorous Woman*, 282–84; Sargent, *The Japanese Family Storehouse*, 235–38; and Hibbett, *The Floating World in Japanese Fiction*, 220.

5. Saikaku probably refers to the 300th anniversary of Kanzan Egen's death, observed in 1659.

6. Hatsudayū may have later changed his name to Handayū, since the actor's crest on his robes in the illustration accompanying this narrative is identical to Fujimura Handayū's in 7:1, "Fireflies Also Work Their Asses at Night."

7. A seventeenth-century Kyoto artisan, famed for dye-work the shade of burnt tea leaves.

8. This would indicate that he stopped having sexual relations with his wife, the most likely cause of resentment in the household.

5:2 He Pleaded for His Life

1. Kabuki was originated in 1603 by Okuni, a shrine dancer from Izumo, and after her death in 1613 was continued by the actress Tayū

Kurōdo (or Kurōzu) until the Tokugawa authorities banned women from the stage in 1629.

2. Kurōemon was the third head of the Shioya Theater, which moved to Osaka from Kyoto soon after kabuki's inception in 1603. After female kabuki was banned, it reopened with boys' kabuki, and in 1653 regrouped once again as men's kabuki.

3. Utanosuke was an actor of female roles, Shizuma an actor of boys' roles at the Shioya Theater in the years prior to 1652.

4. Saikaku is indicating that homosexual relations between men and boys were widespread and not limited to the worlds of the samurai and kabuki theater depicted in *Nanshoku ōkagami*.

5. This barb is directed at the fifth Tokugawa shogun Tsunayoshi's unpopular edicts protecting the lives of dogs. Cf. Shively, "Tokugawa Tsunayoshi, the Genroku Shogun," 95–96.

6. Though Sakai (Osaka) was Japan's largest port in the seventeenth century, all foreign trade was conducted from Nagasaki. This was part of the Tokugawa policy of national isolation begun in 1616 and completed in 1641 when the small Dutch colony at Hirado was abolished and the remaining colony confined to the tiny island of Dejima in Nagasaki harbor.

5:3 Love's Flame Kindled

1. Sennojō was an actor of female roles in the Murayama Theater in Kyoto between 1650 and 1660, spanning the shift from boys' kabuki to men's kabuki. Theater records indicate he performed in Edo in 1661 at the Nakamura Theater in Sakai-chō, and died in 1670 at the age of 35 or 36.

2. A lover of Arihara no Narihira's in *Ise monogatari* and subject of the Noh play "Izutsu."

3. According to superstition, 42 is a dangerous age for men; the phrase may simply mean that Sennojō played female roles until his death.

4. "Kawachi gayoi" established Sennojō's popularity with Edo audiences in 1661 at the Nakamura Theater. The play was based on the *Ise monogatari* story of Arihara no Narihira's nightly visits to a woman called the Takayasu Lady in Kawachi.

5. *Yarō mushi* (1660) says of Sennojō: "His face, form, and artistry are beyond criticism. He is slightly past his prime, however, like a twenty-day-old moon, and will soon become a man, which we find most regrettable." For excerpts from the preface of *Yarō mushi*, see Shively, "Bakufu Versus Kabuki," 240–41.

6. The Han emperor Yuan decided to send a concubine as a good-will gesture to the king of the Huns, with whom he was forming an alliance;

in order to make the choice, he had artists paint likenesses of each of his more than 3,000 wives. Because Wang Chao Chun failed to bribe the painter, Emperor Yuan thought her the least beautiful of his concubines and sent her as consort to the Hun king, though she was in fact a great beauty.

7. Poems were composed to go with pictures as a form of elegant amusement.

8. That is, the Buddhist abbots forgot their vows of chastity and acted like laymen. *Hakama* were trouser-like skirts not normally worn by priests.

9. Kabuki performances began early in the morning and played until dusk.

10. Reference to the Lover's Tomb (Koizuka) in Toba. See 4:2 note 5.

5:4 Visiting from Edo

1. The broad-billed roller gets its name, *buppōsō*, from its call (actually the call of a species of owl), which sounds like the words for the Three Treasures (*sampō*) of Shingon Buddhism: the Buddha (*butsu*), the Law (*hō*), and the Priesthood (*sō*). It is traditionally linked to Mt. Kōya, the center of Shingon Buddhism. The connection to Matsuno-o in Kyoto comes from *Shinsen waka rokujō* poem 2555 by Fujiwara Mitsutoshi: "The peak of Mt. Matsuno-o looms silent in the dawn; looking up, I hear the cry of *buppōsō*." The link to Kōki-ji comes from a poem in Chinese by Kūkai composed after hearing the bird's song during a stay at the temple.

2. The name in the headnote, Tamagawa Shuzen, is the correct one. He was an actor of female roles in Kyoto in the years immediately surrounding the banning of boys' kabuki in 1652. In 1661 he moved to Edo and established a theater in Sakai-chō, later forming a joint venture with Ichimura Takenojō. He left the world of kabuki in 1673 and took the priestly name of Kaken, according to *Kokon yakusha monogatari* (1678).

3. Tamai Asanojō was an actor of female roles in Tamagawa Shuzen's (note 2) kabuki troupe. Theater records indicate he was active from 1661 to 1681.

4. According to *Yarō mushi* (1660), Yamamoto Kantarō was an actor of boy's roles. He moved to Edo in 1661, the same year as Tamagawa Shuzen (note 2), and returned to the Kyoto-Osaka area in 1675 or 1676, after which disappears from theater records.

5:5 Kichiya Riding a Horse

1. An actor of female roles, Tamamura Kichiya left Kyoto in 1661 and moved to the Inishie Theater in Edo; there is no record of him after 1673.

2. Ebisuya Kichirōbei was a well-known actor of female roles from 1652 to 1657.

3. See 2:1 note 1; the attribution is doubtful.

4. The incident occurred in the sixth month of 1652.

5. It was traditional at the Setsubun Festival, occurring on the spring equinox, to eat the number of beans equivalent to one's age.

6. The bridge across the Kamo River at Shijō was destroyed in a flood in 1676; the temporary bridge that replaced it was popularly called *kuzurebashi*, "crumbling bridge."

7. Yamashiro Kinai, a well-known contemporary jōruri chanter.

8. Bandō Matakurō (d. 1700) was an actor of jester roles. In 1661 he moved to Edo and established two theaters, his own and the Mori Theater.

9. According to *Yarō mushi*, Yoshida Iori was working in the Murayama Theater in Kyoto in 1660; in 1661 he moved to the Inishie Theater in Edo, where he acted boys' roles.

10. Nogawa Kichijūrō was an actor of female roles, active 1661–81, first in Kyoto and after 1666 in Edo at the Nakamura Theater.

11. Kagawa Ukon acted in the Ebisuya Theater in Kyoto from 1658 to 1673.

12. Woodblock prints or paintings of actors were presented to temples and shrines as offerings.

13. Active in Edo from about 1665 to 1681, Bōzu Kohei established the original "buffoon" stage-type that was imitated by other actors of jester roles.

6:1 Winecup Overflowing with Love

1. Because they have renounced all worldly attachments and desires. The sentiment is expressed by Sei Shōnagon in *Makura no sōshi*: "There is nothing more difficult than seeing a son you love become a priest. He grows more dear because you must think of him as a scrap of wood."

2. An actor of female roles and the second to bear this name, Itō Kodayū began his acting career in Kyoto, but in 1661 moved to the Inishie Theater in Edo. He returned to Kyoto in 1672 and with Uemura Kichiya became one of the great onnagata actors of his day. He is believed to have died in 1688.

3. A misquotation, as Saikaku recognizes, of *Hyakunin isshu* poem 67 by Suho no Naishi: "Spring nights are but a dream, pillowed in your arms; I hate to see my good name fold for something so pointless."

4. The original sense of this poem by Tu Mu (803–852) is more like "The will of the emperor is the will of the nation," but Saikaku suggests an emotive interpretation of the word *kokoro* (Chinese: *hsin*).

5. Unknown.

6. Based on Kokuraya Gembei's ransoming of the top-ranking cour-
tesan of the Shimabara, Yoshino, for the sum of 1,000 gold *ryō* in 1679.
The play had a highly acclaimed run of six months in 1680 with Itō
Kodayū playing Yoshino.

7. The usual fee for a boy actor was one piece of silver (one *chōgin*),
but Itō Kodayū commanded three times that. His nickname derived from
the fact that three pieces of silver (*sammai*) sounds like the word for graveyard (*zammai*).

8. The weight of three silver *chōgin* coins, about a pound of silver.

9. *Akusho*, a pejorative name for the pleasure quarter (normally, *yūri*
or *kuruwa*).

10. *Tsutomego*, a euphemism for actors engaged in boy prostitution.

11. *Tōjin* referred to Chinese and Korean people and in popular slang
meant "idiot" or "fool."

12. A pun on *asa murasaki*, "pale purple; morning purple."

13. Unknown.

14. One of the top four actors at this time in the Nakamura Theater
in Edo, Hanai Saizaburō first played boys' roles and, after he matured,
switched to men's roles.

15. When the Murayama Theater in Kyoto failed in 1661, Kumenosuke was among those who sought work in Edo, where he appeared
with Tamagawa Sennojō on the Inishie Theater stage as Imamura
Kumenosuke.

16. A theater proprietor in Kyoto, also known as Gombō Shōzaemon.

17. This may refer to the samurai riot at Kamisuki-chō in 1656
sparked by problems between the onnagata Hashimoto Kinsaku and a
samurai named Kawashima, after which theaters in Kyoto were temporarily closed by the authorities. Cf. Shively, "Bakufu Versus Kabuki," 243.
The exact location of Kamisuki-chō is unknown, but a reference in 7:1,
"Fireflies Also Work Their Asses at Night," places it near the no-longer-
standing Great Buddha in Kyoto.

18. Kitano Tenjin Shrine, dedicated to the spirit of Sugawara no
Michizane (805–903), celebrates his death day in the second month with
a festival on the 25th of each month.

6:2 Kozakura's Figure

1. The flower imagery in the opening lines is inspired by the name
Kozakura, "little cherry." Said to be the adopted son of Murayama Matabei, he played female roles from about 1673 until relinquishing his name
to a younger onnagata in 1686. He then played men's roles under the

name Murayama Heiemon. In 1683 he was earning an annual salary of 100 *ryō* at the Araki Theater in Osaka.

2. A reference to a Chinese "never cry wolf" story, in which Emperor Yu during the Chou Dynasty lit signal fires summoning all his ministers and armies in order to amuse his concubine, Pao Szu. Later, under actual attack, the signal fires were ignored and the empire fell.

3. Patron saint of actors and courtesans, enshrined at Shitennō-ji in Osaka.

4. Matsumoto Kodayū was a minor actor of boy's roles in Kyoto and Osaka, 1661–80.

5. The son of the onnagata Masanosuke who died in 1694, Ima-Masanosuke (Masanosuke II) began as an actor of boy's roles, then in 1684 switched to female roles at the Araki Theater in Osaka. In 1691 he moved to Edo and gained fame there for his stage depictions of old women. He died in 1724.

6. Brother of Suzuki Heihachi (see 6:5 note 1), Heishichi was an actor of boys' and later men's roles in the Yamatoya Theater in Osaka from about 1684 until 1693, when he moved to the Yamamura Theater in Edo. Nothing is known of his career after 1699. See Dunn and Torigoe, *The Actor's Analects*, 64, 190.

7. Araki Yojibei lived from 1637 to 1700. He was the adopted son of Saitō Yogorō, founder of the jester role in Osaka, and was an outstanding actor of men's roles in his own right. He ran the Araki Theater in Osaka. See Dunn and Torigoe, *The Actor's Analects*, 174.

8. Matsumoto Bunzaemon is known only from a reference in *Kokon shibai hyakunin isshu* (1693), in the section on Matsumoto Nazaemon (see 8:1 note 6).

9. Symbolizing the close bond between husband and wife.

10. According to myth recorded in the *Nihongi*, the sexual union of the god Izanagi and goddess Izanami produced the islands of Japan and the sun goddess, Amaterasu, who ruled them.

11. A mythical one-winged bird that required its mate to fly (see 1:2 note 13).

12. The headnote states that the tryst took place in the man's lodgings at the Sasanoya.

13. Probably Tanaka Jiemon, a student of Saikaku's who contributed 24 verses to a haikai sequence in *Kubako* (1679), a collection of poetry by Saikaku's students. His haikai name was Teihō.

6:3 Man Who Resented Another's Shouts

1. An epithet for Ikkyū (d. 1481), rector of Daitoku-ji in Murasakino, Kyoto. In responding to a parishioner's questions about salvation, he

preached that since even innocent fans were unable to keep the Buddha's commandments, sinful people could hardly expect to keep them without great effort. When asked what he meant, Ikkyū explained that paintings on fans were false images and thus broke the Buddha's command against committing deception.

2. A family of artists, beginning in the twelfth century.

3. Sung Dynasty poet and painter, also known as Su Shih (1036–1101).

4. Tsukubane has a famous waterfall, and the name Takii contains the word "waterfall." His short but brilliant career began in 1661 in Kyoto, and in 1663 he achieved great popularity as an onnagata in Edo at the Ichimura Theater. He returned to Kyoto the same year and did not go back to Edo until the year he died, 1667, when he joined the Nakamura Theater. In the last year of his life he enjoyed the patronage of a Tokugawa magistrate, Shimada, Daimyo of Izumo.

5. See 5:3 note 6.

6. The kabuki stage developed from Noh prototypes and was framed by four corner posts, of which the *shite* column was on the far left, closest to the walkway (*hashigakari*, or, on the kabuki stage, *hanamichi*) that led to and from the stage.

7. Bandō Matajirō was an actor of jester roles at the Ichimura and Morita Theaters in Edo during the years 1661–80.

8. A multi-talented (*mannō*) jack-of-all-trades in the theater, Mannō-gan Gorōbei got his name because he could act, sing, chant jōruri, and perform comedy routines and acrobatic feats.

9. From a Chinese treatise on death, *Chiu hsiang shih*.

10. The Morita and Yamamura Theaters were located in Kobiki-chō, Edo.

11. Forests were said to have died and turned white after the death of the Buddha.

12. No independent information corroborates the kabuki connection with Negi-chō that Saikaku implies here.

6:4 A Secret Visit

1. Uemura Kichiya (d. 1724) was a protégé of the Osaka actor Saitō Yogorō but achieved his greatest fame as an onnagata in Kyoto at the Nakanoshima Theater at Shijō. He retired in 1681 and afterwards made his living selling face powder. His haikai verses appeared in *Dōtombori hanamichi* (1679), a collection to which Saikaku also contributed.

2. Ukon Genzaemon moved to Edo in 1652, the year boys were banned from the kabuki stage, and became one of the first great onnagata actors in the era of men's kabuki. He is said to have invented the use of a purple kerchief to hide the shaved part of his head.

3. Murayama Sakon predated Ukon by almost two decades. Originally from Osaka, he took the acting of female roles to Edo around 1640 and performed at his brother Matasaburō's theater, the Murayamaza. He is commonly linked with Ukon as the finest onnagata of their respective eras.

4. See 2:4 note 1.

5. Resembling parcheesi, a throw of the dice determines the number of spaces a piece is moved.

6:5 He Never Performed in the Capital

1. Brother of Suzuki Heishichi (see 6:2 note 6), Heihachi made his stage debut in 1676 and by 1684 was earning a salary of 90 *ryō* at the Osaka Araki Theater. He died at the age of 23 in 1686, on the eighth day of the intercalary third month, shortly before Saikaku began writing *Nanshoku ōkagami*.

2. See 6:3 note 3.

3. Su Shih (note 2) composed "Ode to the Red Cliffs" (*Ch'ih pi fu*) in 1082.

4. A reference to Suzuki Saburō (Shigeie), trusted retainer of Minamoto no Yoshitsune who died with him in his final battle at Koromogawara (1189).

5. The Jōkyō Era was from 1684 to 1687.

6. This was a kabuki version of Uji Kaganojō's jōruri play performed at the Yamatoya Theater in Osaka in 1686.

7. Amidha Buddhism taught that humankind need only grasp the threads of light extending from Amitabha's hands in order to be reborn in the Western Paradise.

8. The moat at Dōtombori, Osaka's theater district.

9. A major festival day in Osaka, when people went to worship at the Sumiyoshi Shrine and gather shellfish at low tide along the Sumiyoshi cove.

10. A form of smelling salts.

11. Sakata Gin'emon was a minor actor of men's roles at the Yamatoya Theater in Osaka from 1673 to 1688.

12. Takemoto lived from 1651 to 1714. From a family of farmers, he took the name Gidayū in 1684 and became one of the most prominant jōruri chanters of the Genroku Era. His chief rival was Uji Kaganojō (1635–1711). In 1701 he changed his name to Takemoto Chikugonojō. See Dunn and Torigoe, *The Actor's Analects*, 191.

13. See 5:5 note 9.

14. An actor of boys' roles beginning in 1680, Sakurayama Rinnosuke

switched to men's roles in 1696 and changed his name to Sakurayama Shōzaemon. He is one of a handful of kabuki's greatest actors, excelling at both domestic and historical roles.

15. See 6:4 note 1.

16. From a Chinese treatise on death, *Chiu hsiang shih*.

17. Buddhist sutras chanted in the original Sanskrit were thought to have the power to fundamentally alter a person's karma.

18. Exactly one month after the girl's death. An additional month was added every three years to make the lunar calendar consistent wih solar time.

7:1 Fireflies

1. Cf. "In the Edo Period professional male entertainers, corresponding (very roughly) to European jesters, buffoons or 'allowed fools'; they would accompany customers on drinking expeditions to the gay quarters, where they often had the role of elegant panders. They would frequently supervise the entertainment at fashionable parties and had considerable influence over the courtesans." Morris, *The Life of an Amorous Woman*, 294.

2. See 5:5 note 9.

3. Fujimura Handayū was an actor of female roles in the Kyoto theater of Murayama Matabei from about 1658 according to *Yarō mushi* (1660); he moved to the Morita Theater in Edo in 1675. He is thought to be the same actor called Hatsudayū (see 5:1 note 6) in 5:1, "Tears in a Paper Shop," because the actor's crest on their robes is identical.

4. An all-night entertainment district by the Kamo River at Shijō named for the stone wall that lined the river bank; the Ōtsuruya was one of several eating and lodging establishments in that district.

5. *Teki*, special term for a paying "patron" used by boy actors and courtesans.

6. *Massha*, literally "secondary shrine," was another name for drum-holders that derived from their secondary status to the paying patron, who was called *honsha*, "main shrine."

7. Kagura Shōzaemon was one of the four most sought-after and influential drum-holders in Kyoto in the years 1673–87.

8. Pantomime dance with musical accompaniment, performed at shrine festivals.

9. "Narutaki no nusubito," kabuki version of a Noh play "Hana nusubito" ("The flower thief").

10. Each weighing one *bu* (¼ *ryō*) of gold. According to Saikaku in *Shin-yoshiwara tsunezunegusa* (1689), the name derived from the fact that

the temple Chōtoku-ji in Sugaru rented entertainment rooms for that amount.

11. *Sumata* was a technique of intercrural (between the thighs) copulation that produced the sensation of intercourse without allowing actual penetration. Apparently used only rarely in Japan, it was the preferred method of intercourse between men and boys in classical Greece. Cf. "When courtship has been successful, the erastes [man] and eromenos [boy] stand facing one another; the erastes grasps the eromenos round the torso, bows his head on to or even below the shoulder of the eromenos, bends his knees and thrusts his penis between the eromenos's thighs just below the scrotum. [...] The original specific word for this type of copulation is almost certainly *diamērizein*, i.e. 'do ... between the thighs (*mēroi*).'" Dover, *Greek Homosexuality*, 98.

12. Eight bells would have made it 2 A.M.; seven bells, 4 A.M.

13. "Heianjō miyako utsushi," a jōruri play by Uji Kaganojō (1635–1711). The michiyuki is generally the play's final scene in the puppet theater. As characters set out for their final destination, their emotions and thoughts are revealed through descriptions of the countryside and places they pass. The michiyuki in "Heianjō" begins, "In truth, I am like the cicada or the firefly; I cry, I burn, yet know not which way to go."

14. *Ise monogatari*, chap. 39.

7:2 An Onnagata's Tosa Diary

TITLE: The tenth-century *Tosa nikki*, an account of Ki no Tsurayuki's return to the capital from Tosa by boat in 936, used the fictional guise of a lady in his retinue to record his grief over his daughter's death. Saikaku's narrative is a parody, reversing the direction of the trip and cleverly reworking lines of the original.

1. An actor of female roles, Matsushima Han'ya retired from the stage at age twenty in 1686, the year Saikaku wrote this elegiac narrative. In the actor-evaluation book *Naniwa tachigiki mukashi banashi* (1686), he is listed as earning a salary of 30 gold *ryō* in the Araki Theater. His haikai verses appeared with those of other Saikaku students in *Dōtombori hanamichi* (1679) under the name Matsumoto Chisen.

2. Hiragi Hyōshirō was an Osaka actor of men's roles and brother-in-law of Sakata Tōjūrō (see 8:1 note 19).

3. Unknown.

4. Unknown.

5. Shirinashi, literally "No ass," is a tributary of the Yodo River on which the boat is traveling.

6. He is reminded of Han'ya by a word play involving the phrase "half visible," where "half" is the character *han* in Han'ya's name.

7. Abducted from the capital in *Sagoromo monogatari*, Lady Asukai drowned herself in the sea at Mushiake. Her farewell poem read, "Breeze from my fan, blow and tell them that I have become a weed at the bottom of the swift-flowing sea."

8. Tosa was a major producer of inkstones.

7:3 An Unworn Robe

1. The word for fee (*hana*) also means blossom; thus the phrase "available for viewing pleasure."

2. Only Kyoto, Osaka, and Edo had permanent theaters with resident troupes that performed regularly throughout the year; dramatic entertainment in the provinces was performed by itinerant actors. See "The Structure of Kabuki" in Dunn and Torigoe, *The Actor's Analects*, 15–20.

3. Sanskrit: *Ksitigarbha bodhisattva*, a guardian deity of children.

4. Sanskrit: *Mañjú srî bodhisattva*, deity of wisdom.

5. The provinces around Osaka: Yamashiro, Yamato, Kawachi, Izumi, and Settsu.

6. *Rokujizō*, Jizō of the Six States of Existence.

7. Highest ranking boy actor of female roles in the kabuki theater.

8. An actor of boys' roles, Togawa Hayanojō committed suicide on the second day of the New Year, 1686, unable to pay his clothier bills. In the third month of the same year, another actor named Takikawa Ichiya killed himself for the same reason. Saikaku wrote about both suicides in *Wankyū nisei no monogatari* (1691).

9. Yamatoya Jimbei lived from about 1650 to 1704; he began as an actor of boys' roles by the name of Tsurukawa Tatsunosuke and in the 1670's adopted the name of his father, founder of the Yamatoya Theater in Osaka. The actor-evaluation book *Yarō tachiyaku butai ōkagami* (1687) describes him as a very handsome actor popular·particularly with women, as Saikaku demonstrates in 8:5, "Who Wears the Incense Graph Dyed in Her Heart?" See Dunn and Torigoe, *The Actor's Analects*, 64–66, 193.

10. Fujita Koheiji originally worked in the Ebisuya Theater in Kyoto, but in the 1680's he switched to the Yamatoya Theater and was active there until 1695. He was best known for samurai roles and wielded the sword with skill onstage. *Yakusha rongo* (1776) says of him, "Fujita Koheiji was an actor who won fame for the portrayal of *jitsugoto* parts. On one occasion he said, 'When slapping one's sword one should glare straight into one's opponent's eyes.'" Dunn and Torigoe, *The Actor's Analects*, 89, also 94, 177.

11. An actor of boys' roles in the Yamatoya Theater, Onoe Gentarō was the first of a long line of kabuki actors to bear the name Onoe.

12. Merchants sold material goods and were entitled to collect money

due them at the end of the year, but those who sold services—such as courtesans, actors, and doctors—were expected to wait for their customers to come and pay.

13. Sakata Kodenji was an actor of female roles in Osaka from the 1670's to late 1680's. Saikaku mentions him in 5:7, *Kōshoku ichidai otoko*.

14. An actor of boys' roles in the Yamatoya Theater, Yamamoto Sagenda appears in the actor-evaluation book *Yakusha hakkei* (1680). According to 8:4, "The Koyama Barrier Keeper," he was raised as a child by the famous onnagata Ukon Genzaemon (see 6:4 note 2).

7:4 Bamboo Clappers

1. Tamamura Kichiya was an actor of female roles from 1658 to 1660 in the Kyoto Ebisuya Theater, where he scored a great success as Yang Kuei Fei in the play "Hanaikusa" (see 1:4 note 8). In 1661 he moved to the Inishie Theater in Edo, but nothing is known of him after 1673.

2. *Fubokushō* poem 11307 by Fujiwara no Ieyoshi: "Fragrant on the banks of the Hitsukawa, the late-blooming birch cherries drop their petals, signaling the blossoms' final end."

3. *Shinchokusen* poem 657 by Minamoto no Tamenaka: "Since first parting the luxuriant growth of dew-covered grass on the mountain of your love, how damp my sleeves have grown."

4. Founder of the Akita dynasty of actors, Hikosaburō played jester roles in Kyoto and Osaka in the years 1661–80. *Yakusha hyōban gejigeji* (1674) describes him as a master of mime, acrobatics, and humorous monologues.

7:5 Nails Hammered into an Amateur Painting

1. *Fubokushō* poem 11631 by Fujiwara no Tameie (d. 1275).

2. Okada Samanosuke's career spanned approximately 1680 to 1700. He was an actor of female roles in 1684–85 in the Osaka Araki Theater, and in 1686 he moved to the Okamura Theater in Kyoto. He joined the Murayama troupe in Edo in 1696. See Dunn and Torigoe, *The Actor's Analects*, 185.

3. Arashi San'emon (1635–90) was a tremendously influential actor and theater proprietor from 1673 to 1688. He scored great successes in Kyoto with the play "Tamba no Yosaku" in 1677, and again in 1680 with "Yoshino miuke" where he played opposite Itō Kodayū (Kodayū played Yoshino; see 6:1 note 2) in the role of her ransomer, Kokuraya Gembei. Around 1682 he moved his theater to Osaka. His name appears in many actor-evaluation books of the day, including *Naniwa tachigiki mukashi*

banashi (1686) and *Yarō tachiyaku butai ōkagami* (1687). See Dunn and Torigoe, *The Actor's Analects*, 138–39, 175.

4. Arashi Monzaburō lived from 1661 to 1701. The son of San'emon, he played female roles beginning about 1680 and by 1683 was playing boys' roles in his father's theater in Osaka, the Arashi Theater, according to Saikaku's actor-evaluation book *Naniwa no kao wa Ise no oshiroi* (1683?). At his father's death in 1690, he took the name San'emon. See Dunn and Torigoe, *The Actor's Analects*, 175.

5. Sawamura Kodenji lived from about 1665 to 1705. He began as an actor of boys' roles in Kyoto and by 1682 was working in the Arashi Theater in Osaka. After Suzuki Heihachi's death in 1686 (see 6:5 note 1), he was ranked as the top actor of boys' roles in the Kyoto-Osaka region. According to *Naniwa tachigiki mukashi banashi* (1686), he was 22 years old in that year and earned an annual salary of 75 gold *ryō*. Saikaku includes him in *Naniwa no kao wa Ise no oshiroi* (1683?). See Dunn and Torigoe, *The Actor's Analects*, 188.

6. Fujita Tsurumatsu was an actor of female roles in the Yamatoya Theater in Osaka from 1682. Saikaku says he was a member of Arashi San'emon's troupe in *Naniwa no kao wa Ise no oshiroi* (1683?).

7. "Ransan" was Arashi San'emon's (note 3) nickname, made up of an alternate reading of the character for Arashi and the "san" of San'emon.

8. Possibly a nickname for Fujita Tsurumatsu (note 6).

9. A type of glaze, usually black with iridescent spots.

10. Brother of Uemura Kichiya II (who succeeded the first Uemura Kichiya after his retirement in 1681; see 6:4 note 1), Tatsuya was an actor of female roles and earned a salary of 130 gold *ryō* at age twenty according to *Naniwa tachigiki mukashi banashi* (1686). It also mentions that he was a heavy drinker who was known on occasion to draw his sword and threaten his patrons. He committed suicide in 1691.

11. Arashi Ima-Kyōnosuke was a minor actor of boys' roles in the theater of Arashi San'emon from 1683, according to Saikaku in *Naniwa no kao wa Ise no oshiroi* (1683?).

12. The visit to Sumiyoshi Shrine occurs in the Akashi chapter of *Genji monogatari*, on Genji's return from exile to the capital.

13. *Fubokushō* poem 15165 by Jien (Jichin; see 3:1 note 6).

14. The Onda rice-planting festival was celebrated annually on the 28th day of the fifth month at Sumiyoshi Shrine. If it rained on that day, it was referred to as "Tora's tears" in reference to Tora Gozen's tearful farewell to her lover, one of the Soga brothers, as he set off on his fateful vendetta.

15. A koto tune composed by Yatsuhashi Kenkō (d.1684).

16. The Hsun Yang River was near Kiukang, Kiangsi Province in China. Reference is to the story of a red-haired orangutang living on the river that presented a man with a bottomless keg of liquor, theme of the Noh play "Shōjō" (Orangutang). The unkempt, dry hair of the fishermen with its reddish color evokes the orangutang image.

17. In the Noh play "Hakurakuten," the great T'ang Dynasty Chinese poet Po Chü-i (Pai Lo-t'ien, 772–846) comes to Japan to measure the learning (*chie*) of the Japanese people. He encounters a fisherman, actually the god of Sumiyoshi Shrine in disguise, who confounds Po Chü-i with his knowledge of poetry. Po returns to China in amazement, declaring that the learning of the Japanese people must be unequaled since even fishermen are great poets! Saikaku uses the word *chie nashi* (lacking learning, "idiocy") to refer to their foolish drunkenness.

18. *Ezōshi*, a one-page scandal sheet sold for a small sum on the streets of the major cities.

19. An encyclopedia in twenty volumes of linked verse poetic diction and word associations, published in 1669.

20. The story is told of a Chin Dynasty monk named Hui Yuan who swore never to leave his hermitage in Kiangsi Province beyond the bridge at Tiger Gorge. One day he became engrossed in conversation while sending two other monks on their way home, and inadvertently crossed the bridge, whereupon the three monks shared a hearty laugh. It became a favorite theme of Chinese painting.

21. In the shape of a cherry blossom seen from below.

22. Sadoshimaya was one of the houses of prostitution in Osaka's Shinmachi. Yoshida was listed as a courtesan there in *Shokoku irozato annai* (1688).

23. The story appears in *Taiheiki* of Aoto Fujitsuna, a thirteenth-century counselor to Kamakura regent Hōjō Tokiyori, desperately searching for coins lost during a river crossing. Saikaku has a rendition of it in *Buke giri monogatari* (1688). See Callahan, *Tales of Samurai Honor*, 31.

24. Theme of the Noh play "Tsuri-gitsune," in which an old fox turns itself into the monk Hakuzōsu in an attempt to dissuade a hunter from continuing to trap and kill foxes.

25. To ward off evil; that is, "knock on wood."

26. Listed in the guide to pleasure quarters *Shokoku irozato annai* (1688).

27. Araki Yojibei, proprieter of the Araki Theater in Dōtombori. See 6:2 note 7.

28. Born in 1659, he began his acting career in Kyoto as Takii Namie and changed his name to Namie Kokan in 1680 when he moved to Dō-tombori in Osaka. In 1681 he acted female roles to great acclaim in the

Araki Theater opposite Arashi San'emon (note 3). His name last appears in theater programs around 1694. See Dunn and Torigoe, *The Actor's Analects*, 64, 184.

29. Yoshikawa Tamon was an actor of female roles at the Araki Theater from 1680. In 1684 he was earning 110 gold *ryō* to Namie Kokan's (note 28) 90-*ryō* salary, according to records in the Araki Theater. Late in 1686, he moved to the Okamura Theater in Kyoto according to *Yarō tachiyaku butai ōkagami* (1687) and continued to perform into the early 1700's.

30. Ueda Saizaburō was an actor of boys' roles in the Araki Theater, according to Saikaku in *Naniwa no kao wa Ise no oshiroi* (1683?).

31. See 6:2 note 1.

32. Son of Araki Yojibei, Yoshikawa Gempachi is listed by another name, Genzaburō, as being 22 years old in *Naniwa tachigiki mukashi banashi* (1686); it states "Though he plays the drum well, his acting is poor. He draws no salary, as he is supported by Yojibei."

33. Mitsue Kasen was an actor of female roles in the Araki Theater, according to *Yarō tachiyaku butai ōkagami* (1687).

34. Nakagawa Kinnojō was a highly acclaimed actor of men's roles; his acting career spanned the years 1681–1704. See Dunn and Torigoe, *The Actor's Analects*, 87, 94–95, 184.

35. *Kokon shibai hyakunin isshu* (1693) mentions Namboku Sabu as a jester specializing in the roles of country bumpkins and fools. He is first mentioned in theater records in 1674 and made his last appearance in 1695 at Takeshima Kōzaemon's (see 8:5 note 12) theater in Osaka.

8:1 Goblin with a Beautiful Voice

1. A legendary man from Han China whose longevity was the theme of a Noh play, "Tōbō Saku."

2. An illustration of a treasure boat (*takarabune*), in which rode the seven gods of good fortune (*shichi fukujin*), was spread under one's pillow on the last night of the year to ensure pleasant dreams and wealth in the New Year.

3. One bean for each year of age. See 5:5 note 5.

4. Fujita Minanojō was the adopted son of Fujita Koheiji and began his highly acclaimed career as an actor of girls' roles in 1674 at the age of eighteen (*Yakusha hyōban gejigeji*, 1674). *Yarō tachiyaku butai ōkagami* (1687) is the last actor-evaluation book to mention him: "Though lovely as cherry blossoms and autumn leaves combined, everyone knows that Fujita's nickname is 'handy folding screen' because he is so selfish." The nickname is mentioned in a headnote to the story.

5. Fujita Koheiji. See 7:3 note 10.

6. Popular as an actor of boy's roles prior to the ban on boys' kabuki in 1652, Matsumoto Nazaemon later established his own theater, the Matsumoto-za, and in the 1670's was considered the top actor of leading men's roles. He died about 1685. See Dunn and Torigoe, *The Actor's Analects*, 94, 181.

7. Asaka Shume was the boyhood stage name of an actor later known as Ichimura Shirōtsugu. He began as an actor of boys' roles under the proprietor Komai Shōzaemon in Kyoto and Osaka. He moved to Edo after reaching adulthood and began acting men's roles, returning to Kyoto in 1684. In the eleventh month of 1686 he joined the Arashi Theater troupe (*Yarō tachiyaku butai ōkagami*, 1687).

8. Unknown.

9. *Kokon yakusha monogatari* (1678) lists Uemura Monnojō as a young Edo actor living in Fukiya-chō.

10. Unknown.

11. A Kyoto painter and dyer (*Jinrin kinmō zui*).

12. Unknown.

13. The kabuki playwright Tominaga Heibei (fl. 1670–1700) became the first to break the tradition of anonymity and have his name appear in a theater program as author. His popularity waned after Chikamatsu Monzaemon began writing kabuki plays. *Yakusha rongo* (1776) reports, "Tominaga Heibei was a writer who came after Yagozaemon, and his was the first instance of a writer's name appearing, as it does now, along with the list of actors in the program of the first performance of the year. This was at the *kaomise* late in 1680, and on that occasion it brought him a good deal of enmity from all sides." Dunn and Torigoe, *The Actor's Analects*, 95, also 192.

14. Ranshū no Yozaemon, literally, "heavy-drinking Yozaemon," was numbered with Kagura Shōzaemon among the four top drum-holders of the day.

15. Kawashima Kazuma was an actor of boys' roles in the Arashi Theater, Osaka, in 1686 (*Naniwa tachigiki mukashi banashi*, 1686).

16. Tamamoto Kazuma was an actor of boys' roles in the Ebisuya Theater, Kyoto (*Yakusha hyōban gejigeji*, 1674).

17. Unknown. The same name appears in 7:2, "An Onnagata's Tosa Diary."

18. Hanasaki Sakichi was a Kyoto drum-holder in the 1680's and 1690's. His name appears again in Saikaku's *Kōshoku seisuiki* (1688).

19. Sakata Tōjūrō (1647–1709) was the definitive actor of leading men's roles in the Kyoto-Osaka area during the Genroku Period. His career is intimately linked with a fruitful collaboration with Chikamatsu

Monzaemon. He wrote comic linked verse and contributed to several collections containing the work of Saikaku's students. For a synopsis of his
career, see Keene, *World Within Walls*, 251–53. He receives lengthy treatment in *Yakusha rongo* (1776). See Dunn and Torigoe, *The Actor's Analects*,
67–105, 122–37, 187.

20. Fujikawa Buzaemon (1632–1729) was an actor of male roles from
the mid-1670's. *Yarō tachiyaku butai ōkagami* (1687) called him "the
best actor of samurai roles in Kyoto." He retired from the stage in 1722
after a long and successful career. See Dunn and Torigoe, *The Actor's
Analects*, 176.

21. Arashi Saburōshirō (1663–87) began his brief career in the Edo
theater of Nakamura Kanzaburō, where he went by the name Nakamura
Kannosuke. In 1677 he moved to Kyoto and joined the theater of Arashi
San'emon and adopted a new name. His suicide in 1687, in circumstances
involving both love and money, became the topic of a story Saikaku published in 1691, *Arashi mujō monogatari* (*The tale of Arashi's brief life*).

22. From *Shūishū* poem 88 by Kakinomoto no Hitomaro: "I shall
pluck a garland of wisteria, fragrant even reflected in the bottom of Tago
Bay, for the sake of my parted love."

23. Fujita Minanojō's name contains the word "wisteria," linking him
to the Tago Bay poem (note 22).

8:2 Siamese Roosters

1. In Saikaku's actor-evaluation book, *Naniwa no kao wa Ise no oshiroi*
(1683?), he records that a rich patron from Sakai presented Mineno Kozarashi with a pillow two *ken* (about twelve feet) in length.

2. In *Genji monogatari*, chap. six. Cf. "It was [Genji's] first impression
that the figure kneeling beside him was most uncommonly long and at-
tenuated. Not at all promising—and the nose! That nose now dominated
the scene. It was like that of the beast [the elephant] on which Samantab-
hadra rides, long, pendulous, and red. A frightful nose." Seidensticker,
The Tale of Genji, 124.

3. Kamakura Shinzō was an actor of jester roles in Osaka for a decade
from the mid-1680's. For a time he ran his own theater (*Yakusha ōkagami*,
1692).

4. See 8:1 note 6.

5. Miyazaki Denkichi began as an actor of boys' roles in Kyoto and
moved to Edo around 1660. With Ichikawa Danjūrō and Nakamura Shi-
chisaburō, he came to epitomize the emerging Edo style of acting. In the
1680's he began writing plays under the pen name "Bayō."

6. Mineno Kozarashi was an actor of boys' roles in the theaters of

Osaka's Dōtombori (*Yakusha hakkei*, 1680). In 1683, he was described as being at the pinnacle of his career in the troupe of the Arashi Theater, but his name is missing from the evaluation book *Yarō tachiyaku butai ōkagami* (1687) where one would expect to see it. He contributed verses to collections of linked verse by Saikaku's students such as *Dōtombori hanamichi* (1679).

7. Also known as Gorōzaemon, Hirakawa Kichiroku was an actor of old men's roles in the Takeshima Theater in Osaka (*Yakusha ōkagami*, 1692).

8. Kojima Tsumanojō played boys' roles in the 1660's and 1670's, and around 1681 he switched to men's roles and changed his name to Hikojūrō. He began to write kabuki plays in 1688 as the house playwright of the Takeshima Theater in Osaka. His linked verses appeared under the pen name Kojima Tachibana in several collections connected to Saikaku, including *Kubako* (1679) and *Dōtombori hanamichi* (1679).

9. Onoyama Shume was an actor of boys' roles in Kyoto, and in 1681 he switched to men's roles and changed his name to Ujiemon. He excelled in villain roles, according to *Yarō tachiyaku butai ōkagami* (1687), and contributed verses to Saikaku's haikai collections under the pen name Onoyama Koibune.

10. Mihara Jūdayū began as an actor of boys' roles and around 1681–83 switched to playing villain roles in the Araki Theater in Osaka (*Yarō tachiyaku butai ōkagami*, 1687). He remained active on the stage until about 1712. *Yakusha rongo* (1776) says of him, "Mihara Jūdayū was short in stature, but nevertheless when he made his entrance wearing his long pair of swords and struck his vivid pose and walked his swaggering walk, he looked a big man and struck terror. Nowadays there is no style in entrances." Dunn and Torigoe, *The Actor's Analects*, 113–14, also 181.

11. Shibasaki Rinzaemon (d.1722) was known as Rinnosuke as a boy actor and changed his name when he began playing men's roles in 1684. In the actor-evaluation book *Yakusha tomoginmi* (1707), he was ranked as the top actor of men's roles. He continued active performance until about 1716. See Dunn and Torigoe, *The Actor's Analects*, 189.

12. The name Sawada Tarōzaemon appears once in *Yakusha ōkagami* (1692), but nothing is known of the actor.

13. Sakurai Wahei acted men's roles in the Araki Theater in Osaka (*Yarō tachiyaku butai ōkagami*, 1687), then in Kyoto at the Murayama Theater, where he played old men (*Yakusha ōkagami*, 1692). He is last mentioned in the evaluation book *Yakusha shurobōki* (1698).

14. Originally from Edo, Iwakura Man'emon performed at the Yamatoya Theater in Osaka after 1682. *Naniwa tachigiki mukashi banashi* (1686) states that he was earning an annual salary of 35 gold *ryō*. He was

listed in the troupe of the Okamura Theater in Kyoto in *Yarō tachiyaku butai ōkagami* (1687) and in 1701 was still ranked as one of the top leading men of the kabuki stage.

15. See 6:2 note 8.

16. A minor actor of men's roles, Yamamoto Hachirōji performed in the troupe of the Mandayū Theater in Kyoto (*Yakusha ōkagami*, 1692).

17. Masaburō first appeared as Matsumoto Kozen in the evaluation book *Shin yarō hanagaki* (1674) as an actor of boys' roles. He later played female roles (*Yakusha hakkei*, 1681) and in 1683 was listed as an actor of men's roles in the actors' register of the Araki Theater in Osaka. He continued to perform until about 1693.

18. Kokan Tarōji first appeared on the stages of theaters in Dōtombori in the 1670's, and by 1683 he was playing old women's roles at the Yamatoya Theater. His reputation as the best actor of such roles was still unrivaled in 1703 when he moved to Edo and joined the Yamamura Theater (*Yakusha gozen kabuki*, 1703). He performed until his death in 1713. Examples of his comic linked verse appear in collections by Saikaku's students including *Kubako* (1679) and *Dōtombori hanamichi* (1679) under the name Kokan Shigeyuki. See Dunn and Torigoe, *The Actor's Analects*, 63, 180.

19. Tsurukawa Somenojō's name does not appear in any actor-evaluation books, so nothing is known of him. He is mentioned only in Saikaku's *Kōshoku ichidai otoko* (1682) as an actor of boys' roles.

20. Matsumoto Tsunezaemon was an actor of boys' roles in the 1660's, later played girls' roles, and finally ended as an actor of men's roles. He may have died in 1687. He is mentioned in Saikaku's *Koshoku ichidai otoko* (1682) in connection with Tsurukawa Somenojō (note 19) and Yamamoto Kantarō (see 5:4 note 4).

21. Unknown.

22. Nakamura Shuzen was an actor of female roles in the Araki Theater in Osaka according to theater records from 1683. Details of his later career as Rokurōemon are not clear, but he may be the Matsunaga Rokurōemon mentioned in *Yakusha ōkagami* (1692).

23. Nishikawa Shōdayū debuted as an actor of female roles in the Araki Theater in Osaka in 1682. Saikaku mentions him in *Naniwa no kao wa Ise no oshiroi* (1683?), but his name is missing from *Yarō tachiyaku butai ōkagami* (1687), an indication that he may already have died.

24. Miyata Okinosuke appears in *Yakusha hakkei* (1680) as an actor of female roles, but nothing is known of his later career.

25. About 2 A.M.

26. The ninth bell tolled midnight, the eighth at 2 A.M.

27. Yoshikawa Tamon was an actor of girls' roles at the Araki Theater

in Dōtombori (*Naniwa no kao wa Ise no oshiroi*, 1683?). In 1684 he was earning a salary of 110 gold *ryō*. He retired or died in the early 1700's.

28. "Risshi" is a rank of Buddhist prelate. The name Kakuhan is an error; it should be Chōhan.

29. *Goshūishū* poem 953 by Risshi Chōhan (Tomonori): "If you bore me no grudge, you would not bother to revile me; I am grateful for that sad pleasure." The poem is included in *Iwatsutsuji* (1676).

8:3 Loved by a Man in a Box

1. Also known as Tashiro Magoemon, Jofū erected a monument at Tennō-ji in Osaka in 1650 in penance for the lives he had taken in battle, said to number 1,000 (*Setsuyō kikan*, 1833). Saikaku mentioned the same legend in *Shoen ōkagami* (1684).

2. Bizen Province was governed by the daimyo lord Ikeda Mitsumasa from 1632. He was an avid follower of Yōmei (Chinese: Yang ming) neo-Confucianism and established a clan school where Yōmei studies were taught. As a result, Bizen for years had a reputation for upholding Confucian orthodoxy.

3. The wisteria at Fuji-dera in Yasui, a section of Higashiyama, is named *tasogare no fuji*, "twilight wisteria."

4. Higashiyama.

5. In the early 1680's, Takenaka Kichisaburō acted in the troupe of Iwamoto Kenzaburō (*Yarō tachiyaku butai ōkagami*, 1687), and in 1688 he changed his name to Takenaka Fujisaburō and began acting men's roles at the Araki Theater in Osaka.

6. Fujita Kichisaburō was an actor of female roles and protégé of Fujita Koheiji (see 7:3 note 10). In 1688 he was in the troupe of the Yamatoya Theater in Osaka.

7. See 6:2 note 5.

8. Mitsuse Sakon played leading men's roles in the Kyoto Murayama Theater in the 1680's, excelling particularly in warrior roles (*Yarō tachiyaku butai ōkagami*, 1688). His comic linked verse appeared in *Dōtombori hanamichi* (1679) under the name Mitsuse Gyokusen.

9. He played female roles in Kyoto in the 1680's first under the name Takii Sawanojō and then changed his name to Toyama Sennosuke. In 1687–88, he moved to Edo (*Yarō yakusha fūryū kagami*, 1688).

10. The narrator is referring here to himself with a touch of irony. Some commentators equate the narrator with Saikaku. Cf. *Nihon koten bungaku zenshū*, 39: 581, note 33.

11. Purple; from the purple wisteria (*fuji*) of his name, Fujita.

12. Iwai Hanshirō (d. 1699) was famous for his singing. In his youth he acted on the Osaka stages of the Shioya and Araki Theaters. Later, he

established a theater in Osaka that competed with the Araki Theater (*Naniwa tachigiki mukashi banashi*, 1686). *Yarō tachiyaku butai ōkagami* (1687) described him as exceptionally handsome and the top actor of samurai roles.

13. Horse-cart drivers and river-forders appear in the Tōkaidō Road scenes painted on Toyama's robe.

14. This is the next-to-last stop on the Tōkaidō Road where Sanjō-dōri crossed the Shirakawa River in Higashiyama. The terminal point of the road from Edo was the Sanjō Bridge spanning the Kamo River.

15. There were believed to be 108 evil human desires that could be warded off by ringing temple bells 108 times on the last night of the year.

16. The 88th night counting from *risshun*, the first day of spring in the lunar calendar, was thought to be the last time frost would settle.

17. Younger brother of Fujita Koheiji (see 7:3 note 10), Fujimoto Hei-jūrō was an actor of men's roles from 1680 to 1710. In the course of his acting career, he appeared on all of the major stages in the three cities of Kyoto, Osaka, and Edo. In 1687, he was in the troupe of the Yamatoya Theater in Osaka (*Yarō tachiyaku butai ōkagami*, 1687).

18. Sakakibara Heiemon began his career in 1683 in the Yamatoya Theater in Osaka and appears in the actor-evaluation book *Yakusha ōka-gami* (1692).

19. Sugiyama Kanzaemon began in 1673 as an actor of men's roles in the Osaka Araki Theater. He later switched to the Murayama Theater in Kyoto (*Yarō tachiyaku butai ōkagami*, 1687).

20. Sakata Densai was an actor of men's roles in the Mandayū Theater in Kyoto (*Yarō tachiyaku butai ōkagami*, 1687). In 1691 he joined the Ya-mamura Theater.

21. A legendary emperor, said to have reigned from 29 B.C. to A.D. 70. Figurines were buried in imperial tombs in place of live attendants to ensure that the needs of the deceased were met in the afterworld.

8:4 Koyama Barrier Keeper

1. During the Edo Period, one of the more popular pilgrimages was *saikoku sanjūsan meguri*, visiting the 33 temples housing statues of Kannon in the region of the capital, the so-called "western provinces."

2. The fifth bell tolled 8 A.M.; Naniwa Temple was another name for Shitennō-ji in Osaka.

3. The anniversary of Ieyasu's death on the fourth month, seventeenth day, was observed in Edo by the shogun's visit to Ieyasu's mausoleum at Nikkō and in other cities by a ban on entertainment activities.

4. At the temple of Tennō-ji.

5. Sumptuary laws were common throughout the Edo Period. Here,

Saikaku may have had in mind the strict regulations promulgated in the second month of 1683 that defined proper attire for townswomen, courtesans, and actors, all of whom tended to dress more ostentatiously than the authorities thought appropriate.

6. A temple established in Sumiyoshi, Osaka, by command of Toba Tennō in 1127.

7. Someone named Mori, elsewhere called Mori Go and Mori Gorō, also appears as the narrator's cohort in pleasure in *Kōshoku ichidai otoko* (1682), *Shoen ōkagami* (1684), and *Saikaku okimiyage* (1693).

8. Possibly Takii Gen'emon, who appears on the actors' list of the Murayama Theater in 1693.

9. See 7:5 note 5.

10. Takenaka Hanzaburō was an actor of boys' roles in the Araki Theater, Osaka (*Naniwa no kao wa Ise no oshiroi*, 1683?).

11. Unknown.

12. See 7:3 note 11.

13. The first part of this sentence consists of a rhyme along the lines of "Roses are red, violets are blue," which Saikaku uses to introduce the color red.

14. Uemura Kichiya; see 6:4 note 1.

15. Uemura Tatsuya; see 7:5 note 10.

16. Merchants from Mogami, a section of Kyoto, had a reputation for driving a hard bargain. By extension, anyone who was ruthless in business was called a "man from Mogami."

17. Certain days each month were dubbed "festival days" in the pleasure quarter when courtesan's fees were doubled or tripled. This practice had not yet been adopted by boy actors but would be in future years, just as Saikaku predicts.

18. This appears to be a variation of a legend contained in *Konjaku monogatari* and *Ujishūi monogatari* about a man who sold fabric dyed with human blood. Saikaku made the change to link it with the wine shop owner in the following line.

19. See 7:3 note 14.

20. See 6:4 note 2.

8:5 Incense Graph Dyed in Her Heart

1. The theater district of Dōtombori was south of the Yodo River in Osaka.

2. During the Edo Period, most shrines in Japan had an annual celebration in which a heavy portable shrine bearing a sacred object was wheeled through the narrow streets by drunken men. The San-ō (Sannō) Festival in Ōmi Province was particularly known for its violence, which

usually produced several fatalities, since the gods of the shrine were thought to be placated only by the sight of blood.

3. The so-called "Genji names" became popular among both actors and courtesans in the years prior to the Genroku Era (1688–1703) and represented the cultivation of a mood of increased opulence and refinement in the pleasure quarters and theater districts.

4. Sodeshima Ichiya began acting female roles at the Yamatoya Theater in Osaka in 1681, moving to Edo in 1684 where he joined the Nakamura Theater and became one of the four leading actors in the troupe (*Yarō yakusha fūryū kagami*, 1688).

5. An actor of boys' roles in the Arashi Theater (*Naniwa tachigiki mukashi banashi*, 1686), Kawashima Kazuma later appeared on the stage of the Mandayū Theater in Kyoto, according to theater records from 1688.

6. See 6:5 note 14.

7. See 6:2 note 5.

8. See 7:5 note 33.

9. An actor of men's roles, Suzuki Heizaemon moved from Edo in 1684 and achieved great popularity at the Yamatoya Theater in Osaka performing in a variety of acting styles. He returned to Edo in his later years and died in 1701.

10. Later called Kōzaemon, Yamashita Hanzaemon was a protégé of Arashi San'emon (see 7:5 note 3), to whom he initially played opposite in men's roles. He later achieved fame at the Yamatoya Theater in Osaka. He earned a salary of 200 *ryō* at the Araki Theater (*Naniwa tachigiki mukashi banashi*, 1686). During most of the Genroku Era (1688–1703), he managed his own theater in Kyoto. See Dunn and Torigoe, *The Actor's Analects*, 193.

11. First mentioned in *Yarō daibutsushi* (1668) as an actor of boys' roles by the name of Yamakawa Naiki, he changed his name to Naiki Hikozaemon in the early 1680's and began playing men's roles (*Yarō tachiyaku butai ōkagami*, 1687).

12. Takeshima Kōzaemon moved to Osaka from Edo in 1684 and debuted as an actor of men's roles in the Arashi Theater (*Naniwa tachigiki mukashi banashi*, 1686). His reputation increased until he was ranked along with Fujita Koheiji (see 7:3 note 10) and Araki Yojibei (see 6:2 note 7) among the top actors of leading men's roles of his day (*Yakusha ōkagami gassai*, 1692).

13. Properly known as Hōzen-ji, a temple south of Dōtombori. The popular name derived from the fact that sutras were read there for 1,000 days (*sennichi*) during the Kan'ei Era (1624–43).

14. See 7:3 note 9. The archaic pronunciation "Jimbyōe" is indicated in the text.

15. The thousand-hand Kannon at Kachiō-ji was the 23rd of 33 Kannon images worshipped in the western provinces. See 8:4 note 1.

16. The crest was apparently adapted from those used in incense-judging games in the Heian court. In the illustration accompanying the text, the graph is clearly visible on the robes of both Jimbei and the young lady admirer.

17. Each of the items—the unicorn's horn, the buffalo stone (possibly a gallstone from the stomach of a water buffalo), and Buddha image—seems to be an object of veneration at the temple. A priest would explain to worshippers the legend related to each during their tour of the temple.

18. This was the home of the Danrin haikai poet Saikin (Mizuta Shōzaemon, d.1709) built around 1673 in Toyonaka, outside Osaka. He was originally a disciple of Nishiyama Sōin and later studied haikai composition under Saikaku. He was the woodblock copy artist (hanshita) for Saikaku's Kōshoku ichidai otoko (1682).

19. The men in the narrative, who deemed themselves connoisseurs of boy love, were apparently disappointed that their host made no distinction between the refined pleasures they enjoyed with kabuki actors and the unsophisticated pleasures of buying a common boy prostitute.

20. This term is mentioned in Yodarekake (1665).

21. Also mentioned in Yodarekake (1665), it seems to be a colloquial Chinese term for anal intercourse. Literally, "intimacy [with a] brick [oven]."

22. The Isle of Men (otokojima) stands in ironic juxtaposition to the Isle of Women (nyogogashima) for which Saikaku's hero, Yonosuke, set sail at the end of Kōshoku ichidai otoko (1682).

Works Cited

Asō Isoji and Fuji Akio, eds. *Taiyaku Saikaku zenshū*. Vols. 1–16. Tokyo: Meiji Shoin, 1978–80.

Aston, W. G. *Japanese Literature*. London: Appleton, 1899.

————. *Nihongi: Chronicles of Japan from Earliest Times to 697*. London: Allen and Unwin, 1956.

Bolitho, Harold. *Treasures Among Men; The Fudai Daimyo in Tokugawa Japan*. New Haven: Yale University Press, 1974.

Boswell, John. *Christianity, Social Tolerance, and Homosexuality*. Chicago: Chicago University Press, 1980.

Brandon, James R., William P. Malm, and Donald H. Shively. *Studies in Kabuki: Its Acting, Music, and Historical Context*. Honolulu: University Press of Hawaii, 1978.

Callahan, Caryl Ann, tr. *Tales of Samurai Honor*. Tokyo: Monumenta Nipponica, 1981.

Carpenter, Edward. *Intermediate Types Among Primitive Folk*. New York: Arno Press, 1975.

Childs, Margaret H. "*Chigo monogatari*: Love Stories or Buddhist Sermons." *Monumenta Nipponica*, 35: 2 (Summer 1980), 127–51.

Danly, Robert Lyons. *In the Shade of Spring Leaves, The Life and Writings of Higuchi Ichiyō, A Woman of Letters in Meiji Japan*. New Haven: Yale University Press, 1981.

Dover, K. J. *Greek Homosexuality*. Cambridge, Mass.: Harvard University Press, 1978.

Dunn, Charles J., and Bunzō Torigoe, tr. *The Actor's Analects (Yakusha Rongo)*. New York: Columbia University Press, 1969.

Giles, Herbert Allen. *A Chinese Biographical Dictionary*. London: Quaritch, 1898.

Gunji, Masakatsu. *Kabuki*. Tokyo: Kodansha International, 1969.

Guth, Christine. "The Divine Boy in Japanese Art." *Monumenta Nipponica*, 42: 4 (1987), 1–23.

Heike monogatari. *Nihon koten bungaku zenshū*, vols. 29–30. Tokyo: Shogakkan, 1973.

Herdt, Gilbert H. *Ritualized Homosexuality in Melanesia*. Berkeley: University of California Press, 1984.

Hibbett, Howard S. *The Floating World in Japanese Fiction*. London: Oxford University Press, 1959.

———. "The Role of the Ukiyo-zōshi Illustrator." *Monumenta Nipponica*, 13 (1957), 67–82.

———. "Saikaku as a Realist." *Harvard Journal of Asiatic Studies*, 15 (December 1952), 408–18.

Hirade Kōjirō. *Katakiuchi*. Tokyo: Saigetsusha, 1975.

Iwata Jun'ichi. *Honchō nanshoku kō*. Ise: private printing, 1974.

———. *Nanshoku bunken shoshi*. Ise: private printing, 1973.

Johnson, Irmgard. "Takigi Nō: Firelight Performances in Sacred Precincts." *Japan Quarterly*, 30: 3 (July–Sept. 1983), 301–5.

Karsch-Haack, Ferdinand. *Forschungen über gleichgeschlectliche Liebe, Das gleichgeschlechtliche Leben der Ostasiaten: Chinesen, Japaner, Koreer*. München: Seitz & Schauer, 1906.

Keene, Donald. *Dawn to the West, Japanese Literature of the Modern Era, Fiction*. New York: Holt, Rinehart & Winston, 1984.

———, tr. *Essays in Idleness, The Tsurezuregusa of Kenkō*. New York: Columbia University Press, 1967.

———. *World Within Walls*. New York: Grove Press, 1976.

Keilson-Lauritz, Marita. *Von der Liebe die Freundschaft heisst, Zur Homoerotik im Werk Stefan Georges*. Berlin: Verlag Rosa Winkel, 1987.

Kitagawa, Joseph M. *On Understanding Japanese Religion*. Princeton: Princeton University Press, 1987.

Kitamura Kigin. *Iwatsutsuji*. In Ōta Nampō, ed., *Misonoya*, vol. 1.

Kokinshū. *Kokka taikan*. Tokyo: Kadokawa Shoten, 1963.

Lane, Richard. "Postwar Japanese Studies of the Novelist Saikaku." *Harvard Journal of Asiatic Studies*, 18 (June 1955), 181–99.

Leiter, Samuel L. *Kabuki Encyclopedia*. Westport, Conn.: Greenwood Press, 1979.

Maeda Kingorō. *Kōshoku ichidai otoko zenchūshaku*. Tokyo: Kadokawa Shoten, 1980.

Mathers, E. Powys, tr. *Comrade Loves of the Samurai*. Rutland, Vt.: Tuttle, 1972.

McCullough, Helen C., tr. *Kokin Wakashū: The First Imperial Anthology of Japanese Poetry*. Stanford: Stanford University Press, 1985.

———, tr. *Ōkagami: The Great Mirror, Fujiwara Michinaga (966–1027) and His Times*. Princeton: Princeton University Press, 1980.

———, tr. *The Taiheiki: A Chronicle of Medieval Japan*. New York: Columbia University Press, 1959.

———, tr. *Tales of Ise*. Stanford: Stanford University Press, 1968.

Miner, Earl, Hiroko Odagiri, and Robert Morell, eds. *The Princeton Com-*

panion to Classical Japanese Literature. Princeton: Princeton University Press, 1985.

Mishima Yukio. *Kamen no kokuhaku. Mishima Yukio zenshū*, vol. 3. Tokyo: Shinchosha, 1974.

Mitamura Engyo, ed. *Saikaku rinkō*, vol. 5. Tokyo: Seiabo, 1962.

Morris, Ivan, tr. *The Life of an Amorous Woman (Kōshoku ichidai onna*, by Ihara Saikaku). New York: New Directions, 1963.

————, tr. *The Pillow Book of Sei Shōnagon (Makura no sōshi*, by Sei Shōnagon). Baltimore: Penguin Books, 1974.

Munemasa Isoo. *Kinsei Kyōto shuppan bunka no kenkyū*. Tokyo: Dososha, 1982.

Murray, Stephen O. *Social Theory, Homosexual Realities*. New York: Gai Saber Monograph, 1984.

Nihon koten bungaku zenshū, vols. 1–51. Tokyo: Shogakkan, 1970–74.

Noma Kōshin. *Kinsei shikidō ron. Nihon shisō taikei*, vol. 60. Tokyo: Iwanami Shoten, 1976.

————. *Saikaku nenpu kōshō*. Tokyo: Chuo Koronsha, 1983.

————. *Saikaku shinshinkō*. Tokyo: Iwanami Shoten, 1981.

Ortolani, Benito. *Das Kabukitheater*. Tokyo: Sophia University Press, 1964.

————. "Das Wakashu-kabuki und das Yarō-kabuki." *Monumenta Nipponica*, 18–19 (1963–64), 89–127.

Ōta Nampo, ed. *Misonoya*, vols. 1–3. Tokyo: Kokusho Kankokai, 1917.

Phillipi, Donald L., tr. *Kojiki*. Princeton: Princeton University Press, 1965.

Pollack, David. *The Fracture of Meaning, Japan's Synthesis of China from the Eighth through the Eighteenth Centuries*. Princeton: Princeton University Press, 1986.

Rivers, J. E. *Proust & the Art of Love, The Aesthetics of Sexuality in the Life, Times, and Art of Marcel Proust*. New York: Columbia University Press, 1980.

Sargent, G. W. *The Japanese Family Storehouse*. Cambridge: Cambridge University Press, 1959.

Schalow, Paul Gordon. "Literature and Legitimacy: Uses of Irony and Humor in 17th Century Depictions of Male Love in Japan." In Wimal Dissanayake, ed., *Literary History: East and West*. Honolulu: University of Hawaii Press, forthcoming.

————. "Saikaku on 'Manly Love.'" *Stone Lion Review*, no. 7 (Spring 1981), 3–7.

Seidensticker, Edward, tr. *The Tale of Genji (Genji monogatari*, by Murasaki Shikibu). New York: Knopf, 1976.

Shin'yūki, in Noma Kōshin, ed., *Kinsei shikidō ron*.

Shively, Donald H. "Bakufu Versus Kabuki." In John W. Hall and Marius B. Jansen, eds., *Studies in the Institutional History of Early Modern Japan*. Princeton: Princeton University Press, 1968.

———. "Tokugawa Tsunayoshi, the Genroku Shogun." In Albert Craig and Donald H. Shively, eds., *Personality in Japanese History*. Berkeley: University of California Press, 1970.

Strauss, Leo. *Persecution and the Art of Writing*. Westport, Conn.: Greenwood Press, 1976.

Teihon Saikaku zenshū. Vols. 1–14. Tokyo: Chuo Koronsha, 1951–53.

Teruoka Yasutaka. *Saikaku shinron*. Tokyo: Chuo Koronsha, 1981.

———, ed. *Nanshoku ōkagami*. Nihon koten bungaku zenshū, vol. 39. Tokyo: Shogakkan, 1973.

Thornbury, Barbara E. *Sukeroku's Double Identity: The Dramatic Structure of Edo Kabuki*. Michigan Papers in Japanese Studies, no. 6. Ann Arbor: University of Michigan, 1982.

Walker, Janet A. *The Japanese Novel of the Meiji Period and the Ideal of Individualism*. Princeton: Princeton University Press, 1979.

Weatherby, Meredith, tr. *Confessions of a Mask* (*Kamen no kokuhaku*, by Mishima Yukio). New York: New Directions, 1958.

Yoshida Kenkō. *Tsurezuregusa*. Nihon koten bungaku zenshū, vol. 27. Tokyo: Shogakkan, 1971.

English Translations of Ihara Saikaku

Befu, Ben. *Worldly Mental Calculations (Seken mune zan'yō*, 1692). Berkeley: University of California Press, 1976.

Callahan, Caryl Ann. *Tales of Samurai Honor (Buke giri monogatari*, 1688). Tokyo: Sophia University Press, 1981.

de Bary, Wm. Theodore. *Five Women Who Loved Love (Kōshoku gonin onna*, 1686). Rutland, Vt.: Tuttle, 1956.

Hamada Kengi. *The Life of an Amorous Man* (abridgment of *Kōshoku ichidai otoko*, 1682). Rutland, Vt.: Tuttle, 1964.

Hibbett, Howard S. *The Floating World in Japanese Fiction* (selections from *Kōshoku ichidai onna*, 1686). London: Oxford University Press, 1959.

Kondo, Thomas M., and Alfred H. Marks. *Tales of Japanese Justice (Honchō ōin hiji*, 1689). Honolulu: University Press of Hawaii, 1980.

Leutner, Robert. "Saikaku's Parting Gift: Translations from *Saikaku Okimiyage* [1693]." *Monumenta Nipponica*, 30: 4 (Winter 1975), 357- 91.

Mathers, E. Powys. *Comrade Loves of the Samurai* (selections from *Nanshoku ōkagami*, 1687; *Budō denrai ki*, 1687; *Buke giri monogatari*, 1688; and *Yorozu no fumihōgu*, 1696). Rutland, Vt.: Tuttle, 1972.

Mizuno Soji. *Ihara Saikaku's Nippon Eitaigura* [1688]. Tokyo: Hokuseidō, 1955.

Morris, Ivan. *The Life of an Amorous Woman* (selections from *Kōshoku ichidai onna*, 1686; *Kōshoku gonin onna*, 1686; *Nippon eitaigura*, 1688; *Seken mune zan'yō*, 1692). New York: New Directions, 1963.

Nosco, Peter. *Some Final Words of Advice (Saikaku oridome*, 1694). Rutland, Vt.: Tuttle, 1980.

Sargent, G. W. *The Japanese Family Storehouse (Nippon eitaigura*, 1688). Cambridge: Cambridge University Press, 1959.

Takatsuka, Masanori, and David C. Stubbs. *This Scheming World (Seken mune zan'yō*, 1692). Rutland, Vt.: Tuttle, 1965.

Index

Library of Congress Cataloging-in-Publication Data

Ihara, Saikaku, 1642–1693.
    [Nanshoku ōkagami. English]
    The great mirror of male love / Ihara Saikaku ; translated, with
an introduction, by Paul Gordon Schalow.
        p.   cm.
    Translation of: Nanshoku ōkagami.
    Bibliography: p.
    Includes index.
    ISBN 0-8047-1661-7 (alk. paper): ISBN 0-8047-1895-4 (pbk.)
    I. Schalow, Paul Gordon. II. Title.
PL794.N37E5   1990
895.6'33—dc19   89-31182
                                                           CIP